NIGHTWOLVES COALITION

(Book One of Memoirs of the Nightwolves Series)

by

Clarrissa Lee Moon

World Castle Publishing, LLC

WCP

World Castle Publishing, LLC
Pensacola, Florida

Copyright © Clarrissa Lee Moon 2010
ISBN: 9781937085100
Second Edition World Castle Publishing, LLC June 1, 2011
http://www.worldcastlepublishing.com

Cover: Fantasia Frog Designs
Editor: Lea Ellen Borg

NOTE FROM THE AUTHOR

I realize that the names of the dark Gods in this book (and future books in this series) are completely fictitious, yet I used the correct names for the Gods and Goddesses of the Light. Orochi is actually a Japanese demon, not a dark God, so using his name won't matter. Those who are in the know, will know why it is so. For those that don't, read the books on Magick, then you'll understand why.

I used the spelling for Magick with a 'k' to differentiate the magic (no k) being used by magicians and stage artists from those who actually practice real magick and run with WILL on the astral planes. Though there are some stage magicians whom I wonder if they should have the 'k' included. Some are just that good to be hiding in plain sight. However, like them, this book was made to entertain you and I hope you enjoy all of my new exciting worlds and travel with me often as more are created.

I'd like to thank my boys, Jerimiah, Cody and Cameron for letting me use the computer for hours on end. I want to thank Jerimiah, personally, for being the one who came up with most of the chapter title names. I want to personally thank Cody for keeping me fed when I would forget. And I want to thank Cameron, for reading all of my stories and giving me feedback and ideas when I would write myself into a corner. Thanks, also, to Laurie and Kenny for getting me the research I needed for more authenticity in my stories. Finally, thanks to my own personal editors, Liz and Lea Ellen, who kicked butt on editing. Good work, guys. Keep on astral running. Ride hard, ride free!

I'd like to thank my favorite Rock band, Nickleback, and my favorite Heavy Metal rock band, Godsmack for rocking me through my writing. Keep rocking! Also, thanks to my two favorite Rap bands, ICP and Twiztid. The love scenes were inspired by a CD mix I made with my various favorite "Mood" music. Oh yeah, it worked, HA!

(The Typos Below are Deliberate)

Just one More note: i have Three very special people i hope read the whole series. You know who you all are. if you do, hey, i am here, still Alive, bring me in from The cold. Sushi and Margaritas until the End Of time On our own island in Nature's paradise.

TABLE OF CONTENTS

CATRINA'S PROLOGUE

Finding your soulmate is a great gift. No gift of the Gods, however, comes without a price and when you are a child of the Gods, the price can be even steeper. Staying celibate until we could find one another and tacking on a save the world quest, I knew I would be in for an interesting time.

Thanks to a prophecy that is told in many of today's religions by the end of 2012, four and a half billion people or more could die. Great plagues, famine and wars will take their toll. "The end of days", which is really not the end of mankind as most people think, but a change of life as we know it.

The reason for this is twofold; one scientific and one metaphysical. The scientific side is this: A major shift in the Earth's gravitational pull has been happening slowly for the past ten or so years. Surprisingly, not a lot of people know this, but it is a scientific fact. December 21, 2012 will see the full end of the "Shift" in the polarity of Earth. Even its' axis will be tilted more than it is now. Minor Shifts have happened to some degree every 5,000 years or so. Some shorter and some longer time spanned between the shifts. With these shifts, depending on the severity, they can cause earthquakes, tsunamis, flooding, earth temperature changes and many other weather deviations. Some believe that in 2012, we will see a shift on a magnitude that hasn't been seen in thousands of years. At one time, our Earth's surface was one solid piece of land. Then, after the first 'Great Shift', the tectonic plates moved so far that many smaller continents were made. The Ice Age happened and the Neanderthals perished.

For the metaphysical side: Myths and legends record that during this time, all the magickal races (dragons, vampires, werewolves and the like) were sent to other various dimensions through portals and astral doorways, which can only be opened or closed during a major polarity shift. Hence, the reason they are myths and legends in today's cultural histories. This was done to protect man from races that were stronger, faster, smarter and much more lethal in magickal uses than man who had no way of protecting themselves. Man too, eventually would have been wiped out as the Neanderthals were. The Gods and Goddesses decided to separate the pure magickal races and let ingenuity and science rule man for a time. Not all magick was lost to earth, but the greater magicks and the beings that can wield it were removed. Science has ruled heavily, but with science too, there is a price. Pollution, skepticism, a disregard for nature and natural cycles, as well as the imbalance of feminine and male roles in most cultures and newer religions got the attention of The Gods once again. Now They want the door opened, to hopefully bring back balance between the female and male aspects, as well as a healthy respect for the Earth and The Gods themselves. Therefore, a great change is coming and most are completely unaware. And with great change, always comes a great price.

The Gods and Goddesses of many of the older religious pantheons of Earth got together and decided to have children that would be mated to other pantheons, to combine and amplify power like in the days of old on Earth. The merging of two powerful houses of Lords in marriage would have influence over a more vast area. By putting us in human physical bodies that were birthed by human women, it gave Them a channel of power here on Earth for a more effective use—to help bring down the death toll, ease those left through the new changes here on earth and to protect them from the more aggressive magickal races that are coming back. I am one of those children, the first born daughter of the Triple Goddess and Her Consort, from an ancient Celtic pantheon. There are six of us—three daughters and three sons, all placed into separate physical mothers at conception. Only my youngest brother and I share the same physical father—a High Dark Adept, who also happens to be a Mafia Don. Lucky us. Searching for my soulmates using astral magicks opened a whole can of worms on my astral spiritual heritage; more than I was ready for in many ways. It could be part of the reason why it took fifteen long years to find my mates on the physical plane.

The prequel to this story (which may be written sometime in the future) will tell the tale of how I had learned to use my powers and astral project out of my body. Using this method of astral projection for finding my soulmate, I met Antonio, one of my mates, briefly, for about three seconds. I tried again sometime later and made it to Demitri's mansion, Antonio's eldest brother. Their middle brother, Andre, had felt me coming; curious, he followed me home using the same technique. I fell in love with all three of them and when made to decide which one, I said all or nothing. They chose all. We found out later, that's the way it was supposed to be and made peace with it. I had also met my brothers and sisters (who had different physical parents then me), but we have the same spiritual mother and father. During this time, my evil physical father, a High Dark Adept, tried many times to keep us apart and even tried to kill me a few times. Then, another new enemy joined the fray. The outcome was me being cursed and my powers brought down to minimum levels. Many of my psychic powers were blocked and without those powers, I could not find the physical location of my mates (though we now lived in the same city). We had gotten that far before I was cursed. Even blocked, I would not stand down, and many magickal battles ensued, leading up to a battle with the dark God Orochi. We won, and that lifted my curse; but lost, because we died. The Goddess brought us back and "Blessed" us by modifying our physical bodies. I then finally got to meet my mates. They brought my brothers and sisters to their home and I got to meet them physically as well. We were then wed by my youngest brother, Gerard. Unfortunately, fifteen years of darkness had left its toll on me and I froze on my wedding night. This story is what happened after that. And I thought the hard part was over....yeah, right.

These memoirs I have written, were not only written by me, but by the other Nightwolves. Even months before 'The Great Shift' happened, I think of the Nightwolves as the true heroes of this tale. I can't really claim to be a hero, since I was born and made for this job. To me, a real hero is one who chooses the path of great danger even though they may be the most ordinary of us all. It takes great courage to face the Great Shift with no extra tricks up ones sleeve, so I had them write their own memories from their view point and put them together within this story here and there as best I could. This story is for them, as it should be, for the truly great heroes of our time.

CHAPTER ONE
On a Wing and a Prayer
On Flight 1409

You'd think I would be home getting some wild monkey love from my soulmates after fifteen years of celibacy, right? Wrong! After finally finding my soulmates, fifteen years of saying "no" to any man who asked me out; it was hard saying yes—even to my mates. And yes, you read that right—soulmates with a plural. Lucky me had not one, but three soulmates, who were all brothers! We finally got together on the earth plane after a nasty battle with the dark God Orochi and his odious minions. We won, but also lost our lives. We were battling on the astral plane in partial physical form. It was a dangerous, but necessary, move. The Goddess apparently wasn't done with us and our fates, bringing us back as modified vampires 2.0 with retractable fangs and all the magickal attachments that went with it, but with half of the side effects. We were now super vamps that can stand sunlight, unlike the vamps of myths, and we only needed a mouthful or two of blood every two weeks or less.

We also had heightened senses; smell, hearing and sight, along with strength and speed (all of which were much better than regular humans). She, The Crone aspect of the Triple Goddess, called it a blessing; I called it "a new pain in the ass" I had to deal with. At least the powers that be (on the astral plane) allowed my mates and me to find each other on the physical plane after removing the curse that was laid on me by one of the dark God's minions. I was glad to finally be with them. But, seeing as they were upper class, and I came from the streets, I had to not only start trying to overcome my habit of keeping anything male at arm's length, but fit into their lifestyle as well. This is not easy for a street rat who ran away from home at the age of twelve and hung around bikers for most of her life.

We got together and married on the physical plane with the blessing of The Triple Goddess, but I couldn't finish with the physical consummation part of it. Our wedding night would have been the stuff made for vaudeville if it wasn't so sad seeing a tough biker chick shudder with the nerves of a fragile virgin. Then my mates got a frantic call from New York and they had to leave on their private jet out to deal with their corporation's problem. Two days later they talked me into coming out to be with them since it was going to take longer to deal with the situation then they had first thought. I could see it was going to be yet another kind of battle for us, in trying to juggle corporate problems in this economy and working on a new physical relationship at the same time. I consoled myself that I was flying to New York to hopefully end my very long drought of no sex and find a middle ground with them on lifestyles of the rich and shameless, and I was flying first class no less.

A week before, I wouldn't have even been able to afford to fly coach. You'd think I would be hopping up and down for joy at my luck; rich handsome men who were all mine… but this only seemed to make the walls I had built around myself seem even taller and thicker. Add to that, I was used to being a single mother of three sons from pervious relationships that had left their own special brand of emotional scars. Downscaling the shields I had built would take a lot of work and patience. If someone glanced at me, their main word (if they were female and kind) would be "biker chick". Males would say "easy lay". They would be wrong on the latter, but more than once, I had to get my point across with a good right hook. "Biker chick" I may be, but I am also a High Priestess and daughter of the Triple Goddess and Her Consort. "Easy" I have never been, even before I started my quest for finding my soulmate with astral magick and got more than I had bargained for. Between learning that I had three soulmates, two sisters and three brothers (who also had three mates each), I also found out I was the spiritual daughter of the Triple Goddess and Her Consort. The Goddess had placed me inside of a human pregnant woman, like my other siblings, making us half blooded Demi-Gods with physical bodies.

It sure explained all the 'weird' things I was able to do as a child, causing my physical mother to scream 'demon child' at me and threaten to have me exorcised. I wasn't a bad child. I just had to learn how to control my powers, especially when I got upset. Slamming cupboards and rattling knickknacks while I was standing in the middle of the living room having a tantrum seemed to really freak my physical mother out. Not that she was the best parent to begin with. June Cleaver she wasn't. More like Mommy Dearest, if you get my meaning. Leaving home at a young age to avoid anymore abuse actually helped me to get in touch with people who showed me how to control and hide what I could do. Hiding was what I got really good at, but the more I did it, the lonelier I got. I had several relationships and even was married once for exactly one year. None of my previous relationships worked out. Some of it could have been my fault (as never being able to be just myself—even in a relationship). Most of them were just assholes. Who could feel safe enough to be themselves with an asswipe?

I made a deal with myself at the age of twenty-nine. I would settle for nothing but my soulmate and since dating never worked, I thought I would try using my powers to find my mate. I figured with a soulmate, I would be able to be myself. I found him (and his brothers) and did a high bond with them on the astral plane which can only be kept if we were true in spirit and body to each other. No matter what lifetime we are in, we will always be together from here on out. The last thing we needed to do, to cement the bond between us, was to physically consummate the marriage between us. That would also tie their Egyptian pantheon to my Celtic one on a magickal level.

I had frozen on my 'wedding' night—the night before they had to leave for New York, and they were sweet about it. Even their astral Mother and Father, Isis and Osiris, were being really understanding with me. Which, truth be told, was grating on my nerves. I am not used to people or Deities being nice and sweet, or considerate. I felt like looking for the fine print, their ulterior motive for being so patient with me. People in general just weren't that damned understanding, no matter the situation. Maybe I was more upset with myself because usually I am one ballsy bitch. I've never been afraid of doing anything before and sex had usually been a pleasant experience. Yet, when I had the chance in my hands, almost literally, I froze like some damn frail virgin damsel in those sappy old movies that set my teeth on edge.

'What in the seven hells was wrong with me?' I snorted to myself? This drew the attention of my neighbor sitting in his own throne, I mean first class seat, and then realized how upset I was getting. This could be a very bad thing to do on an airplane thousands of feet in the air with a host of electrical things around me to blow out in a fit of uncontrolled temper. I have been known to blow out TV's and microwaves from being pissed off. Losing my cool in the airplane, with the cockpit not fifteen from me, was not a wise thing to allow myself. Electrical things and my temper have never been good friends. I gave up wearing watches years ago due to the anomaly. Besides, with the kind of bond my mates and I shared, they felt everything I felt. If they felt me get upset, they would want to know why and use telepathy to find out what the problem was if it lasted too much longer. That wouldn't be a good idea either, so I silently started my deep breathing, thinking about a calm pool of blue water, which was my usual fall back in controlling my feelings. Then, I heard a soft voice say, "Excuse me." I snapped my eyes open and tensed, looking at the stewardess (although I think they prefer flight attendants or some such PC thing) who had a stack of magazines in her hand. "Would you like something to read Mrs. Garcia?" she asked me, with her eyebrow slightly raised. Maybe she thought I couldn't read or something.

"It's Ms. Garcia", I replied.

"Would you like some champagne, Ms. Garcia?"

I thought about it for a second and said, "Sure, why not?" She smiled slightly and took off to get my drink.

So this is first class, huh? Plush chairs, soft lighting and being waited on hand and foot. I didn't even need to wear my black sunglasses to shield my eyes. Leg room to spare, too. I eyed my black carryon bag which carried all of my toiletries, my journal (for writing down dreams or nightmares), my book of shadows (BOS), two paranormal romance novels and a book on quantum physics. It usually held a few choice weapons as well, but I had to keep those in my main luggage due to the rules at the airport. Still, I liked the first class area of the plane. Lots of room, no one sitting so damn close to me, invading my personal space, and no one bugging you for your entire personal history to while away their time. This was obviously going to take some getting used to. I also appreciated the soft lighting due to my sensitivity to bright lights. I've had that problem even before being modified. That's why my mates had me booked on a late flight, so I wouldn't have to deal with the sunlight. I can be in the sun, but it did hurt my eyes and made me feel tired quickly. Avoiding daylight hours was just easier for us. The stewardess came back with my drink and I smiled, thanking her. She rushed off to another passenger and was looking after their comfort. I took a sip and wrinkled my nose at the bubbling cold bite it gave me and decided I definitely hated champagne. Yuck, how could people drink this stuff? All it is, is carbonated white wine, which I hated even on a good day. I liked red wine from time to time though. I sat back and watched the flight attendant and wondered how far her nose would get out of joint if I asked for a Bud instead. If she acted the way they did at the check-in station, then I say, "Forget it." At check-in, they looked at me, then my ID, and thought it was a fake, because I'm 44 and they said that I looked like I was 24. I told them about my physical mother being carded when she was 46 (even back when checking people's ID wasn't done) and praising great genetics, to make them finally back off. It was a true story too. I hated lying for the most part, and tried to avoid it. The next time I flew, I was hoping my mates had ways of fixing this problem for all of us. They obviously missed this nuisance due to their private jet and not being bothered by airport security as much as the masses were. As I stated: a new pain in my ass. Don't get me wrong. I liked looking younger, being stronger and faster. I also liked the modifications The Crone made to us with only needing a mouthful or two of blood for regular maintenance (unless we took heavy damage). It could even be animal blood. If we did take from a human, The Crone was adamant that we asked for it and received the donor's permission. Mind wiping would be against everyone's free will and one of our Laws was to respect anyone's free will (even the bad guys). I thought that blew, but I could see why, in the 'big picture' scheme of things.

Do what you wilt, with harm to none, be the law. But, what if they were hurting you first? I knew we had the right to defend ourselves, but did that include taking an enemy's blood without permission as well? Always check the fine print when dealing with Gods, even if you were related to them; especially if you were related to them. I added this question to ask my spirit guide when I hit the ground. I was so not going to call up astral power on an airplane. Crazy I may be, but insane I wasn't. There is a difference.

I felt the plane hit what seemed to be some turbulence, bouncing us around a bit and then slowly decline in altitude. I assumed it was the pilot going to a lower level to avoid anymore bouncing, which was making me nervous as well as others, from looking at the passengers around me. Everyone looked nervous except one guy in the corner, who appeared like he was sleeping thru the whole thing. Maybe he flew so much and bouncing around like that didn't faze him? The plane continued to decline until I felt a sudden leveling off and then it was steady once more. I blew an inward sigh of relief and tried to relax my tense muscles. A few minutes later the flight attendant came out of the forward section looking white as a ghost, with a phony smile on her face. My mouth drew down in concern and I sharpened my gaze and my ears in her direction.

She first went to the sleeping man shaking him gently saying, "Sir. Sir?" But, he didn't rouse. She pulled away with a concerned look on her face, but then went to another male passenger. I heard her ask him if he knew how to fly a plane. Right then, I knew we were in deep shit. The guy she asked was an older business gentleman who also now looked extremely concerned, and started firing questions at her.

She replied, "No sir, no problems at all. The pilot just wanted someone up with him at the cockpit to show a customer around. A small tour to help build up business for more frequent flying, by sharing with certain passengers the unique experience of being a pilot for a huge airline. I assure you, sir, there is nothing wrong. We do this all the time now as a promo." He looked at her, not thoroughly convinced, but it seemed he was willing to go along with (what I thought was) a truly bullshit storyline. She smiled with more assurance at the man and drifted off to another passenger, looking at me out of the corner of her eye. I motioned her over with a no-nonsense, 'come here,' flick of my fingers.

She came over, if reluctantly, asking, "Yes, may I help you?"

I said, "No, I can help you. I can fly and I would love a tour." Ok, it was small planes and Cessna's twenty-five years ago due to a more illegal time in my life…but she was bullshitting too. I needed to know exactly what was going on in the cockpit. The only way that was going to happen was to invite myself in. I knew she was looking at my black leather jacket and jeans, black Harley tee shirt and biker boots. I knew my look inspired fear and mistrust in most 'decent' society type of people. That was the point, but she didn't know that.

How could she know I lived in an area in Tucson called, 'felony flats', by the cops? It was a neighborhood where nine out of ten kids had probation officers by the time they were fifteen. Not my kids, I got lucky, but most of my neighbors did nothing but bitch about the trouble their kids were into and mention how jealous they were of my kids who never caused problems. I always thought a few classes in parenting and reading child development books helped me out the most, but most of the parents I knew only read their TV guides.

Home schooling helped a lot also. Public school, in my opinion are nothing but glorified free day care centers where kids could learn to be bullies, join gangs and do drugs. Not my boys, not on my watch. So home schooling it was. Now that my youngest was sixteen and my eldest turned twenty, I could take a break without worrying about their well being or their teachings as much. I knew they were safe at home, and right at that moment I was really glad they weren't on the plane with me.

"Well, do I win the lottery?' I quipped. She frowned at me slightly, but motioned for me to follow her to the cockpit. We walked down the aisle and passed a small galley area off to the right. To the left was a small sleeping area suggesting that there should be more than one or two pilots aboard. I was asking myself what could have happened to all the pilots. That question was answered as we moved into the cockpit area. Three men, two up front, and one off to the side were all slumped over their equipment with trays of food scattered nearby each of their bodies. Yup, 'bodies' because only the dead lay with such a disregard to comfort for their positions and I could hear no heart beats from any of them, nor see any auras glowing off their corpses when I switched my vision. The light they may have had, had definitely gone out. I breathed deeply and then instantly regretted doing that. Inhaling the air, I could smell a sweet sick smell coming off of their bodies which made me think they were all hit at the same time by the same thing. I looked at the scattered food and then again to their bodies. I was putting clues together very fast. Poison. I'd bet my Harley it was poison.

The flight attendant was watching me closely gauging my reaction to the macabre scene before us.

I raised my own eyebrow at her and said, "No problems, eh?" I sighed heavily, shaking my head, "Understatement of the century if you ask me."

"Can you really fly?" She replied, voice heavy with doubt, I thought it would be best to check this attitude at the door really quick.

"Listen and *hear* me. I can drive anything with wheels, I did fly small planes. What you need to do is stop treating me like white trash with no brains. I may be white trash, but I have more of an education with college as well as street smarts and skills then you will *ever* learn. I have four degrees on my wall, so never think I can't do better than most of those people out there, including you. I'm all you got, and I will do the best I can for all those people out there and you because it is not only your asses on the line, it's mine too."

She took a step back, since I was definitely invading her personal space, and said to me. "Ok, I hear you."

I said, "Good. Now answer me honestly, who fed the pilots their dinner?"

She answered," I did."

"Fine. Did anything unusual happen?" I questioned further.

She shook her head, and then blurted out, "The only thing was a passenger coming into the galley to ask for a drink. He didn't wait for any of us to make our usual rounds. He seemed really impatient." She looked a bit miffed at this.

I asked, "Which one?"

She replied, "The man who is asleep out there." I thought to myself, 'What were the odds?'

"Ok, let's go look at him, but if he is in the same condition these guys are in—don't react just follow my lead," I cautioned her.

Her expression was puzzled, but she followed me out as I had asked. We went to the corner chair and I shook the guy as I took a whiff at the same time. Yup, same smell.

"Sir," I said loud enough to be overheard, "You've had too much to drink we are going to take you into the galley and get you some coffee." I looked at the flight attendant and motioned with my head for her to take his other side. She looked doubtful, but did what I wanted. Taking most of his weight wasn't a problem for me, and we faked taking a supposedly drunk guy out of sight of the other passengers. I laid him in a corner and went to wash my hands just in case. I motioned for her to do the same.

"What's your name?" I asked her.

She glanced at me and said."Lisa, Lisa Wright." I looked at her hands as she washed them and noticed no ring, tidy black hair and pretty hazel eyes. She was slightly shorter then my 5'6.

"Miss Right?" I couldn't resist teasing with a small smile on my face which she answered in kind.

"Don't start with the jokes please. I've heard them all." She gave a tiny smile.

Now that we were on more comfortable footing, I asked her, "Notice anything about the guy on floor?" She looked him over, taking in his short, dark curling hair. He had a lanky medium build with a dark cinnamon cast to his skin.

She answered, "He seems to be in the same shape as the pilots."

"Anything else?" wondering if she could make the connection herself. I was disappointed as she shook her head.

"He's of a Middle Eastern decent." I said. Her eyes grew wide. I noticed her breathing starting to come faster and shorter.

I put my hands on her shoulders and said in a calm voice, "Breathe. Calm down. He is not a threat anymore. He obviously got caught in his own crap." She was shaking her head up and down rapidly, breathing deeper and slowly passing the point of possibility freaking out on me. I couldn't blame her, considering what our country had gone through a few years ago, but losing it now wasn't going to help.

"Look, we're strong, we're tough. We can handle this. What we need now is some gloves and the other first class flight attendant. What's her name?" I said, getting back to business.

"Gloria. We do runs all the time together. She's good." She was still trying to calm down.

I asked, "But she can't fly either?"

"No, none of us can. We're just the aides. It's not in our job description to fly a plane like this. I told Tower this. They told me how to make the corrections and put this plane on autopilot, but that's all I can do. I am not trained for anything more than that. And first aid. I can do first aid." She was rambling now, her voice getting more strident.

Again, I got eye contact and said, "Breathe. We're fine. Everything is going to be fine. I need you to get Gloria, find some latex gloves and you two need to move the bodies into the bunking area. I don't want them laid out with this asswipe, ok? They deserve better than that." She bobbed her head again, tears threatening to spill over.

"Make sure you and Gloria wear gloves when moving the bodies and cleaning up the food. Do NOT touch that food with bare skin." Again I got a rapid compliance from her. I had ruled out a viral exposure for the simple reason she carried the food to them and was fine. Whatever this was it hit them fast, but didn't touch her. Poison was looking more likely by the minute. And since it hit the passenger as well, it must be strong enough that touch alone could be deathly quick. I sure as hell wasn't going to rifle through his pockets, just in case, and I cautioned her against the same thing. The main thing was to keep her busy and get in touch with what she called 'The Tower'. It was a chore I wasn't looking forward to, knowing how most men are towards strong females. I was betting a hundred bucks that I was going to get some flack when I finally got into the head gear and made myself known to them.

CHAPTER TWO
Attitudes, Altitudes and Latitudes
Still on Flight 1409

Lisa came back with Gloria and the gloves. I took notice of the new girl. She was an inch or so taller than me. She was sturdier looking then Lisa, who was very slender, but I thought the two of them could handle things.

I nodded a greeting to Gloria, saying, "Hello, I am Catrina. I will be your pilot for the evening."

She looked at me with brown eyes slightly shocked and looking like she didn't quite know how to take me.

"Never mind, I throw everyone off-guard like that. It's just my way of easing stress for everyone." I smiled at her.

She gave a small smile, which tightened at the sight of the slumped pilots and just that quick, the small awkward grin was gone. I again cautioned them against touching the spilled food with bare skin and helped muscle the bodies down the aisle into the small sleeping quarters they had. It was a very tight fit, but I was damned if they were going to be next to the one responsible for their present condition.

I oversaw them gingerly cleaning up the food spill and made a request, "Can you ladies make sure you put all that into a single plastic bag so it can be examined closely by the proper authorities once we reach the ground?"

Lisa looked up and asked, "Are you some kind of cop or something?"

"Hell no, though I did study criminology in college. I know they will want to screen the food for poisons or other contaminates when we get to the ground."

"What else did you study in college?" Lisa asked. Gloria was listening, but still efficiently cleaning away.

"I studied astronomy, physics, political science, computers, business law and criminal law. I also have a certificate for specializing in certain theological histories. Actually, I have been studying theology and history for much longer, but did class time as well." I wasn't going to say for the past twenty-five years. They wouldn't believe me at this point, and by judging the look on their faces they looked shocked at my list of accomplishments.

Lisa said, "You're kidding, right?"

"Nope," I said, "I have one of those really unusual brains. I can learn anything and kick ass at it. I was always at the top of most of my classes."

"Wow," Gloria said, "Your folks must be proud."

I snorted and shook my head, "My folks could give a shit. My mom and I haven't seen each other since I was twelve, except a phone call every now and again. My father was never in the picture. He took off the minute my mom told him about her pregnancy. I wound up with my stepfather's last name which I will be changing shortly, if I have my way."

Lisa said, "I am sorry to hear that. It must have been rough."

"Some parts yes and some no. I learned a lot. The main thing I learned how to do was to survive no matter what. The odds may be against me, but I know I'm strong enough to kick ass, take names and forget the prisoners." They both smiled at that, as I had meant them to do. "That's how I know we will be fine, no worries."

Keeping them calm would help me stay calm as well. I didn't mention the psychology classes I took as well. If I could have made a career of being a college student I would've stayed there forever. It was the only good thing from my past, besides my kids.

"How do you know we'll be fine if you've never been trained to fly a huge airplane such as this?" Lisa asked, bringing me back to our situation.

"Small aircraft, big aircraft; they've got to have the same basic principles. I can drive anything with wheels from a Harley to a big eighteen wheeler. Same difference, just with wings is all." I tried to sound like I knew what I was talking about, but from the corner of my eye I could see many pretty colored buttons and gauges and small red wheels with steel bars between them and toggles galore. Everywhere. I threw a quick and silent prayer to The Lady and made my way to the seat I had assumed was where the main pilot sat. There was a small black head phone with a mic and I picked it up, putting it on my head. I looked around for a switch that would turn the mic on and found one near the headset rest that look like a good candidate. I switched it on and got a static sound in my ears. I gave myself a mental pat on the back.

"Cat to Tower." I waited for a reply.

"Tower to flight 1409. What took so long? Who exactly am I talking to? This doesn't sound like the flight attendant that I was talking to earlier." Oh great, just what I needed, an anal retentive prick.

"I'm a passenger she found in first class. My name is Catrina Garcia."

"What do you know about flying a commercial plane?" he asked with a condescending voice. Now I knew why Lisa was so high strung earlier.

"More than you know about women obviously," I shot back.

Silence stretched out for a long minute.

"Do you have any real experience flying planes or not?" He still wasn't convinced Go figure.

I gave a short answer, "I flew small aircraft and Cessna's."

"That's nice, but any larger planes?" The condensation went on.

"No," I said simply.

"Then I don't think this is going to be much help." He had just gotten on my last nerve.

"You're right. You're not, get me someone else," I demanded. I knew starting a war with this guy wasn't the smartest thing to do, but I had trouble with my attitude about guys like this.

"Excuse me? I am the one in charge and I say...," he started to rant.

I cut him off, "Shut up. I am the one behind this wheel and I will land this fucking plane by myself if I have too. Then I am coming for you and kicking your ass all over the tarmac. Get me, asshole?"

He sputtered, "Just who..."

Again, I cut him off, "Listen, the flight attendant was asking people if they knew how to fly a plane which was starting to get the passengers upset and asking awkward questions. If you send her back out there for some male you'll feel more comfortable with, but who knows even less than I do about planes, we'll have an even more serious situation up here then what we already do. Now, get me someone else with less attitude, and more brains or there will be hell to pay when I get to the ground."

"Hello, Catrina?" A new voice said in a calm business like voice. "My name is Richard when I am not in the tower. We have call signs when pushing tin, but I think we'll just stick with names for now. That ok with you?"

He was trying to feel me out with a 'talk a jumper off the roof' kind of voice. I knew I had to get this guy on my side, or this would escalate. He just started the conversation with using his first name and trying to get a connection between us. The first step in a potential jumper or hostage situation; establish a friendly bond.

"Thanks, Richard. Names are fine with me. They call me Cat back home." I used the same tactic back at him.

"Great. Now how much flying time do you have and is it on record? Maybe a pilot license?" He sounded hopeful.

Now here was the tricky part. The flying I had learned was from smuggling, and telling these guys I used to do illegal runs wouldn't boost their confidence in me. In fact, they'd have kittens if they knew just how illegal I used to be.

"I flew over 2500 hours. Probably more, but you won't find any record of it. My ex-boyfriend taught me how to fly and we spent a lot of time in the air with mostly me doing the flying." I skirted around the truth.

"And this ex-boyfriend, does he have a pilot license and a flight record?" he continued.

"Yeah, most likely," I said vaguely.

"His name?" he wouldn't be put off.

Fuck it, I wasn't dating him anymore. I gave his name, "Joey Caboni."

"All right then, thanks. Why didn't you get your pilot license though? It sounds like you have enough hours under your own belt?" Richard inquired.

There wasn't much legal work for an underage kid to get, so I had done lots of illegal things to get by. I hadn't done illegal things since I had my first son, wanting to use clean money to buy him things, but old habits die hard. Staying under the radar of the government had just become second nature for me. All of this wouldn't inspire those on the ground.

So again, I skated around the truth, "Never had any reason too. I wasn't going to make a career out of it."

"But you know the basics of flying aircraft?" He wanted clarification.

"Sure, that part is easy." I sounded way more confident then I felt, as I looked at all the bells and whistles around me.

"Good, then we should have an easier time of it showing you how to land a commercial plane." And he did sound more relaxed, but I knew they were running Joey's name through their computers. If they dug deep enough, which I knew they would, he wouldn't sound so relaxed then.

They wouldn't be relaxed when they ran me through, either. I wasn't able to keep my name totally clean, even with precautions taken. I was hoping by then to have enough instruction from this guy to carry off what I needed to do in the meantime. By then they would be out of time trying to find someone else on this plane to fly it. I knew in my gut there would be no one else with the knowledge of flying (no one I could trust)—and I always followed my instincts.

"Now, what we need to do is this, Cat. We need you to take the plane off of autopilot and make some corrections. You're flying on a low flight pattern right now and that could cause some problems later." He started with the instructions.

"That wouldn't be a good idea right now, Richard." I deterred him.

"Oh, why is that." He was sounding a bit on-guard again.

"Well, I hope you've called the FBI because we have one dead man up here that looks like a bad guy of Middle Eastern decent. Though, I hate to racial profile. Shit happens though and these guys usually run in small groups of three or four. Lately, they've been known to recruit new members who actually live in the country they want hit; but I don't think that's the case this time."

Lisa and Gloria both went pale and I mentally kicked myself for not preparing them for this part.

"Why weren't we apprised of this before?" he sounded worried now.

"Because I didn't want to sit or step in food that's probably been poisoned, which is what took out your pilots," I explained.

"What makes you think it was poison?" his tone was doubtful.

"It hit too hard, too fast, and got all three pilots plus a passenger in first class, who had been asking the flight attendant for a drink during the time she was getting the dinner trays ready for the pilots. I'm thinking he handled it wrong and got a touch of the poison on his skin, which took a bit longer to kill him. He made it back to his seat after dosing the pilots. That's my best guess at this point. The main problem I think is, we may have more bad guys up here and I'm afraid of changing anything right now which might alert them to the problems we're having and have them come running up front from coach."

He asked, "Why wouldn't more be in first class?"

"Because that's where Lisa, the flight attendant, started asking people if they knew how to fly. If there were any more bad guys in first class they would have made their move then." I had been thinking about the series of events that might have taken place and this made the most sense to me.

"If you're right, then we have a much more serious problem then we thought."

Again, with the understatements, I thought to myself.

To aid the ladies in calming down, I made eye contact with Lisa, who seemed the shakier of the two and said to Richard, "I have a plan if you're willing to listen?"

He said, "Ok, what's your plan?"

"Hear me out all the way before you say no to this, but these ladies need to get back to their routine and act like nothing is amiss after they get me some weapons. Are there any guns in the cockpit?"

Both girls shook their head no and Richard said, "No, there isn't," he said firmly.

"Ok, old school time then; how about knives?" I sighed deeply thinking of my suitcase in the cargo area.

Richard was saying, "No, I don't…"

But Lisa piped up, "Steak knives are in the front galley for people in first class."

"Steak knives in the galley, Richard. I can use those easily." To Lisa I ordered,

"Go get me four knives and anything I can use as a club maybe."

Meanwhile, Richard was sounding worried, "What do you plan to do with steak knives?"

"Fillet me some bad guys if needs be, but first I have to check the coach area to even see if we have more to deal with. Hang a sec, Richard." And without waiting for a reply, I cut off the headphones and got up as Lisa came back in with the knives. I took them from her and slipped one up each of my sleeves of my leather jacket. I put the other two in my inner jacket pocket for now. I told them both to stay where they were and walked back down the aisle until I was in first class section again. When I got to the partition that separated the coach area, I peeked through the opening. I slowly scanned those seated in rows, looking at each passenger, one by one. I saw one guy with dusky skin, a bald head with a beard and mustache staring intently at the wall that separated coach from where I was and thought to myself, 'Movie screen?' What else is on the wall if I was looking from the seat to the wall? I remembered from the times I flew coach there was a red sign that would go on and off that said, "fasten seat belt", when one had to remain seated for taking off and landing. I kept scanning others and there was another guy five rows away with dark hair, same kind of skin tone with darker shading. He was flicking his eyes up every now and again from his magazine to the wall in front of him. Again, could be a movie screen, but I couldn't angle around without showing myself to see what they were looking at. I saw one other young looking guy on the other side of the aisle, gazing at the bald headed guy, then up front every few seconds, yet he was two rows back and to the side. I seriously doubted it was true love. And, if they all knew each other and were legit, they would be seated more closely together. I also saw another flight attendant pushing a cart, but going towards the back area where I supposed another galley area was for food and drinks for those in coach.

I went back up the aisle to where the ladies were waiting with worried looks on their faces and I asked, "Is there a movie screen or TV on the wall facing everyone in coach?"

"Yes," Lisa said.

"Where exactly is it placed?" I dreaded the answer.

"In the middle," she replied.

Shit, they were looking to the right. I had to ask, "Where is the, 'fasten seatbelt,' sign?"

"On the right—up high," she motioned with her hand. Yup, we were in for it. I stood there thinking of plans, scouting the aisle, and the off-shoot of rooms. I looked at the ladies and evaluated each as a potential fighting partner.

I asked them, "Do either of you have any training in fighting, martial arts or hand to hand combat?"

You never knew; one of them could have been military before becoming what they were now. But neither of them gave off that kind of stance in their walk or speech, so I doubted it. They both shook their heads confirming this assessment.

Gloria stopped and said, "I took self-defense classes."

Self-defense was better than nothing, if you were on the streets looking at a normal street fight, but not so much in this kind of situation.

To mentally empower them I said, "That's great. Once I get these guys subdued you can stand watch over them so I can fly and not worry." Giving her a look that said this would really be a great help, and it would in the bigger picture of things.

But they both gasped and Lisa said, "You aren't going to start anything with them are you?"

Gloria at the same time spurted, "You can't be serious?"

I looked at both of them and saw the redness around their eyes from crying earlier when they found the pilots and saw the tension in their shoulders from the fear of this situation and now knowing there were more terrorists on the plane. Half of me sympathized with them and I was surprised they hadn't had a complete melt down. I also knew that if we didn't do something, and soon, things would go downhill very fast. And things were bad enough.

"Look, those guys out there—and there are three more- won't wait until we land. I have to take them out now before we do anything else. If I get the jump on them the odds will shift back into our favor."

"How are you going to do that? You're one woman against three men. If we lose you as a pilot, we won't have a chance to land safely," Gloria said. Lisa was nodding her head in agreement.

"Number one—I can take three guys out. I've done that and more before." This was true even before I got "blessed" with the super vamp modifications. Street fighting 'down and dirty' became necessary when you're a young girl alone. "Number two—I've had martial arts training my whole life. This isn't as hard as you think for me." This, too, was a true statement. I was trying not to lie to them, but damn, they were making it hard for me.

They both still looked doubtful, but I knew they would eventually see things my way, which better be damned quick, if baldy was staring at the sign already. Besides, I'd just knock them out if it came down to it. I'd hate to do it, but I didn't need anything or anyone else working against me when I already had a mountain load of trouble to deal with coming from all sides.

At least, that's what it felt like.

I sat back down into the seat and grabbed the 'phones again and hit the switch, "Cat to Richard."

"This is FBI Special Agent in Charge Williams of the Homeland Security office for Counter Terrorism," came a clipped, no nonsense voice.

"Wow, you got there quick. I was only gone for ten minutes," trying for rule one of establishing friendly relations.

"Eleven and a half minutes exactly. What the hell do you think you're doing? You need to leave the operations up to the professionals." Apparently, he wasn't having any of rule number one.

"Oh really? Ok, I'll just sit back and let the he-men run the show. Am I to assume that you have a tactical unit up here then?" my voice dripped with airheaded sweetness.

"Well no, but that's doesn't ...," he started. I cut him off, "Then, am I to assume you have some FBI agents on board already? They must have magickally appeared if they are. I didn't know you FBI types could do Copperfield shit, you sly dog, you."

The ladies started laughing and even I was smiling a little.

"Now see here, we have rules we have to follow and I expect you..." again I cut him off from his tirade and orders.

"I expect you like acting like an asshole, but that doesn't mean I want to date you and I didn't even take this shit from my exes....main reason they're exes, you see. You...you are everything I have come to expect from my government and I bet you represent the best of them. And from what I've been reading about you dillrods, that doesn't amount to shit. So, if you are not going to be a part of the solution, quit being part of the problem and shut the fuck up."

"Excuse me, children," I heard someone else say with a bit deeper and gravel sounding voice. "Cat, this is Captain Vincent O'Hara, Delta squad leader from Ft. Hamilton. They call me 'The Rock' in the field though, but Vincent is ok."

Great, we were back to rule one. Progress! Although, I heard the hesitation in his voice. He really didn't like his first name being used so easily. It told me a lot about him right there. One, he was ready to do anything to get some progress going and two, he was ready to bend a bit for me on a personal level. But, only to a point.

"How-de-do, Captain O'Hara, My full name is Catrina Lynn Garcia. I prefer Cat though," I said to keep things friendly with him, but show respect at the same time.

"How-de-do? There is nothing in your file that would suggest you spent any time in the south, or near Louisiana where that particular phrase is used most often?" confusion and curiosity lacing his voice. His knowledge of phrases and cultural identity also let me know I had someone with half a brain...maybe more? Here's hoping.

"I spent some time here, there and everywhere and picked up bits and pieces from different places. I was a truck driver for four years, so I saw a lot of this country and its melting pot of cultures," I expounded.

"A real rambling rose, huh? There is also nothing in your file about truck driving." he sounded a bit put off.

I smiled, though he couldn't see it. "You have a file on me, eh? Bet it's thin."

"It is," he said, like he didn't like that part and it made him suspicious. This was both good and bad. I needed him smart, but I didn't want to let the 'cat' out of the bag either. I had a feeling I was about to be screwed blue and tattooed on that hope.

"It does have a very long juvenile record. But, surprisingly you never did any hard time. Always seemed to slide right out of anything you got into. We also ran your ex, Joey Caboni. He, unlike you, has a very thick file and is currently spending time as our guest in San Quentin for drug smuggling and murder. DEA caught him five years ago with a plane full of cocaine. Any comments on that?" Now he was in interrogation mode.

"Nope, I haven't seen him in twenty-one years. So whatever he has done since then ain't my biz." My dialect was slipping back to street terminology which would also tell him too much. I always do that when put on the defensive. And I sure as hell wasn't going to tell him Joey was my eldest son's biological father.

"Ok. Well, why don't you fill me in on the whole situation you're in now?" He was toning it down a bit.

"Now wait a minute, I am in charge of this operation," Special Agent sunshine cut back in, "and you're not even here so if you..."

Captain O'Hara cut him off, "Our ETA is 15 minutes and this *is* our area of expertise. So we will take over from here."

"Fine, you have her until she hits the ground. Then she is mine," he growled.

"I ain't your anything, sweetcakes. Now shut up and let me fill in the nice Captain." I could imagine the amount of shit that will hit me when I did get to the ground; assuming if we even made it there (alive that is). Until then, screw him.

I gave Captain O'Hara what I had figured out so far. "The situation is this. We have three dead pilots, all killed at the same time after the flight attendant brought them their dinner. I'm assuming poison, rather than a biological viral agent since the man who dosed them is also dead, but it didn't kill the flight attendant. I'm assuming he didn't handle the stuff right and he touched it somehow, where a mere touch of this stuff can kill. Since the dead man looks to be of a Middle Eastern descent, due to the hair and eye color, as well as skin tone, I assumed there would be more, since they tend to roll in groups of three or four men cells. So, I went to look in coach, considering that when the flight attendant started asking passengers who were seated in first class if they could fly a plane and no more bad guys came forward at that time. So, I went to look in coach for them. There are three more men that look from the same cast staring intently at the 'fasten seatbelt' sign since the screen for recreation is in the middle and that sign is to the right. That's where they keep looking. So I'm assuming we have a terrorist cell up here that used poison and is waiting for the 'fasten seatbelt' sign to go on, so they can take over the cockpit and pull off whatever dumb ass idea they have. Although, you have to give them props on thinking of poison since security is so tight these days."

"How do you know so much about terrorists and how they operate?" He sounded suspicious.

"I read. A lot. I know it's racial profiling and lately they've been recruiting natives from whatever country they want to cause shit in, but since this guy is Middle Eastern, I know they don't like to roll with anyone but their own kind. Three men fit that profile," answering him truthfully—sort of.

"How would *you* know these things?" he repeated.

"Why? Are you thinking you're talking to one of their recruits?" I laughed. "I can nix that idea right now. One, they don't roll with others not their kind when on a mission, as I said. Two, they don't roll with females, period, even from their own country. To them, women are inferior, and their cattle mean more to them than women. They'll strap a bomb on one and send her in alone, but they won't roll with her."

"*How* do *you* know these things?" he repeated more strongly.

"How about, because I pay attention. Look, I can't explain it any better than saying I just know. I recall everything I've ever read, watched or learned. I've seen a lot, done a lot and survived a lot. It may not be in my file, but you wouldn't believe the shit I do know."

"I am not disagreeing with you. I believe from your observation alone, you are most likely dead on, but there is nothing in your file that would support *how* you would have learned these things. Unless you were more a part of the underworld then is reflected in your file, and if so, since it isn't in your file, you must be damn good at being bad."

"Can I plead the fifth?" I tinged my voice jokingly.

"No, won't work here," he said in a sharp tone. "Your file says for the past twenty years you look like Miss Mary Sunshine. Not even a parking ticket, but you talk Mata Hari? That makes me nervous."

Exactly what I was trying to avoid.

"I get that. I really do, but you're just going to have to trust me. I am one of the good guys, and will do my best, which ought to be done soon, before the three stooges in coach get jumpy. So what say you let me do what I do best, and take these guys out? Then, show me how to land the plane and we'll have all have coffee when we touch the ground, Captain." I put force in my voice to show him I had strength. Any warrior of any flavor can hear it in another; I was counting on him knowing that tone of voice.

"You're asking me to take a lot on faith. And I don't do faith real well right now. And I don't know what your best is." From his tone he sounded like he had been recently burned, and burned bad.

"I understand that, Captain, but the point is, you haven't got anyone else but me. So let's get this show on the road," wishing he would just drop it.

"What's the plan?" Good, right where I needed him to go.

"I'll send the ladies out one more time to settle the passengers again. Then I'll have them sit in here behind these nice comfy seats where they'll be safe and flip the sign on for me. Meanwhile, I'll wait outside the cockpit for Larry, Curly and Moe to make their move. Then take them out."

"Just like that, huh?" he sounded skeptical.

"Yup, Hey diddle diddle, straight up the middle," I quipped.

"That's a Marine quote. You weren't in the Marines." he sounded sure of that, if nothing else.

"Nope, but I dated quite a few of them."

"That doesn't make you an expert in tactics." I could almost see him shaking his head.

I said dryly, "You'd be surprised."

"See, there you go with the Mata Hari shit again," he spouted.

"Then isn't it lucky I'm on your side?" I said slyly.

"You don't like the government. With your juvenile record and your attitude toward authorities, you are prime for recruiting; and you're asking me to trust you?" He just laid it out for me.

"I get that. I don't fit anywhere in most profiles and I'm ok with it, but you have no frame work for it. That keeps you off-balance, which you don't like. I may hate the government, but I love my country. I wouldn't betray my country, no matter what. Besides, what other choice do you have?" laying it right back out for him. "What can you do from there? Helicopters—even if you can get one out here fast enough, it can't keep up with a huge airliner such as this. Not to mention the back draft from the engines on this beast. An F-14? Can't jump one from another with any hope of survival. Your best bet would be an F-14 ready with a missile and shoot us down before we get near whatever target these asswipes have in mind. Because in the end, it's about the numbers. Two or three hundred people compared to a thousand or more; if it were me, I'd take out the plane and call it a day."

"Could you?" he asked.

I paused and thought about it. "I don't really know, honestly. I'm not the one in your shoes. So it's me or a missile. Your call, not mine. Trust what your gut tells you," and I let him stew over that.

CHAPTER THREE
Attitude Adjustments
In the skies of New York

Wizard, what's the status of a visual?" Captain O'Hara looked at his newest team member who had the unfortunate timing of joining when the shit hit the fan on the last mission. The mission that had gotten him and his team stuck stateside and not out in another country where they could do the most good.

"Good to go in two minutes." Sergeant Mark Logan aka 'The Wizard' didn't even look up from his screen. His blond hair was in a military buzz, and his bright hazel green eyes just kept going back and forth over the flow of data.

O'Hara took a deep breath and closed his eyes. He was confused and he didn't like that. 'Cat' represented a variable that couldn't be factored. She sounded confident enough. She knew enough. She knew too damn much. How does an ex-street kid know so much? Looking at her file was like looking at two different women, one really bad, and one really good; well three, if you counted what he had to deal with at present time, and this version had attitude galore. But not malice, he thought to himself. She'd said, "I don't know," when confronted with a hard decision no one with a conscious would want to have to make. She'd also said, "Let me do what I do best and take these guys out." A conundrum and contradiction like that could make a cluster-fuck out of a situation like this. The last one was one too many, and he didn't want another FUBAR on his hands. 'Trust what your gut tells you,' is what General Pierce had said to him many times. He listened to his gut last time, and look what happened. However, the General was right about trusting his gut. He must have been right in his decision on the last mission, but it didn't stop the shit from hitting the fan and his ass being roasted over the fires. And now his gut was telling him something impossible once again.

"We're up, Rock," Wizard cut through his thoughts.

"Have you got the cockpit?" he asked as he leaned over and looked down at the screen. He saw her sitting there with what looked like a manual reading it fast. Too fast, for much comprehension, he thought.

"What's she reading?" Babyface asked curiously, though his tone was dead flat; a contradiction to his soft round face. If you didn't look into his cold steel eyes, you would think him a nice mellow guy; he was anything but. Babyface was his call sign, but he was Major Jonathon Harris, one of the coldest killers O'Hara had ever known. They had been on many missions together; fought and bled together. O'Hara trusted this man at his back any day of the week.

"It looks like a flight manual. Doesn't look like she's waiting for instructions. Fits with the personality we've seen so far," O'Hara answered. At least she was consistent in that aspect.

"Where are the flight attendants?" This from Romeo, figures. He always zoned in on the women. His name may have been Sergeant Theodore Watson, but it should have been Don Juan. He could smell a chick from fifty miles, and with his lanky down home boy good looks—he got them.

Wizard tapped at the board and got a picture of the women taking drinks and pillows to their respective passengers in first class.

"Looks like she's moving forward with her plan, boss," Babyface looked at O'Hara with hard eyes. "Seems like we've got two options, her way, or the missile way. Which way we gonna jump?" his tone reflected that he really didn't care which way they jumped. So long as the job got done.

O'Hara turned back to Wizard, "Click it back on her."

The screen flicked back to the cockpit, which showed she was more than halfway through the book already.

"How could she possibly get enough information out of the manual going that fast?" Wizard asked O'Hara.

"Maybe she's skimming, speed reading?" O'Hara took a wild guess.

Right then she stopped, leaned back, and he got a good look at her face.

"She doesn't look like she is pushing fifty; she looks more like mid-twenties. This can't be right." O'Hara picked up the file again, scanning for the date of birth and her drivers' license, which matched. He looked at the screen again, seeing her with her long brown hair down to her ass and it didn't even look like it was going to grey any time soon. She could be using hair dye. She was pretty though. Her license said she had blue eyes. She looked fit from what he could see with her sitting. Built really nice, too. He moved his thoughts from that. Her records from her youth showed a girl who didn't give a fuck about anything. No school records past the sixth grade. A series of assault charges and even an attempted murder charge at age twelve. The charges were dropped for no apparent reason. Her college records showed an above average intelligence level and a wide variety of classes. Damn, what did she do, take every course offered? Mostly A's, graduated with a 3.8 GPA. A Board of Governors Award, and many high achievement awards. Not bad for a street kid, almost unheard of actually. A contradiction in mind and living. It also said a single mother of three boys. None of them had a record. They were squeaky clean. Also, no school records, but there were affidavits for home schooling. College *and* home teaching her children? A living contradiction all around. Most single parents are too busy surviving to teach their own kids. How the hell did she pull it off? Only one other paper, a Business License was registered to her for an online store for pagan supplies. What the fuck was a pagan?

"Anyone know what a pagan is?" O'Hara asked out loud to the group.

Wizard answered, "Someone who doesn't follow one of the main religions and follows a pagan faith."

"Muslim isn't a pagan religion, is it?" O'Hara sounded doubtful.

"No, it's considered one of the main ones. Christianity, Jewish or Muslim are considered 'main stream'. Any others are considered pagan," Wizard said.

"Got that thing tagged for the coach area?" O'Hara looked up from his papers to Wizard who nodded and clicked the pad again.

The screen switched to a view of the coach area and he intently scanned the passengers sitting in rows.

"Too bad we can't ask her to point them out. Think she knows about the cameras?" Babyface asked O'Hara. Cameras installed on commercial liners were a relatively new thing. Some planes still didn't have them, but this one did. They got lucky on that.

"It's not widely known yet. She shouldn't know about them. Then again, she shouldn't have known a lot of things about cell operations either," he answered back. He spotted a couple of likely candidates and pointed those out to Wizard. "Snap those and send them through the data base, see if we have a match." If they could find any corroboration to what she has been saying, it would give O'Hara a lot more to work with.

He felt the chopper lowering slowly and knew they were at the airstrip, landing as close as they could to the tower. Time for the face to face pissing contest with, what did she call him? 'The dillrod'? Yeah, that would fit.

He and his team walked into the control tower and saw several men seated at their stations, each with their monitors and keypads and various other types of equipment needed to guide their planes in and out. One man was standing wearing a grey suit and he was betting this would be 'the dillrod'. Grey suit turned and O'Hara saw a grey and silver tie around his neck. Shit. FBI agents come in one of two flavors. Those who wear a standard black tie are all about the job and nothing but the job. Those that wear designers ties are bureaucrats and not always about the job, but the politics that can get them up the ladder.

Those kinds can cause more problems even after the job is done. Plus, he was here alone. These guys usually worked in pairs. That made him a glory hound looking for the big win. Shit.

"Special Agent in Charge Williams, I am head of the Homeland office here." He stuck his hand out, but his face was hard. He was in his late forties and still fit-looking for being a bureaucrat. But he had eyes like a cobra, and that put O'Hara on edge even more. His gut was telling him something was off with this guy, but he couldn't pin point it yet.

"Captain O'Hara and this is my team, Jonathon Harris aka Babyface, my second in command, Theodore Watson aka Romeo, and Mark Logan aka The Wizard. He's our tech guy." He put his rank out there because it would matter to this bureaucrat, but he didn't add his men's rank to the list. Special force teams usually don't fuss much with rank. If you live, you're a bad ass. That's your rank. He shook the Special Agent's hand and noticed he was also wearing a ring. FBI Agents usually don't wear any jewelry what-so-ever and yet this big sterling silver ring set had a black onyx stone with an engraved symbol embossed with more silver, another odd thing with this agent (to be considered later).

"So, you lead; Harris is your second in command and Logan is your tech. What does Watson do?" Williams asked. O'Hara could tell he wanted rank and abilities of the whole team.

"He gets the girls." He gave Special Agent Williams a dead set stare with a raised eyebrow. He was 6'3 at 225 lbs of rock solid muscle, but it was the eye habit that got him named.

Williams drew himself up and asked, "What kind of progress have you made so far?" in a cold tone.

"Wizard?" O'Hara clipped.

Mark knew what he wanted without having to be asked; it's how he made the team.

"We have a hit on two of those pics we took. No joy on the third, except his passport and visa having been cleared by a University Professor that is under FBI surveillance already for forging and passing said passports and visas to undesirables of the Middle Eastern flavor. The fourth picture is just a Mexican national and he checks out."

O'Hara turned to look at Williams again with the eye.

"The Professor's name?" O'Hara asked.

"Professor Haji Rammondon of Boston. Harvard," Wizard answered before O'Hara could ask which university.

O'Hara was still looking at Williams who answered the silent question, "We are aware of Professor Rammondon's activities. He's been under investigation for two and a half years."

Romeo snorted and Williams took exception to that. "Investigations take as long as they take. You know that."

Romeo answered, "A lot of buildings could be blown to shit in two and half years."

"No shit," this from Wizard.

"We have to have enough evidence, concrete evidence, before we go against someone with his standing at a prestigious university," Williams said snidely.

"Meanwhile, we have this to deal with, gentlemen." He was trying to turn the focus.

O'Hara could see him trying to slide back into a position of power again as well and he shot it down. "No, we have the combat training. WE will deal with it. You don't have that plane or anyone on it until they touch the ground. Then that's your jurisdiction." The hard look was back in his brown eyes.

"And how do you plan to deal with that hellion?" Williams said with an air of superiority. "*You* can't even touch her right now, but when she hits the ground, if she does it alive, she'll wish she hadn't even bothered." His thin lips slid into a cruel smile.

"Why, what are you planning to do to her?" asked Romeo before O'Hara could.

"If she lands the plane alive, I'll throw the book at her. Obstruction of Justice, obstruction of an FBI terrorist investigation and anything else my department and the FCC can come up with. If she doesn't land that plane right, she'll be implicated with the terrorist," he smiled smugly.

"Damn, so she's fucked no matter what she does," Romeo looked disgusted.

"She should have thought about that before she stuck her nose where it didn't belong. And if she does manage to take those men out—which I seriously doubt—I'll have her for assault and murder as well." O'Hara noticed he'd said, 'stuck her nose where it didn't belong.' He filed that away for later consideration.

"Guys, we need to do something soon. Flight 1409 is about 30 minutes away from some heavy air traffic. I can steer some of the planes on an alternate path, but I would rather have the plane climb higher to make things easier." The air-controller spoke up from his seat before the monitor which had the trajectories of all incoming and outgoing flights in the area.

"And you are?" O'Hara looked at the medium built man with dark hair and worried hazel eyes.

"Richard Thompson. Air Traffic coordinator for this section for now, since I took over for Hank, who just got on her nerves. Not without reason. Hank can get on anyone's nerves, given enough time," he said with a half smile.

"Good to meet you. Glad you could at least get her to talk without the temper. It makes things easier for everyone," O'Hara said to Richard, but was looking at Williams from the corner of his eye and saw him tighten in his stance.

"Wizard, status of those on that plane?" O'Hara turned to where Wizard had taken over an unoccupied station and had set up his laptop and gear.

"She's still in the cockpit, just finished reading. Flight attendants are headed her way. Hoppy is getting anxious."

"Hoppy?" O'Hara queried.

"Yeah, the younger one, Rajul Kidar Mousal his passport says, age twenty, is moving around in his seat like he has A.D.D. or something." His tone of voice sounded concerned.

O'Hara's eyebrow went back up, "The other two?"

"Cueball and Snake? Tight, real tight. Snake isn't reading a magazine anymore and he took off a metal leg brace he had on his right leg." Meaning they've been waiting for that sign for too long and were getting edgy. Just like she said they would, thought O'Hara.

"She didn't say anything about a guy with a metal leg brace." He walked over and bent down to watch the screen more closely over Wizard's shoulder.

Wizard shook his head, "She wouldn't have seen the leg brace from behind that curtain separating coach from first class. Snake's leg is out of line of sight from that position." Wizard showed him the angles on the screen.

O'Hara nodded, mostly to himself and straightened back up. He had made his decision. "Ok, Richard let us know when the flight patterns become just this side of 'oh fuck'. Wizard, record everything from all cameras. The one in the cockpit, one in the aisle, one in the first class area and the two in coach. Can you split screen so we can watch more the one area at the same time?"

"Can do, Rock." Wizard started tapping away at his computer again getting it set for the way O'Hara wanted it.

O'Hara walked over to Richard's station, "Can I borrow your mic?"

"Sure can. Everyone on the other flight patterns are settled for now, but don't take too long at this," scooting aside so O'Hara could use the mic.

Richard had it ready for talking to flight 1409, so he just turned the mic on. "Tower to Cat."

Back on Flight 1409

"Hey, there. How come you sound like Captain Vincent O'Hara?" I could guess why, but I was being cheeky anyways.

"We made our ETA and we are set up in the Tower here at La Guardia now. I need to know if you really can handle these guys on your own." He was getting right back to business.

"Why? What's up?" I was curious.

"Let's just say I believe you about the fact that there are more bad guys and things could go south if you don't get a move on soon. Now he sounded like he was the one evading something.

I sat and thought for a bit as I started braiding my hair. I tied a black hair band to the bottom of it then shove the braided tail down the back inside my jacket to keep it out of the way.

"I can do it if things go my way." I sounded sure.

"Do you have a plan?" He was sounding more open to me than before. I was wondering what was up with him, but I let it go for now.

"I got a rough outline," I said truthfully to him.

"All right then, go for it, but don't get any civilians up there killed." He made it sound like an order.

"Sure," I said back. Like that was no problem. I shook my head and the girls had come back. I turned to them, speaking to them both.

"Ok, here's what I need to you to do. Lock this door when I leave. Then in exactly one minute flip that switch for the sign. Hide behind the seats and don't open that door for anyone but me. No matter what, ok?" The cockpit was the safest place I could think to put them.

They both looked scared as hell, but nodded their heads. They were holding hands, for crying out loud.

I walked out and closed the door. I turned and looked at my options. I didn't like the fact that once these guys were coming up front, they would see me and be ready. That wouldn't be a good thing. So, no hey-diddle-diddle this time. A bit more of an old fashioned ambush would be more like it.

41

The first place I would look if being a bad guy would be the galley which would most likely have a person there. They'd be ready for that too.

I looked at the bunk area. It was the only other option, since taking these guys out in front of a bunch of people in first class was out, for so many reasons.

Shit, this isn't going to be pleasant. I moved in, taking my knives out of my jacket. I kept the curtain opened and waited; ignoring the bodies behind me and the one on the floor at my back heels. I made a note to myself not to drop back my left foot this time and I waited.

Back at the Tower

"How's she doing?" O'Hara directed his question to Wizard.

"She's in an ambush position. She looks calm and ready. Total focus mode," Wizard answered back.

"That's my problem with her. From the start she has been calm. No fear. No hesitation. That's not normal. I say she's in league with these men and we're letting her set them up with the plane. Just handing it over to the enemy," Williams added his opinion loudly.

"Sure, that's why she's ambushing them as we speak," O'Hara growled. This guy was really getting on his nerves.

"With steak knives? Please, O'Hara," Williams snorted in disbelief.

"Captain O'Hara, Williams. But, you're right; three men with steak knives would be hard even for one of us in such close quarters," he said that last part under his breath.

Harris, aka Babyface, piped up to the room, "Fifty says she does it with two minor injuries."

Romeo joined in the customary betting before a mission is a go, "Fifty says she takes two down with one major injury."

"What? She doesn't make the full mission?" asked Babyface.

"No. Three men against someone of her stature? That's too much weight. Plus she's a civvy, no way." Romeo was a bit of a sexist too.

Wizard added his bet, "I see that fifty and raise you another she takes them with one minor injury. Rock?"

He looked around at the room. The operators looked appalled that they were betting on the outcome, but a few looked like they wanted to join in the fun. He smiled. "A hundred she makes it, but with one major injury." He had read her juvy file.

Williams looked at him with his mouth hanging open in shock. He snapped it closed when O'Hara turned to look him full on at his face with a tight smile.

"How can you be so cavalier, Captain?" Richard said. "There are innocent people up there."

He looked at Richard and his face hardened. "We know that and we know what's at stake, but we can't do anything, personally, about it. So to de-stress we add the fun before a mission. It takes the edge off for us, and makes our job easier to deal with mentally, because we have to face this kind of shit every time we go out."

Richard sat back at this mild rebuke.

The ball Babyface had got going in black humor had stopped and everyone turned grim-faced toward the screen where the drama would unfold. All of them were hovering over Wizard's terminal. The tension was back to being thick as ice and almost as cold.

Back on Flight 1409

I could feel them coming, like a dark cloud of malevolence and hate, thick black swirls of negative energy rolling toward me. I realized I had tapped into my power, and stopped the empathic wave. Instead, I focused on becoming as invisible as possible. I knew doing a 'blending into my environment' using power was risky, but I needed the curtain opened so I could move fast and unimpeded before striking. If anything electrical did go freaky, I knew I could call out to one of my mates. Andre was real good at fixing electrical power circuits even from a distance. Of course, he'd have to astral project here, but oh well; I would cross that bridge if and when I came to it.

And then there was the bald one. I pegged him as the leader when I first saw him. He was followed by the youngest one. The one with a mustache was bringing up the rear. As baldy neared the doorway for the bunk, his head was still slightly turned toward the galley door. He was looking like he was expecting someone to be in there, which gave me the few seconds I needed to rush out and jam his right shoulder hard. He was thrown hard into the opposite wall. With the momentum, I took my knife in my right hand and quickly slit his throat. Blood sprayed the wall in front of him and coated it red over the blue paint. With one motion I put my weight back on my left leg and kicked the younger one three times with my right, each harder and faster than the kick before. I heard a crack and felt a rib or two cave in. The Mustache guy was right behind him, mouth opened wide with shock. His right hand was moving up. I thought I saw a weapon, but didn't give a thought to it as I drew my hand back fast. I threw the knife with power into the middle of his chest. I then heard a pop and felt a burning sting in my right leg and looked down, seeing blood welling out from a wound that had appeared.

I took a deep breath and dropped to my left knee, pain throbbing from the wound in the right thigh. I grabbed a bandana from my inside coat pocket and wrapped it around my upper thigh, right over the wound. I was hoping to catch all the blood before any got on the floor, but looking down, I saw some already there. Shit, I hope they have bleach on board this airliner. I took a look at the terrorists and baldy was dead. No aura off him anymore. The younger one had passed out from the pain with his hand clutched at his side, curled up in the aisle. Mustache guy had fallen backward after he had fired his shot and no light was coming off of him either. He was gone. He was laying there with a knife sticking out of his chest, buried to the hilt. I stood up slowly, feeling a burn in my leg again.

'What the fuck happened?' I heard Andre in my head. He must have felt my pain as I got shot; then again when I stood up. This was the down side of the high bond we had. We could feel everything from the others all the time. Pain, happiness, even if one of us were hungry, we felt it. I had kept such tight control of my feelings ever since this had started just so they wouldn't know I was in deep shit up here. There wouldn't have been too much they could have done about it, even if they had known. And using any power would be bad for the systems up here as well. I knew that when they found out what I had been up too for the past hour, they might seriously think about spanking me. Hey, that could be good, I thought to myself with a wry smile. Shaking my head clear from the graphic pictures I was giving myself, I answered him quickly.

'I'm safe. Still in airplane with too much electrical shit around. Not safe to talk. Will fill you in when I hit the ground. Love you.' I cut him off while I grabbed mustache guy by the shoulder and dragged him to the galley, since he was closest to it. I threw him next to the first dead guy and went back for the younger one. He was still alive, but out cold.

I dragged him in and looked around the place searching for something to tie him up with. I went back out to the aisle and saw the curtain that hung to the side of the door for the sleeping area had some long plastic cords for drawing the curtains tight. I cut those off and went back to the galley, tying the young guy tight. Then, with one more trip, I got baldy lying next to the other two dead guys. I walked back to the cockpit feeling tired already.

CHAPTER FOUR

Cat out of the Bag
Back at the Tower

Did you see that shit? Did you see that fucking shit?" Wizard was looking around at the rest of them as if he couldn't believe what he'd seen with his own eyes.

"She moved like lightening and almost as fast. Go back to where she's in the bunk area and slow it down." The hair on the back of O'Hara's neck was standing on end. He had never seen anyone move so fast. The first kill had happened so quick, they didn't even know he was dead, until they saw the blood spraying on the wall. By then, she was already moving onto the second target. All three went down like dominoes, but so fast you would have missed it if you blinked. That wasn't normal. That wasn't even human. She obviously had the skills of an assassin, but he'd never known of any assassin who could move that fast, that supple.

They watched the replay in slow motion and again, a few of the men were spouting 'man, you see that shit' comments. It had looked like she'd come out of nowhere and the bodies started falling. Then they watched again, until they reached the part where she dropped to her knee.

"She got hurt. What hurt her?" Babyface asked. Even he looked impressed and he wasn't impressed by much.

"Look at the last guy. He had something in his hand. Can you zoom in on that?" O'Hara asked of Wizard.

"I'll try," his hand was shaking a bit as his tapped the controls on his pad. It looked like a toy gun. It was one of those specially made guns that come apart like a jigsaw puzzle and made of strong wood instead of metal. It had a polycarbonate coating that hardened so the barrel wouldn't blow apart expending a bullet. They only hold one or two shots and were for shit on accuracy, but for threat, they would do the job for a hijacking. How the hell did he get that past security? Being made of wood and poly-ceramic, it wouldn't set off the metal detectors, but the pieces, even separated, should have been found by security. And what about the bullets? They were made of metal. Those would not have passed thru security at all. O'Hara mentally snapped his fingers—the metal brace. If they took a good look at that metal brace, he would bet they would find empty holes where the bullets had been and maybe even a small metal barrel that could fit into the wooden one.

"Look at her now. She's dragging those bodies practically one handed and one of those guys must weigh about 210," Romeo pointed this out to the group.

"I want a copy of everything before we leave here," Williams demanded. "When she hits the ground, we'll need this for evidence." O'Hara knew he was telling the truth about needing it for evidence, but he didn't miss the hard gleam in his eye either. His face was hard and had turned white when he watched her move the way she did. He knew something, but what could he know? O'Hara asked himself. Something is off about this whole thing; his gut was screaming at him now.

Back on Flight 1409

I knocked on the door of the cockpit saying, "It's just me. Bad guys are down. Everything is cool, open up."

The door clicked and started to open slowly. I could see Lisa peeking through the crack, still looking scared. When she saw it was me she opened it wider and gasped as she took in my state of being.

I was a bit of a mess, so I asked, "Can you find me some clean towels, a pair of tweezers, some iodine, a plastic bag and some bottled water. Oh, and some bleach, if you've got it?"

She looked at me like I was speaking a foreign language for a minute, then nodded and went around me. I grabbed her before she could go much farther. "One of the bad guys is still alive. He's hurt and tied up. Under NO condition are you to even speak to him, go near him, or offer any aid. I don't care if he starts crying about his momma, he doesn't exist for you. They lie. They'll lie about anything to get close and kill you. Don't believe a fucking word he says. Just ignore him." I moved closer to her to make sure she got the point, "If you do anything for him, I will personally kick your ass. Believe that."

She nodded fast and went down the aisle. I turned to Gloria and said, "Same goes for you. I can't worry about him and fly at the same time. I need to know he's down and out of my hair." She nodded almost as rapidly as Lisa did, eyeing the blood on my leg.

Well, there goes our great friendship. Show a bit of roughness, kick some ass and people start treating me like I'm Typhoid Mary or something. I sighed heavily.

Lisa had come back with the things I asked for and I laid down two hand towels on the seat and sat down. I moved the towels so they were right under my wounded leg to catch all the blood and liquid I would be spilling on it. I took out one of the remaining unused knives from my sleeve. I'd put the one I had used on Baldy in the sink before dragging the bodies in there. And thought to myself, 'well that was stupid'. "Hey Lisa, there's a knife in the sink. Go get it and bring it here, please."

I started cutting into my jeans just enough to get the wound exposed properly, putting the pieces into the bag. I took the bottle of water and poured it over the wound and saw a gleam of dark metal. I had to get it out quick before it started to poison me. Not because of the Super vamp stuff, but because I was naturally allergic to any metals unless it was sterling silver or pure gold. With this in my leg, I was slowly being poisoned and would soon become really ill. I took the tweezers and doused it with iodine, then did the same to my leg. Hissing a bit from the pain, I could feel my teeth starting to descend. Shit, just what I needed, my fangs showing and really scaring the shit out of these girls. I kept my head down because Gloria was watching in gross fascination as I dug the tweezers into my leg and grabbed at the expended bullet. I pulled it free and a wet meaty sound popped as the bullet came out. Gloria started to gag as blood welled up and spilled over from the wound. I let it bleed to get any contaminates out and put the bullet into the bag with the tweezers. I poured more iodine over the wound then I took a towel and wrapped it around my leg, tightening it to staunch any more blood flow.

I took the soaked towels from under my leg and put these into the bag, too. I grabbed the bleach and went back into the hall. I looked around for the spots that were my blood and mopped that up with my remaining towel. Then I poured bleach over the area. I knew this wouldn't destroy the DNA completely, with forensics having come so far these days, but I had one trick up my sleeve that would have to wait until neither of the women was around to see it. Everything that had my blood on it went into the bag and I put it in my inside jacket pocket. This made my jacket really pooch out on one side, but I didn't care. I wasn't leaving this laying around for anyone to grab, even by accident.

Lisa was back with the knife and asked, "What do you want with this?"

"Just put that on the other pilot seat. I don't want to leave it for the dipweed to find in there."

Since that blade didn't have my blood on it I didn't give a shit what happened to it. Finger prints, yeah, but they had those already from my driver's license. It would be an exercise in futility trying to wipe all my prints.

I picked up the toy looking gun from the floor and looked at it. It looked like it was made of ironwood which lived up to its name. It was a bitch to carve. It was also lined with a plastic ceramic bond. Man, the things these bad guys come up with I thought to myself. I dropped the gun next to the knife on the other seat and sat back down. The girls had gone back down the aisle to take care of their passengers again and I had a few minutes to myself. I leaned back, smelling my own blood and Baldys, and felt my teeth with my tongue. I was thirsty and not for water. Made sense since I was hurt, so I needed to replace the blood soon, but there wasn't any way of doing that on the plane.

Back at the Tower

O'Hara and Wizard were watching as she doctored herself with nothing more than a pair of tweezers. Williams had made a sound of disgust and moved to watch the monitor Richard was sitting in front of with the scope for the planes on their courses.

O'Hara never moved. If she could take it, then he could stand witness. A warrior didn't flinch when another warrior was going through pain whether it was torture or medical. And warrior she was. She kept those ladies safe. In fact, everyone on the plane was safe and kept away from the worst of what was going on because of her. That was a miracle in and of itself; if he still believed in such things anymore.

"Holy..." Wizard was cut off when O'Hara clamped his hand down on his shoulder and squeezed hard shutting him up. He had seen the same thing Wizard had.

Williams turned to look and asked, "What is she doing now?" and started to walk over.

O'Hara quickly answered, "Nothing, just more blood poured out of her leg. It gushed pretty badly," he lied. He didn't quite believe what he saw, but he lied nonetheless. His gut told him too.

Williams took on a look of disgust again and stayed where he was, which was just what O'Hara wanted.

Wizard was looking at him intently, his eyes begging questions. They had both seen the fangs.

She moved like an assassin. She wasn't human. O'Hara didn't know what she was, but she wasn't human. Still, she'd kept those people safe. She kept her cool through the whole thing. It was the one point he couldn't condemn her for. She was working for them, not against them in every action she took. He noticed her cleaning up her blood. She didn't give a shit about the blood on the walls, ignored it even, but her blood, she meticulously cleaned up and separated from everything else. She bagged her things. Something a professional assassin would do as well, but she didn't bother with finger prints. She knew she would be in custody when she hit the ground. But she cleaned up her blood anyway and anything that touched her blood.

O'Hara's lips went thin and acting on his instincts, he bent down and whispered in Wizard's ear, "Copy everything from the time she was in the bunk area right before her attack to just now. Then make it look like a glitch so those scenes don't show up anymore and hide our copy. This dillrod doesn't get that." And he straightened back up with Wizards face going into shut down mode; he went to work on his computer. His second in command gave him a hard look, and then a slight nod of his head. Romeo, too, was looking serious, which wasn't his normal façade, and nodded his assent. O'Hara nodded back at them and went outside to make a phone call.

Back on Flight 1409

Goddess, I was tired. I needed blood. I needed sleep. If I tapped into the bond between my mates and me, I could draw energy from them to keep me going. I couldn't function at top level like this. And we still weren't out of the woods. I was thinking about the blood I could take from the wounded terrorist. They did owe me blood, since it was them that had cost me blood. The Goddess was all for an eye for an eye justice system, so I knew I could get away with it in this situation. However, the idea of taking it from him made me feel slightly nauseous. I needed to do this even though it was second best to taking blood, the risk to the equipment around me notwithstanding. I stood up and swayed. I backed away from everything as far as I could get. Closing my eyes, I focused on the bond which had settled right on the top of my solar-plex chakra and opened it up. Three shining bonds were glowing from it and I drew energy from those cords and into me.

"Baby, are you ok?" Andre asked.

"Yeah, I am really tired and need to do this fast. Please trust me," I begged.

"Anything, anytime, anywhere, just come to us," he pleaded.

"I'm almost there, I think. Now hush, shit is starting to flicker around me. Love you," I said to him with my heart.

"Love you more," he replied.

I drew the energy I needed, then shut down the connection completely. I looked around and the flickering had stopped. I blew a sigh of relief. Nothing blew up or sparked. I felt for my teeth with my tongue and noticed they had retracted. I sat back down into the seat and grabbed the head phones again.

"Cat to Tower."

"You got Richard, Cat. How are you doing?" He asked sounding genuinely concerned.

"Score one for us. Bad guys down and now we're ready for some instructions on landing this beast," I said in a perky voice, even though I still didn't feel very perky.

"That's good news! But we need to do something else first, ok?" he sounded concerned about something else now.

"Sure, what's up?" I asked.

"Your flight altitude is too low. Bigger planes are always sent up higher to avoid collisions with the smaller, faster planes. We need you to make those corrections until you are close enough to the airport where then you need to start coming down. Do you understand that?" he asked.

"Yeah, makes sense to me. So, what do I need to do first?" All business now.

"First, do you see the horizontal gauge? With a symbol of a plane with wings hovering over a middle line? That's called a planer," he started directing.

"Yup, the horizontal. Got it." I saw it off to my right at about the middle of the console.

"Ok, once you turn off the auto pilot, you need to keep your eye on that gauge," he instructed.

"No worries." I grabbed the wheel for the plane with one hand and saw the switch that said autopilot.

Richard said, "Do you see the switch for the autopilot?" falling a step behind me.

"Yup, got my eye on it already. You want me to hit it?" Just to help keep in line with him.

He said, "Yes, then watch your horizontal gauge."

I flicked the switch and felt the plane drop out of autopilot. I could feel the weight of the plane through the wheel that I was now holding in both hands.

"Oh, this thing feels like driving a bus. A really big bus. Loaded down," I remarked dryly.

"Good, you are already getting the feel of the plane. You're doing great," Richard sounded encouraging.

"Richard, I appreciate the props and such. I really do. It's way better then getting asshole 'tude from other guys, but this will go so much faster if you just run it down by the numbers. Just like any of the other guys, ok bud?" I was trying to be nice about it, but the 'handle with care because I'm a girl thing', I didn't have the patience for right now.

"Sorry, I'm just trying to ease you into this," he sounded a bit put off.

"No worries, Richard, I'm just out of sorts, tired and want to get this done. So what's next? Just run it down for me step by step," I tried my friendly voice.

"Ok, now pull back slowly and gently on the wheel until the plane matches up with the floating ball on 15 degrees and hold it there until I tell you otherwise," saying in a more instructive tone, as I'd asked.

"Got it." I pulled back carefully and watched the plane symbol and the floating black ball with numbers on the side and pulled until it hit the requested degree altitude.

I held it there steady, waiting for further instructions from Richard.

"Ok, now level off. Get the ball back on zero degrees again with the plane symbol," he said.

I did as instructed and said, "Ok, now what?"

"You're a bit off course. Now do you see the gauge for latitude?"

"Yup, got it." It was a bit more toward me on the console, but near the horizontal.

"Good. Turn the wheel to the right by 5 degrees until I say stop," getting to the point faster now.

I did and felt the shift in the plane.

Lisa and Gloria had come barreling into the cockpit and stopped to watch me.

"Ok, stop. Get it back on zero degrees," he said.

"Ok," and I leveled out the turn and watched the gauge go back to zero.

"Good," Richard said, "You're back on course now at the right altitude. We don't have to worry for another 20 or so minutes. Meanwhile, we'll go over the preparations of landing a plane if that's all right with you?" he asked.

"Yeah, no worries I'm having fun up here, dude." That got him laughing.

I turned to look at the girls and Lisa said, "You need to tell us when you're doing shifts like that. I spilled a glass of wine on a passenger out there."

"Oh, my bad, I didn't think of that. I'm really sorry." I kept my voice contrite though I felt like using sarcasm. They were still shaky. I can forgive them for that.

She sighed, "It's ok. You're doing really well with the plane. It was a very smooth shift, otherwise."

I grinned at her and said "Coolbeans. See, landing won't be so hard. You watch," trying to bolster them both once more.

CHAPTER FIVE

Close Calls
Back to the Tower

Hara walked back in and went over to Wizard. He glanced down at the screen, watching her talk to Richard on landing procedures. Wizard touched his leg and he bent down to listen.

"She did another freaky thing so I copied that too and glitched it for Dillrod."

"Good job. What did she do?" dreading the answer.

"She backed up against the door. Then the lights and stuff in the plane started to flicker really badly. I thought they were going to blow out there for a second," he sounded awed.

"That's it?" O'Hara was feeling relief at the news. He was afraid Wizard was going to tell him she was sucking necks or something.

Wizard's eyes were wide. "Yeah, believe me when you see it, you'll know what I mean by freaky."

"I believe you. Run a check in the data base for any murders that even resembles what we just saw." He had to dig. He had to know. Did he have a killer, or did he just have Twilight Zone.

"Got it, Rock." And Wizard went to work on his computer again.

Williams had ambled over, "What's going on, gentlemen?"

"We're just running a check for any felonies she may have committed. Just in case." O'Hara stayed close to the truth.

"I thought you had everything in that file already? I have my own copy, and since the birth of her first son, she hasn't done anything." Williams looked confused.

O'Hara sat down next to Wizard to wait for the information. "Maybe she has another identity. We just want to be thorough."

"Investigations are our department, yours is anything combat worthy. You're not detectives, you're soldiers. You really should leave that to my department." He'd started to sound pompous again.

O'Hara raised his eyebrow, "Then your department should have done their homework, the right way, the first time. No way did she get that kind of training raising babies and going to college. Even if that training was learned twenty-five years ago, something has to be on record somewhere. And if that training was learned twenty-five years ago, no way would she still be that sharp after all this down time. My men and I will be boarding that plane to take her into custody for you, and we need, *as soldiers,* every bit of information on her that we can get to keep those people on that plane safe. To keep my men and I safe. Everything about her is necessary for us *soldiers* to do our job. Or are you saying we don't need to do our job?" As he talked he stood up and took a step toward Williams with every sentence he spoke until he was nose to nose with the agent.

Williams made the mistake of taking a step backwards. He realized he gave ground and tried to make up for it by making it look like he meant to turn around and go back to Richards monitor waving his hand carelessly saying, "No, I am not. Do what you think you need to do." Williams was trying for an air of not caring about anything but the plane coming in. Then he turned sharply, "But remember, she is mine once she touches the ground with her feet." His smug smile came back in place at that thought.

O'Hara narrowed his eyes thinking to himself, 'we'll see about that'.

"Hey Rock, you won the bet." Romeo said with his usual cocky grin.

"No, I won," Wizard argued still working at the pad.

"How do you figure that, Wiz?" Romeo asked.

"She pulled those guys into the galley no sweat, and then she took the bullet out.

"No problem for her. To her, it's a minor wound, so I win," he explained.

"She got shot, that's a major wound," Romeo glared at Wizard.

"She treated it like it was nothing. It's minor," Wizard stated.

"It's a wash boys. It's a major wound she treated like it was minor. Both of them win, they split the take," Babyface said, stepping in as referee. Not many would be crazy enough to disagree with him.

"Damn, there goes my lap dance money," Romeo said and they all laughed.

Back on Flight 1409

Richard had just gotten done giving me the 'lo down on landing procedures. It was more difficult than I had thought. It was akin to backing a 40 ft trailer into a small dock that's angled and sliding down. Believe me parking a trailer backwards into that kind of small space can drive even the most professional of truck drivers' nuts. They often have to start over from scratch, over and over, pulling back out into oncoming traffic to get the proper angle. Like a trailer of an eighteen wheeler, the angle of the nose of the plane was essential to landing properly. If you're too low or off by too much—BOOM, your ass is grass. Looking at the gauges and steering, going over and over again the steps needed to land, I heard in the background pleading coming from a male voice. I slammed out of the seat and went to the galley where I saw Lisa, a mere two feet away from my prisoner. He was pleading with her and crying about the pain in his chest. She looked way to compassionate for my liking. I walked over and she took a step back, looking scared now. I glared at her and looked at the kid on the floor. And kid he was to me. He looked about the same age as my eldest son.

He was saying, "Please, please it hurts. It hurts to breathe." Tears were running down his face unashamedly.

"If it hurts too much to breathe, you wouldn't be able to talk." I walked over to where he was laying and pulled my fist back and hit him square in the jaw, knocking him out again. I turned on Lisa and barked, "What did I tell you?"

"Not to go near him," she said in a shaky breath.

"What did I say I would do if you didn't do as I ordered?" I barked in a hard voice.

"You would kick my ass." She started backing away from me and edging towards the galley door.

"Exactly. He just took what I should have given you, if you had loosened his bonds. If you go near him again, I swear to the Gods I will slice his throat and knock you out because there won't be anyone else to take your due. Are we clear?" Not caring how bad I scared her now. Better scared, then dead.

"Yyyes," she stammered with lips trembling.

I looked behind the counter that had a bunch of drawers and saw one slightly ajar.

"Open that drawer," I ordered her.

She looked down at the cupboards and did as I asked.

"What's in that drawer?" my voice cold.

"Steak knives and utensils for eating," she stammered out.

I looked back down at the kid and rolled him over using my foot and saw a handle. I reached down and picked it up and showed it to her. It was a steak knife.

"All he was doing was waiting for you to get close enough. You probably came in right as he was going to cut his bonds off and he switched his plan. He would have sliced you, gotten free and came after whomever else until he completed the mission he was set to do. That's all they know.

That's all they do. The younger ones are even more brainwashed and stupid then the older ones, 'cause they feel like they got something to prove. Youth being what it is. Young, dumb and full of shit. You wouldn't have seen tomorrow if you had let him loose, and that would've sucked for you and yours. Don't disobey me again. Pull out that drawer and move it to another section out of here." And I walked out of the galley and went back to the cockpit fuming over the stupidity, but understanding it too. Compassion for your fellow man. Doesn't matter who or what he or she is. You feel for them. It's human nature. But at that moment I wasn't feeling very human or humane. I was *thirsty*.

I had put my headphones back on and Richard was soon talking in my ear, "Tower to Cat."

I answered simply. "I'm here."

"You are about to need to start with step one. We have a landing strip on what we call, 'the back nine,' ready for your exclusive use." He tried to sound cheerful, confident even, but I could hear the tension in his voice had gone up a few notches.

I was willing to bet that the 'back nine' was where they had trouble planes coming in to land in an area that would keep an exploding plane from doing any damage to the terminal or other planes. A place far enough away that if shit went wrong, only the plane would be at risk.

"Oh, that sounds sooo special," I quipped.

"All for you. Now you need to push forward and start coming down like we talked about," he reminded me. I did as he said.

Richard piped up, "Looking good there Cat, just keep coming."

I could see we had dropped a lot of height already. The flight attendants had already started with their routine in getting passengers in their seats before they went into their nice and calm emergency procedures and, 'not to worry there is only a slight problem and we'll be all right speech'.

Richard told me how to turn the plane to angle it right for the runway that he wanted me on. As I approached the air field I could see the long row of lights down on the ground, but still a good bit of distance. I sent a prayer up to the Lady and went through the procedure of slowing down and getting ready for that tail wind he warned me about.

Back at the Tower

The Tower supervisor came up behind Richard, and said, "How's it looking?"

"She is doing well, a bit too low though, I think," he answered fast.

"Your others?" the supervisor asked just as quickly.

He touched the screen. "Racked and stacked. There will be some delays. I've already punched those in for the main."

"Good luck, Hammer." And with that, the supervisor got out of his way so Richard, aka The Hammer, could push his tin in and hope it didn't turn into a fireball.

On Flight 1409

"Cat, bring your nose up just a bit and put a bit more on your flaps," Richard advised her.

Yeah, he was right, it felt wrong. I ease it up and gave more to the flaps. It tilted the nose up higher.

"Good, looking good. Now let's get your landing gear down. You'll feel some resistance when you do that because it'll cause a drag, don't worry about it. That what's supposed to happen," his voice pattern was speeding up and the tension getting tighter. I pulled the levers for the landing gear down and felt the drag and pull in the wheel.

"Good, now slow it down some more," he spat.

"Slowing down." I put more into the flaps which slowed the plane down, but it felt like it angled the nose off a bit.

"Good," Richard said, "Now line up with the runway and we'll bring you in."

The lower I got, the more the unease hit my stomach. Richard kept encouraging me though and he would know, right? I was close to hitting the runway with tires when I just felt this deep bad feeling and pulled back on the wheel and gave the plane speed to get back in the air.

"It's wrong, it's wrong," I kept saying to Richard. I pulled up, getting some altitude and speed.

"OK, it's ok. We can try it again," he was lying, I could hear the strain in his voice.

I assured him, "Good, just get me turned around. I can do this, but that felt wrong."

His voice went soothing on me, "I believe you, you're the one in there not me. Are you sure you're good to go for a second try?"

"Yeah, I will get this; just get me lined up again." I kept my heavy breathing to myself. That scared the shit out of me, but I wasn't going to tell him that.

He steered me through and got me lined back up for a second try.

On my second approach, I took some deep breaths and found my center, letting myself be one with the plane. I listened as he guided me, but adjusted when I felt the nose angle was wrong to me (not to him). I let the plane's back wheels touch the tarmac this time and felt the jolt as we hit. It felt like it bounced a few times before making more solid contact. Then Richard was going faster with the slowing down method and guiding me for the front wheel to touch the ground. It seemed to take too long to get that front wheel to make contact. I got the plane to slow down some more. I finally got it to kiss the ground and got my flaps pulled back enough for more drag which would slow the plane faster. I got the plane at a decent speed for the second braking system, which I pushed lightly at first, then with more force. I could hear the stress in Richard's voice getting higher, urging me to slow the plane faster. I knew why. We were running out of runway, but this damn thing felt like a moving boulder on wheels with too much weight for fast braking. It finally listened to me and slowed to a stuttering stop. My hands were white on the wheel from gripping it so damn hard. I could hear Richard whopping over the mic, "You did it, Goddamn, you did it." I heard cheers in the background.

On The Ground in the plane

My heart was pumping with an overload of adrenalin. Now I was scared. I always did that. During a crisis I can stay cold. But after the crisis is over, win or lose, it seemed everything I had bottled up, spilled out in one big rush. Tears were threatening to spill over, as I saw the black top of the runway ahead of the plane. There wasn't much room left from where it had a steel gate and then nothing but field after it. Slowing down this airbus had been hard. I took deep breaths (in through my nose, out through my mouth) and put up a second shield around me to make sure my mates didn't feel anything from me. The questions wouldn't stop then, but the extra shield would cost me energy and I was still very thirsty. I saw flashing red lights out the starboard side window of the plane. I couldn't hear the sirens, but I could see the wave of emergency vehicles coming down the tarmac, looking like they were heading for war. I thought to myself, suck it up, the crisis isn't over yet. I knew they would arrest me for this. I knew I was looking at hours in a grey interrogation room. Hours of having them yell questions at me I couldn't, nor wouldn't, answer. I knew I wouldn't get a hero's welcome for doing this act. No good deed goes unpunished. And it's so true. I'd lost count of the number of times I had done good deeds on this plane of existence and the astral plane, only to get butt fucked with no 'I love you' and no KY either. Never have I gotten a thank you from anyone outside of my family (barring my Mother, who never thanked me for shit). Then again, she didn't know how many times I'd protected her without her knowledge, even though I had left home so young.

Blood takes care of blood. That's rule number one.

I sighed deeply and leaned my head back, waiting for them to come. Waiting for the hand cuffs. I really hated handcuffs. Well, except in one instance, I smiled to myself. Who was I kidding? I choked on my wedding night. No spanking and no handcuffs for me until I got over my damn mental problem.

I could hear Lisa explaining to the passengers how to get on the slide and exit the plane safely. She was saying, "And if you will be patient, we will get started as soon as I get the all clear." She wouldn't get the all clear until all threats to them and those outside were neutralized. That was SWAT 101 or any law enforcement rule.

They had to come in here first to subdue anyone and everyone they thought a threat. Then, and only then, would people be allowed out of their seats and guided to the slides, which hadn't even been deployed yet. I could see the reason why it hadn't. The mobile staircase was coming along with the pack of emergency vehicles. The staircase was for SWAT or whoever they had coming. Probably Special Forces, I thought. Can't get into a plane fast with a slide.

I took all the weapons I had on me and placed them on the co-pilot seat.

Pitiful pile of tools I thought, but they had gotten the job done. I pulled my braid out of my jacket and loosened the hair from the braid. I shook it out. I needed a brush, but it would do.

Then, while the girls were busy in first class, I took the plastic bag I had filled with the bloody towels and whatnot. It was safe to do magick now, so I focused and breathed. In through my nose, out through my mouth and '*pushed*'. There was a POP and the bag was gone. One more thing to clean up. In through my nose, out through my mouth. Think of a soft flame and '*push*'. Then I smelled smoke mixed with what smelled like burnt bleach. Nasty smell, I thought to myself. I also smelled burnt wire and looked around to see some of the gauges spark and crackle. Oops...didn't focus well enough or I should have moved away. But we were on the ground now so we didn't need that stuff working properly anymore.

Soon after I cleaned my mess, I heard gasps coming from the passengers in first class and knew that the marines had landed and were swarming. I smiled at myself. I knew Special Forces were made from men in all branches. The only requirement was that in rank, they had to be an E-5 or higher. Nothing less. And their skills had to be exemplary. Otherwise, these days, a Special Forces team could be made of army, navy, marines or air force. Didn't matter anymore. I thought that fact was cool.

I heard a voice saying from outside the cockpit and down the aisle, "One alive and wounded, tied up. Three dead in the galley."

Then I heard, "Three, all dead in the bunk. Clear."

The next sound was a directive to me, "Don't move and place your hands on top of your head. Lace your fingers together. Do it now," a deep gravelly sounding voice commanded.

I slowly raised my arms up to my head, lacing my fingers together.

"Stand up," he ordered. I stood up swaying a bit from the dizziness. I had expended way too much energy. I was in the danger zone now.

"Do you have any weapons on you?" the gravel voice asked.

"No, they're all there on the seat," I answered with the same tone of voice I received.

A different voice from behind him said, "Covered."

I heard steps behind me get closer, then a hand searching me professionally and thoroughly for weapons, not missing anything.

He tugged my hands behind my back and snapped the handcuffs on. I sighed again.

"You're being awfully calm about this, Cat," the voice behind me commented.

"Would it do any good to throw a hissy fit, Captain?" I answered him back in a tired voice.

"No, not really. Let's go." Then I heard "Clear" one more time. I turned around and saw a man pointing a gun right at my head. He was tall at 6'2 and about 200 lbs of lean mean muscle. He wore all black, with a black tactical vest. His grey steel eyes were as cold as the dead of winter, but framed with a face that looked smooth and round like a baby's. But for those eyes, I would have said, 'Here is a nice man'. Those eyes gave him away. They told me he had seen enough, done enough and kicked ass on the way. His gun was a SOCOM with a laser sight. His aim didn't waver and was dead on. I knew from his eyes he could pull the trigger, hit what he was aiming at, and not have any thoughts about it afterwards. I wondered if there was anything soft left in him at all, other than his face. I nodded at him out of respect. I held no hard feelings for them. O'Hara gave me a slight push and we walked out.

"Why is there a burning smell in the cockpit and here in the aisle?" O'Hara asked me.

"Malfunction, I suppose. You want to get this circus going or what?" I was starting to lose patience and my teeth were threatening to come down again. I held them back with sheer will and kept walking. We walked down the aisle and out to first class.

No one nodded to me. No one said thank you. At least Lisa had the decency to look at the ground with an air of embarrassment. I didn't want a 'thank you' really, but a 'hang tough' or something would've have been real nice. Some kind of show of support, but I should've known better. I sighed again.

We went down the staircase and into a black vehicle, a big, black SUV type. The kind most government agencies use. I didn't know my modern cars as well as I knew my older muscle cars. I could tell you everything about those. They were the last *real* cars ever made. These modern cars sucked, in my opinion. You couldn't work on a new car on your own anymore without a machine to tell you all the electrical shit on them. Totally useless, in my book. And off we went to the grey room that I knew was coming.

CHAPTER SIX
Trojan Interrogation

I was wrong about the room being grey. It was worse. It was a sick colored peach shade with white trim. Whoever decorated this room didn't know shit about mental interrogation techniques. Colors have power, even the mundane know this. Colors can influence the mind. Nine times out of ten, any room that an assassin lives in, is dark grey and spartan. Mental hospitals have soft green shades to their walls, because this is supposed to be calming for the disturbed mind. Put a schizophrenic in a red room and you'll see him go off on a tirade in mere minutes. Children's hospitals usually have light blue walls with Disney characters painted on them and this makes the kids feel safe and happy; it also aids in healing them. Colors work. And this peach thing? Well the only thing it was doing to me was making me nauseous. It wouldn't intimidate me as interrogation rooms were supposed to do to those who get a forced invitation. It wouldn't even intimidate June Cleaver. She'd be thinking of what colored roses would go with the walls. Sheesh. It must be because this was the airport's 'interview' room. Didn't want to scare the masses, I supposed.

O'Hara had brought me in and sat me down in a chair. There was a desk and another chair on the other side of it, opposite of me. His unit followed us in and stationed themselves around the room. I got a good look at the men. O'Hara was standing next to me. He looked about 6'3, maybe 6'4 and was about 225 lbs I would guess. He was somewhere around the age of 35, with brown eyes and a look of one who was hardened by things that would never be mentioned. The cold grey eyed guy was stationed off to his side, gun at rest, as they all did now.

At least the guns were no longer pointed at me, and I sighed again. I looked at the one standing on the other side of the room. He was tall like the other two, but lankier. His face still held smiles in it, but he wasn't smiling at the moment. He looked really leery of me for some reason. I couldn't quite put my finger on why yet. I hadn't done anything to warrant such a reaction from someone who had never seen me before now. The last guy looked the youngest out of the bunch. Most likely around 25, with green hazel eyes and blond hair cut really short, but more in a surfer style then a military one.

O'Hara looked down at me and stared at every feature of my face. Not like he was interested in me as a woman, but like he was trying to figure out a puzzle or something. A puzzle that's a problem, was my gut feeling.

"Why are your eyes so bruised looking?" he asked.

I took a deep intake of breath and looked down as if in embarrassment. But his question told me that I was on the edge and wouldn't last too much longer. Already my stomach was rumbling for both food and blood. Soon the pain would begin and then my shields will drop. The shit would hit the fan at that point and it would all be out of my control.

"Tired I guess," was all I said. I started my breathing exercise again. Staying calm, thinking of blue waters. The door to the room opened. In walked a man I knew would be 'the dillrod'.

It was going to be hard to look tough with bruised looking eyes, but I hardened my face as he sat down at the table in front of me. In his hands, he had a cup of coffee and a sandwich wrapped in see-through cellophane. He placed them down on the table in front of me and took a seat.

"My name is Special Agent in Charge Williams. I thought the coffee and food will help, since we need to have a statement from you about the attempted hijacking." He looked so sure of himself and his place in the world. He reached over, as if to shake my hand, while he was giving his name then realized his mistake. I was still hand-cuffed. Then I saw his ring. It was a sterling silver ring with a black onyx stone embossed with a sigil that said he was a High Dark Adept and the sigil invoked protection with a dark God's blessing. I knew this, because my physical father had one like it and he had tried to kill me, twice. I couldn't tell what dark God this dillrod served yet, but I scooted my chair away from the table and got tense for action. Even with my handcuffs on, I could still do a lot of damage, one way or another. O'Hara watched my every move, my every reaction. He looked back and forth from the dillrod to me, looking not very happy about the situation.

"I'm sorry. Maybe we should remove those handcuffs, so you can eat and drink," he said, looking at me with snake eyes, waiting to see what I would do.

O'Hara stared at me like he knew I was on sudden alert for a reason, but he didn't understand *why* I went to that extreme.

He reached down to unlock the handcuffs and whispered, "Behave," in my ear. I looked at dillrod to see if he noticed the exchange, but O'Hara must have said it so softly, not even his second in command heard it.

The handcuffs were off, but I didn't rub my wrists like most people do when released from them. I wouldn't give dillrod even that much.

Again, Williams motioned to the refreshments and said, "Go ahead. I know you must be famished by now." His smile was tight. I think he was going for friendly but was failing, miserably.

I said with a flat tone of voice, "No, thank you. I want a phone call and a lawyer."

"That shouldn't be necessary, right now. Why don't we talk about happened on the plane while you eat?" His voice sounded so oily to me.

"I want a phone call and a lawyer," I repeated.

"We haven't charged you with anything at this time. We just want a statement from you. We are getting statements from everyone who was on that plane. So why don't we start with you?" He was trying again for slick.

"Listen and hear me well. The only two things you are going to hear from me over and over again—is 'I want a phone call and a lawyer.' Until I have those two things, you don't get shit," I said, my voice cold and emotionless.

"You don't need a lawyer if you haven't been charged with a crime. We just need to know what happened from your side." I heard what he was saying...we haven't charged you—yet...but it will come. And the food and drink thing—no way. Only an idiot takes food or drink from an enemy. And enemy he was, if he worshiped a dark God.

"I want a phone call and a lawyer. These are my constitutional and civil rights." I knew what my civil rights were worth in this day and age. Not squat, since the Patriot Act. But I wasn't going to relent.

"How about you explain to me how you took out three men, so fast, the cameras almost didn't pick it up?" he asked with a smug tone in his voice.

My blood went cold. "Cameras?"

O'Hara interrupted, "After the last attack, some of the planes have been outfitted with cameras. Most have them, not all, but most. Your plane did. Everything was taped."

I could feel my face turn white and I got dizzy. Even sitting down, I was dizzy. The impulse to fight or flee was pumping through my system. Then O'Hara did a strange thing. He put his hand on my shoulder and squeezed tightly. It didn't feel like a restraining squeeze, but one with a 'cool down' feel to it. I chilled and tried my best poker face again.

"If you really do have it all taped, then it would show that I wasn't with those terrorists. I fought for America, not against her; never against her." I was trying to get my poker face going.

"But with no sound, it doesn't help us fill the gaps. Pictures can only tell us so much. Why don't you fill in the gaps for us?" Williams was again trying to be endearing...and failing once again.

"I want a phone call and a lawyer," I repeated.

"Wizard, why don't you show the tapes to Cat?" Williams turned to the blond haired guy.

He stepped forward and said to Williams, "Sergeant Mark Logan is how I prefer to be addressed."

Ahh, dissension in the ranks. This was looking better for me. He brought out his laptop. Then again, this could be really bad.

He opened it up and started to go to work on it. Pictures came on and started to play out the scene I just had lived through for the past two hours.

"Skip to the most interesting part would you, Sergeant Logan." Williams sounded so smug I wanted to slug him.

Logan complied, and then the screen went blank.

"What is this?" Williams asked his tone not so smug now.

"I don't know. Let me try something else." Logan replied.

Again, he clicked and poked at the pad. Logan still got nothing but a blank screen.

"It's gone, looks like a glitch of some sort. Maybe a virus or a worm," he started to explain.

"A virus or a worm? How the hell does that happen with the equipment you have?" Williams was damn near roaring by now.

"I was all over the net tonight between three satellites and two data bases. I could have picked up something that isn't recognized by the anti-virus software programs. There are always new things coming out every day. The software can only catch so much." I could tell he was trying to cover his tracks.

"It just happened to wipe out the most damning parts, is what you're telling me?" his voiced laced with sarcasm.

My mind was racing with the implications. I agreed with Williams that it wasn't likely this happened. Oh, it could, but the odds... well let's just say I wouldn't bet on them. And it pointed to this team covering up for me, but why? Wizard would have only out blanked those parts on command. So this had to be a group effort, but for what reason? I mulled that over and kept my face blank. Besides, I was still having my own internal problems going on. My stomach rumbled so loud, I knew the whole damn room had heard.

Williams was still going on his rant, "I am going to make a call. I will have a tech look at your equipment and we *will* get to the bottom of this. You had better not be lying." He stormed out the door, slamming it closed.

"Oh, I miss him already," I quipped, and then I looked at O'Hara with the question in my eyes. I knew better than to say anything out loud in an interrogation room; where the walls, literally, had ears.

He just shook his head and motioned with his head towards the food. I motioned with my hand going across my neck. No one mistakes that gesture.

His face looked doubtful. Then he nodded to the door with what looked to me as a, 'Him? Really?'

I nodded, 'Surely'.

Again, he squeezed my shoulder and I warned aloud, "You're too close." I could smell his blood under his skin and it was making my mouth water. But he just proved himself an ally, if an uneasy one, and I wouldn't disrespect that by biting him, but I was so thirsty. Besides it was against our law to bite without permission.

He looked hard at me with an eyebrow raised.

"Please, I am hungry and you're too close." My eyes were begging him to understand.

He did, finally. His hand dropped from my shoulder and he moved away.

"Thank you," I said to him and took a deep breath. This was a mistake because I could smell them all now. I got up and moved to the rear wall as far from them as I could get. I started groaning when the door opened again. O'Hara's face eased with relief, like he had been waiting for this person to show up.

A Four Star General walked into the room and took a look at the scene before him. I was un-cuffed and backed up against the wall groaning. His men moved slowly away from me to the other side of the room. Grey eyes raised his SOCOM at me again. Except O'Hara. If I wasn't getting so weak, I could have sworn I saw a look of pity in his eyes.

The General said, "What's wrong?"

O'Hara moved close to him whispering in his ear quickly and urgently. The General's eyes widened and I started to slide down to the floor. I couldn't hold myself up anymore. My breath was coming in short gasps and fast paced. I was close to hyperventilating. Pain started to twist in my gut. Next, would be the feel of flames in my stomach. The General quickly opened the door and spoke to another man in uniform outside. I heard footsteps go down the hall, double time. Then they came back and someone whispered to the General.

He moved over to me slowly, saying, "The recorder is off. You have my word you can speak freely. What can we do?"

I debated the situation. I could tell him what I needed, but then hiding what I am would be a bitch. I could try and hold out, but I didn't think I would make it. They had seen the tape in the first place, so hiding what I am was a moot point now.

Also, it sounded like the truth when he gave me his word. I followed that tiny voice in my head. "I need food and drink that hasn't been opened to be tampered with. It's all I will trust at this point; and I need blood. Blood freely given."

"Blood?" he drew back a bit.

"Please," I was getting too close to going on a free for all. It would get me into serious shit, but I wouldn't be able to stop, if this went on too long.

Everyone was quiet for a minute, until O'Hara looked like he had come to a decision.

"I'll feed her," O'Hara offered and he started walking to me. He bent down slowly. He nodded to two of his men to cover the door. They moved to keep it closed.

He looked back at me and asked, "How do we do this?"

"Offer of your own free will," I groaned, "Offer is ritual, you must speak the words or I can't feed, legally."

"It won't do anything weird to me, like make me your slave or something, will it?" he was cautious.

I laughed weakly, "No, that's movie crap. Wrong kind of vamp for that kind of thing."

"Ok, what do I say and where do you bite?" his voice softened.

"Wrist is good enough, since I'm not mortally wounded. You say as you offer your blood, "I offer my blood—warrior to warrior—from heart and soul. Of my own free will. So be it."

He offered his wrist and said the ritual words, "I offer my blood—warrior to warrior—from heart and soul, of my own free will. So be it.

"I take your offering with honor, warrior. So be it." And bit down on his wrist. The sweet coppery taste slid down my throat and I groaned in pleasure as his blood fed me. I tried not taking any of his life force, since he didn't know just how deep the feeding could go. I only took the energy of the blood into me. I could have taken life force as well, but he would be tired for a few days until his astral subtle bodies replenished it. If he knew how to energize his chakras, which I doubted, then the drain wouldn't be so bad. So I didn't take that which he couldn't replace easily on his own. It would have been rude to do so. And I doubted he would know how to stop me if I took that kind of feeding too far. The only sign of discomfort he may have had, is the thinning of his lips, but he didn't make a sound. I knew the wrist was more sensitive than the neck since it had more nerve endings. But for me, feeding at a neck is just too damn intimate.

I 'thought' cool blue energy at his wrist, and was rewarded when I saw his lips relax. I had to force myself to stop and lick his wrist, sealing the wound. I pushed back away from him.

"You ok?' I asked him.

He took a deep breath and stood up. "Yeah, I'm fine. No dizziness."

"Good, thank you. Now move away from me, please." I motioned him back with my hands.

He looked at me with a question in his eyes and I answered, "I didn't want to take too much. I have enough for now, but will need more of a deeper feeding later. Regular food right now will help me stand being close to others." And as if my stomach was agreeing with me, another loud rumble gurgled in my tummy. Everyone heard it.

O'Hara ordered the tall lanky one and said, "Romeo, go find a vending machine. Don't let anyone else touch the food or the soda."

"What kind of soda?" the one called Romeo asked, looking at me.

"Whatever they have is good, please," I told him.

"Gone." And out the door he went.

"Well, while he's doing that, let me introduce myself. I am General Pierce." He looked a bit shaken by what he had seen, but tough as nails as he looked, he was rolling right along as if this was an everyday occurrence. He seemed to be in his early fifties; still fit and trim at 6'0. He had an air of power to him that I recognized and respected. The vibes coming off him felt like this was a man that had honor and would back his men to the gates of hell if need be. His uniform not only showed the four stars on his shoulders; on his chest there were the pins that showed him to be an Army General. I wanted to trust him, but trust had become a four letter word for me a long time ago. I was willing to be nice though, since he was playing fair... so far.

He continued with the introductions, "Captain O'Hara you've already met. This is his second in command, Major Harris, otherwise known as Babyface. The one who left to get your refreshments is Sergeant Theodore Watson. His code name is Romeo." I grinned at that one. "And last is Sergeant Mark Logan, also known as The Wizard."

"I'm Catrina Lynn Garcia. Cat for short." Rule number one when in a hostage situation. Technically, I was a hostage, since I was here against my own free will. My civil rights thus far had been ignored. I didn't blame these guys. I had a feeling there was a lot more going on here. The General didn't disappoint.

He offered his hand and I nodded my head in a short bow instead, and added, "Where I come from shaking hands is a big no-no. A nod of the head is good enough."

"That's interesting. Why is that?" He sat down and waited for me to do the same.

Since he had sat down first, I knew he was comfortable with his status and didn't need to posture.

I took my own seat and asked instead, "Do you want me knowing everything in your head at this time?"

His eyes went hard and said, "No," very firmly.

I continued, "Then shaking your hand would be bad. Besides do you know how many germs get passed around like that? If everyone in this country would stop shaking hands, colds and flu's alone would go down by fifty percent."

"Let me get this straight. You can read people by touch and you can get sick?" the General wanted clarification.

"Yes to the first. I don't know anymore about the second." I grinned, "Just being honest."

"You could have just shaken my hand. You could have just not told me, period. Why did you do that if it's true?" So, he had a skeptical side. That's good actually.

"One—you turned off the recorder. Two—you let me feed. It would have been bad form on my part if I took advantage after that. I returned your favors. Now we're even." This let him know anything else he wanted to know was going to be like pulling teeth.

He heard what I wasn't saying. He looked at the uneaten sandwich and cup of coffee. "Why didn't you take this?"

"Because it's been tampered with," I stated plainly. I wanted to know what he would do about it.

"By whom?" he asked.

"Most likely, Williams," I guessed. I knew I was right, though.

"How can you tell it was tampered with?" he queried.

I said simply, "I can smell it."

His eyes widened, "Your sense of smell is that good?"

"Yes, it is," I confirmed.

"General, if I may?" O'Hara had cut in.

"Go ahead." General Pierce gave him the lead.

"I thought I saw you react to Williams because of the ring, but it was the food?" he sounded slightly confused.

"No, you were right the first time. I reacted in defense because of the ring at first. Then I smelled the food and drink. The food and drink have an agent in it, either poison or a sleeping aide."

O'Hara nodded his head as if vindicated on his original idea and the General looked at us both. "What about the ring? I assume we are talking about William's."

O'Hara spoke first, "I saw the ring on his hand when we first met at the tower. It struck me as odd, because most agents don't wear jewelry. Especially those going out in the field."

The General then looked at me, his eyes questioning. "You wouldn't believe me if I told you," I answered.

At that moment Romeo walked in with a can of soda, a lemon fruit pie, and a vended sandwich.

I looked at the fare and smiled, even though I really hated vended sandwiches.

"Thank you," I said, as he handed the meal to me. "No one touched this after you took it from the machine?" I asked him, watching his aura.

"No one touched any of it after I bought it from the machine," he stated and his aura didn't flare any reds. His aura would flare with red colors if he were lying, unless he was a habitual liar.

"Please don't take offense, but I don't know *you* well enough yet," and I sniffed the food. I looked closely for needle holes. I then wiped the rim of the drink with my shirt before I popped the top and gingerly drank it. Romeo watched me with an amused look on his face. The General just looked curious. I opened the fruit pie and said, "Excuse me for a few moments," and ate. I kept eating and chewing, taking a drink now and again as I thought about how to answer his question.

As I finished, I decided to go for most of the truth.

"The ring, General, is the mark of a Dark High Adept with a sigil that gives him magickal protection and shows he serves a dark God. I waited for his reaction.

He just stared at me, digesting what I had told him.

He looked at O'Hara who shrugged his shoulders, "I have no clue. I don't know anything about this kind of stuff, but Williams has been acting weird from the start, atypical of an FBI agent. That's all I can corroborate."

"And that's the problem, O'Hara. None of us knows anything about these kinds of things. Not you, not I, but something is happening. A lot of unexplainable things have been happening everywhere and we can't do anything about it, because we don't know what we have or how to deal with it when it happens," General Pierce explained.

"You mean magick rings and dark Gods?" O'Hara sounded shocked at the answer he got from this man. His superior.

"I have files and files of things I can't explain and it's getting worse. It was why I asked you to keep an eye out for anything out of the ordinary in the field. Whenever logic fails to answer a question, the impossible, however improbable, is possible. Something big is going on and we have no frame of reference for answering any of these questions or dealing with the situations as they come up."

"Yes, but…" O'Hara began.

"A plane gets hijacked in a most improbable way and she's there. She wiped the floor with those men, landed the plane safely on the ground, saving hundreds, and she drinks blood. Proof that the impossible is possible."

Feeling stronger from the food, my mind started working again properly. I said, "You saw the tape." Half question, half statement.

General Pierce confirmed, "I saw the whole tape."

So, he had gotten an unvarnished copy, while they deleted anything that would be considered weird from William's eyes. That was interesting.

Did this obligate me for another favor or piece of truth? If it did, it would be a pretty huge piece or favor. Damn. I didn't have to ask why. I knew why. They wanted something. Or more specifically, the General wanted something. This was going to be good. I needed coffee for this shit.

CHAPTER SEVEN
Yours, Mine and Ours

The General looked back at O'Hara continuing, "So, she's a vampire?"

"Sort of," I cut in.

His face got serious again, "How can you 'sort of' be a vampire? You drank blood. You have fangs. You move faster than a human and your sense of smell is more than human."

"It's a long story," I sighed heavily.

The General urged, "We have time."

"You don't have clearance. I answer to someone higher than you, metaphysically speaking, and She, I won't piss off," I spoke in a no nonsense tone of voice.

"Who is this "She"? He was digging for more information. Information I really couldn't give him.

"Again, clearance," I repeated.

He started to look frustrated, when suddenly his face cleared. "You said, 'clearance'. Are you part of some secret military organization?" O'Hara took a deep breath in shock.

"We are not affiliated with any government agencies," I answered quickly.

He sprung on my mistake, "You said, 'we'. There are more of you?"

I closed my eyes, realizing just how badly I needed some coffee. All the men in the room went sharp, waiting for my answer.

"A few, but we never hurt anyone. We can't. Our number one law is 'Do what thou wilt, but harm none be the Law'. Meaning we can do what we want, but we can't hurt anyone doing it. We can't go against their free will," trying to reassure them.

"You hurt those men on the plane. You killed two of them," he sounded firm again.

"We have the right to defend ourselves. And we have the right to do what it takes to keep innocents safe." I was getting nervous now.

"So, you and others like you, protect innocent people? Who decides who is innocent and who isn't?" Pierce was fishing.

"What happened on that plane is pretty clear," I answered as vaguely as I could. If I started talking Goddesses and pantheons, he might think I was delusional as well as dangerous.

The General wasn't slow. He sat back and looked at me then at O'Hara. He finally reached down and grabbed his briefcase, placing it on the table in front of us.

Opening it, he took out one of the thick files he had and put it on the table." Recall your last mission, O'Hara?"

O'Hara's face went tight then, without emotion, "Yes, Sir."

"A mission with a clear objective. The Intel was complete. There was no foreseeable reason for you to go against orders and pull your men back out of the mission, yet you did." The General slid the file to me.

"Yes, Sir, I did," his voice was tight. I took a look at his aura. There was red from being internally angry, but I noticed it was also larger than any of the others in the room. Yet, I knew he didn't know anything about the astral planes or magick.

"It's what landed you and your team stateside on a supposedly low level area. Here, where nothing was supposed to happen, taken out of the main game, so to speak." I had a feeling he was speaking more to me then to his man, because I felt like, if it was at his man, it was cruel to rub salt into his wounds. He didn't seem the type to do that.

"Yes, Sir," O'Hara's voice came out even more crisp.

"Do you know what happened after you were pulled out and sent stateside?" The General was looking at O'Hara more than me now with compassion lacing his voice.

"No, Sir," his voice was still clipped.

"The second best team went in and they were all killed." He said gravely, "If you had tried to complete that mission, you and yours would be dead instead."

That was when Babyface said, "Razor....Joker?"

"Yes, son, all dead," he confirmed.

"Shit," this came from Romeo.

We all sat in silence and I gave a prayer for those men I would never know and prayed that whatever God or Goddess they answered to, their particular heaven would accept them with honor.

"I am sorry for your loss and know that whatever heaven they belong to, they will be accepted with honor due them," I was sad for them.

"There is more than one heaven?" asked Babyface.

I clearly stated, "Yes, several."

"More than one kind of hell too, I suppose?" this was asked from the General.

"Of course. All things must have balance," I answered in teacher mode now.

"This place here," tapping the file in front of me, "seems to be our own personal hell on earth." He motioned for me to open the file, so I did.

"Inside that is all the Intel we have on that location. It is home to a self-proclaimed prince. It's near Preshawar in Pakistan. This was the mission; O'Hara pulled his men two clicks away from hitting the objective. The objective was to gain entrance into the compound and locate their computer, which supposedly has information of other terrorist cells. And to ascertain whether this Prince Babur has a black market nuclear missile. A pretty straight forward mission for the most part, yet he pulled his men back and refused a direct order to complete the mission. There is nothing in that Intel that would substantiate his claim that 'something was off' and the mission was a no-go. Then the Pentagon sent in the second best team we have. They went in and didn't come out. We can't even find the bodies using Sat-com."

As I was listening to him, I was rifling through the mission reports, looking at satellite photographs and some photos that looked like they had been taken by someone on foot. Those were the ones that caught my interest. They were photos of a bushy area with a huge compound. Inside, the compound had many buildings and one grand house that looked something similar to the Taj Mahal type of architect. Just on a very minor scale. It wasn't noticeable to the naked eye, but with my vamp vision and my power, I could see a dark cloud of power overhanging the whole house and the area around it expanding outward of the house. It was most likely in a circular power base, though even I couldn't verify that through this photo, but the way power works it was usually in a circle. I looked deeply into the picture and sent out a tiny thread of astral energy, focusing with intent, to see what I could find through this photo. I started to get a slightly oily taste in the back of my throat. Sending the thread, willing it to the area closer, the feeling intensified and I wanted to gag. Then the photo pulsed and started to heat up, suddenly bursting into flames right in my hands. I dropped and recalled the thread I had sent out and jumped back from the table.

The General too, stood up fast, swearing, and the men were all exclaiming almost at one time "What the hell is going on?"

"What was that?"

"Shit, are we under attack or what?"

Too many questions were being fired at once for me to answer them all.

All I did was start to chill them out, "It's cool. It's cool; I made a mistake is all. I'm sorry." I was trying to reassure everyone in the room as I patted the small flames out trying to not directly touch any more pictures for very long. Just quick pats to put out the small flames.

I got it out and they all looked at me. The General asked, "What exactly did you do? And how is it responsible for that...that spontaneous flame?"

"I saw a dark cloud of power around the house, so I sent out a thread of power to try to get more information. The dark God protecting that area took exception to my astral queries and shut me down. Anyone mundane or null going in there would die. No one of your caliber would have the slightest chance of going into a place like that and leaving alive. They will die and they will die ugly. That's all I got from the picture." I sat back getting ready for the disbelief and onslaught of questions. I just didn't ever want to hear of another team trying and then dying too, because of it. If I could warn them strongly enough, maybe other teams could be saved.

He sat back down as well, "Explain mundane and null," changing his tactics completely and taking me off guard.

"A mundane is a regular person. A person that would have to work really, really hard to gain any real magick and psychic power. A null is a person that no matter what they do, will never have any power—can't sense it, can't work it—ever. It's not in their genetic makeup." I went back into teacher mode.

"You said our, 'caliber'. Why wouldn't the best damn special forces team have a chance in going there and doing what they do best?" He sounded slightly offended and I didn't blame him, but he didn't know what kind of things were really there. Not yet. He was getting a clue, though. I could see that.

"O'Hara answered that already. He can learn to have power. His instincts told him to back out, because the way they were going in would have spelled their doom. He and his men weren't prepared properly for that mission, at that time. He may not consciously understand *why* he couldn't complete the mission, but he knew he and his men wouldn't survive. So he backed out. That saved their lives. The second team must have either ignored their internal warning system or were a null or mundane, thus they died."

"But you and yours would have this ability to go into a place like that and get the objective done?" His eyes gleamed just slightly.

"Possibly," I said, not liking where this was going.

"Could you train these men here to enable them able to carry out a mission like this?" He was fishing again. I just knew it.

"O'Hara maybe; the others, I'm not sure," I tried to skirt a bit.

"Don't you and yours do things like this all the time? Like with the plane. You didn't hesitate at stepping up to bat. You took charge and got the job done. And you did do it well. Don't you and yours do that all the time?" He was letting the lead line go out further.

"Sometimes..." I was trying for vague again. I didn't think it was going to work.

"So you and yours are like a magickal mercenary team. You see a job; you do the job and walk away?" fishing deeply now. Deep sea fishing.

"Kind of..." going really vague now. I didn't want to lie, but damn, he was pushing me.

"And you're not part of the remote viewing operations the military does have?" he threw out of left field.

"Hell no, but I'll tell you what I know about the remote viewing and other psy-ops they have going on. It's going to bite them in the ass sooner or later. They have no clue what they are really doing. And their success rate is so low because of that very fact. It will continue to be that way because of the way they regard remote viewing and psychic talent. And just an FYI, I really, really hate the term 'remote viewing'. It's trying to white wash what can never be scientifically bound. It *is* religious. It *is* spiritual and it will chew them up and spit them out one of these days. I will laugh my ass off when it that happens." I was on my soap box now, a dangerous place for me to be. Honest!

The General nodded as if he agreed, "I have seen the numbers. Not too impressive. So, I have a proposal," he said in a firm voice, coming out of left field again. I raised my eyebrows, waiting.

"An alliance between yours and mine. Combining the teams. You'll work alongside these men here on missions and train them in whatever abilities you can get them to learn." He may have been proposing, but it sounded more like an order.

"Sir." O'Hara was taken aback as well. The rest of the men stared at the General in disbelief, looking slightly bewildered.

"Yes, O'Hara?" his tone dared him to disagree.

"You can't be serious. We're Special Forces. They are mercenaries. Mercs and Military never work together like that. Not on highly classified operations. The Committee would have a fit if they found out," he sounded almost furious.

"The Committee will never know. No one above me, but a select few will know. We've already discussed the possibilities," the General informed him.

O'Hara looked incredulous. "I don't think it could work. It's never been done before; and with vamps?"

General Pierce had a look of total confidence. "I have faith you can integrate the teams. You've already worked with her, so to speak, with the plane. I bet you and your team even gambled on the outcome of her fight with the terrorist. You fed her, even knowing what she was. I trust you to make this work."

O'Hara looked at the rest of his men, as if looking for support against such an outrageous plan.

Wizard said, "This is some nix level shit. This whole day has been out of the ordinary. I'm in," he smiled.

Babyface looked at him still expressionless and simply shrugged his shoulders. He turned to Romeo who just replied, "This is some weird shit. Whatever."

He still looked freaked over the burning picture.

The General smiled and turned to me. "We can get the charges dropped. We'll give you protection while you're here. We'll also start an investigation into Special Agent Williams. What say you?"

"You bet on me?" I asked, cutting him off.

O'Hara had the grace to look uncomfortable. "Yes."

I shook my head, "So, who won?"

Wizard replied, "O'Hara and me. We had to split the take....so ruled Babyface."

When the General saw I wasn't really upset (kind of freaked, but not upset), he said, "See, you can work together."

I was about to shake my head no and try to work my way out of it somehow, when I felt a warm breeze of spring air hit my body, caressing my aura in a feeling of warm sunlight. *'It's all right to say yes'*, then She sent me a feeling of being hugged. *'Good can come from this. More than one world could be saved. You'll need the help later, but tis your choice'*, and She was gone. What in the seven heavens did She mean by 'more than one world could be saved'? My world and Earth? I wasn't aware Trinidad was in danger.

"What was that?"

"I smell flowers."

"I smell trees and earth."

Again, they were all firing questions and looking around for the source, snapping me out of my contemplation.

The General just looked at me like he had a slight clue as to what just happened and that the source was because of me. I wanted to sink to my knees in honor of Her, but I was surprised they were allowed to pick it up. She usually doesn't let anyone else know she is there when guiding me around. And guiding She was. Yeah, She said it was my choice, but I knew it would be in my best interest to just go along with it, whether I really wanted to or not. We had played this game before, and I lost. Though sometimes I had to admit, She was right ...sometimes. I had a problem with authority figures, though. Even Hers.

The General was still looking at me and I took a deep breath and said the only thing I could say." Yes. But I have to clear it with my people."

CHAPTER EIGHT
FBI Gets the Boot

The General had a pleased look on his face while the others looked a bit shell shocked. I could empathize with them. What just happened? I felt like I'd just gotten shanghaied.

I was drinking my soda when I heard someone shouting outside the door to the interrogation room, "But I have a right to be in there. She is my prisoner after all. The military has no jurisdiction over this anymore. Your job is done, now move."

The dillrod was back. The evil dillrod, I noted to myself. He burst through the door and turned to General Pierce and glared, "Why are you here?"

"You forget yourself Special Agent. Or did you not see the stars on my shoulders?" his voice went to a crisp tone.

"I see them, but she is in my custody and I have brought a doctor to tend to her wounds. If you would leave us now, I'll have her seen to. Then, we'll be taking her to the office for more questions. The military has no reason to be here for any of that," he was back to being sure of himself.

I got up from my chair and moved to put the wall behind my back, "I refuse medical treatment as my civil rights say I can." I dropped my left foot back and tensed. No way was I going to let any doctor near me, even if I was dying and was a normal human. Most were nothing more than butchers these days. Might as well bring on the leeches and bleed people again with what doctors have been doing to people lately. But with my 'special condition', if a doctor got a look at me now, I would have a future of being a lab rat for the rest of my life. I would rather be dead. Again.

O'Hara noticed my stance and looked at the doctor that was standing by the doorway, slowly scooting in. He snorted and shook his head slightly and moved away from me. It felt like an invitation to go ahead and kick ass. He made points with me right then. I dropped my chin down and prepared for a fight.

"Come now, you've been shot. It's a good idea to let Doctor O'Reilly have a look at it."

The General hadn't said anything yet. He was just watching the scene play out.

"If that hack comes near me, it'll be his last day in a functional body. He'll need his own doctor when I'm done. Then he might get a taste of what their kind dish out. No-fucking-way." I was getting pissed and everyone knew it.

That's when the General stepped in. "She's coming with us. We'll treat her wound at the base."

"You can't do that. It's not your place..." Williams sputtered.

The General cut him off with a bark. "Yes, I can, and yes, I will. It is now a matter of national security and you don't have the clearance for any further contact with this woman. She will be coming with us. We have our own investigations to do and you will stand down, or by God, I'll see you busted down to filing in the darkest room of your building," he was growling now. I wanted to shout 'way to go General'.

"You don't have that kind of authority. You can't do this. Homeland Security *is* National Security," but he didn't sound so sure now.

"Call your superiors and find out what kind of authority I have. Your office can't interfere in matters of national security when the military deems a situation a purely military problem. You are the one overstepping your bounds." He then turned to the doctor and said, "Move aside. We will be leaving with her," and the team formed up around me. The General looked at O'Hara, then to the table as he was stuffing his file back into his briefcase. O'Hara knew what he was asking him to do because he then picked up the sandwich and coffee the dillrod had brought and then we marched right on out of there. The look on dillrod's face was priceless.

We were in one of those big black SUV's again going down the highway when the General asked, "Why did you come to New York?"

"I am meeting someone here." I needed to make sure things were on the level before I took a chance of bringing in my mates and putting them in danger alongside me.

"Someone who could be of help in this coalition of ours?" he asked.

I was confused or maybe just tired. "Coalition?"

"The merging of you and your mercenary friends to my Special Forces team. A coalition," he explained.

"Oh. Sounds about right. Yeah, maybe, but I'll have to talk to them first. Have a meeting, take a vote." He caught the plural, but didn't call me on it. I was mentally kicking my own ass. I really shouldn't blame myself. I'd had a really rough night already. But damn, I needed to be sharper than this, regardless.

"Where do you need to go? We'll drop you off there," he offered.

Now I was stuck. They were supposed to meet me at the airport, but I wasn't there anymore and they didn't tell me exactly where they were staying. It just never came up in last night's conversation. Then throwing together my bags and clothes.....shit my bags.

"Uhmm, my bags are back at the airport and I don't know where we were going to stay yet. I was going to be picked up at the terminal." I was anxious for my things now. Some of the things were irreplaceable.

"Not to worry, we have your bags. I had my attaché pick those up before I even came into the room. They're in the back. Interesting choice of weapons in your luggage. Swords and knives? The swords and a few of those knives look like they're made out of pure sterling silver." He left the question up in the air.

I was relieved. Some of those cost a pretty penny.

"Tools of the trade, I'm afraid. You might want to think about outfitting your men with some of the same. Silver bullets, too."

"You're joking, right?" he looked like he really wanted it to be a joke.

"No, sir, I am not. There are other things they'll need too," I told him.

He sighed heavily. "Please make a list for me and then explain the why of each item later. We'll schedule a meeting. Do you want to use my phone to call your friend? You can have your friend meet you someplace else which would be safer right now considering who may still be at the airport." He held out his cell.

I looked at it, then at him. If I used that phone he'll have their cell number. After that, it was just a matter of time before having their whole history spelled out for him.

"Can you just drop me off somewhere and I'll call from a restaurant or something? I really need that meeting with them first before I have them meet with you. It's not just me I have to worry about," asking him with my eyes to understand. I wasn't being bitchy, just careful.

"Loyal, protective instincts. Those are good qualities in a soldier. In a leader." He turned to the driver and gave him the order to take us to a nice restaurant. At least it sounded nice. Carrigans, they were supposed to have good French food.

"It's in a nice neighborhood. A safer place to leave you since this isn't your hometown." I appreciated the thought, but found it funny. I had just taken out three terrorists; what freakin' gang member had a hope against me?

"You're from Tucson, Arizona, right? Do you like it there?" he asked me. It felt like he was fishing again though. But what was his intent?

"It's ok. It's served its purpose, though. We've been thinking about moving to somewhere with a lot more water. I miss the ocean something fierce and I feel better near water." This insight was ok to tell him, I thought.

"Ocean, eh?" rubbing his chin like he was thinking of something. The car slowed down and stopped in front of a golden, glowing fancy restaurant. I looked down at my torn and bloody jeans. I thought, no way. "They won't let someone like me in there General. Especially with a bloody towel wrapped around my leg."

"How is your wound? I'm sorry, I should have asked earlier, but it didn't seem to bother you." He looked contrite.

I shrugged it off, "I'm used to pain. It'll heal." I didn't tell him it was already looking like a wound which was days old. With no further aid, it would heal on its own in two or three days. With added healing power, it would heal in mere hours. However, he didn't need to know that right now.

"Don't worry; they'll set you up here after we talk to them. Come along." And we exited the car. The man who he called his attaché, brought my black carryon bag and one long suitcase. I had stuffed my knives and two swords in with my clothes so they wouldn't scratch each other in transit. O'Hara and his team had gotten out of the other SUV. They'd left their heavy artillery in the car, but still had their side arms. Guess they didn't want to scare the civilians too much.

The man behind the podium got bug eyed as he saw our odd group walk up. A General and his attaché, a biker chick with a wound and four Special Forces guys must have made quite a scene for him. I noticed him gulping, and was curious if he was going to faint.

The General's attaché walked up, and the man standing at his station stammered out a greeting and said, "Reservations?"

"The General doesn't have a reservation tonight, but he is often a guest here with his good friend Senator Patiste. He and his party would like a table somewhere private." His tone of voice brooked no argument, like he expected to have the General served, no matter what.

The Matri' de gulped again and said. "Of course, anything for a friend of the Senator. We will set up your party immediately." Hmmm. It pays to have friends in the right places, I see.

He took a look at my leg and swooned a bit.

I leaned over and said to O'Hara, "Twenty bucks says he faints before you guys leave."

He grinned and said, "You're on." A bunch of 'I'm in' and 'I'll that action,' remarks came from the other men.

We were seated in the back of the restaurant, as far as he could get us away from the regular customers. He looked at the General, addressing him, "Your waiter will be out shortly." And he turned to leave.

I said, "Wait a minute, sir." He stopped and looked at me. I unwrapped my towel and said, "Do you have a clean one I can use?" and he dropped in a dead faint. Luckily, the rest of the men didn't have a good view of my wound. If they did, they would have asked questions of why it looked so healed up. But, the Matri' de still fainted over a half healed wound. How funny.

O'Hara started laughing and said, "You're evil."

I answered back, "Pay up" The whole team was chuckling by now, but the General frowned a bit at me like a stern father. "I see I won't be able to take you anywhere if you can't behave." The gleam in his eyes gave him away and I started laughing.

A couple of waiters came over and fussed over the Matri' de. They looked like clucking hens. Sheeesh, he only passed out; I was the one with a bullet wound.

"Are you hungry for some real food? The food here is really quite excellent," the General sounded encouraging.

"That sounds great. Something with a nice red, juicy, totally bloody rare steak. Brussels sprouts with any sauce and mashed potatoes, if they have that here? I'll take baked if not, with sour cream and chives." I gazed around to everyone to see if I had made a faux pas in ordering like that.

"I'll see what I can do." The General just took it in stride. "My men and I will just order drinks so we can leave before your 'friends' come to pick you up."

"Your word that you won't stay around to get a visual on my people?" My eye contact went hard as I looked at him.

"My word we won't stay to see." He looked sincere and his aura didn't flare.

"A word of advice, General. I believe your word on this, but at any time in the future, if you give your word to one of us—keep it. It goes badly for those who lie to one of my kind," I informed him quite seriously.

He went on guard and his men went tense as well. No doubt ready to defend him against me if I went bogy.

I shook my head at them, "No. We don't personally hurt people for lying to us, it's the magick. You ever hear of the Fae?" I asked.

He thought a minute and the others relaxed just a bit, "Yes, aren't they some kind of elves that are Celtic in origin?"

"Kind of. Do you have a paper and pen?" I looked around the table.

He turned to his attaché and was handed a pad and a pen from his jacket post haste. "Oh, this young soldier is my attaché, Major Brandon Stewart. He's my right hand man."

I nodded my head and Major Stewart went to shake my hand. The General stopped him saying, "They don't shake hands as a matter of course. A nod of greeting is good for her and her people. Is that right? All your people are like that?"

"Yes," I affirmed, not looking up from my writing. I finished and handed him the pad and pen back.

"Those first three are a series of fictional books I know, but they hold grains of truth to them, believe it or not. You put those series together and you have what we are. It's amazing how truth can be framed in fiction. The authors are either very lucky guessers or have innate power themselves. Those other books are on magick and astral projection. I put an asterisk besides the ones O'Hara should get started on ASAP. Between all those books, they will give you a real good idea of what you're dealing with. The most important stuff. What we consider totally classified stays that way until I get a go ahead from my superior."

"So, you have a superior then?" He caught everything didn't he?

"Yes, I do," I said reluctantly.

"Then what would your standing be in such a situation?" He was asking my rank, if we had such things.

"That is a tricky question and maybe someday I'll be able to tell you why. For now though, when it comes to all things on this physical plane, I am second in command."

"Good, then you have the authority to make decisions and contracts?" he asked just to clarify.

"Yes, for the most part. There are others I consider my equal and they are in their own...," I searched for a good word, "section. They now have a vote in things I'm involved in."

"Good to know. You've said physical plane a few times now. What do you mean, exactly, by that?" He was curious again.

"Those books will explain it pretty well. If you need more clarification, I will be more than happy to tutor you on it. Meanwhile, I have to use the powder room. The waiter, he comes." He looked oddly at me, at my phrasing.

"A movie line. My 'team' have a game too, where we'll say something straight from a movie or a song we've seen or heard and use it in everyday conversation. Sometimes we twist the words a bit to fit the situation, but then the person we're talking to has to guess which movie or song it came from."

Shaking his head, "Ah, I see. I'm afraid I won't be much good at it. I don't watch movies very often and only listen to classical music."

"You should, they're fun." I moved to get up to find the ladies room. Every man rose at the table and I took the gesture for what it was, nodded, and walked away.

I heard a few gasps as I walk toward the ladies room, but ignored it. I found the sign for the ladies room and walked inside. Looking around the plush bathroom I found a spot that should stay relatively empty. I dropped my shields and got a wave of frustration and anger. Oops, I had definitely put this off for way too long.

'Where in the seven hells are you? We can't find you,' Andre was frantic and pissed. He was the most volatile of the three.

'Calm down, hon. I am very, very sorry, but I'm fine. I have had a spot of trouble though. I cleared it up for the most part. Can you guys get in your car, leave the airport and drive going towards this restaurant called The Carrigan? Do you know where it is?' I asked.

'What the fuck are you doing there?' he barked.

'No wonder we couldn't feel you out here anymore.' That was Demitri.

'I had to leave the airport under guard of a Special Forces team and a General. The FBI dude was a real prick and a dark practitioner to boot. I had to leave fast before he could get his claws into me,' I rushed the information before they could really get worried.

They did anyway. *'Special Forces, what the hell? We're getting whispers and rumors of a hijacking. Don't tell me you were involved in it, babe,'* this from Demitri, who is usually the most stable of them.

'Up to my neck, I'm afraid. The plane had a terrorist cell on it. They were going to take the plane and use it for something. I haven't found out what exactly they were going to do yet. I had to take them out and fly the plane. All the pilots were killed.' I knew they would be pissed.

'Shit,' Andre spurted.

'Only you can find yourself in the middle of a hijacking,' Antonio felt pissed as well, but not at me.

'Babe, are you ok?' It was always the first thing Demitri asks me, before taking me to the carpet.

All three were head speaking almost at the same time. It was getting hard to focus properly. Hard to separate their feelings. The emotions I was getting was fear, grief, anger, vengeance, worry, concern....they just kept rolling in, swamping me.

'Ok sweethearts, you need to just relax as best you can. I'm getting flooded. Let me finish. I took out the terrorists. One died on his own by fucking up the poison delivery, which was what took out the pilots. That's when I had to step in. There were three men left. I killed two and left one

alive. We need to get someone down there that can read him and get more information ASAP. Then I landed the plane. After that I was in custody.' And I waited for the anger. I just hoped it wouldn't be at me.

'Assholes. Whose ass do I kick?'

'You were just helping.'

'You saved them. What the fuck?'

It was rolling in again. *'Chill guys, please. I have had a rough night already.'* The emotions and thoughts trickled down again until one was left. *'And you, are you ok?'* Demitri asked again.

'I got shot, but it's healing.' I figured I had better get it over with now. I added a hasty, *'I am fine though. NO worries. Honest.'*

'Where were you shot?' Demitri asked.

'She was shot in the leg. Weren't you, hon?' Andre supplied the answer.

'Yes, my right leg,' I confirmed.

'I was wondering why my leg ached for most of the night. Now I feel the burn' Demitri said, *'Do you need healing?'*

'Later. Yeah, I will need it,' I admitted.

'Done. Now, what else Catrina?' That came out clipped, from Demitri. He was getting upset. That was never a good thing. It took a lot to get him going, but once he was there—look out. Run.

I took a deep breath. *'They caught me on camera. I didn't know they had cameras. But the damage is contained,'* I hurried to assure them.

'Oh, Good Mother Goddess. Please tell me you're shitting me. Please.' The other two were cursing right along with Demitri. I was flooded once more. I could now add terror to the list of emotions. Terror for me. For my safety and what this meant to us as a whole.

'Oh, it gets better.' And all three of them groaned. I could hear them say, *'What? How much worse could it be?'*

'One of the Special Forces soldiers had to feed me.' And I braced myself for the explosion.

Instead, sudden cold silence ensued.

This was worse. Way worse.

'The fucker dies. He dies tonight.' Andre was pissed.

'You sucked one some guys neck?' Demitri asked hurt and pissed.

'NO. NO. NO. I didn't hit his neck. I took from his wrist only. I swear it. And only blood, nothing else. I swear. I was fading. I would have soon attacked anything and anyone in my way. He stopped that from happening. I swear it.' I was scared now for O'Hara, because Andre doesn't fool around. None of them did.

I could feel them deep breathing. Trying to control their emotions. Trying to hold their anger in check.

'*OK, ok, it was an emergency. It was only the wrist. We can deal with this. We actually owe this guy a thank you,*' Demitri said, trying to calm his brothers. They could share me among themselves, but Goddess help any other man who even looked at me.

'*Yeah, but the camera film?*' Andre asked.

'*The special ops team yanked it. They and their General are the only ones who have it. FBI Special Agent in Charge Williams only saw part of it. The team then glitched the video for him,*' I explained.

'*What do they want?*' Antonio was always quick. I loved his brain.

'*You're going to love this. A coalition of their team and ours.*' I wondered how they would take that idea.

Long silence followed as they thought about it.

'*How much do they know about us?*' Antonio asked.

'*About you guys, nothing. About me, fangs, blood, can move very fast and can read by touch.*'

'*I'm impressed you've it kept it down to so little.*' Praise from Demitri. I loved it. I had never gotten praise as a kid, so now when one of them did it, I got all mushy. It was a stupid reaction really, I thought to myself.

'*And your opinion on joining forces?*' Antonio asked me.

'*Well, given the fact The Goddess showed up and said it would be a good idea, it really might be a good idea. Sooner or later, we'll need military help when the shit hits the fan in 2012. We won't be enough to stop all the death by ourselves and with them behind us we would have the physical authority for the things we will have to do. Most importantly, we would be more effective if we had them on our side now, then becoming an obstacle later.*' I had been thinking of the pros and cons for the past hour and related all that to them.

Antonio said, '*I love the way you think. But can we trust them?*'

I went gooey again...shit. '*Conditionally, for now. Yes.*' The General and his team covered for me, protected me from the FBI and got me loose. It bought them some stock with me and by extension, my mates as well. I could feel that from them as they thought about all of the implications.

'*A trial run then, with minimum contact. We'll keep the exposure down in case it goes south and they turn on us.*' Demitri said, '*What say you?*' This directed at his brothers. They both agreed.

'*We'll have to let the rest of the Coven know, and soon. We'll get their votes as well,*' Antonio said. Meaning we were going to be making a bunch of calls to my brothers and sisters tonight and tomorrow.

'Catrina, I'm still upset that you didn't let us know what was going on. We would have helped. You should never have left us hanging like that for so long. We were worried sick. Andre was about to tear that airport apart because we couldn't get any information on you or about the plane you were on.'

I felt myself shrinking bit by bit. He was right. I fucked up. *'I'm sorry, hon. I'm just not used to checking in with anyone at all. I've been my own boss since I was twelve. I know I need to make adjustments. I honestly didn't mean to do that.'* I was feeling like a jerk.

'We all need to make adjustments and it will be easier when we all live together. It's ok. Just don't do that again, all right?' he asked so nicely.

'I'll try harder.' I couldn't promise. Knowing myself, I most likely will screw up and breaking promises was even worse than lying. But I would try harder. That, I could do.

'Fine, we're about twenty minutes away now. You need to tell us everything. In detail. What happened?' Demitri said. Obviously, I was still on the carpet. I sighed.

'Ok, I have to get rid of the General and his men. I won't be able to talk to you when they're around. They are way too sharp and I don't want them to know about the telepathy we have, but I won't shield, so you can hear what's going on if you drop in my head.' They knew this was a huge concession, because I hated it when someone dropped into my head. Hearing every thought or word spoken to me made me feel very invaded.

Demitri, knowing this, said, *"That's sweet; we'll just keep tabs on you to make sure you're safe. That's all we really need.'* HA! Maybe not so much on the carpet anymore, am I?

'OK, *I'm going back to my table. Love you.'* I said with a smile that they could feel.

'Love you more,' he replied. I walked out feeling gooey again. Ye gad. Some tough bitch I was, sheesh.

I walked back to the table and sat down. I saw that my meal had been delivered already.

"I didn't know what you wanted to drink so I ordered another soda for you since I knew you liked that." The General filled me in as I stared longingly at the plate of food.

"Perfect," I said. "I called for my ride and got a vote of confidence from some of the others already. We're ready to do this on a trial basis. A small group of us will be available for the time being," I informed him.

"Excellent. And it sounds reasonable. But answer me this. How did you call when the bathrooms are over there and the phone is there?" He pointed in the other direction. Like I said, these guys are sharp.

"Everyone in this room most likely has a cell phone, right?" I asked him.

General Pierce looked confused, "Yes."

"Other people have to go to the bathroom, too." I didn't state that this is what I did. I just pointed out a fact and let him assume. We don't like lying, but we were really good at misdirection when needs be.

He didn't look entirely convinced, but he let it drop.

"They'll be here soon, so if you all could make yourself scarce, that would be good. I hate being rude since you bought me such a lovely dinner but..." I let the rest hang in the air.

"Of course. Men, shall we go?" And they all got up to leave.

The General handed me a business card. "Call this number in two or three days. I have some things to get ready, but will have enough done to fill you in by then."

I took the card and put it in my jacket. O'Hara handed me a piece of paper with a number written on it. "Memorize it, and then burn it. Use it if you need us to come running."

"Thanks," I said, truly touched.

"It was very interesting meeting you. This was one of the weirdest missions I have ever had. Though I am sure the weirdness isn't over yet, is it?" he asked.

"Nope, we've only just begun," I said in a romantic singing tone, jokingly.

"Carpenters." He gave a tight smile and they walked out. I sat there shocked that he knew the song.

CHAPTER NINE
United We Stand

I had just wolfed down my dinner when they walked in. Demitri gave the Matri' de his coldest eye and asked to be taken to my table immediately. Damn they all had that knack of getting people to treat them like princes from a visiting country. The man practically fell all over himself escorting them to my table. He started apologizing profusely, and when I had had enough, I told him, "Shut up and go away." I didn't have that upper class knack, but I was good at being rude to people who pissed me off.

Besides, I wanted the man gone so I could ogle my men. And damn, they were fine. All were brothers by blood, so they had the same basic features. Dark hair, deep brown eyes, tall and fit, absolutely mouthwatering. And they were mine. All mine. Andre had a roguish scar on his chin he'd gotten from a sword fight many years ago and a tattoo of a black panther on his arm. Demitri's only scar was on his leg from an axe he had accidently embedded it. He'd been chopping up a Yule tree after the holidays were over and missed the tree. He was embarrassed about the incident, so it didn't get mentioned—much. It depended if his brothers wanted to tease him about it. Antonio was the tallest of the three, even though he was the youngest.

They were each only a year apart and all birthed by their physical mother in the month of December. Demitri's birthday was December 7th. Andre was born December 3rd and Antonio was born December 14th. If one added their birthdays up, you got my birthday; except I was born March 24th, roughly five years younger than Demitri. Even numerically we matched. Children of the Gods and Goddesses tended to do that.

The men didn't look their age either and with their black slacks and silk shirts they looked like they were set for seduction. I felt a bit under-dressed, to say the least. I got up and gave them a hug one by one, kissing each in turn. Then I heard Andre hiss in sympathy over the state of my leg. I quickly sat back down again, trying to hide it.

Demitri looked at me and asked, "Are you sure you're ok?"

"Yeah, I got this." I hated and loved being fussed over by them. I loved it because it never happened before with any of my exes. I also hated it because it made me feel like the 'little woman'. I hated that more than anything. I never had been, and never would be, even if I were purely human. I'm just not wired for that, mentally. Anything soft and womanly got burned out of me when I was little. Literally. With cigarettes. Just ask my step father.

Demitri noticed the look on my face and reached over to grab my hand. "It's all right, hon. We love you the way you are. We got bored with the mousy x-ray women from when we dated before. You'll never be mousy, nor a bag of bones. You're just right for us," he reassured me. "So, tell us what happened."

I sat back and told them everything that had happened. They ordered drinks and some dinner while we got caught up. Andre asked me what I wanted and I told him I had already eaten, but would take a dessert of cheesecake and ice cream. He nodded and told the waiter what we wanted. I finished the tale over their dinner and my dessert.

They were eating their dessert and sharing with me, like I needed more, sheesh. But I didn't refuse. It was kind of sexy being fed. Demitri asked, "What do you think about General Pierce? Is he going to hold that video over you like blackmail or what?"

"I don't know. But I will make it a demand for our help to give it back. They really do need our kind of help by what I saw in that one file alone."

"That is one powerful dark God to reach all the way back here," Andre said.

"I'll do some research about their dark pantheon for that region. We'll have a name and his weaknesses, if any, by tomorrow," Antonio added.

"What about the young terrorist? Can we find a way to him to get a read?" I asked my mates.

Demitri said, "I'll make some calls in the morning and see if I can find out where he was taken. I'll try to work out something from there."

"This FBI dillrod being a dark practitioner is stretching the word coincidence a bit. It seems too convenient that he was the one in charge of the area that happens to have a hijacked plane coming in," I said. "Can we dig into his history?"

Antonio said, "Yes. I'll make some calls tomorrow on that as well."

Demitri signaled the waiter over and asked for the check.

"That won't be necessary, General Pierce has your evening covered," he explained.

"Well, that was nice of him," Demitri said. He left a nice tip on the table and we left.

When we got outside, a long black limousine pulled up. My mouth dropped open.

A freakin' limo. It was a freakin' limo. Adjustments my ass. I was in over my head. Demitri opened the door for me. Andre had grabbed my bags and the driver had opened the trunk. They were settling my luggage. I climbed in and took in the plush surroundings. A mini bar with crystal glasses, TV, CD, all the bells and whistles. I sighed and settled into the most comfortable seat I had ever sat in. Demitri sat beside me and gathered me close to him. I could smell the patchouli on his skin and the scent relaxed me as nothing else could. I looked at the other two and thought to myself, for them, I'll adjust. This was home. This smell, these men. It was home, and here I felt safe, for the first time in my life. I fell asleep on the way to the hotel. Safe and warm.

I woke up hours later in an unfamiliar bed. Naked. I felt a warm body lying next to mine and turned to see Demitri's sleeping face. I didn't think he could get anymore handsome, but he just did. His skin was an olive complexion from his Italian heritage and looked even darker against the white silk sheets. Silk sheets? Shit, where was I? I looked around the room and saw dark, rich furnishing and the huge king-sized bed we were on. I took assessment of my body and wound. The wound had healed and I was washed up. They somehow had gotten me in the hotel room and cleaned me up. They must have healed me and put me to bed in this state. I'd slept through the whole thing? Damn, I must have been more tired than I had thought. OK, fine, superwoman I wasn't. I looked around trying to find a clock. The room was still dark, though I knew it was daylight outside. The heavy drapes gave a sultry twilight cast to everything in the room. I looked back at Demitri and noticed his eyes were open.

He smiled gently, "Hey, sweetheart," and rolled closer to me. My breath caught, either from fear or passion. I really wasn't sure which. Maybe both. I put my hand on his chest which had only a small patch of hair on it; otherwise it was smooth and well muscled. He stopped with a concerned look on his face.

"You ok?" he asked.

In a breathy voice I said, "Yeah."

He smiled again and it was a sexy smile, "Good. We drew stones last night to see who would sleep with you first. We thought it would be easier if you got used to us one by one instead of all at once. That didn't help on our first night back home did it?" he asked.

I just shook my head.

"We made a bag with three stones in it. Two black, one white; whoever drew the white stone wins. We thought that would be fairer for us," he explained the process of elimination.

"It was a good idea," still sounding breathless. He leaned over to kiss me. His lips were soft and gentle, but firm. His tongue slid into my mouth. He kissed me deeply and thoroughly. My toes were curling, my body getting tight and hot. His body moved against mine and I could feel him getting hard.

Then it happened again. I froze.

He stopped.

Panting, he asked, "Honey?"

I was shaking again. He put space between us, but held on with his hands and I eventually got control of myself.

"OK. That's it," I said, out of patience with myself. "I thought this might happen again. So, I had an idea. There's something I want to try, if you're willing to play along?" I looked at him. I was NOT retreating from this battle. I would win the war bit by bit if that's what it took.

"No problem, sweetheart. Anything you need, I'm willing to try." He looked so earnest and still pulled off sexy. Damn.

"OK. If you could let me know your body? Give me total free rein, but don't touch me. We can bring down this fear to where we can make love all the way. But for this time, the first time with you, just let me 'do'. You don't touch me. That's the problem, it's having the touches," I explained to him.

"Let me get this straight. You want to please me, but I don't get to please you this time?" sounding not very happy with the idea.

"Right. It will help me overcome my fear because I would be in total control," I said.

"It's not fair to you though," he still sounded doubtful.

"I don't think of it that way. I would totally get off giving you pleasure. Can we just try it this time? *Please?*" I begged.

"All right. This time. Next time, it's my turn," and the sexy grin was back.

"I'll try. Do you have any oil?" I asked him

His eyes lit up like it was Yule. "I have oil. I even have strawberry flavored!" An evil grin was on his face. He knew I loved strawberries.

"Oh, yum!" I was grinning.

He got the oil and handed to me.

I told him, "Lie down on your stomach. No matter what, don't touch me. No touchy!" I shook my finger at him.

"Emperor's New Groove," he said and lay down.

I laughed and then stopped. He had the finest ass I had ever seen on a man. Tight and perfect. I wanted to bite it. His back was muscled, long and lean. I sighed. This time I had pleasure just from looking.

I straddled him and poured some oil in my hand. I let it sit there as I put heat magickally into the oil, warming it up. I started at his shoulders and rubbed it in massaging his neck muscles and upper shoulders. I let my caresses move to his arms, feeling the muscles there. I worked my way down his back slowly, kneading and stroking his skin in light touches. He was groaning already. When I had reached his lower back and thoroughly massaged the muscles there, I leaned over and started kissing his neck. He hissed with an intake of breath, but stayed still, waiting for my next move.

I moved down his body, kissing and tasting his skin with my tongue. I would alternate between long strokes of my tongue to short ones. He was starting to wriggle around.

I lightly patted his bottom, "Stay still." I ordered. Then I continued kissing and tasting my way down his back. When I reached his ass, I poured more oil in my hands and massaged his buttocks. Then I bent down and started to kiss and lick my way all over his rump.

"Honey, please," he was begging.

I patted his ass again and said, "Shush, be still." I kissed and licked some more until he was panting. So far, so good. I was still here with him. No panic. All I wanted to do was taste. That was the only thing on my mind was his taste. His skin.

I allowed him to roll over; his eyes were hot with passion. "If you keep that up, I won't last long," he warned.

"After fifteen years of celibacy, I would be surprised if either of us lasted long." And with the oil in my hands, I went to work on his chest. His hands fisted into the sheets so he could keep himself from touching me. But I could tell it was costing him. I worked my way down his stomach, touching and stroking his skin. When I got to his groin I stopped and leaned over again this time kissing his lips. His hands started to reach up to grab me, but I pushed them back onto the bed. I moved my kisses from his mouth to the side of his jaw. Then I worked my way around to his ear.

His was moaning again, since this was one of his erogenous zones. I moved down his neck, nipping and kissing.

He started to breathe harder and faster, "Please, let me touch you," he said, his voice deeper and in need.

I told him, "Just let me do this."

He groaned, but did what I wanted him to do. I licked my way down his chest, kissing and sucking at each nipple. His back bowed a bit. Then I worked my way down his stomach with my mouth. When I got to his groin again, I got more oil in my hand, then gently grabbed his cock. I massaged the oil up and down with my right hand while I caressed his balls with the other.

"Baby, please," he was moaning deeply now, shaking from passion. I was getting so hot just watching him writhe under my hands. I bent down and licked the inside of his thigh and he nearly shot off the bed.

I restrained him lightly, again pushing him back down and said, "Patience, I'm getting there." He was breathing hard and his eyes...damn... I never saw such intensity in a man's eyes before, so hot with passion and need. I held his gaze with my own as I bent down and gently licked the tip of his long, hard cock. I then took my tongue and swirled it around the tip, before sucking it into my mouth.

He bowed his head back into the pillow and said, "Fuck, your mouth is so hot," pushing his hips up, trying to get more of his dick in my mouth. I obliged, taking him down as far as I could go. I gently sucked his hardness up and down, in and out of my mouth. With my other hand, I massaged his testicles and played with the perennial, slick with the oil on my finger. His body grew tauter from clenching his orgasm back, trying to make it last as long as possible. I felt his cock throb hard and knew he wouldn't be able to hold back and sure enough...

"Catrina," he cried out and came in my mouth. I swallowed and licked some more. His body shivered. He was breathing so hard.

I moved back up and we kissed again. "That was out of this world, babe. My turn now?"

"Next time. See, I didn't freeze this time." And I kissed his neck.

I snuggled into him and he asked, "But don't you need release, too?"

I looked up at him and said, "I'm so satisfied that I didn't freeze up and gave you pleasure, I'll smile all day from it. Trust me."

"You know, payback is a bitch, right?" he warned with a growl.

"No, sweetheart, I am a bitch," laughing, I rolled out of bed before he could attack.

"Come on, get up. Feed me food and let's get to work. We've got evil bad guys to vanquish." I ran for the bathroom when I saw the intent in his eyes as he crawled towards me. I wasn't stupid.

But I was still laughing as I locked the door. "Bring me my clothes or I could be in here all day, you horny devil."

"Damn, evil woman," I heard him growl. "Fuck bad guys. You're worse."

"Why, thank you, honeybun," I said sweetly. "My clothes now."

I got dressed and left him the bathroom, so he could get ready next. I went to my suitcase and saw how rumpled everything was. I picked through it until I found what I needed and spied my friend.

He was no longer wrapped in the silk scarf I had him in. Shamus, a black pewter figurine of a wizard with a huge crystal ball held over his head, was just laying there. I felt anger rolling off the 6" statue. Then the anger came from the corner as his astral spirit shimmered into existence.

"Do you know how many people touched my physical representation?" he was pissed. "I don't mind your children. I don't mind your mates, but total strangers? How could you be so lax?" he berated me.

He was my very first astral familiar to appear to me. He and I had been through many astral battles together. He'd healed many wounds, both physical and astral, due to me having a physical statue of him which gave him power on this plane. He felt more like a gruff uncle then the astral familiar servant he was supposed to be. And he was pissed that I didn't protect the physical object that tied him to this plane better. I couldn't blame him, but things last night were out of my control.

"I'm sorry, Shamus. I will clean off the statue and purify it again," I promised.

"Don't forget to anoint it again with your astral oil either," he barked. "Did you take a look at your portable altar?"

I gasped, and looked for the small cedar box that held the tools that I needed for a traveling altar. I found it and opened it with trepidation. Sure enough, things were scattered in it. The top had not been put back on right on the bottle for my sea salt and it was everywhere inside the box. I was shaking in anger. Don't these stupid mundane mortals respect anyone's religion?

Any idiot could see this was a religious box.

And they had defiled it.

Andre and Antonio came running in, "What's wrong?"

I held my box out for inspection and nodded toward the figurine of Shamus. I couldn't speak, I was so angry.

"Awe, honey, I am so sorry." Andre gathered me in his arms, hugging me tightly.

Antonio came up from the other side and joined the group hug session. "I have more sea salt. You can have it. You can re-sanctify the rest of the tools and your box, hon. We can put this right again."

"Yes, she can and yes, she will, but my question is how was this allowed to happen in the first place, hmmm?" Shamus asked.

Demitri came rushing out of the bathroom, dripping wet. "What's wrong?"

"Airport security and Goddess knows how many others defiled her traveling altar and touched Shamus." Peeking into the suitcase, "And her weapons," Antonio informed him.

"Awe, shit, hon. I didn't think of that last night. I am really sorry." He looked so sad for me.

"I am waiting," Shamus said gruffly. He was pissed at me, but more for me, really. I could tell.

"It was a small incident of the plane we were on being hijacked by terrorists. I got shot. I kicked ass, but I got shot. I had to land the plane myself because the pilots had been killed. Then, I got detained. Then, was I shanghaied into service for a special force operation," I summarized for him.

His mouth dropped open. His spirit form seemed to grow out bigger and wider. Then he flashed over to me scanning my body for damage. He still wasn't used to me being modified and was acting like I still had a purely human, fragile form.

"You seem fine. Any dizziness?" he barked.

"No," I replied.

"Have you fed on blood?" he asked.

"Yes," I answered.

"Hmm, your aura says different or you didn't get enough. Your energy signature is not at optimum levels. Please feed now," he ordered like a doctor.

Andre was already baring his throat to me and I halted the motion. "First things first. I have to start cleansing this stuff and purifying it." A good High Priestess and warrior always took care of their magickal tools and weapons first. They all understood this and allowed me to start.

"Fine," Shamus said. "You know if you hadn't ordered me to stay away, you wouldn't have had so many problems. And I could have helped in bringing in reinforcements for you. But, noooo, you had to go all Lone Ranger and look what happened." He was back to being the nagging uncle.

"Do you realize how much electrical stuff they have on a plane? Cell phones aren't even allowed to be turned on in a plane. No way could I have had any of you popping in to check on me and taking a chance the plane would crash because of tripping a circuit or something. Are you nuts?" I reminded him.

"We could have been careful," he almost pouted, though this argument didn't work the first time either.

"Astral beings like you probably started the whole gremlin thing," I shot out.

"Hrmphh, I seriously doubt that, Your Highness," he shot back.

Oh, I hated the Highness thing. Even though, technically, it was true, I wasn't used to the title of Princess. The guys were, but they grew up with that sort of thing. I hadn't. So, it made me really uncomfortable to be worshiped and bowed to. It was Shamus' way of getting my goat because he knew this.

"So tell me everything that happened," he demanded.

Well, at least he wasn't mad at me anymore. Demitri went to finish cleaning up. I filled Shamus in as I did my own cleansing and finished dressing. I blessed the altar as best as I could, but I would have to wait until the next full moon to do it properly.

Stupid people didn't realize how much work went into keeping magickal tools cleansed, powered and blessed. They are so used to throwing something into a washer and snap, they got what they wanted. Sick? Pop a pill. Hungry? Go get fast food. If they had to do things that took time and energy, they would not only have respect for the things of other people, but would be much healthier in body and mind as well. True, the fault wasn't totally theirs. Society at large was making people work so hard, for so many hours; no one had time to do things the right way anymore.

"Tell me again why we're wasting energy saving these ungrateful buttwads?" I asked for the fiftieth time."Let them all perish and start over again I say. The only thank you we're going to get, most likely, is a burning at the stake," I grumbled.

Antonio laughed. "They don't burn us witches at the stake anymore honey."

"They would if they knew about our kind. We are not just witches. People fear what they can't understand or control. And they kill what they fear," I told him.

Andre asked Antonio, "What movie did that come from?"

"Several, actually," he answered his brother.

"Doesn't make it any less true and you both know it," I said.

Shamus must have told my whole astral clan of familiars about my being wounded because I kept seeing orbs pop in and then pop out, checking on me. I guess they needed to see that I was all right with their own eyes.

Shamus was my second in command over all of my other familiars. I had usually been too busy surviving, fighting or searching for my mates to keep everyone who served me on the astral in line or to take care of all their needs. So, I made Shamus powerful enough and gave him the authority to oversee everyone else.

Delegation, even on the astral planes.

"True, but you remember that little baby you saw in the park back home?" Antonio reminded me.

I answered shortly, "Yes."

"Sweet kid, huh?" he asked me.

My face softened, as I remembered the pretty chubby cheeks and innocent smile the baby had given me. Then she reached out with her little arms like she wanted me to pick her up and hold her. I melted, remembering how much I ached to hug that kid. Her mother probably would have had kittens though, so I just smiled back at the baby girl. I was a sucker for babies. Any type of babies, human, otherkin or astral, it didn't matter.

He saw the look in my face, "That's why we do what we do."

I sighed in defeat. He was right.

Antonio eased up in front of me, lightly touching the back of my neck and pulling me to him. "Feed from me. Andre has you tonight. I know it's blood and sex that gets our batteries super charged, but I get the blood part now; Andre will give you the sex later." He bent so I could reach and I licked his neck which got my fangs to drop.

I waited. "I offer you my blood, mate to mate, from my heart and soul. Of my own free will, So be it," he intoned the ritual words.

"I take your offer in honor, mate. So be it," and I bit in, closing my eyes. His blood was so rich and strong. Pulsing with power, as it slid down my throat. The room we were in fell away, and it felt like it was just the two of us on another plane. His spirit and mine were facing each other standing close. Then we melded together becoming one being for a brief second in time. Power flared and pulsed though me, through us. More than just a life force feeding, it had turned in an astral melding of spirits. The same thing one had to do to create a mating bond. Now it only reinforced what we already had, making it stronger. I fell back away and we were in the room again. I licked the wounds my teeth made. I knew they would heal in mere minutes. His eyes were heavy lidded, like we had just had sex. But a melding was more than that. Added to the feeding as well, I felt strong, like I had slept for weeks and could go for months on end now, if I needed to. The power surge would fade after a while, I knew, so I took a deep breath and gave him a kiss.

"Thank you, love." I whispered to him.

"Wow, my turn?" Andre's eyes were hopeful.

Laughing, I said, "If I did, I might blow apart from overload."

"Yeah, I am that damn good," Andre said, strutting towards me.

"Dude, check you out." I reached around and smacked his ass. "We need to get to work."

"We have a board meeting at 6 pm tonight. It wasn't easy getting the board members to meet this late. This being New York, the city that never sleeps, it was doable this time," Andre said, shaking his head.

"But we have files for you to look at." Antonio walked over to the desk and grabbed a few files, some thick with paper, and handed them to me. "Here is the dossier on Special Agent Williams. I couldn't find any magickal ties to any black covens, but I am sure you're right about him," he said grimly.

"What makes you so sure?" I asked him, sitting down on a huge couch and using the glass table in front of it to spread out what he'd given to me.

"That young terrorist just happened to die at the hospital. According to the hospital file—yes, it's in there," he answered, before I could ask, "he had three broken ribs and a slight concussion. Yes, people can die from even a slight concussion. I know this, but that's not what killed him. He was hooked up to an IV to hydrate him; someone must have pushed an air bubble into the line, because his heart," Antonio gestured with his fingers, closed, then flicking out, "went boom."

"Shit, how convenient," I said.

"Special Agent Williams tried to add his death to your charges, but there apparently was a call from some top dog military official. Everything against you has been dropped and Special Agent Williams was warned off. Strongly," Antonio told me.

"Ten, says the General had something to do with that," I snorted. I was pleased though. It made things easier for me. But I was also leery of anyone doing me any favors. It always seemed to bite me in the ass later. And not in the good way.

"I ain't touching that bet," Andre said, smiling. They were trying to fit with me. Trying to merge my world with theirs. It meant a lot to me.

Demitri walked into the room looking sharp. They all did. Armani. Tailored to fit.

Even I, being the bohemian I was, could tell that.

I sighed; half because of the doubt of the merge and half because, damn, they looked good. No matter how bad I felt inside or out, just looking at them, finally being in the same room with them after all this time, was a blessing on so many levels. I hope the day never comes where I would take it for granted.

Demitri looked at me and smiled, "Already working, hon?" He had the same workaholic tendencies that I did. "You didn't eat any food yet. We wanted to take you out somewhere nice, but we got up too late. After the meeting though, we could go anywhere you want. Meanwhile, there's room service or a decent restaurant a few blocks from here to hold you over."

I smiled at him. No, that day will never come.

CHAPTER TEN
Base in Black

The time in New York was an experience for me. They wined and dined me. I had always wanted to see a stage show, so they took me to off Broadway. I was amazed at the talent that I saw. I had always wanted to see 'A Midsummer Night's Dream', but it wasn't playing anywhere. Demitri promised if it ever was being played, even if we had to take the jet, we would go. So I had something really neat to look forward to.

We still hadn't fully consummated the marriage yet. Antonio was the hardest to get around that one. Andre got handcuffed to the bed since I knew his penchant of being dominated. Every now and again, he loved it. Antonio, though, no way. He dominated or was an equal. Period. So working around that took every skill I had learned way back when. I had to use my safe word, 'Popeye', a lot. But, I got my way.

They got their corporation back on track, being the trio of power players that they were. Demitri led most of the time, but Andre was the muscle, when needed. He also provided the, 'party favors' that some business men liked to indulge in when closing deals. Women, wine, good times. Whatever they needed, Andre got. My men never joined in after creating the bond with me. I would have blown a fuse if they did, but I knew it was necessary for their business dealings. I felt bad for the wives of the businessmen, even if some of them were just trophy wives. When one makes an oath, it should be upheld, no matter what.

Andre also did the strong arm tactics when Demitri needed that particular talent. Andre's build was thicker than his brothers, since he spent so much time at the gym keeping extra fit. Antonio was the tech guy. Anything technical needed, Antonio fixed, got or circumvented in times of need. Together, the three of them were unbeatable, even in this economy. They were doing very well. They had their fingers in so many pies, it made my head spin. And I could absorb a lot. Export, import, hi-tech, green tech, real-estate and so on. So many things, that I didn't bother trying to remember it all.

The only thing I could contribute, and had been, even before we found each other physically, were flashes of insight or prescient dreams. Like when the stock market in China dropped, I dreamed about it three months before it happened. I told them about it and they were able to save their investments that would have been affected by the crash. Sometimes I knew when a contract was bad or had a mistake in it, when someone in their company was putting it together. I would warn them. They would investigate, find the problem, and fix it. But I could only tell them things if, and when, I got a pre-warning in a dream or that funny feeling. I couldn't make it happen on every deal. They understood this, knowing how gifts and magick worked, and were just happy that I could do what I was able to do. It was enough for them. And I felt like I played a part, however minor, in the grand scheme of things. We also talked to my brothers and sisters. They were ready to go along with the General's plan. With caution.

I had called the number on the card the General had given me. He asked for a meeting in Corpus Christi, Texas at the Naval Air Station, otherwise known as, Truax Field. He set up accommodations for us at the Navy Gateway Inn and Suites. He got us clearance to land at the airstrip 3 miles away at Navy Landing Airfield. He had me write down the authorization codes Demitri's pilot would need. He also said a car would be there to take us to our rooms. I felt like I was entering the militant zone again.

At least I wouldn't have to worry about my luggage being mauled this time. I also told Demitri about the trouble with ID and he said Antonio would fix it. I knew he would, too. Their plane was at JFK, but I was still on edge when we stepped out of the car and headed toward the plane while Demitri dealt with security. It went much faster than when I went through on my own for the commercial airplane.

And his jet sure was pretty. Inside and out. I thought first class on the commercial plane had it going on, but this plane put it to shame. Uber plush chairs. Thick carpeting. The rich color of forest green decorating the interior. The cabinets and bar were made from Mahogany wood. It was gorgeous. We took off smoothly and as soon as the plane leveled out we could move around. Demitri got me a cup of coffee that I'd had been jonesing for. He knew I didn't drink alcohol often. Margaritas, if I was going to cut loose, but not on a plane. No way.

Andre said, "We should introduce her to the Mile High Club," with a mischievous grin on his face.

I stopped that idea real quick. "Not this time, love. It is definitely on my to do list along with that show, but right now I need to focus on what's coming up with the meeting in Texas."

They knew then that I considered myself 'on the job' and wouldn't budge. They looked disappointed, but they were willing to give me the time I needed.

Demitri asked, "Do you want to handle the plane for a bit?"

"Hell, yes." I jumped up.

"You'll love this. Flying one of these…well, there is no comparison," Demitri said.

"You fly, too?" I asked

He smiled. "Yes, we all do. We have the pilot for business meetings so we can just relax or get paperwork ready," he explained.

"Oh shit, we're doomed, Antonio. She's flying," Andre was teasing.

"You know jokes like that can get you couch time buddy." I pretended to glare at him.

He said in mock seriousness, "Shutting up now."

"Yeah, I thought so," laughing and walking up to the front of the plane.

The pilot didn't even bat an eyelash at Demitri's request to show me a few things. He then let me take over.

Now those small planes that I used to fly back in the day, they were like driving a go-cart. That big commercial airline plane I barely landed, that's like driving a huge loaded-down bus. This was like driving the sweetest machine ever made. Not like a SS '69 Nova, but like a Maserati. Smooth, fast, and the lightest touch got you what you wanted.

I had to get me one of these!

Oh, wait. I married into the family. It IS mine. I was grinning widely, having a real good time. The pilot was looking at me like he knew what I was thinking and smiled with me. Demitri felt my happiness and was also grinning. Soon, though, I had to turn her back over to the pilot. We walked back to the main area and his brothers were looking at me, knowing how happy I was feeling.

Antonio was grinning and shaking his head, "You're so easy to please. Not like most of the women we know."

Andre piped up, "Well, we're still alive, so I guess that means we didn't crash," and laughed.

"I see a couch in your immediate future," I gave him a saucy glare.

Andre frowned. "Oh, you're mean, baby."

"You have no idea. Oh, wait you do. She did it to you, too," Demitri teased.

"With handcuffs bro," he nodded with fake sadness.

"She actually brought out the handcuffs?" Antonio started laughing hard.

"I had left my other cuffs at home," I said. "I bought those new, after you told me it was his night. We broke them in," I said, with an evil grin.

Andre agreed with a nod of his head, "Yeah, we broke them in real good." They all laughed at that.

The car with Major Stewart was there as the General had promised, with the temporary clearance passes, and we went to the Inn to drop off our bags. I made a telepathic phone call to my brother, Grant, and to my two sisters, so that they'd be ready to be a part of the upcoming meeting (astrally speaking). He then took us to the staff room for the meeting with the General. It was 10 o'clock at night, so I appreciated the gesture, knowing most military people get up at the crack of dawn, or earlier, philistines that they were. It's just not natural getting up that early in the morning. Even when I was purely human, physically speaking, I never got up early. I gave a shudder and walked into the room.

The General was there along with O'Hara, sitting at a big table. There was a cart that smelled like food, parked against the wall to the right side. My mates flanked me as we neared the table and stopped just a few feet away.

"Good evening, General, Captain," I greeted them formally.

"Good evening to you, Ms. Garcia, "he replied, just as properly. O'Hara just nodded his head, "Is this all who is with you?"

"Yes. I thought just a small group for now, until we see how this plays out. I'm not going to put all of my people on the table until I'm very sure there is no danger. I want to thank you though, for the nice dinner back in New York and your help with the FBI. Your welcome here was nice, as well. May I introduce my men to you?" I was trying to take the sting of mistrust out of conversation.

"Yes, please do," he was looking interested.

"This is Demitri, Andre and Antonio Caberelli. They are my mates. What you would consider my husbands." Turning to my men, "This is General Pierce. The man standing next to him on the right is Captain Vincent O'Hara. He is the leader of the Special Forces team that helped me out back in New York. Special Forces teams don't worry about rank so much though. I think he prefers O'Hara or Rock. That's his call sign." I looked at O'Hara for confirmation and got it with a nod of his head.

"This is Major Stewart, The General's right hand man. His attaché," I explained, and received nods all around and pleased-to-meet you's.

"Three husbands?" the General asked, looking a bit overwhelmed at this. Nothing in his experience gave him a clue on how to deal with it.

I didn't help him out. I wanted to see what he would do or say. I wanted to see how all of them reacted.

"Yes. Husbands. Mates. Soulmates. Truemates. Bondmates. All apply with us as an accurate relationship," I answered.

"Caberelli of Caberelli Corporation?" he wanted clarification.

Demitri spoke up, "Yes. That's us."

"Your corporation ranks pretty high. Just below Bill Gates," he stated. "That's impressive. And you are like her?" he asked them.

"Yes," they said in unison.

"Well, I'll be damned," he said, and sat down.

I laughed. "Wait 'till you meet the rest of my people. You'd be surprised at who they are and their positions."

"After tonight, I don't think so," he said dryly. "Well, let's get down to business. Have a seat, if you will." The General was rolling right along, although he got hit with two things out of left field in quick succession. I was impressed. O'Hara didn't say anything, but sat down at the General's side, looking a tad shell-shocked.

"There's food and drink if you'd like. I got this room because I wasn't sure how many people you'd bring. But the food should be plenty if you're hungry after your flight?" he said, with a query in his voice.

"I could eat." I walked over to the cart to show trust about the food not being poisonous.

I did take a good whiff. Just to be sure. Major Stewart started to move ahead of me, to serve, I supposed, but I waved him off with a smile, saying, "Nah, it's cool. I got it." Looking at my mates, I asked, "Sweeties, you want anything?"

Demitri said, "Sure, we'll help."

We grabbed our plates and loaded them with what appealed to each of us. We sat down to eat. The General and O'Hara grabbed a plate themselves and got settled at the table.

"I thought as we eat, I can lay out a plan for you to consider and a bit of history on this base," he started the conversation.

"Sure, go for it," I said

"The base here is used mostly for training pilots. Other training does go on here that most that don't know about. Like O'Hara here. Special Forces teams are trained in a variety of skills. Some of them right here. That's why this base is perfect for what we have in store. Hide in plain sight, so to speak. This used to be the biggest Navy Air Station in the world, but due to budget cuts and military cut backs, this base has been downsized. Dramatically. Army still does repairs on helicopters and Coast Guard does search and rescues and so on. However, if you looked about the base, you would see about one tenth of the personnel that used to be here even ten years ago." He stopped to take a drink.

"Ok, I'll take your word for it," I said.

He continued, "Besides being able to hide in plain sight, there is the advantage of having access to land, air and sea from here. We would have the advantage to go in any direction yours and mine would need to go. With a base this big, but mostly not in use, we can take over a section of it and use it for a base of operations. Furthermore, we would have access for Intel through Surveillance Support Center, right here on the base."

I got where he was taking this. "You want us to move here?"

"Yes, it would be more convenient to have you closer. Time could be saved, and would add to the percentage for a successful mission," he explained.

I stopped eating and sat back thinking. I glanced at my mates and noticed they were mulling it over.

We all looked at each other, *'We have a branch office here in Corpus Christi already, hon,'* Demitri told me. *'It would be advantageous actually, for us at this time, to move here.'* I snorted at that. They had branch offices everywhere, even overseas. I wasn't surprised by this fact.

'We did decide to move from Tucson, but are you sure you guys would be happy here?' I asked them all.

'Would you?' they replied.

I thought about it. I could smell the sea air from here. I could also smell grease. Airplane fuel. Exhausted airplane fuel. And the noise! They may have downsized, but they still flew in and out. A lot.

'We would have a home off base,' Demitri said.

Ah ha! That's true; I would only have to be here for missions. I wouldn't be here day in and day out. That, I could live with.

'It's cool with me if you guys are down with it?' I offered feeling a bit nervous.

Demitri looked at his brothers, each giving a slight nod. He turned to look at me, smiled and said, *'Done.'*

I smiled at them and closed my eyes, reaching out mentally to my brother Grant and my two sisters, Cassie and Cendra. I had to work harder to establish mental contact with them, since our bonds were not only just the sibling kind, but I haven't spent too much time with them on the astral planes, yet. Sporadic at best. And I still held a grudge against my sister, Cendra. My three siblings had zoned into our signatures when I'd called them after we landed here in Texas. They had astrally come along for the ride, so they'd heard everything in the meeting room.

'What's your vote, oh siblings of mine?' I asked them.

'I heard that they had an awesome resort. A padre something or another. I'm in,' Cendra said, always seeing the good in it ...for her. She

had red hair, a slim figure and bright green eyes. I had a hard time not hating her. Not because she looked better than me, but because of 'the incident' that had happened a long time ago.

'I can be there in three days with my mates, sister. If we like it, we will stay,' Cassie answered. I liked her so far. She had black hair, brown eyes and was half Japanese. She was a wiz at numerology. She and I could really put away the sushi. I loved sushi.

My brother, Grant, chimed in, *'I like the idea personally. It feels right to me.'* His feelings were rarely wrong. *'I don't know how I would get transferred over fast enough to be of help to you though.'*

He was the closest already since he was a Houston, Texas detective. He took all of the hard, extremely dangerous cases. Drug smuggling, serial killers, you name it. I once saved him when he got nabbed by a serial killer. He found out too late that the serial killer, a real John Ritter looking kind of guy (but the most evil human I had ever seen), was working with two other people that my brother didn't know about. I got him loose, and we caught the bad guys. Even before then, if I ever needed anything, Grant has always been there ... no questions asked.

'I have an idea, but would have to tell the General of your existence now. Name and all that, all right?' I asked him.

'Go for it, sis.' See, no hesitation from him when I needed back up. I valued him highly for that.

The General was still looking at me. "Sorry I was taking so long. I like to think things out thoroughly, first."

"Take your time," he said, alert though to what I may be doing.

O'Hara was looking a bit curious and suspicious. I don't think he bought it and neither did the General. They must have read some of the books.

"I have a brother who is a Houston Police Detective. He wants to come and be near me here, ASAP. Do you have any contacts on the Corpus Christi Police force that could transfer him over?" I asked.

"Yes, we do, actually. It would be a simple matter. I know the Police Commissioner." The General looked amazed.

"Then yes, we are in. More of my people will be coming here in a few days, but they mostly want to be on the sidelines for now, if that's all right?" I asked him.

"So you'll move here and more of yours will be close at hand if we have need of them?" He looked as hard as any businessman did over a huge deal, but I could see in his eyes he was happy.

"Yes, I am committing our abilities to you and your special forces team," I stated more formally.

"That is acceptable," he replied with seriousness. I could tell he was thrilled though. "Just write down your brother's information and we'll get on it in the morning."

I nodded and took the paper that Major Stewart handed to me and wrote the information down.

When I finished, the General went on, "All right. On to the second part of the meeting. Remember that file I showed you back in New York?" he asked me.

"Yes, the place in Pakistan," I affirmed for him.

"I have some updated Intel on the area and the objective. I want your opinion on what will be now a third run at the place." He was testing me, I could tell.

You get a close hit on a place on the first run, but fail. It may or may not trip off any alarms for the target. You go a second run and fail, they know you want something. Going for a third run, they will be waiting and loaded for bear. It was a suicide run. A real 'mission impossible'.

I couldn't wait.

I was looking over the additional information and saw a denser perimeter of guards. Spots of light grey indicated a person standing there at that moment. I saw a pattern and thought we could get about a half a mile out from the compound, but that last ring was so dense, only one person who was fast and silent could get all the way to the compound. Then there were more men stationed at various entrances and exit ways. Also, there were four watch towers. I could tell from these papers what may be inside the compound and where in the middle of it, was the house. I was wondering where their mainframe computer would be. In the house itself (which I doubted), or in another one of these buildings surrounding the house? I wasn't about to send another tendril of power through the photo to find out.

I looked up to the General, who was watching my face. "With a third run, they will know we are coming. No doubt there. There are more men in what I call an echo pattern. I don't know what your label for it is. So where is the mainframe? In the house or in one of these buildings? I'm betting building," I said in a cavalier voice.

"You have a plan for getting into the compound already?" His eyes were wide now.

"I have ideas actually, but I need the exact location of the computer you want hit." I looked him dead in the eye and didn't flinch.

He took the photo and pointed to the closest building to the house. I almost groaned. It figures it would be there. The house was where the center of dark power would be, but having that kind of technology in the house would either screw up the magick or screw up the computer. Usually the tech stuff goes first. But having it close to the house, means it will be heavily guarded and not by just physical things.

"That is where the most energy is going to and would most likely be where they would have their computer mainframe," the General said.

I knew why he would want to send O'Hara and his team on this particular mission. His team needed to save face. To regain their lost status. They wouldn't be able to do it alone. Not with the dark God Kalim protecting this place.

I turned to one of my mates. "Antonio, file please." He reached into his briefcase and pulled out the file he gave me back at the hotel in New York.

"Antonio put this together while we were in New York. This place is protected by the dark God Kalim. Before Pakistan went Muslim in 711 A.D., they had pantheons of tribal Gods too. This guy is dark, way dark. Likes the sacrifice of virgins. So you most likely have a lot of young girls going missing near this place. Apparently, this dark God rapes them, and because his penis is so deformed, it kills them. He has four arms, and is a warrior God that has a penchant for knives. He also has some wicked fangs and claws. He protects and gifts to those who war. If they give him virgins, he gives them strength and power. He also enslaves djinns and forces them to use their power to aide in those who serve him. He also has bacakuls', and they are your basic demon types with a nasty attitude and they eat meat from fresh kills."

"You're serious about this dark God?" O'Hara joined in. "And djinns and bacakuls'? We are back in X-files again." He looked like he was trying to fight off a headache.

I shrugged my shoulders at him. "This is what we do. He'll most likely also have efreets. They're an elemental being."

The General asked, "After seeing that photo burn up by itself, I am willing to go on a little faith. Plus, that target has been more difficult than it should be. That is unusual in itself." Which meant a lot. If anyone outside this crew found out about that this mission was being treated like this, his career and O'Hara's would be over. They would be laughed out of the military. However, I could still see doubt in his mind.

"I can't refute that, but the rest of the team is going to be hard to convince," O'Hara said dryly, knowing he was going out on a limb with the General. He doubted more than the General did, too.

I looked around the room and by the wall behind us was a table that had a stack of black colored folders and a stack beside that of white papers.

I couldn't read what they were from here, but that's not what I needed them for.

I stood up and said, "See that stack of papers and folders over there?"

They both nodded.

"Watch this." I turned around and gathered my energy which had been so nicely topped off from Antonio a few days ago. I made an energy ball and threw it at the stacks. They exploded in a swirl of flying papers drifting down to the floor now. Folders flew in all directions.

"I never went near that end of the room as you all know." I saw their stunned eyes watching the papers scatter and drift everywhere onto the floor. "Magick is real, dark Gods are real, as are many things that go bump in the night. You guys haven't seen anything yet. There is more out there then you all realize. I mean, you have a small clue, obviously, or you wouldn't have us involved now, but there is more. So, believe me when I tell you something. This stuff I don't mess with. I wouldn't lie about any of it. Things tend to bite the ass of the one who does."

The General cleared his throat and said, "Ok, that is impressive. I thought what you did on the plane was otherworldly. How much more can you do? How much more is out there that we might run up against?"

"A lot and a lot; too much to cover in one day," giving him the short answer.

The General just closed his eyes and then slowly nodded.

O'Hara looked a bit shell shocked himself. "I knew you were different but..."

"Yeah, I get that a lot," I sighed and walked over to the mess I'd made and started picking things up. My guys came over to help and I smiled a thank you at them. If I make a mess, I try to clean it up. It was one of my better quirks.

"When is the next full moon?" I asked, getting back on track.

"Why do you need a full moon?" O'Hara was curious. "Most missions are best done during the dark of the moon. It makes for better stealth."

"Ah, but you're dealing with a dark God and evil practitioners' now. The dark of the moon is their time of greatest power. The full moon is ours. We won't leave on the night of the full moon though, a few nights after that would work. I need the full moon to empower the necklaces and stones I will be making for our team," I explained.

"Maybe that's why previous missions went south so fast. They were on the dark of the moon," O'Hara said. Watching him trying to wrap his head around the metaphysical facts, I almost felt sorry for him. He was trying to overcome years of conditioning and mental training both from the military and society in general. It would be hard for anyone who was purely human.

"Now, if we go in during a bright moon, how do we avoid the dense pattern of patrols? It would be incredibly difficult even with the dark moon," O'Hara asked, getting back to the strategy. Something familiar to him. I was about to drop more unfamiliar things on his head. Hope he had some aspirin.

"When we go in there, I will be able to feel their life force. I can steer our men through their lines," I laid it out for him.

"You can feel other people's what?" He was getting overwhelmed again.

"Life force, energy signatures...well if they have any type of soul, that is, I can pick them up," I stated.

"Is this part of being what you are?" O'Hara asked.

"Yes and no," I answered. "If someone is gifted enough, they can be taught how to do it, too. Their range might not be quiet as wide as mine, though."

"That is unbelievable," he sounded incredulous now.

"The rest of the team is 24 ft in that direction, all together. Call them and find out," I told him to prove my words, yet again.

"That won't be necessary. I asked them to be there, in case," the General stumbled, trying to explain.

"In case my people were more dangerous than could be handled," I answered for him. He gave me an apologetic look. O'Hara went back to having his hard face on.

I laughed. "You're right to treat us like we could possibly go buggy. Some of us have issues. Some things can trigger us into a dangerous mode. We do try to keep a handle on it, but sometimes...well, shit happens." I tried to reassure, but I wasn't going to bullshit him on us being all fluffy bunnies just because we worked in the light. We weren't fluffy. We do try to do the right thing, but we weren't fluffy. It was best for the General and O'Hara to fully understand this now to avoid any incidents later.

"Like nitro?" the General asked. "You can use it to make your job easier, but handle it wrong and it could blow up in your face?"

"Yup, exactly that way," I told him.

He didn't look so embarrassed now, which I bet was a rare feeling for the General.

O'Hara got back to the issue, "Ok, you say that you can steer us to here, then you take off from that point to the wall of the compound. How are you going to get into the compound itself? The gates are too heavily guarded and the walls are 16 ft high with barbed electrified wire. Plus, you have the four watch towers to avoid being seen by."

"I'll jump the wall, not to worry. My worry is that building. They're bound to have motion detectors and alarm systems on the door. If they have a guard I can take him out, but there could be many metaphysical booby traps, too. That's the hard part for me," I clarified.

"You can jump ...never mind. I don't want to know. So the building, that's your bug," shaking his head.

Until now, the guys were quite willing for me to take the lead; like I would be quiet for their business meetings and dealings, unless I had something concrete to add.

Andre said, "Hon, I can make a crystal that will detect most dark-side traps."

Demitri added, "I can come up with a few general spells and incantations you can memorize for deflecting and searching."

Antonio added his contribution, "I can put together a bag or two of herbs; throw them at something and any darksider will have a major problem. Something for those bacakuls' and djinns', too."

O'Hara groaned out loud this time, and then caught himself. The General was looking a bit put off as well, but dealing with it. "So, I see where you three fit with this, but you don't seem to mind her going out on a very dangerous mission by herself?" he stated this, but it came off as a question, too.

Demitri spoke for the three of them, "We do mind, believe me. But, we can't keep her from doing what she needs to do. All we can do is support her or fight by her side and watch her back, depending on the situation."

The General nodded understanding of what they weren't saying. He was sharp.

O'Hara spoke up again, "So once you're in and get the data we need, you'll feel out the nuke in the same way you feel for life force energy?" He was sharp, too.

Nodding my head, "Yes, radioactive things have an energy pulse, too. Different, of course, then from a human's, but all things put out energy waves. Just at different frequencies. Once you learn what wave they represent—in respect to what thing, person or being—you can detect them accurately."

O'Hara nodded, like this made sense to him and he could agree with that much. He still looked a bit skeptical though, but I had a feeling things would happen that would make believers out of them all. Sometimes, that was a sad thing, because then comes the fear. But I didn't want to think about that yet. I had to focus on what we needed to accomplish. And that was getting that data, finding out if a nuke was there; if there was, disarm it and wipe them out. A good thing, because then it would be easier to close the vortex that Kalim was using, which could be its own magickal nuke if not dealt with.

The General cleared his throat and said, "Well, it seems like we have a good idea of what we are all doing. You'll need some things now from me as well as signing some papers." His attaché opened a briefcase and pulled out another file.

He gave it to the General. "You'll need these," and handed me a badge that would get me through the gates of the base and a card with a black strip on the back of it." That's a high security pass. There are various buildings you won't be able to get into without the clearance. Just swipe it through the lock by the door. Here are your security codes for different places here on the base. Memorize them, and then burn this." The General gave me the run down on each item and the code for it.

"You're giving me a lot of access for only knowing me for a short time and for not being military," I said to him.

He grinned a slightly evil smile." I want your word that you or your people will not go to these places here, here and here. Oh, and these four buildings on the south side."

I admired his tactics, "I give my word I will not go to any of the areas or buildings you have designated and I will keep my people from them as well," I promised him.

A promise like that was binding. I would not break trust. I could not. I would lose power if I did and I'd just gotten it back.

"That's good enough. Now these papers will show you as an independent civilian consultant. We do use them for various things on the base. But your base pay will have to be what we would pay these kinds of people. However, after each completed and successful mission, I can authorize a bonus and hide it as a consultant fee for another job."

I handed the papers over to Antonio and he looked through them for me. He understood the legal side of this better than I did. He read them fast and handed them back, nodding his assent. "One of them is a promise, basically not to tell anyone about the missions or the people on the teams or anyone on the base." I nodded, expecting that. I signed them and handed them over to his attaché.

"Your mates and any others that need access to you on the base or will be involved will have to give their ID over to the Major here. He can provide them with the security badges and card passes. They'll have to sign the same paperwork as well," he said. My mates fished out their drivers licenses and handed them over to the attaché.

"Major Stewart took them and said, "I'll have these done by tomorrow afternoon and bring them with the necessary papers to you."

O'Hara cleared his throat, "We have also started an investigation on Special Agent Williams. It seems you were right about the food and drink being loaded with something. Our labs found a high dose of tranquilizers in both; enough to knock an elephant on its' ass."

"Now, why would an FBI agent need to drug a prisoner?" I said in my most innocent voice. "That doctor probably had a loaded syringe ready to use, since Williams figured out I wasn't going to bite, no pun intended, the food." I gave them a crooked smile.

O'Hara eyebrow rose, "It is obvious he knew he needed such extreme measures with someone like you. My question is what was he going to do with you?"

Antonio stepped in, "We haven't connected him to a specific black coven yet, but our thoughts are that he was going to use her for their own agenda or kill her if she posed too much of a problem to handle."

General Pierce added, "We've had Wizard digging into Williams' past. There's a pattern in his movements that seem suspicious to us. Wherever he moves to, an incident happens there. To what purpose, we haven't figured out yet, but we have posted surveillance on him now. Anything we find out, we'll let you know about."

"That sounds good," Demitri said and we got up to leave.

"Oh, General, one more thing. I would like that disk and a promise it is the only one," watching him.

He pursed his lips and nodded to the Major, who took out an envelope that felt like it had a disk in it. "I thought you might want that," Pierce sighed.

Taking the disk, "Is this the only copy anywhere?" I was making sure I tied up all the loose ends.

He nodded, "Yes, it is."

I nodded in respect, "Thank you." Looking at O'Hara, I said, "Tell the guys I said hi, and a hundred says we get through and get the data."

He gave a half smile and said, "I'll let them know it's on."

"We need to get together later, smooth out the plan and I need to know exactly how many men will be in our group," I said.

He nodded and said, "I'll call your cell."

I looked confused because I didn't have a cell, and then he handed me two items. "Here, this is your cell and this is your pager. If your pager goes off, then you have to call in immediately for orders. No matter what you're doing, no matter where you are. You answer the pager. This is non-negotiable." I'd have to find a way to carry them without blowing the damn things out in case I got upset while wearing them.

"Oh, I get it. We have something like that, too for our people." I knew this was an important thing.

He looked like he wanted an explanation, so I gave it to him. "An astral Red Alert. We send out a red orb along our bond cords and it has to be answered immediately."

He groaned again. "I'll find out later. I don't suppose I could learn to see a red orb?"

"No, not fast enough for now. Later though, maybe. In the meantime these will work better for everyone involved. There's lots of training involved for red orb sending and receiving."

He groaned again. I laughed; I thought he sounded like an old bear.

CHAPTER ELEVEN
Coven Gathering

Over the next few days, we were busy getting settled into our new hometown of Corpus Christi. Demitri had found a nice huge home right on Padre Island. My boys were ecstatic, being the young men they were. Padre Island was the place that, during spring break, there were college girls galore. They had wind surfing, scuba diving, swimming and other great amusements for young adults and military soldiers on leave. Lots of distractions. I hadn't told my boys everything about what we were doing there. Yet, I could feel my youngest, 16 year old Craven, peeking around the corners of the small mansion we were living in, trying to eavesdrop on our conversations every now and again. Keeping secrets from my boys was going to be hard because of Craven.

Craven was the youngest of the three and the biggest. A big, burly kid with dark blond hair, almost brown, and the biggest blue eyes you'd ever seen on a male. He used those eyes too, even as a baby, staring at every woman walking by; whipping his head back and forth trying to ogle all the ladies. Already 5'10 he was going to be a bear of a man when he reached adulthood.

Crimson, at eighteen, had dark brown hair and was 5'11 but I didn't think he was done growing yet. A master of Tai Kwon Do, he was the most studious of my kids, always reading, mostly on the civil war and World War 2. With eyes that were almost gun metal blue, he looked the most mischievous of my kids, but he'd given me the least amount of trouble growing up. That is, unless Craven, with his cherub angel good looks, was blaming Crimson for something he had done, getting Crimson in trouble for it. It worked for a while, but I soon caught on.

Christoph was the eldest. His hair was the blondest of them all and he had sky blue eyes. He was sweet natured for the most part, and hardworking, always willing to help me with the younger two. He was physically lean, built for speed and used it with his martial arts. As a kid, he had always wanted to be a Ninja when he grew up. All three had different biological fathers, but it was during a time that for some reason, I would only date guys with blond hair and blue eyes.

I loved my mate's dark hair and brown eyes though. The intense looks they had would always make me catch my breath. My mates and my boys were spending time together, trying to acclimate to each other. Andre and Craven got along the best with each other, both having a strong interest in Japanese weapons and martial art fighting styles. Antonio and Crimson clicked pretty well, both being quiet and burying their noses in books at most times. Demitri and my eldest, Christoph, hit it off since they were both the serious-minded type of personalities. It was going well, so far.

My brother, Grant, packed up his family from Houston. He left it to his three wives to get a home, settle into it and get to know me while he settled into the police force in Corpus Christi. I didn't know his wives from before, physically, but they seemed really nice so far. They were a trio of cousins that could have passed for sisters with their blue eyes and blond hair. One of them was 6 months pregnant expecting their 9th child as a family unit. So, she and I spent the most time together, since we all wouldn't let her do anything but stay off her feet. My sisters, their mates and kids made it into town quickly, as well.

I was expecting Cendra to take the longest, but she surprised me with the speed she lit under her mates in moving on down. I still growled under my breath whenever she and I crossed paths. I did give into my worst personality trait and pulled her aside one night. I warned her that if she ever went near Antonio again, sister or no sister, I'd kill her. I couldn't understand why she wasn't satisfied with her own mates. They had been together for 15 years, both astrally and physically. They had children. She had been able to touch her mates, spend time with her mates and give her mates physical children. But she had moon eyes for Antonio and my other mates, but mostly Antonio. She was always complaining, even way back when we were finding our mates and settling into our bonds, that her mates didn't spend enough time with her. They didn't do enough things with her. All that translated into they weren't fawning all over her and worshipping the ground she walked on. They would go out and do things together, being guys, and leave her at home. This, of course, had her bitching and complaining.

Even before my mates and I found each other physically, they would hang around me astrally all the time, spending time with me and trying so hard to get the curse removed so they could re-establish the telepathy with me. I think our closeness, despite the curse, made her jealous. I couldn't figure it out though; she has had her men in her physical life all this time.

She was way luckier than me. But my men were in my physical life now, and I would kill to keep them there.

Cassie and her family rolled into town as well. We had a huge family dinner at the mansion. We had the barbecue going and music was playing. Everybody was having a good time when one of my favorite dancing songs, Jungle Love by The Times, played on the stereo. I couldn't resist getting up and dancing.

I was out in the backyard dancing under the twilight skies, swaying and bumping to the music. About halfway through the song, Andre had joined me. It was great. I was having fun and then the song ended. We laughed and turned to walk back to the table. Everyone had a look of either being incredulous or smiling and enjoying our antics. That was when one of Cassie's mates hit us with his idea.

Lee announced in an excited voice, "I can find a building and turn it into a bar where we can relax. There would be drinking and dancing. We could also have a band area for those of us who play instruments. None of our houses are big enough for us to get together regularly and really cut loose when we need to. This would give us our own place!"

I agreed with him, "Awesome idea, dude! Our own private bar and grill with a dance floor. I love it. What do you think, sweeties?" I turned to look at my mates.

They were all nodding and Demitri added," We'll be happy to invest in it."

I had a thought, "Wait up, though. We would have to let our military guys hang, too. So we can be more cohesive. Kind of a bonding thing for our teams. A place to 'kick it' after a mission and unwind. What do you think, Lee?"

He nodded, "It would be rude to exclude them out of our bar and grill. We will include them, too."

"You should have a pit area though," I added the thought.

He looked confused, "A 'pit' area?"

I said, "Yeah, these guys are military and sometimes they can get rough in play. If we had a pit area, a place where they could work out their differences with their fists and have a beer together after their dominance sport is done, we would avoid having the base MP's coming in, breaking up the party."

Cassie added, "It would keep the General from having to deal with any complaints from the local police force or the MP's. It's a good idea. We too, may have a need to get a harsh feeling or feud out of our systems," giving Cendra and me the eye. Cendra looked affronted, but I was looking forward to any opportunity she gave me. I know I'm a bitch, but, oh well.

The men had gathered around in a circle, planning finances and a liquor license, even though it would be a private club. Though it was for family and our military brothers, we felt that if we charged for food and drink it would keep anyone from drinking too much, too often. Excessive drinking would cause too many fights to break out, more than we could even contain 'in house'. They then discussed interior decorations, sound systems and floor plans in a rough draft. I kept out of that. Most of the women did too, except when it came to the women's bathroom. We had plenty to say about nixing any fluorescent lights. Although, with the whole Coven being together physically, we were now all immortal. But, only my mates and I had been modified so far. The only ones with fangs.

As the full moon rose, we gathered the children indoors for the eldest children to watch over them and to keep them entertained with movies and game systems. My children were the oldest of all the children gathered. In fact, the oldest of the children of the whole Coven, but I had the least amount of kids, with only three, and none of them physically with my mates. My youngest brother was next, in having the fewest children, and he also had the youngest. Gerard and his Eskimo wives were still in Alaska waiting in the 'dark'. Just in case. The three siblings I had there, were the best choice for my mates and me for backup, in case we needed to be extracted from the military.

I kept my two other brothers where they were, because for one, Gerard had the youngest children. Mere babies. And Gaston had the most children, making them both the more vulnerable of us. But they were also good muscle and could call in other types of nefarious people to come to our aid, if we, who were already in Corpus Christi, needed it. Gerard had his Mafia connections, since our physical father was a Mafia Don. Gaston had assassins and other Mercs as acquaintances. We could bring in some serious heat if the shit hit the fan here. I was worried about Grant, since one of his wives was pregnant. But, with him already in Texas, he would have been pissed to be kept in the outside 'dark' ring. So, I made sure Grant's wives had two bodyguards, made up from my sister's husbands and mine, alternating them in shifts, so Grant's wives would never be alone. Grant could go to work in peace knowing his wives, especially the pregnant one, were being guarded while he was away. We had to do this, since we had exposed his name to the General, and we just wanted to be cautious.

Now that the children were occupied, we gathered in a circle and I looked at our group. We weren't complete, but the power already flowing around us was strong. I had cleansed and sanctified a corner of the backyard for our circle the previous night. We cast our circle and called the watchtowers. We had placed the crystals, stones and necklaces I had made in the center of our circle and spelled each to do a specific job. Antonio had added his medicine bags and we also empowered those for their jobs. Then we asked The Goddess and Her Consort to bless our family, that they be protected and kept safe from harm while I was gone. We also asked for a blessing that our team would perform our mission with honor. We asked further, that our team and any soldiers fighting with us, make it home alive and give strength to those waiting for them at home. We thanked and released the watchtowers. Then we closed down the circle. My sisters, brother and their mates went to get their children ready for going to their respective homes and called it a night.

I watched the cars leave, heading towards the highway. Cassie's and Grant's car went toward S. Padre Island Dr. to get back to Corpus Christi and Cendra went east, toward the house she bought on the island as well. Go figure. I blessed their trip home though. They had shields and wards on their cars, I knew, but I still worried for them. After seeing the tail lights fade out of sight, I walked back through the house and out to the back again. I stood staring up at the moon with so many thoughts going through my head.

I felt Andre come up behind me, encircling my waist with his arms holding me from behind, "What are you thinking, Baby?"

"I'm thinking about the moon, and the mission. Many things," I whispered.

"How do you feel about the mission?" kissing my neck.

"Like we're in the middle of a hurricane. The eye of the storm. The air feels so heavy. Everything feels heavy," I leaned back into him.

"The calm before the storm type of feeling?" he asked

I sighed. "Yeah, just like that."

"Maybe we should go with you?" he suggested.

I shook my head, "No, I need you here with the others in case I need an extraction. If I get taken overseas, with your jet on standby, you can use it to extract me there."

He hugged me tightly. "I don't like you going in alone, but your strategy is sound." He kissed the side of my face. "Do you think we'll be burned by the General and his men?"

I thought about it, trying to get an astral read. "No, I don't think so, really. But why be stupid, and trust too much, too fast? Better to test the waters first, just to be on the safe side."

"You're rarely wrong," he stated.

"Rarely, true. And I got cocky, lax in taking precautions because of my belief that we were invincible, and would never be wrong. When I was wrong, it bit us on the ass and I got cursed. I never want to make that mistake ever again." I closed my eyes, remembering the long nights of crying myself to sleep because I didn't have their physical arms around me. Not being able to see their smiles or do things to make them smile. My sisters and brothers had their mates in their physical lives. They were loving together and having children together. I was left alone with no one, but my three sons. They couldn't fulfill every aspect of my life and I felt like I was withering bit by bit in spirit. Dying a slow death every night I went to bed alone. Woke up alone. I'd fought to put food on the table and to keep my kids healthy and learning. All alone. It had left a deep, bleeding wound on my soul that I didn't think would ever heal.

Andre hissed in empathy. He was feeling my pain, as I remembered. An echo that felt like a slash of pain across his heart and I knew the other two were feeling it as well.

"Hush hon, we're here now. We've got you," holding me tighter, spilling blue light through his spirit to mine, and trying to calm my soul.

I took deep breaths, trying to forget the pain. But I felt like screaming in rage. I knew I was with them now. But the rage, the despair, and the loneliness of fifteen long years had been torture. A never-ending torture of them being so close, but kept just out of reach. It was a literal hell with them being the heaven I needed to reach, just beyond the horizon. But it had always been a mirage. A dream that would refuse to come true because of that god-awful curse. So many times, I'd thought that finding them would never happen. Never end. I would grow old and die....alone. Always alone, as I had been my whole life, with the curse slowly eating at my soul. My boys were the only thing that kept me sane, that gave me hope. And hope can be its own form of torture when it's not fulfilled for so long; another tool to slowly drive me insane. I'd had to kill any sexual feelings in me so I wouldn't howl at night in frustration. The curse, too, was cruel in that area of my life. I would feel their astral bodies give a kiss. A touch or two here and there, just enough to tease. To get me going sexually, then the curse would cut off any feeling from them, leaving me empty, unloved and unfinished. Masturbation got boring and empty, so I just quit that, too. I knew my astral bodies were loving my mates, keeping them satisfied, but I couldn't connect with my astral selves either, to feel through that part of me. The curse had cut that off as well. The emptiness was slowly consuming me, as year after year passed by. Now they were here and I couldn't turn on the sexual side of myself. I had killed that part of me years ago. I had killed so many parts to stay sane.

I bent over, shaking from trying to hold back the pain. Demitri and Antonio had run out of the house, took one look at us and grabbed me from either side.

"Let it out, baby. We've got you." Andre was crying for me because I couldn't.

I kept shaking my head back and forth, "I can't, I can't. If I do, I'm afraid I won't stop. I'll start screaming and I won't be able to stop. I can't lose it now. Not now, maybe not ever." And I pushed all that rage, all that hopelessness deep back inside my soul.

"No, don't do that." Demitri felt what I was doing. "Please don't do that. We've got you. We'll help keep you together," he was pleading. He knew what this would cost me. More wounds on my soul that wouldn't heal. Not until they were cleansed out, but this wasn't the time. Maybe it would never be the time. I ruthlessly pushed it all back inside the bottle.

"Shit," Antonio said, sadly. He knew I'd had to kill another piece of me to do it. Sacrificed another bit of my soul.

I slowly stood up straight, but Andre was on his knees, still crying for me.

I bent down and held him. "I'm so sorry. I never meant to cause you pain." I looked at all of them. "I never meant to cause any of you pain. I am so sorry." I was at a loss at what to do. We all ended up holding each other, while I tried to take their pain from them, spilling blue light back at them.

"You can't hold on to this forever, Catrina," Demitri was saying. "It'll eat you sooner or later if you do."

I nodded, "I know, but now is not the time for soul therapy. We have a mission in two days. I can't be dealing with an emotional breakdown right now." I was still breathing hard from the effort of containing everything.

He nodded, understandingly, but hating the necessity of it.

I wound up with all three of my mates in the big bed, all of us holding each other tight, so I wouldn't be alone that night. I fell asleep, peaceful, but the nightmares still came.

CHAPTER TWELVE
Dominance Games

The next day we went to the base, knowing I had my back and others covered well. My mates would be at the base while the operation was going down; scanning everybody periodically, to make sure they were doing what they said they would. My sisters and brother would be off the base ready to extract my mates if they should be detained, and then depending on where I was, to come and get me out. My other two brothers were outside of it all, ready to call in some wicked forces, both mundane and magickal, if we were all cluster fucked here.

I thought I had done well with the plan. It was noon when we got to the first gate. We had to remove our sunglasses so the guard could compare our faces with our I.D. badges. My brother, Grant, had gotten his security badge and pass, too. He had also filled out the paperwork, but I wanted him off base for now. We moved onto the second security station where Major Brandon Stewart was waiting to show us our new military headquarters and introduce us around. We walked by several hangers, and large, squared grayish buildings until we came to one that said ML-30. We had to use our card pass and codes here, and then walked down a long hall with many doors until we came to what looked like a war room once we stepped inside. The General was there with the whole team and a Marine Captain. Also, there were four Marine Sergeants, all looking as tough as nails.

The Marine Captain turned out to be Captain Robert Holland and he was the leader of the marine platoon, Alpha 53rd Recon, which the General had put together under his command. The Captain had no hair, with hard blue eyes and a bulldog mug. He didn't like us at all. I could tell from the flare of his nose every time he looked at us. A real by-the-book Marine, whom I think resented Mercs being included in this mission.

He looked at me while we were being introduced by Major Stewart and he practically sneered when the introductions came to me. I think, because I was a woman, he was even further insulted. I bet he didn't have any females in his platoon. The squad leaders were there and two of them didn't like us either, it felt like, judging by the vibes in the air. The other two didn't seem to care or were better at hiding it, if they did.

Major Stewart passed down a file with the list of people in the platoon and their basic stats. Sure enough, from the quick glance I took, no females.

"Why does she need a list of names of the men in my platoon?" Captain Holland barked, addressing his question to the General, who was watching the whole exchange.

"Cat." The General nodded at me to answer the question. He didn't really know why I requested the list, but promised I would have it when we met in the war room. He'd seemed pretty busy when I had called the other day, most likely from making it possible for us to have this platoon and getting the go ahead from some heavy hitters in the Pentagon for this mission.

"I need the names and will need to meet each of these men to memorize their energy signatures, so I can tell friend from foe in the field," I answered in a clipped voice.

"Energy signatures?" he practically sneered. The General just nodded like he now understood the reason for the request.

"Each human gives off an individual energy pulse. This is a scientifically proven fact. Just like auras, they can be read now using a machine." Though, I didn't like that fact myself. "When I meet someone, I can feel that signature and commit it to memory. I will then know, instinctively, where each and every man is in the field. That way, I can keep them from being hurt by friendly fire."

"And how is a little thing like you going to keep my recon safe? Look at you. Sure, you have a bit of muscle, but what do you really know about fighting? Can you even shoot straight?" he was snarling now, almost nose to nose with me trying to intimidate me with his height and weight.

I narrowed my eyes at him. "Shooting is not a problem. I am a crack shot, but my strengths are with a fist and blade."

"A real sell-sword huh, little girl? I doubt you could take any one of my men," he both sneered and growled at the same time. I was impressed.

"Where is your platoon?" not backing away from him.

"In the exercise room in this building," he snapped back.

Good. Two birds, one stone, I thought to myself. I snapped back, "Take me there," adding my own growl.

And we all trooped out of the room following the Major, who had a suspicious gleam in his eye. O'Hara's team followed along, making bets under their breath as we went to the sub basements of the building. We walked into a room that had various weight machines, a boxing ring and mats lying all around. Various other equipment was there for building strength and speed. But it was the mats I walked too, taking out my eight inch blades from their sheaths I wore on each side of my hips. The captain's eyes narrowed at the move, until I handed my blades over to one of my mates. Demitri took them from me with a slight bow and a grin on his face. He knew what was up and thought it would be hilarious.

I walked to the edge of the mat opposite of Captain Holland.

He barked, "Alpha Recon." The men stopped and snapped to attention. Then they started gathering around the mat.

I walked to the middle of it, bowed and looked inquiringly at the Captain.

"Pick anyone," he clipped.

"Who's the toughest, meanest son of a bitch?" I inquired.

He smiled a cruel smile like it was Christmas for him."Why that would be me. Watts over there holds the boxing title for the group, but for hand to hand, I still whip ass."

I flicked my fingers at him in a 'come on' motion, and he smiled wickedly.

He came forward; I dropped my left foot back and set myself.

"Anything goes?" he asked.

"Give me your best," I answered simply and dropped my chin down, bringing up my guard.

"Just don't go crying to the General asking for a hanky when this is over little girl, "and swung with his right hand in a brick-like fist.

Waiting for the move, I shifted my body to the side slightly, grabbing his right wrist with my right hand, pulling him further towards me, much faster than he had intended to come. I then put on speed and whipped around to his back, right wrist still in my hand. I pulled it towards his back bending it, finding the nerve endings to send shooting pain up his arm and keeping him immobilized. I put my left hand on his left shoulder, pushing him down as I took my right foot and hooked his leg, sweeping him down to the floor. Then, I landed on his back keeping his right arm bent towards the rear and pulled up, putting pressure on his shoulder socket. I kept him plastered to the floor with my weight and the strength of my left hand. If I had been purely human, he might have been able to buck me off and counter move, but I wasn't human anymore and he didn't believe that or didn't know about it yet. I had no idea what the General had told anyone else about us. But it gave me an even bigger edge on him either way. He grunted on the floor trying to buck me, ignoring the pain I was sending up his arm. He then tried to rotate his hips, hoping to use his body weight against my lighter one and throw me off. It might have worked if I wasn't what I was, but he wasn't going anywhere. I could have killed him in so

131

many different ways, so many different times as he tried to twist, turn and buck.

The rest of the room was held in silence. I didn't take my eyes off my opponent; I couldn't hear anything beyond the Captain's grunting. Like the bulldog he was, he wasn't going to stop trying. He was a marine through and through. They don't stop coming, they kept on going against all odds. It was one of the things I had always respected them for. Shoot off a leg of a marine, and he will still get up and use anything around him to kill you, including his shot off leg. If left with nothing but fists and teeth, they used that too. An unstoppable fighting force. And this man represented that. It made me sad we couldn't be friends, but I could still respect him regardless.

I whispered in his ear, "Do you still need another lesson in respecting the Cat?"

He grunted and twisted. "Apparently, you do." And I jumped off him and moved back two feet. I set myself again. He got up, pissed as hell and got his fists up, but kicked with his leg, aiming it to my stomach, trying to get the wind out of me. I just grabbed his foot. I pulled it back towards me again, putting him off balance and he landed on his back. Most purely human females wouldn't have been able to do that, but I could. He got up and came at me again, going for a right hook. I used the same move to get him pinned to the floor as before and held him down longer this time.

I leaned down after a time and said, "Do yourself a favor, tap out, and the lesson is over." But he couldn't, because I had his left arm pinned under his body and his right was again being curled up towards his neck. His shoulder was going to hurt tomorrow, bad.

"Tap," he wheezed and I let him loose. I kept my guard up just in case.

He got up off the mat and glared at me. "Fucking sell-sword," then he stomped away. I bowed to his retreating back and turned to my mates. Andre was having a hard time not busting out laughing and Demitri was smiling, shaking his head. Antonio gave me thumbs up and blew me a kiss. O'Hara's team was exchanging money.

I looked at the rest of the 28 male soldiers. Most looked incredulous, some looked leery. A few were just outraged. I took my blades back from Demitri and sheathed them. Then I took out my list and called out the first name on it. I went to each man, covertly smelling him and taking in his signature, as I asked position and strengths of each one. There were four NBC's, (Nuclear-Biological-Chemical specialists), one in each squad. A medic for each squad too, but they had other skills as well. Getting this particular platoon must have cost the General a few favors. It was a well detailed platoon. I looked over the squad leaders again and picked the one who seemed to have the least animosity towards me.

"Sergeant Miller." I looked up at him. He was 6'4 and a wall of a soldier. He had hazel grey eyes, a brown buzzed haircut and talked with a Brooklyn accent. You could tell he had worked at it though, since it was barely noticeable. I don't know why people find themselves working on their accents. A Brooklyn accent was especially sexy, I thought.

"Yes.....Ma'am?" he ended with a questioning tone.

"Just Cat; if I had a rank, it would be Captain. Like Special Forces though, we don't sweat it," I informed him. He looked like he could accept that.

I scanned the crowd, "Can you call the rest of your squad behind you?" I asked, because it was his squad. The only one who could order him was O'Hara, since the Captain hadn't come back yet.

He sounded out a, 'yuuuppp!' and his men formed up around him. Seven men, with only two, seeming out of sorts with the leadership role I was putting myself in. The rest were just taking in the scene. The NBC was also a Sergeant and his gaze was curious, but not hostile. Good enough for me.

I turned back to get O'Hara's attention and nodded my head towards the squad, silently asking for his approval. He looked them over too, and nodded back.

I turned back to the squad leader who caught the silent exchange between O'Hara and me. "Your squad will be going in with us." I didn't give him a chance to argue. I just about-faced, nodded my head to my mates and they formed up with me. I assumed O'Hara's team would follow, as well as the squad leader I had just taken over for this mission.

We walked back up to the war room where Major Stewart was waiting with the General. He must have left while I was screening the platoon and I told the General the outcome. "Are you done now? We need to get back to planning the operation." The Captain was there as well, and all four squad leaders had come in. I nodded my head and focused on the table where papers, satellite photos, and a map were laid out.

"Cat, you have a way of getting O'Hara's team and a squad to this point, is that right?" The General pointed to a spot on the map.

I answered, "Yes, Sir."

The Captain snorted. No one acknowledged it though.

"Do you have the tools necessary for getting these men here?" the General went on, ignoring him.

I looked at O'Hara and Sergeant Miller. "Yes, I do, and when I give you these things, you need to put them on and wear them exactly as I say.

You can't move them or take them off. If you do, you will expose the rest of the unit. FUBAR city after that." O'Hara nodded as well as Wizard. Sergeant Miller looked extremely curious.

"Sir, if I may?" Sergeant Miller broke in.

"Yes, Sergeant." The General looked at him.

"What kinds of tools do my men and I need to wear?" he asked.

The General turned to me and I answered the question. "A necklace and a few stones worn on the left side of your body in a pocket. Once there, DO NOT, under any circumstances, remove them or move them anywhere else," I explained.

The Captain coughed, "Necklaces and stones. What is this hippie shit?"

The General backed me up. "Those necklaces and stones will keep the men cloaked enough so they can get close to that compound undetected. They are not your run of the mill jewelry."

"I fail to see how..." the Captain started.

The General cut him off, "I don't care what you think you know or what you don't know. I am making it a direct order that those men do as she says when it comes to getting them to this point. Anyone failing to follow her direction or O'Hara's will face a court martial. Is that clear?"

The Sergeant's hesitation, which had been wavering on following the directions of what I was going to give his men, vanished at the mention of a court martial. I could tell from his eyes, that he would follow this order even if it sounded stupid. He was also smart enough to realize O'Hara and I shared leadership on this mission. The Captain just shut his mouth and stared straight ahead with his teeth clenched.

"All right then," moving right along, the General again turned to me, "from there, you go alone to the first objective. The team will hold. How are you on computers?"

"Decent, but if it's complicated or in another language, I'll have problems. If I could borrow Wizard for a minute?" looking to O'Hara for permission.

He nodded and Wizard walked over to me.

I nodded to the far corner of the room and we walked over there together. I turned to him saying, "I need you to keep an open mind. Quite literally, actually." He looked confused.

"Just look at me." And I tried tapping into his mind. *'Can you hear me? Hello Wizard of Oz. Come in Houston.'* A shocked look went over his face and I said aloud, "What did you hear?"

Stammering, he said, "Hello Wizard of Oz. Come in Houston." Ok, he missed the first one because his brain and mine were syncing.

"That's telepathy. You received me. We can use this, if you are willing to help me hack the mainframe if I need it?" I watched him.

He nodded his head, but didn't say anything, still freaking over the contact. He'd get used to it. He was Special Forces after all.

I took out a business card of Demitri' and held it in front of my eyes and 'pushed' the image to Wizard. "What about now?" He rattled off everything on the card.

"Good job. Are you all right?" I asked concerned.

"Fine, but that was weird." He looked frayed.

"You ain't seen weird yet, but you will." I walked back to the table, "Ok, I can use Wizard for help in hacking the mainframe. No worries." I didn't tell them I would be using Antonio, too. They didn't need to know just how far my range was with telepathy when it came to my mates. It was our ace if we needed it.

The Captain asked, "How in the hell are you going to do that when we'll be in complete radio silence unless shit goes south, or if you find a nuke?"

I gave a half smile, "I have my ways."

"Bullshit..." The General cut Captain Holland off again, "If she says she can do it, then she can. Leave it," the General snapped. The Captain again went back to staring straight ahead.

"Now you get the data, confirm the nuke, and then get out. Once..." I interrupted him.

"General, I won't be able to leave that quickly," I stated firmly.

His eyebrows went up, "Why not?"

I gave him a look that conveyed, 'do you really want the others to hear this?'

The General got the hint. "Captain, take your marines outside for a few minutes. The Major will come to get you when we're finished."

If the Captain was pissed before, he was infuriated even more now. A mere "sell-sword", a derogatory word for Mercs, meaning 'bitch for hire', was privy to top secret information that he and his wasn't included in. He did an about face and walked out, every line of is body was vibrating with anger, though. The rest just followed him out, eyes forward.

After the door shut I said, "I didn't know if you had informed them of our other abilities and conditions."

Shaking his head, "No, I didn't tell anyone outside of those who already knew. The Major did have to have the information in order to arrange things for you and yours."

"I appreciate that. How are you or O'Hara about the information about the dark God Kalim?"

O'Hara let the General go first. "Well, I assume there are more things out there if you and yours exist. Dark Gods are a bit much to take on faith though."

O'Hara nodded his agreement with the General.

"All right, understand that our job is important to us and should also be important to you. As you came to find out with that second team being wiped out, there is a clear and present danger to people at large that normal people or soldiers can't handle. I am willing to help you obtain your personal military objectives, but be aware that we have our own as well," I stopped to see his reaction.

"Go on, "he urged

"Going in, I can hide for a while, but sooner or later, that dark God is going to notice me. It can't be helped. I'll move as fast as I can, but I will be found. It's my job to fight him in order to contain or push him back into his own astral realm. The vortex that has been made in the center of that house will have to be closed. Especially if you bring in fighter jets and start to lay down missiles on the place. Missiles and death will only feed that vortex, since it is evil. It feeds on death and destruction, making it stronger and denser. More of your men will die and more people later if it isn't dealt with first. That's my job. I have to close it with any means at my disposal," ending the lecture.

He frowned and thought a moment, "It is really hard to believe that dark Gods are here and they have enough power to be that dangerous."

"I can agree with that, Cat," O'Hara spoke up. "I have seen you do some incredible things, but they have been things we can see with our eyes. I mean you're not a God. You may not be human, but we can see you. Feel you. That makes you real, but Gods of any flavor have to be taken on faith and that is harder to believe in."

Antonio choked a bit on the 'you're not a God part', but I shot him a look. Besides, I was a child of one, not a full one. Big difference, really.

"I understand that O'Hara, and we would like to show you something," I left off.

The General groaned, "Every time you show us something, things get blown around."

I laughed, "No, nothing like that this time. Just don't go shooting anything or anyone. It wouldn't do any good anyway, but I'm worried about the ricochet."

"Oh, no," O'Hara said and closed his eyes.

I laughed again, saying "Shamus, come here, please." The men looked around anxiously.

Shamus shimmered into existence. He wasn't dense enough to be completely solid, but everyone could see that he was there and glowing the purple that was his astral color.

Gasps and 'oh shits' followed.

"It's ok; I promise there is no danger whatsoever. This is my friend. My second in command on the astral planes. Gentlemen, meet Shamus, a very powerful wizard. A real wizard, Wizard," I laughed as I looked over to where Wizard sat.

The General gaped. He actually gaped. Then he shut his mouth, closed his eyes and breathed very deeply. O'Hara and his team were staring, trying not to believe what they were seeing, but couldn't deny.

O'Hara, not yet over the shock, breathed, "What is that, exactly?"

My amusement flew out the window, "He is not a 'that'," I snapped.

O'Hara looked at me, and then his eyes narrowed when he saw mine were filling with anger, "Sorry, but it's a little overwhelming."

"He isn't an 'it' either," I growled and took a step forward.

"What, exactly, then?" he growled back.

"I, too, would like to know," the General joined in again.

"Shamus is mine. He is my second in command. My General. My friend. My astral healer. He is a person who died thousands of years ago and decided to not be reborn again, but continued to learn more wizardry on the astral planes. When I came to be, he decided to serve me. His allegiance is to me only. NO one else," my tone still held anger, but I was slowly calming down.

"Your General?" the General asked. "You mean you have more than him serving you?"

I smiled a wicked smile, "A whole army and not just wizards."

"Shit," the General actually swore and sat down on a chair behind him. I think I'd overwhelmed him, too. My mates were trying so hard not to laugh.

"Shamus, this is General Pierce. That is Captain O'Hara. On his team is Major Harris," pointing to each man, introducing them to Shamus, "Sergeant Watson and Sergeant Logan. Otherwise known as Rock, Babyface, Romeo and Wizard. And that soldier over by the General is Major Stewart, the General's attaché."

"Pleased to meet all of you." Shamus looked highly amused.

Babyface asked, his usual cold eyes showing a bit more life than usual, "Can I touch his hand?"

I looked at Shamus, who shrugged. Babyface, bold as brass, walked over to him and reached out. Shamus held up his hand and Babyface pressed his to Shamus'. Then he pushed and it didn't go through as he expected.

"He is a very powerful wizard, Babyface," I told him. Suddenly, Shamus went misty and Babyface lurched forward, his hand sliding through Shamus'.

Shamus chuckled.

"That was mean," I scolded, smiling.

Babyface turned to look at me. "There is no temperature change. Isn't he supposed to be cold?"

I shook my head at him, "That would be a ghost, and Shamus isn't a ghost."

"Then what is he if he isn't a ghost or a God?" Wizard had gotten over the shock and went into curious mode.

"An astral familiar," I explained simply.

"What's an astral familiar?" O'Hara walked forward for a closer look.

"There are many spiritual beings on the astral plane. For that matter there are many different levels on the astral planes," I snorted.

"You forgot to tell them about the many different kinds of planes. There are more than just the astral, as you know," Shamus added.

"I know that, but don't you think these guys are freaked enough as it is? Information overload isn't going to help." I walked back to the table now that I was sure these guys weren't going to start shooting. For nothing. Bullets wouldn't do shit against an astral or spiritual being.

"Harrumph, 'freaked' about covers it." The General recovered enough to stand up and squared his shoulders. "Nice to meet you, Shamus." The other men took their cue from the General and nodded their greetings.

"And you, General. Thank you for getting Cat's butt out of the fire back in New York." He solidified and walked closer to the table cautiously. Babyface walked with him, still staring out of the corner of his eye.

"You're welcome," General Pierce nodded. "As unsettling as this introduction is...he still isn't a God."

I shook my head, "No, and you really don't want me to call one here either. Not for show and tell. That would be bad. And I can call quite a few to me now. But The Gods and Goddesses are old, powerful and they can still be capricious. I try to stay out of their way, but you all felt one in the interrogation room in New York."

He harrumphed again, "So, that's what I felt. I knew something very unusual had happened, but a God?"

"Goddess, actually. Take my word for it," I said dryly.

Shamus looked at the General, but pointed at the table, "May I?"

He nodded an assent. Shamus bent over and scanned everything laid out there. He placed his hand, palm down and 'felt' the photos and maps.

I cautioned him, "Watch it, Shamus. The last time I used power to find more Intel, the photo burst into flames in my hands."

He pulled back, "You didn't tell me that."

I shrugged my shoulders, "A lot happened that night. I must have forgotten."

"A minor ancient Pakistan dark deity had enough juice to reach out with fire all the way to New York?" he looked appalled.

"There has been much death over the years in that region. The people on both sides are war hungry. It's been feeding and feeding well. Add all that to The Great Shift happening soon and voila, you've got a bad ass," I tried to joke about it.

His expression grew grim, "This is not a joking matter, Your Highness," and again I heard gasps from the men around the table. "You're just healed from the last battle with a dark God." Remembering the men around the table, he went vague "You know what happened last time. What makes you so sure something like that won't happen again?" his tone was serious.

"Who you gonna call?" I said, just to piss him off. I was the only one allowed to do that.

"This isn't Ghostbusters," he snorted. Then with a loud pop, he winked out of existence. It was his way of stomping out of a room.

"Where'd he go?" O'Hara was looking around, his hand searching for a gun unconsciously.

"He's off fuming somewhere," I sighed. Demitri came up from behind me, placing his hand on my shoulder.

General Pierce was giving me a hard stare. "What exactly are you? He said 'Your Highness'."

Demitri squeezed my shoulder slightly. "It's a title he uses to make me uncomfortable." I was vague, but still truthful at the same time.

"And is it a true title?" he pressed. Damn.

"I have many titles actually, but for these purposes, plain old Cat will do," trying to steer him away and back to the game board in front of us.

"If you're royalty, that changes many things. If anything happens to you, we could be looking at a possible international incident," he persisted.

I looked him in the eye, "An inter-dimensional incident to be accurate. I hold only one title here on Earth and that's a High Priestess. Not quite important enough for an international incident," I smiled wryly.

"Your file said you were born here in America." O'Hara interjected.

"You're right. The file is right. So see, no international incident potential. Now can I have the time I need to kick Kalim's ass and close the vortex so my job with this will be finished? Then you guys can come in and lay waste to the place for all I care. Shit, I'll help." I was getting tired of the third degree already.

Andre came up on my other side and placed his hand on my other shoulder. They knew I was getting cranky.

"Will doing this have a direct positive effect for my men?' General Pierce asked.

"I can absolutely guarantee fewer losses of men if I close that vortex. Believe that," I said firmly.

He studied my face for a full minute. "You'll have your time. Call in the rest of the teams when you're done." He'd do it for his men. That was good enough for me.

O'Hara asked, "Is there any way we could help?"

Shaking my head, "No, this thing will eat you up and spit you out, and not even remember what he ate. You'll need a lot more training in the arts before you'd be ready for anything close to this." I answered truthfully. "You take care of the mundane and we'll take care of the metaphysical. Together, we can then kick some serious ass."

He gave me a half grin, nodded and said, "Hooorah!"

The rest of the meeting was tense. When the rest of the marines were allowed back in, the Captain was so not a happy camper. I didn't care; I'd gotten what I wanted and we were moving forward. The Sergeant that I had inducted to our group kept giving me sideways looks, as if he was trying to figure out just how much pull I had and what I knew that they didn't. He was a sharp one. I took this as a good sign. Having stupid people at your back is a recipe for disaster. Although on a mission like this, keeping our unusualness a secret may be impossible in the long run. Sooner or later, one of them will see something or something will slip, but until that happened, we would try to keep it as contained as possible.

Like that was gonna happen, sh'yeah!

CHAPTER THIRTEEN
Saving Face

An A C-37A Gulfstream plane, with in-flight refueling capabilities, took us from the Navy Air Station base, so in roughly thirteen hours it landed us at the base in Kadar, Afghanistan. My mates were really uneasy about letting me go alone with no other backup from our side other than Shamus. He didn't make another appearance and wouldn't, unless it was absolutely necessary. I had put his physical representation in the backyard at our new home to gather energy from the sun when it was up and gather the moon's energy when it was night time. I had placed him in a protected magickal circle with my sister, Cendra, to guard him physically while my mates were waiting on the base. It was also a good way to keep her from sniffing around Antonio while I was gone. I smiled to myself. I was such a devious bitch. Cassie and her mates, as well as some of the other clan, were close by the base on S. Padre Island Drive. Lee, one of Cassie's mates, had found a building that was vacant. They were busy refurbishing it for our new clubhouse. They did that while they waited for word from my mates, who were about roughly five miles down the same road. They could be there in mere minutes the way some of them drove. Could we take the base if things went south? Oh yeah, but it would take an awful lot of power and we might have to break a few rules to do it. But it could be done. We would then be absolutely useless, having to be on the run after something like that, so I hoped everything stayed the way I was feeling it was. I felt General Pierce was genuine is his coalition ideas. I felt that O'Hara and ours could get along and work well together. But one other time I had felt good about something, and I was wrong. That had cost me and my mates fifteen years of hell. So I had to be sure. General Pierce had talked me into putting a tracking device under my skin, in my arm, so they could tell which mark I was at on the mission. I didn't like it, but telling them about the ability for my guys to track me would have given away our ace. So I let them, and grumbled about it all the way to the plane.

The base in Afghanistan was hot and arid; dusty as hell, too. The country had an odd charm to it, an ancientness of quiet pride that I felt while walking out to a field away from the main buildings and airstrip. Ignoring the planes taking off and choppers floating in and out, I stretched my senses out and around me, taking in life of the area for miles around. I found ghosts from recent deaths. One, a child crying quietly in a corner of an abandoned building, not too far away from where I was. I sent white light to the child, trying to comfort his spirit. He sniffled and said 'Momma?', but in a language I couldn't understand. It just felt that he was saying that. I shook my head, 'no', knowing he would feel the response, if not understanding my words. He sniffled again and bent back over his knees, hugging himself. I felt so bad for this lost soul. I made a portal appear over him, a tunnel of white light that would take him from this physical plane of existence to the spiritual plane he needed to be on. I called for any relatives that had passed on before him to be there on the other side of the tunnel to guide him, to take him to his rightful place on the spiritual planes. I mentally tapped him on the shoulder and he looked up, seeing the tunnel of white light. I offered for him to cross over, where there would be someone who loved him to guide him on the other side. He looked through the tunnel and gasped. He said what I thought amounted to 'Papa'. His father must have passed away before his own death. He stood up and ran into the tunnel and was gone. I smiled and closed the portal. There were many ghosts around. Some recent, some had been dead a long while. I did the same for any that I came across. Opening a portal, calling deceased relatives and offering them the chance to cross over. Some went gladly, some were still so angry, they refused. I let it go. I didn't have the authority, or the right to make them cross over unless they were a danger to a living being. Nor did I have the right to make them cross over to the Summerland's, which is my own kind of heaven. Some people go to another kind of heaven. That is their right and their free will. The portals I opened would automatically know which spiritual heavenly plane a particular person needed to be in. Anyone who tried to convert a person on their death bed or after death or force them into their own heaven, was in for a very nasty surprise when they passed over themselves. It wouldn't be their own heaven they would be going to when they died. Serves them right too, to be so arrogant to think their way and their heaven was the only right one. I blew off those thoughts, knowing those that did it would get their just rewards later on. Karma can be a bitch.

We were waiting for twilight when we'd be able to climb into a Black Hawk helicopter, which would take us about 20 clicks away from our target drop-off site. We would hoof it to the first mark from there. There were other Black Hawks waiting to take the rest of the squads to their own drop-off points and they, too, would be hoofing it to their respective marks. I walked back to the building I had been cleared for. It had bunks and a few tables for our unit. Some of the guys were playing cards and drinking bottled water. Others were going over their equipment, checking it for dirt or damage. A few were sleeping. I thought it might be a good idea for me as well, since I'd just done what amounted to a spiritual cleansing of a huge area. I was drained, but it had been worth it. O'Hara squinted his eyes at me, taking in my appearance. I nodded at him and went to the bunk farthest away from anyone, falling into it. I fell asleep instantly.

It must have been some time later when I felt a hand grab my shoulder to awaken me. I screamed, coming out of a nightmare, and flung myself out of bed, reaching for my blades at my belt. I found the wall and put it to my back. I looked around me, trying to clear my head and figure out where the fuck I was. Where was the danger? Who touched my shoulder? I spotted a person and slow recognition came in my mind. I knew him, Romeo. He was friend, not foe. The rest of the team was at his back, watching me back against the wall, knives in both hands, ready to slash. I was breathing hard, taking deep breaths to calm my pounding pulse.

"Whoa, it's ok, Cat. It's just us. Breathe. Calm down," O'Hara said, hands away from his sides. Romeo took his cue from O'Hara and turned his palms face out. Shaking, I put my knives back into their sheaths, nodding my head to let them know I recognized them. Knew they weren't a threat. I was conscious now.

"Post Traumatic Stress Syndrome, huh? Lots of us get it from having a bad battle or too many of them. You should have told us." O'Hara was relaxed now, but still concerned about the incident. It could have gone badly. With us being Captains, we both knew it.

"I'm sorry. My bad," my breathing was slowing down. "I should have told you before I went to sleep. There were just so many and I was tired."

"So many what, Cat?" O'Hara looked serious.

"Never mind. Just next time, call from a good 10 ft away. Even my kids call from the doorway at home. I'll still wake up battle ready, but no one will get hurt if there isn't a person near me." Only my mates had been able to sleep next to me, needing only to rub my back if I was coming out of a bad dream. Their scent was the first thing I smelled and it seemed to take the fear right out of me, making me feel immediately that there was no danger. No need to hurt anyone in defense.

When my kids were little, it was fine. They often slept with me. But when they hit about twelve, they learned quickly to call from the doorway. Something about them changed, too, where I didn't quite recognize them anymore when first waking up. It got worse as they got older. I never could figure out why. Maybe it's an age and male thing.

143

O'Hara cut into my thoughts, "We're about to leave. You need to get your gear and get going. We leave in 10 minutes." Good, I only needed that.

I nodded my head and sat down on the floor. "No problem, give me a me a minute here."

He nodded. They all turned away and left me alone. I opened the bond between my mates and me, '*Hey sweeties,*' I greeted them.

'*Are you all right? Demitri wouldn't let me contact you when we felt your fear spike. He said to give you a chance to call first,*' Andre grumbled. '*What happened?*'

'*I came out of a bad dream. Being in an unfamiliar place and a hostile one at that, I woke up bad. I'm fine now. No worries. I swear it,*' I assured him.

'*Ok, sorry you're having problems sleeping. If I was there, I would hold you.*' Aaahhh, I fell in love with him all over again. Egads, mushy stuff. What am I thinking?

'*I do need energy, hon. I spent a lot of it earlier easing spirits across the Veil in the area.*' He knew I wouldn't be able to not answer my calling as a High Priestess and didn't berate me for expending much needed energy that should have been used for mission details only.

He just quietly answered, '*Take what you need*', and opened up. They all did, and power flowed from them to me along our bonds, filling me up, taking the strain away that sleep didn't ease anymore. Most people, while sleeping, recharge during REM. Their bodies turned it to healing the days stress away, so they woke up feeling rested, refreshed. Due to my nightmares, my REM only took more energy away from me, battling in my sleep, as I battled during the day. Most times, I would wake up feeling even more drained then before I had slept. Since making the bond to them, I had access to the energy I needed, so I could refresh that way. They would recharge their chakra's, replenishing what I took. It took them about 15 to 20 minutes to recharge. So it worked out for us. Even this, though, was finite. If I got seriously injured, and they used everything they had to heal me, they would be down themselves, for a long while. They would need more than a simple chakra recharge to regain what was given to me.

My energy had filled up and I said to them all, '*Thank you. I have to go; we are going into stage two. So far all has been well. Love you*'

'*Love you more*', was the answer I got and they cut the connection. Our telepathy range didn't have a limit, but it did take energy. So conservation was important.

As I got up, I grabbed my bag. I found the bathroom and used it. I braided my hair tightly and put in my black band on the bottom. I noticed the men had their tactical gear on and were armed to the teeth. I took out my own uniform and put it on. We had ours specially made. And we had our own name for it too, calling it a Gaileyah. It looked very much like what a ninja would wear. Tight fitting, black cloth and specially made to resist tears, with a wrap for my face that would hide all but my eyes. Then I put on my own tactical vest, but not like what Special Forces would wear. It, too, was black, but very thin. My vest was lined with a dual metal of sheets of silver and lead. The lead was thin. Too thin to stop a bullet, but it would protect me from knives and sword slashes. The silver would protect me from most magickal attacks. They had to be thick enough to do the job, but light enough for me to run—fast. With this vest, I could run for miles and not get out of breath. Over the vest went my belts. Two of them crossed my chest loaded with knives and throwing stars. Others went across my back for my silver seventeen inch swords. Around my waist, went a wide belt. It held more knives and had pouches for the bags Antonio had made for me.

I grabbed the purple bag filled with stones and necklaces and set those on my belt tying it with the handle of the bag. Most of my knives, my two swords and my Shurikens were made of pure silver, but everything was coated with black special paint, so as to not ruin the metal. That way there was no gleam that would reflect off of anything I was carrying that an enemy could see. I tucked my head wrap into my wide belt, grabbed my bag and walked out. They were waiting outside for me, and they all did a double take at my mission uniform. Or, maybe it was my body? I knew I was built like a brick shit house, but damn, you'd think these guys got laid often enough not to be affected by it. Most of them were cute enough. Shit, a few were damn handsome, where a mere smile could get any woman to say 'yes'. Ahh, me being a woman was it, period. Well, they would just have to get used to it. I gave them a dangerous look back. A few cleared their throats and gazed away.

Some went stone faced and O'Hara let out a, "Hherrummp!" And they all fell in as we marched to the chopper. Maybe it was all the knives and no gun? Damn, this mission didn't come with a dress code rule book. Maybe Martha Stewart could come up with something?

We flew low, through the darkening skies heading towards the Pakistan border. I looked around the cabin of the chopper and thought to myself how cool and dangerous looking it was. It felt like a second home to me. O'Hara had handed me a headset, and I put it on, but no one was talking much for the long flight. I scanned each man. There were eight of them, plus O'Hara's team and me. This was a thirteen man squad. I thought, 'way cool. Good number'.

Most people believe the number thirteen was unlucky, but it honestly wasn't. The myths had started when the Catholic Church helped King Phillip of France to detain all Templars on Friday, October 13th, 1307 and tortured them into confessions of devil worship. King Phillip wanted their treasure and bribed the reigning Pope Clement into helping him steal it from the Templars. Jacques De Mollay, Grand Master of the Templars, and his second in command had rescinded their confessions and were ordered to hang.

Most people thought it had to do with Jesus' last supper, there being thirteen people at the table and Judas turned on him, but it really got it's bad name because of the Pope's betrayal of the Templars.

The Templars were revered by peasants because of their mandate to protect those who journeyed in pilgrimage to the Holy Land. After the massacre of Templar's, peasants and travelers were again at the mercy of highway men and the like. Hence, Friday the 13th became a bad day in memory of those lost to the greed of the Church and King Phillip.

Being pagans, we do honor those like the Templars, because of their strength of faith and how they did start out with great intentions. The number 13 is a power number for us. Not feared, but desired. I took this as a good sign that we would be ok and get back home. I sent a prayer to the Lady for a blessing on these men and that we would all make it back home safely.

The chopper banked to port and a voice came over the headset, "ETA, 2 minutes to drop zone."

O'Hara acknowledged the warning and added for the troop, "Remember the best missions are those done with all of us making it home," echoing my earlier wish. We drifted down fast and the chopper landed. We all hustled out and moved away to the far right, some dropping to their knees, automatics held out ready to shoot. The chopper took off and it was soon silent in the dark night. We went under the cover of some trees that were dark and heavy with leaves.

I motioned to O'Hara, "I need to give these out to everyone." I pulled off the purple bag from my belt.

He nodded and brought everyone in with a signal of his hand. Everyone fell in. I pulled out the necklaces first holding them up for them to see.

"They have to be worn on your neck, close to your skin. This will help me cloak you all from enemy sight." Some looked at them oddly or skeptically, but they took theirs and started to put them on, tucking them under the tactical vest and black shirts. Each necklace was the same, a black leather cord with a sterling silver pentagram that had a black quartz crystal hanging from it.

I pulled out two smaller bags within the purple bag. One held the clear quartz crystals, the other apache tears. I had an affinity with apache tears, and was able to invoke them to do many things that most other practitioners wouldn't be able to pull off.

I handed a clear quartz crystal to each man. "This goes in your left pants pocket. This is a power stone, it will help protect you." I was vague on what exactly it protected them from, because I didn't want to get into djinn, efreets and bacakuls' right now with those not in the know. The apache tears went around next. "Put these in your upper right pocket on your vest. Do not move any of these things I have given to you. Don't touch them and don't lose them. If you do, you screw the pooch, got it?" I looked hard at each man. I put the bags in my black carry pack and zipped it up.

I turned to O'Hara, "I should take point." I put on my head wrap and tied it loosely around my neck, tucking in the ends, so they wouldn't get caught on anything.

O'Hara nodded, then turned to everyone saying, "Hand signals only from here on out. Cat's on point." Then, with a signal from his hand thrusting forward, I moved to lead them towards our first mark.

I opened up my senses and moved through the forest, hardly making a sound. The troop behind me did a damn good job of being silent themselves, despite all the gear they were wearing. I started out normally, but then picked up the pace, as I got used to the pulses I felt around me, getting in sync with the environment and life-forces echoing through the dense forest. I was surprised with the greenery. I had always thought anywhere in the Middle East would be nothing but sand and dunes. I was wrong. The trees were oddly shaped, bending in ways no tree at home did, but they had wide leaves and a musky scent to them with tan to whitish coloring in the bark. Red colored boulders and rocks were here and there, with reddish to dark brown dirt for the most part, but there was tall grass, too. After about six or more clicks, I heard some of them breathing harder behind me. I slowed, to take a look at them. I'd been pushing too hard, going at my pace and not remembering they were purely human. I held up my fist for the signal to stop.

O'Hara came up to me, bending to my ear. "What?" Apparently, he went monosyllable when on mission, which it made sense when in silence mode.

"Sorry, went too fast. Give them ten minutes to catch their breaths. Then we'll pull out again," I whispered back. He nodded.

Some went to guard, while others sat back taking a rest. A few looked at me with respect and awe that I could move so fast and not be tired. Only two were sweating; I was impressed myself. But this wasn't a race. We could go at a slower pace. We were making good time.

Once I felt them rested, I looked at O'Hara and he signaled for everyone up and out. Pointing to me, he thrust his hand for me to take point and go.

I set off again at a better pace for everyone. We were clear until we were about five clicks away from our first mark. Then we hit the first ring of guards. I signaled 'stop' again. Everyone froze. I glanced back at O'Hara and held up two fingers and pointed off to the left at about 30 degrees from our position. I then held up three fingers and pointed dead ahead of us. Two more fingers showed men stationed off of our right hand side. O'Hara made the motion for slashing across his throat, and I shook my head. I took my hand and motioned a snake like S pattern around two of the groups slowly. He nodded and motioned for me to go.

I went much slower and didn't make a sound. All of them knew we were sneaking around the line without a kill. It took us longer, but we got through the first line with no confrontations. I picked up the pace again, but still slowed it down from our previous hike even more, so I could catch every pulse around me. Two more clicks in, and we hit the second line. This was denser with larger groups of men. I signaled for 'stop' again and showed O'Hara how many and where they were. Again we snuck around the guards. The third line was a bitch. We had to wait until there was enough space to slip around the groups of men stationed really thick, but we made our first mark, and there was a bit of room between us and any other enemy. From here I would go on alone. I took my black bag and pulled out a double terminated fifteen inch long clear quartz crystal about five inches in diameter that had been treated with copper. It allowed me to send energy through fast and hard, much more so then regular clear quartz. My powers didn't do so well with wood, but give me copper and I can make it sing. Too bad I was allergic to it, or I would make magickal rings and wear them. I placed the crystal's small end down into the ground and then drew a circle around it. I said a spell under my breath and the crystal was set.

I leaned into O'Hara and whispered, "Do not let anyone break this circle. Have everyone stay within 50 ft. of it. When I call you in, then break the circle, grab it and put it in my bag." I took my bag to a nearby tree and hid it as well as I could. I took the stick Wizard had given me and put it in my pouch on my belt. It was like a memory stick, but odder shaped and did way more than a simple memory stick does. But I would have to find the right port to stick it into.

I bent to his ear and whispered, "Be ready for me to send in your head. You don't have to answer aloud, so think your directions and I'll pick it up." He nodded, eyes a bit wide, but I knew he would do the job. If not, I had Antonio. I turned to O'Hara to let him know I was ready for stage two. He nodded, setting his men with hand signals.

He came over and leaned to my ear, "Don't get killed." I nodded and took off.

I moved like a shadow through the forest, going into a Zen-like zone, reading my environment, making corrections and avoiding enemy pulses. I never slowed down. I reached the outer wall of the compound quickly. I found a shadow and became one with it. I blended into my environment, waiting for the guards in the watch towers to all be looking away for the split second I needed them to. I finally got my opportunity, and with a burst of speed, I ran to the wall and launched from the ground, up and over the wall in one smooth, silent move. Landing on my feet jarred my hips a bit, but this was one of those times I loved being modified. I ran to another shadow, blended, and looked around. There were many pulses of life force here and there. Most were sleeping, but some were patrolling, even inside the compound itself. I slipped from shadow to shadow, halting here and there until the way was clear to the next shadowed area. My target was designated building two. The main house was building one. I felt around for an energy signature that would say they had a nuke and I found it in building eight. It was farthest away from building one on the west side of the compound.

I took a deep breath and tuned into Wizard's mind, *'Nuke, building eight'*. I felt his first feeling of shock at the contact, but then he settled. I opened my eyes and broke contact, knowing he would relay this to O'Hara. I kept going through the shadows getting closer to my target. I slipped around building one because I wanted to stay as far away from the center of power as I could and came at building two from the east side.

It took an extra few minutes, but it was worth it to me. I slid up to the side of building two and there was one guard standing in the front of it. He had an AK-47 set diagonally across his chest, resting in his arms. I took out a knife and slipped around the corner, trying to come up between him and the door so I would have his back. I moved silently and quickly, reaching around his throat with my knife hand, slicing his throat, while my left hand caught him as he fell in a gurgle of surprise. I dragged his body to the rear of the building and put him in the darkest part. I cleaned the blood off my blade on his shirt and went back to the door. I stopped in front of it.

I first searched for any more pulses around me, then cautiously sent out a power thread to gently feel what kind of wards this door had. There was a huge sigil and a psychic shield behind it. I looked up and down with my eyes and saw a laser alarm system on it. They'd thought of everything, they did. I took out one of the bags Antonio had made for me of a powered herb mix that was spelled. I put some in the palm of my hand and blew it gently onto the door in a wide circle. It cut through the ward and shield, leaving a nice gaping hole for me to step through.

First, I had to deal with the physical alarm system. Electrical things are so easy to mess with when you know astral magicks. I sent another tendril of power, this time through one of the lasers lights, not disturbing the laser beam, but just adding to it, riding it to its source. It was in a box somewhere inside the building. I sent a pulse of power and it turned right off for me. I looked both physically and with power to make sure I had gotten everything before touching the handle of the door. To move the metal locks out of the way, I opened it using telekinesis. I slipped inside and found the mainframe. I didn't move toward the computer yet. I scanned the whole area looking for traps, both physical and magickal. I didn't see anything physical, but I saw a black circle around the computer with an unknown mark in the middle of it. Not an inverted pentagram, but something else I hadn't seen before. Then I heard chewing sounds coming from around the back of the computer which was set in the middle of the room.

That was unusual for most computers, but they did that here, I thought to myself, so they could put the mark around it. Silently, I moved around the computer, being careful not to break the circle to see what was behind it. It turned out to be a bacakul chewing on what looked to be the left arm of a human. Several fingers were missing, but one perfect thumb. It looked female due to the shape of the nail and the manicure. Figures; these terrorists would feed their own women to a demon, I thought, disgusted.

Taking my right hand, I threw an energy ball at the bacakul, entrapping it with a bubble of white light. With my left, I took the second bag Antonio had given me and spilled it on the black circle and there was a small burst of power then a sick rotten meat smell wafted through the air. The bacakul was spitting and hitting at the bubble it was surrounded by, trying to get at me. About three and half feet tall, it had grey greenish skin and looked like a cross between a gargoyle and an imp. Sharp pointed teeth filled its mouth, and red cat-like irises were the biggest features on the small demon. With it eating, it had been distracted from guarding the inside building, which explained not needing anything else physically to guard the inside. Bullets wouldn't do anything to this thing but piss it off. I added an extra layer of power in a silver color to further strengthen the bubble entrapping it. I opened a portal from this plane to a lower astral plane and sent it, bubble and all, where it belonged. Killing it might wake the dark God and have him come running. I thought it best to just try to remove the thing first. Then I moved quickly to the computer, recalling the instructions both Antonio and Wizard gave me for finding the correct port. Then I bent over the key pad looking at it. The keys were not in English. Damn them. The hard way then.

'Wizard, look,' and I showed him the keypad in my mind to his.

He thought to me, 'ok,' and showed me which key strokes to hit and in what sequence. It took longer, but we got the job done. The information was being downloaded into the weird looking stick.

I was waiting impatiently for the download when I smelled, and then felt, it coming. The smell was the scent of a dead skunk and the power was dark and rolling in like a Category 4 hurricane. He solidified, standing seven feet tall, inside the room. His body was slender, but for his huge erection with barbs on the head all around it. He had two feet, with six toes on each, and a tail on the back of him. It swished back and forth showing his anger, I assumed. Two twelve inch horns of black curled up from his head with a mouthful of teeth. His eyes looked reptilian, glowing grey and black. His greenish-grey skin was mottled over his entire being. But all that came second to the four arms with wicked 9 inch blades in each hand. He was a dark God all right; a minor one, true, but a God, nonetheless. The power signature told me that.

'What did you do with my servant?' he spoke in my mind. The funny thing about telepathy with any being of any flavor (except ghosts on the physical plane)—was so long as they used mind-speaking, one can understand what they are saying. If they spoke verbally, it came out in their native tongue.

I said, "I sent it back to the hell it belonged to," I answered, being flippant

He hissed, 'You will take his place.'

"You can kiss my white rebel pagan ass. No, wait. Skip that. You're too fucking ugly," and I slid my swords out and started to slash at him. His guard went up, and he returned blows and blocked my attempts to cut him at the same time. He soon had me on the defensive with his four to my two blades, even though mine were longer. I smiled and kept thrusting, down stroking and spinning into, then away from him. I tried slashing in close, then using my foot to kick him in the gut. He just grunted and kept coming at me.

We moved around the computer and I forgot about the half eaten human arm and stumbled. It gave him an opening and he didn't pull back, slashing with his blade across the right side of my stomach. It sliced right through my tactical vest, damn it. The cut was deep enough to bleed heavily, but not enough to kill. Well, it could be worse, I thought to myself. I stepped up my blocks.

I then tried distracting him with a stroke to his head with one blade, then slashing downwards towards his leg with the other, trying to ham string him. He just casually brushed it away with one of his lower arms with the knife in that hand. I was going to lose. I knew it. I didn't have anything that would make a dent in this minor dark God. I had to figure out something else quickly.

I backed around the computer again, trying to get us both away from it before I tried anything with magick. I finally got him around where I wanted him, and then I opened a portal right behind him. Taking my right foot, I kicked him in his balls. THAT got his attention, bending over just like any man, fire sparking out of his eyes. I grabbed the other bag Antonio had made for me and quickly opened it to throw at him, as I chanted a banishing spell. I swept my left blade across his front, moving his hands away from his middle torso. Then I kicked him again and he fell through the portal. He screamed, but had no way and no time to counter it. The portal closed.

I was panting and shaking. That had been the second scariest thing I had ever fought. But I must be getting better. I wasn't dead this time. I stumbled to the computer to check the progress and thankfully it was done. I grabbed the stick and put in my belt pouch. Unfortunately, the battle with the dark God had gotten someone's attention out there, because I could hear men running towards the building I was in.

'Hey Wizard, tell O'Hara I need that distraction now.' I knew O'Hara would break radio silence and tell the other three teams to start moving in, killing anyone in their path. I was hoping that would turn the direction of these guys back to the outside walls. It sort of worked. Some went to the walls, but some just kept coming. I ran outside so I wouldn't be trapped inside the building and started to make my way to building one.

My job wasn't done yet. I had a vortex to close. If I gave enough time for the adept or priest to recall the dark God, I would be starting all over again. And I was already tired. I threw a star at the guard who was closest to me and got him in the neck. Another came and I dodged behind a wall before he got a shot off, then snapping around the corner, I threw a blade into his chest. I went back behind the wall and skirted the other side of the building trying to avoid anymore guards. I looked around; no one would be there for about thirty seconds. Time enough for me to make the roof. I faced the building and jumped up, right when another guard was making his way towards me. I backed away from the edge and made it to the middle of the flat, squared roof. I looked around at the walls and saw the south side watch tower guard shooting down. That's the direction I came in from. That meant O'Hara and his team were backing up towards the wall since we left every enemy alive behind us. They were going to be trapped and that guard would pick them off like shooting fish in a barrel.

I took out a three inch throwing blade and drew my hand back. I snapped it, letting it go at the right angle. It thunked into his back and he fell forward. The shooting stopped. O'Hara could now use that wall to guard his team's back. I felt for their energy signatures. All twelve were still alive, only one was throbbing heavier than the rest, telling me we had one wounded. I felt beyond them and saw enemies closing in, the outer rings of guards collapsing into O'Hara and his team's position. This wasn't good.

I sent a spell of confusion and darkness at the incoming enemy. They would now be confused and seeing double. Also, the night would seem even darker to them, giving O'Hara's team an edge. I couldn't send a death spell or move the earth which was dangerous to begin with. Any other spells I could do would take too much energy that was needed for the closing of the vortex.

I had to hit my target.

O'Hara would breach the walls as soon as he could, and make for building eight, if no other team made it there before his. I left O'Hara and the team to do what they did best, praying they would be all right while I turned back to my main target.

I peered cautiously over the side, checking for roaming guards. It was clear enough for me to jump down and hit the next shadow. I blended in again. I could hear gunfire all around me, hand grenades going off sporadically, but not in the compound, yet. I moved towards the main house. I got next to it and slipped up to the door. I checked it for spells and seeing none, I walked in with my shields up.

I strode into what seemed to be a foyer with two sets of staircases going up and around to the second level of the house off to the left of me. Coming down one of those sets of stairs was a man in his thirties, in his dressing robe, looking like he had just gotten out of bed. He had two guards at his back. This must be the self-proclaimed prince.

He had a radio in one hand, so he must have been up on the upper balcony guiding his troops until he saw me coming in. In his other hand wasn't a gun. In fact, it was empty except for a tattooed circle with a mark in the palm of his hand. He was gathering energy and his guards had so much confidence in him they didn't even draw their guns on me.

I could see why they thought he was all that with that mark on his palm. It gave him access to the dark God's powers and he could do a lot of damage from using it. Guess he didn't get the memo yet, Kalim got sent on vacation. I took out two small throwing knives and waited. As he sent his spell at me I threw my knives at his men. His spell got deflected by my shield and my knives took down his men. They had looks of surprise on both their faces as they fell, dying. He, himself, looked shocked and he actually checked the palm of his hand.

I didn't know if he would understand me, but I didn't really care, "Without your God to back you up, you must be an amateur. What level are you at? Grade school still?" If he had been a master, I would have had more trouble with him, so he must still be in the beginning stages. He had gotten overconfident in relying on his God and probably took his learning as a matter of course. If he had been studying it seriously, he would have known what I was. I was way over his head.

Prince, my ass. I drew one of my long swords as I moved towards him. He must have realized he was now in deep shit, because he started backing up. I sped up, spinning in the swing, as I brought my blade up and severed his head from his body. His head went one direction and his body fell backwards with blood spurting from his severed neck. With any practitioner, small or large, you cut off the head. Some can get back up from mortal- seeming wounds. I felt out and around me again, ignoring the spreading blood. One strong source of evil was below, with another lesser pulse of darkness coming down from upstairs. A few guards were about, but on the upper levels still. The lesser darkness though, that one had my attention. He came down the staircase that the now deceased Prince had come from. He wore all black with a black turban too, but you could see his face. He had the typical beard and mustache most men of the Middle East wear.

Dark eyes glinted in anger, his lips pressed thin, as he regarded the headless body and pooling blood. He flicked his gaze back to me with a promise of death in them. He was spouting angry words at me, but they didn't sound like a chant or a spell. He was just running his mouth. I had my blade in my right hand and I tilted my wrist so my blade was lying horizontal. It looked like I was handing him the sword. I flipped my middle finger at him in a universal sign anyone could understand. I backed away from the body, keeping my left hand free. I didn't need any stinking mark on my palm. But I did need it clear of anything in it, unless using a wand. He cussed at me some more while coming down the rest of the steps, following me to the middle of the foyer. Probably spouting how 'I would be dead and my soul would roast in the belly of his master', yadda, yadda, yadda.

So long as he was here with me, he couldn't throw any more nasty spells at our men coming in. I bet things were easing up for them out there and I smiled. This priest or magician (having no clue what they called themselves), must have felt my smile because he really let loose with his cussing. And then a spell chant in quick succession of his tirade. I crossed my arms before me in a blocking motion and with power; I threw his spell to the side. The wall on the right hand side blew apart. A nice big hole was left there with debris floating down to the ground. His eyes widened a bit, and I laughed at his expression; serves him right for disregarding me for being a mere woman.

I chanted a protection spell, and then a spell for The Lords of Karma, throwing a beam of white bluish light at him. He put his hands out, palms up towards me, blocking with a magick shield. While he was doing that I used the sword in my right hand, cutting off his hands. He screeched as blood pumped out from the stumps. I ended his misery by swinging again, this time cutting his head off. I didn't even watch him go down as I raced up the stairs. I made quick, quiet work of killing the rest of the guards. I found a room with terrified women huddled in a corner and left them alone, but locked the door just to be safe. Some of the women, even being treated like crap, will still fight for their men. It's how they're raised; they didn't know any better.

I went back down the stairs and felt for the door that would lead me to the vortex. The closer I got to it, the more my stomach got nauseous. I was now in front of the door. It had a ward on it like the one on building two. I took out the powered herb and blew the mix on it. It released the ward and I opened the door. Going down a long flight of stairs, my stomach was roiling, threatening to vomit. The bottom floor was made of marble with blood stains marring it everywhere. In the center were two pillars where the vortex was spinning between them. Two efreets were about to hit me with their fire, but I threw a water spell at them and they died in a mist of steam, adding to the smell of rotting meat. I breathed with my mouth, trying not to give in to the urge to spew and fought it down. So long as I didn't breathe too deeply, I should be alright. I put my sword away because it would be of no use in this.

The vortex was stronger and denser than I thought it would be. It was the worst one I have ever been up against. All others seemed like closing a jack in the box compared to the magnitude of this one. I could feel it trying to tug on the edges of my aura, seeking a way to suck my soul from me.

I didn't dare call Shamus here and take a chance he would be sucked into it. I knelt before this thing and I prayed. I felt for the bond between my Goddess and me, tugging at it spiritually. I prayed to The Lord and The Lady for the power to close this portal; that the evil may be banished and no other innocents could be thrown into this hell, feeding this dark God. I prayed, while taking the energy I had and the energy that was flowing through the bond, and pressed the edges of the vortex together. I mended it shut with the power of my Goddess and Her Consort, pulling it tighter and tighter, closing the edges and sealing it with a band of golden white light. All of a sudden, with the absence of dark energy, when the vortex suddenly shut, a blast of power swept through the room. It felt like a psychic bomb just went off, throwing me into the far side of the wall.

I laid there, stunned. Breathing deeply, I tried to form a coherent thought and it was slow in coming. I finally got my head back together. I looked at the space between the pillars. It was shut, the air lighter and cleaner than before. I could tell that much. I sat up slowly, shaking my head, trying to clear the sudden dizziness. I was hurt, and astrally bleeding. My aura had been shredded because of the strength of the blast of power.

I needed help.

I called out to Shamus and waited. Nothing happened. He didn't come. I called out for my mates. Again, I got nothing. I felt for my inner self and that part of me lay huddled, shaking in shock. I sent feelings of warmth and love to my astral subtle body. She didn't respond. I'll be damned. I'd gotten hit with an equivalent of an EMP blast; of the psychic kind. My telepathy was gone and I had no idea how much more of my power got shut down. I needed blood now.

I pulled myself up off the floor and made my way outside where I could hear gunfire getting closer. Of course it had to be off to my left where I had come over the wall. I walked back to the south wall, flinging stars at running guards who saw me too late. I made it to the watch tower and climbed up it. This way, I wouldn't have to waste energy jumping up. I would only need pure strength for the landing on the other side. The Prince had put garrisons of guards at the east and west gates. He had only put a few guards at the north and south towers, probably thinking the walls were high enough for a deterrent. And he had emptied out a lot of his men for the extra guards on the outside.

This is why we had chosen this point for entry. The other three teams would have an easier time because they were killing anyone they came across, not leaving any live enemies at their backs. I looked down, noting the progress of the live enemies we'd left behind us, and felt all around our position. The other teams were doing well coming in. They would be here soon, but because of their success, the enemy was falling back towards the compound, pushing more closely to us on both sides. The enemy guard would be easier to take, though, because their leadership was gone; hence, all the running to and fro within the compound.

No one knew what they should be doing now their commanders were dead. I jumped down, landing harder than I did before, and it took me a second to catch myself this time.

I heard a 'Holy shit' off to my right and made my way over. The team was there in various defensive positions firing at targets that would pop around a tree or a boulder. It was harder for O'Hara's team because they had had enemies all around them. They had a core center with two wounded. One looked bad. The medic was working on him, trying to staunch the blood flow from a gut wound.

It was Ridgewood, Sergeant Howard Ridgewood. I recalled his file saying that he'd recently just had a new-born, with a wife and a three year old at home waiting for him. The other man down was Ensign Roger Peterson. He had two wounds, one in the right leg and the other in his shoulder. Neither was life threatening at the moment and he was lending his good hand to handing gauzes and other things to the medic as needed. I didn't have a gun, so I wouldn't be much help, unless the enemy came within my range of throwing knives. I made my way over to them, to see if I could help. The rest of the team was circled around these men. Ridgewood looked bad. Peterson's shoulder wound wasn't field dressed yet, so I grabbed the things needed for that out of the medics gear and went to work. The medic, Sergeant David Ashline, looked grim faced and eyed what I was doing. Then he grunted when he saw that I knew the basics of field dressing. Noticing the blood on my stomach, he said, "You're hurt. How bad?" nodding towards my stomach.

"Nothing I can't handle," I answered. I couldn't tell him about the astral wounds which was life threatening for me, but he wouldn't have been able to do anything about it anyway.

He nodded, "Field dress it when you're done with him," and focused back on Ridgewood. I was taping the white padded gauze to Peterson's shoulder wound when I saw another one of the men go down. It left a hole in the defense and I saw three guards heading our way. I looked at the medic asking, "Got a gun?" Peterson handed me his nine mil. "Here, go." I took off running and stood over the newly wounded soldier and fired the gun. I got two of the enemy, but wasn't fast enough for the third before he got a shot off at me. The bullet hit my shoulder, spinning me around. As I went down, I saw a fourth guard coming through the heavy tree line. Then suddenly he went down, along with the third I had only wounded. Sergeant

Miller and Corporal Thompson came in close the hole. I got back up, gun pointing towards the tree line.

Sergeant Miller's eyes widened, saying, "Hey, I got this. Fall back. Thompson will help you with Corporal Bannock."

"I got it. Thompson can stay here," and I lifted the wounded soldier up in a fireman carry-hold and took him back to the area for the wounded. I was sure I was leaving behind looks of shock. But this wasn't the time for playing human. This soldier's life was in the balance, and the faster we got him seen to, the more likely we could get him home alive.

I eased him next to Peterson and took a look at his wound. It was bleeding pretty badly. I put my hand over the wound and tried to 'lift' the bullet out of his chest. It didn't work. I packed it with gauze and put pressure on it to stem the flow while I thought of what I could do.

I looked at Peterson's leg and asked, "How bad is that one?"

He shook his head saying, "Nothing to really worry about, it's just a graze. It's the bullet in my shoulder that held me up, but you got it covered. Just take care of him, and your own shoulder," he nodded to the man lying next to us who was breathing hard from the pain.

I crawled over to his side and took the dressing that was on Peterson's leg.

Peterson asked, "Hey, what are you doing?"

"Hang a sec, I want to see something." I put my hand over the minor wound and gathered energy, pouring healing power into it. It started to heal over quickly. I stopped. Cool, I still had this. Healing worked on another level of psychic power then did levitation or telepathy. It used a slightly different frequency, if you will. One which I could still tap into. I noticed my stomach wound wasn't all that bad. My shoulder, once I got over the punch of the bullet, didn't do a continuous burn, letting me know I still had my natural healing abilities going on. If I can still heal my physical body quickly, then I can heal others, too. In fact it was easier to heal others than yourself. Much like a doctor trying to take care of himself, sure he could to it an extent, but he was much more effective treating others.

"What the..." Peterson started to say.

"Don't worry about it; just help me with this guy." I went back to him and grabbed a pair of forceps from the bag, ripping the sterilized wrap it was in.

"Hold him down." I started to dig for the bullet. Corporal Timothy Bannock, I noticed, as I took in his face, was now trying not to scream as I found the bullet and pulled it out. Then I put my hand over his chest and poured healing into it. The bleeding slowed down and the wound started to close.

Corporal Bannock groaned, "Ahh that feels hot, what are you doing?" then he shut up, looking amazed the wound was sealed and the pain, for the most part, was gone.

"You never saw me do this," I glared at both of them, then went to Ridgewood. The medic looked at me, his eyes wide in amazement.

I asked him, "Have you taken the bullet out?"

"Ah, yeah," then he shook his head as if to clear it. "The problem is, it nicked his liver. He's bleeding internally. I don't have the means to stop the bleeding from his liver."

Shit, when a liver is hit, they bleed and don't stop. He'll bleed out, filling his stomach and he'll die. There was no way we could help him here. He was a goner. It was only a matter of time. I could heal his liver easily. Livers regenerate even in a normal human pretty well on their own, once whatever damage to them is fixed. It was the blood already in the stomach that would give me a hard time. It would take a tremendous amount of energy to break up the blood that was filling him up. Plus, I would have to replace the blood that he lost. I had to do all of this quickly too, because he was running out of time. A brand new baby at home was waiting for him. Fuck it.

"Tell O'Hara I'm going to need a lot of what he did for me back in New York. He'll know what I'm talking about." I went to work. I laid both palms over Ridgewood's stomach and poured it on. I healed the liver fast, then stimulated his blood reproduction in minutes, which would have taken weeks normally. I used his own life force to aide in this. He'll be tired for a long while, but he'll live. I then went over the excess blood in his belly, willing it to flow out of the wound. When enough came out, I sealed the wound in his gut. When I felt the last inch close, black darkness swamped my vision and that was all I knew.

"Shit," the medic stated, as he saw her fall over Ridgewood. He pulled her off and laid her on her back. He went back to Ridgewood and swiped at his stomach wound that was now healed, with a new pink scar in its place. Ridgewood was coming around.

He checked his pupils."Hey, buddy. You're ok?"

"I feel like I haven't slept for days," he groaned.

"Any pain?" the medic asked

Ridgewood thought about it for a minute then shook his head, "Damn fine pain killers, Doc."

"It's not the pain killers," Doc said and went back to Cat. He checked her pulse and got nothing. "Shit." Then a weak pulse-beat came.

"Ok, come on. What did you do?" He waited for another pulse, which it was long in coming. This wasn't normal. Her skin was white and her breathing so shallow she should be dead. This was impossible.

He got on his Comm, "Rock, come in."

"Yeah," he sounded busy.

"Your girl is down. I think she's either dead or dying. She did some weird shit here." He didn't even know where to begin to explain to O'Hara.

"What did she do?" came the bark over the Comm.

"She healed two of our guys and with her hands, Rock. Nothing else, but her mother fucking hands, then collapsed. I think I'm losing her. Or we lost her. I can't tell. The pulse rate is one beat every 15 seconds. No one can live with that." Doc was trying to make sense of everything.

"Anything else?" O'Hara pressed for details.

"She said to tell you that she is going to need a lot of what you did for her back in New York. She said you would know what was she is talking about."

"Fuck," was all the answer he got for a minute. "We're still cleaning up here. Is there anyone there willing to donate blood?"

Peterson nodded his head. Bannock too said, "Yeah."

"Yes, I've got three men here. What's her blood type? I can get a transfusion going."

"No, not like that. Wizard is coming in. He'll explain," and he cut off the transmission.

Two minutes passed before Wizard came into the temporary medic station and rushed to her side. "Shit, this ain't good."

"You're a blood match with her?" Doc asked.

"We all do, in a way. Just watch, 'cause it will take more than me to get her through this." He removed her head wrap so he could get to her mouth. "Rock didn't want it on the airwaves, but if any of you guys in our group mention this outside of us, you will be in deep shit. This is top secret. Need to know only. Now watch." He lifted her head and put his wrist to her lips. "I offer my blood, warrior to warrior, from heart and soul. Of my own free will. So be it." And waited for the bite. It didn't come.

"Shit, her teeth aren't even dropping." Wizard was getting really concerned now.

"What?' Doc exclaimed.

"Cut my wrist. Just a small cut. Maybe she needs the blood flowing to get it going for her," trying to figure a way to get her teeth into his wrist.

"You're nuts," Doc said.

"No, I'm serious. Do it. Do it now," he ordered.

Doc, shaking his head, grabbed a clean scalpel and made a small incision. Blood seeped out and Wizard again put his wrist in her mouth.

Her teeth dropped and her mouth clamped down.

"Fuck, I've seen everything now," Doc looked on, still not quite believing what he was seeing.

Peterson asked, "What is she? She ain't normal, that's for sure."

"She is different." Wizard was gritting his teeth.

"She's a vamp isn't she?" Howard was engrossed in watching the feeding.

"Sort of," Wizard answered. He was feeling a tad dizzy now and he tried to pull his wrist out, but her mouth wouldn't let go. "Shit, help me, I can't get her loose."

Doc bent over and pried her mouth open and Wizard popped his wrist out. "Ok, next."

He looked around at the men in their group.

Peterson said, "Fuck it, she protected Bannock when he was down. Healed him, Ridgewood and even me. She can have it," and put his wrist near her mouth.

"First say the words or she might get in trouble. It has to be of free will," Wizard informed him.

He repeated the words which Peterson recited and then he placed his wrist in her mouth which automatically bit down and fed.

Doc checked her eyes. "Pupils aren't responding."

"Let's see after this feeding." Wizard was praying, but he didn't know if they were doing the right thing. Maybe there was more they should do, but what?

He scanned her body and saw the wounds. "Have you checked those?"

"Shit, no," and Doc went to work. He cleaned and field dressed them both.

"She'll need stitches for the cut in her stomach. We'll get her to the base to remove the bullet."

"No, we can't do that there. You take it out." Wizard was firm on that.

"It would be safer to do it back at the medical facility at the Afghan base," Doc argued.

"No, take it out here and now. I know what Rock will say," Wizard ordered.

Doc shook his head, "Ok." And he grabbed what he needed and started in on her shoulder. After he pulled the bullet out, he cleaned the wound again and patched it up.

O'Hara was on the air again. "We're pulling in."

Wizard breathed a sigh of relief. They must have gotten the area cleared enough and were making for the wall now, but first he'd see to the wounded.

Wizard was helping Peterson get loose from her mouth when the rest of the team came in.

"Comms off." Everyone complied. They were all protectively standing around those who were down, but watching what was going on with eyes wide at her extended teeth.

"What happened?" O'Hara asked.

"She was helping with the wounded when Howard got hit. Peterson gave her a gun and she stood over Bannock protecting him and us. She got hit. Those two filled the hole. She brought Bannock in. Then she did some weird shit, healing Ridgewood and Bannock," Doc filled him in.

Peterson spoke up, "She healed my leg, too."

"Ridgewood was the worst when she got to him. He had almost checked out. His liver was nicked and he had a bad wound in his gut. Once she healed it, she collapsed and now we're doing weird shit to fix her," Doc finished up.

Deep intakes of breaths all around. Everyone knew once your liver got hit, you didn't have much time left. Unless you could get to an operating table within 20 to 30 minutes, the reaper was coming. No stopping it. But she did.

Sergeant Miller added, "She picked up Bannock like it was nothing and brought him in here. What is she?"

"What she is, is top secret. No one outside this group will dare speak a word of this to anyone else including the Captain. If the Captain needs to know, General Pierce will let him know himself. Until then, you are all under orders not to repeat what you've seen here. Is that understood?" O'Hara warned them.

All around, 'yuuupps!' sounded off.

"Shit, she saved my ass. I won't betray her," this from Corporal Timothy Bannock.

"I won't either," Ridgewood was still down; exhausted, but well.

"Yes, she protected our wounded, and took a bullet for one of us. We'll keep quiet about this Captain, not to worry," Sergeant Miller assured him, his face serious.

O'Hara bent down and said the ritual words and gave her his wrist. When he gave as much as he could without tiring himself out, he pulled his wrist out.

"Doc, check her," he ordered.

"No, response. It's like she's in a coma. If she was normal, I'd say she was still dying, though her pulse is picking up a bit, but not enough. Not nearly enough at four beats every 15 seconds." Doc shook his head at Rock.

"What do we do Rock?" Wizard asked him.

"Did she get the data?" O'Hara asked him.

Wizard looked in the pouch. "Yup, she got it."

"Atta girl," O'Hara said. "She needs her own kind for aid. Where is Shamus? I thought he was to be here if she needed him?'

Wizard just shrugged, looking around.

"Who's Shamus?" Doc asked.

"You'd have to see him to believe it," O'Hara said. "Shamus," he called out aloud, looking all around him.

Nothing happened.

"She said he was hers. He only answered to her. Maybe he won't come unless she calls him," Wizard looked at O'Hara.

He nodded, "I bet you're right. He won't come unless she calls, and she can't do it now. We have to get her home. They'll know what to do for her better than us. But next time, I'm going to demand I have better Intel on helping her if she winds up like this again."

Babyface bent down, looking at her, "How'd she get this?" pointing to the bandage on her stomach.

Doc shook his head, "I don't know, she came in with that."

Babyface turned her head and saw blood in her ear and checked the other side with the same results. "She was near some kind of explosion, it looks like. You only get this kind of thing from the concussion of an explosion."

"That loud booming sound we heard earlier that sounded like it came from the compound? Maybe it fucked her up bad?" Romeo reminded them of the sound they'd heard earlier and wondered what the hell she was doing in there. But they'd been too busy themselves at the time, to come running.

O'Hara said, "We'll get her back home, but first we need to finish what we started." Looking around at the formally wounded, he said, "Who's good to go?"

Bannock and Peterson got up, slowly, but they got up.

Ridgewood groaned from trying to sit up, "Fuck, it feels like I haven't slept in months." He was trying to keep his eyes open.

"Peterson, since your arm is fucked for now, can you carry her?" O'Hara questioned him.

"Sure," he said simply.

"Good. Bannock and you," pointing to one of the other corporals, "Pick up Ridgewood and bring him along," O'Hara ordered, then turned to Sergeant Miller. "Get one of your men to make me a hole in that wall."

"You got it, Rock. Gus, make a hole." Sergeant Miller relayed the order to their bomb expert in his squad.

"We'll finish this, and then get her home. We'll keep feeding her every few hours and see if we can at least keep her going." O'Hara looked worried though. "We'll scramble a call stateside once it's safe, and let her mates know. Maybe they can send help."

CHAPTER FOURTEEN
Family Reinforcement

O'Hara had a hell of a time keeping her out of the medical facility once they got back to the base in Afghanistan. The base commander was not happy, but knew of his team's reputation. He knew O'Hara would not put anyone in his unit in danger unnecessarily, so he let it go with a note that it was against his own advisement. Bosses always knew how to cover their asses with paper from anyone over head. That tactic didn't change in the military. He scrambled a call to the base at the Navy Air Station while they were on route flying over international waters.

"Echo one to base one," O'Hara called into the SAT-phone.

"Base one to echo one. Go ahead," the base operator responded.

"Get General Pierce on the line ASAP. We have an emergency," O'Hara ordered.

"Stand by, Echo one." The line was quiet for a while.

Then the General's voice was on the line, "What happened, O'Hara?"

"Cat's down in what looks like a coma. We can't bring her around, even with doing what I did in New York," O'Hara filled him in the immediate part.

"Her mates have been going bug crazy. If it wasn't for the tracking device, they would have been out there themselves tracking her down. To hell with security, I'm bringing them up here and putting them on. I assume it looks bad for her?" General Pierce asked in a heavy voice.

"I think we are losing her, Sir," O'Hara answered honestly.

"Stand by." Silence again ensued. Then one of her mates was on, "O'Hara, it's Demitri. Tell me her condition."

"It looks like a coma; she has two wounds, one on her shoulder, and one in her stomach. She is feeding, but her pulse rate is 4 to 5 beats per every 15 seconds. Breathing shallow and no pupil response. Both of her ear drums look like they were busted from an explosive concussion," O'Hara finished up what he knew about the situation.

"We can't feel her. We would have thought we lost her, if it wasn't for that device in her arm. I'm sending help now," Demitri told him.

"How...?" O'Hara started to ask, "Fuck!" Shamus popped into the plane. They all saw it. Guns were pulled and aimed at this intrusion from what seemed out of thin air.

"Stand down. Stand down, it's a friendly. Hold your fire," O'Hara ordered loudly. Talking into the phone, "Great fucking job. We had this contained up until now."

"I'm sorry about that, but we don't have time to pussy-foot around. Right now, she's a priority. Nothing else matters," Demitri told him straight out. He didn't give a shit. He just wanted her healed and now. O'Hara could understand that, but it was still a FUBAR situation. And he'll have to clean it up.

"Fine. Echo one out," O'Hara slammed the set down.

"Do you mind telling me, Captain O'Hara, what the fuck is going on? Who is this ...person? How the fuck did he get on this plane?" Captain Holland was yelling questions at him.

"I don't have time for this. He's needed in the back STAT. The General will have a meeting about this; until then, it's top secret. Keep your mouth shut." Motioning for Shamus to follow him, "Your boy back at base sure fucked this up, sending you in like this. How did you even know where, exactly, we were?"

"I knew your signature from the first time we met. Once I got an order to zone in on you, it's a simple matter from there. No one could feel her at home. We had no way of knowing what was going on, and we didn't want to step into anything without a go ahead."

"So, Demitri can order you?" O'Hara asked curious.

"Yes, he can, because Cat gave him that power over me. When she was cursed, it was necessary. She couldn't hear me or see me anymore. It was a dark time for all of us," Shamus told him.

"Cursed?" sounding really curious now.

"Ancient history. Don't bring it up with her. It still gives her nightmares," Shamus shut down the questioning. They reached the back of the plane, where O'Hara pulled back the drapes where they had the wounded laid in their stretchers strapped in for safety. Cat was as alone as they could make her.

"Sweet Mother Goddess." Shamus exclaimed, rushing over to her, laying his hands over her body. "She is shredded. Worse. She is off-kilter inside as well. Like something blew her apart from the inside out. All of her spirit levels are compromised, out of balance," Shamus was saying out loud, but O'Hara didn't think he was talking to him. He asked anyways, "Spirit levels? I thought we only had one soul."

"You have seven actually. So does she. Spirit and soul are two different things. The Egyptians call it The Ka, The Ba, and so on. Read the list of books she gave you. It's all there. Each level controls certain things in a person's life. All of hers are off kilter. They should be aligned and in sync. Hers aren't anymore. It's one of the reasons she isn't healing. Her power level is bottomed out. What was she doing right before this happened?" Shamus demanded.

O'Hara gave him the whole run down of the healing she did on the men.

"Ah, that explains some of it. She gave everything she had. With the damage already done to her spirit, she had no way of keeping any energy for herself to keep going. She is quite literally bleeding out on a spiritual level. Even her chakras are perforated," his tone sounded sad.

"Chakras?" O'Hara had to ask.

"Orbs of energy in a person's body. There are seven main ones. Each has a different color and they have their own specific duties. Over three hundred smaller ones. Again, read your books," he was getting grouchy now.

O'Hara decided to back off that line of questioning. "What can we do? We've given her blood, but it doesn't seem to be working."

"It won't either, not until we heal this damage. You might as well try to hold a pile of water in your hand for all the good it would do. But what tiny bit is making it into her system is keeping her alive. So thank you for that," Shamus nodded at him. "Now I have to call for more help. I don't have a choice."

O'Hara sighed heavily, "Go ahead."

Shamus called out, "Danny, you're needed."

A small orb popped into the air, then solidified into what look like an honest to god fairy. O'Hara couldn't believe it. He watched as the fairy zoomed over to where she was laying. O'Hara could see small tears trailing down the little fairy's face. He was only about four inches tall with brightly colored wings that were moving fast. It looked male and he was wearing a small green colored outfit that didn't interfere with his flying. He even had a small sword hanging from his waist. He had blond hair and bright blue eyes; he looked like a ten year old but, for the eyes. His eyes were filled with knowledge that only comes from living a long, long time.

One of the wounded men asked, "Umm Rock, tell me I am seeing this?"

"You're seeing this. Top secret, not to be repeated to anyone." O'Hara gave him a serious look.

"OK, good, 'cause I thought the morphine Doc gave me was making me hallucinate." He did look relieved to be validated on what he was seeing though. O'Hara shook his head.

"What happened to the Princess, Shamus?" the fairy asked in a small tinkling voice.

"I don't know what caused the initial wound to her soul, but she drained herself afterwards by healing others."

"The Princess gives too much again, Shamus," he nodded sagely.

"She has an irritating habit of doing that. I wish she would learn to harden her heart more," he said gruffly.

Danny shook his head, "She wouldn't be our Princess if she did that, old friend."

"You're right," Shamus agreed, "Can you sprinkle some fairy dust on her aura and inner selves?"

"Happily." He went to work. The air was soon filled with brightly colored flakes floating down all over and around her. O'Hara touched some, and it tingled when it met with his skin.

"Leave it alone. Her aura needs it and her aura spreads out widely around her body," Shamus was growling now.

O'Hara felt that Shamus had resisted the urge to slap his hand like disciplining a child. His eyes tightened over the slight insult.

A little pop interrupted his response to it. Then an even smaller fairy came into being.

"Why not you calls, The Trixie? Mean Shamus." She gasped, holding her tiny hand to her mouth. "Oh, poor, poor Princess. What's happened to hers? The Trixie will pix thems, she will. Trixie pixes them goods." She flew over, stopping in front of O'Hara's face. "Who's the ones responsible fors this? The Trixie demands to know," she looked so infuriated, but he wanted to smile.

She was so tiny in her anger, it was funny.

"Don't take a pixie's anger lightly there, Captain. She can do things that can leave you wishing for death. Trixie, come away from the Captain. He didn't do anything. If you insist on being here, spread dust on her to heal her inner wounds so we can stop the astral bleeding," Shamus ordered her.

"The Trixie can dos that. The Trixie is goods healer, too. She saved The Trixie, she dids. Gave a homes to The Trixie, she dids. The Trixie will helps the Princess." Just as quick, she was adding her own pixie dust to the efforts of the male fairy. They looked like they had worked together before because they didn't fuss about who did what. They just complemented one another's work.

"How come she is smaller than the other fairy? Is she a young one?" O'Hara couldn't stop watching them, finding it fascinating to see this happen before his eyes. She was only half the other fairy's height and had black hair and brown eyes; a small dagger was also in her belt around her tiny waist.

"Again, read the books. She is not a fairy, but a pixie. Two different beings. If she catches you calling her a fairy, she'll pix you," Shamus warned him.

"Noted, but there hasn't been a lot of time to study yet, so don't growl at me about it." O'Hara wasn't going to let the last one slide. Wizard or no Wizard.

"My pardon. I am upset over her condition," bowing his head at him again.

Contrite, O'Hara asked, "I understand. Is she going to be all right?"

Shamus turned grave eyes to him, "I honestly don't know."

O'Hara didn't like the sound of that, "Can't her mates come here to help?"

"They are conserving their energy for hands-on healing. The rest of the Coven will be there as well," Shamus answered him sadly.

"Will it make a difference?" his gravel voice gruff.

"I hope so," Shamus answered quietly.

O'Hara noticed it was Andre who was in the ambulance that came out to the plane and loaded her up. As soon as she was put into the bed of the ambulance, Andre stuck his wrist in her mouth after reciting his ritual words to her. O'Hara, Doc, and Shamus had also joined the ride. Doc knew he couldn't do much but monitor her heart rate and other vitals; he mostly did it because *the way* they were trying to heal her was fascinating to him. When Andre had put his wrist to her mouth, her pulse rate jumped up more encouragingly. Shamus had told him earlier to put an IV in her; that it would help to keep her body hydrated. But it was the glowing hands and sprinkling dust that were really interesting to see.

"Giving her my neck wouldn't be a good idea in a moving vehicle," he said to Shamus.

Shamus snorted, "Wouldn't do any good anyhow. She can't soul feed; look at her solar plex chakra."

Andre looked at her stomach area and hissed. He bent down to her ear and started whispering words of encouragement in a loving tone, "Come on, baby. You can make it. You have to. We're here now, you can't go." Over and over he kept it up until they got to the wing of a building that would get them into the hospital.

O'Hara nodded his head to Shamus, "Solar-plex chakra?"

169

Shamus sighed, "Here is your solar-plex chakra," (right about where the liver would be), O'Hara noticed. "It's perforated with holes and the bonds going to her solar-plex chakra are compromised as well. That's why shooting energy down the bonds between them," Shamus pointed to Cat and Andre, "or between her and I, wouldn't do anything but bounce right back. She is getting nothing. Her bonds can't intake right now."

O'Hara started to ask another question, before Shamus cut him off. "Read the books. Or ask Simon; he doesn't mind teaching. I am not built that way."

They climbed out of the ambulance, "Simon?" O'Hara was moving with the whole group.

"Yes, she has six other wizards in her compliment. Simon is one of them. You'll have to ask for permission first, though," Shamus said in a rush. And then they were inside. His eyes were wide at the waiting horde that was there for Cat, some of them children. They made an aisle for them to push the gurney she was now on down the hall and into the wing that was reserved for their family. Demitri had requested a whole wing just for their use from now on. With the downsizing of personnel on the base, it was easy to accommodate the request. There was still room galore for the rest of the base hospital that would never be used.

General Pierce was standing by the nurse's station that was in the middle of the widened hall. Two other wings branched off from this station. Cat was in one of them and in her own room. He noticed when the main monitor at the nurse's station started beeping, slowly. The other wounded, were taken off to the left wing to be settled and seen by base doctors, evaluated, and then given treatment for whatever they needed. Cat's people went down the right wing, some carrying chairs to place in the hallways to wait. A few went into the room where they'd put her and didn't come out for long periods of time. When one did come out, they were weak looking and pale. They were led to other rooms and placed in there to rest and another person would walk into Cat's room to take his/her place. He also noticed that all of the adults and even a few of the young adults were armed to the teeth.

Captain O'Hara was closely watching what was going on down that hall, but that wasn't the only reason he was there. He was there for all the wounded. Like the General, he would stay until each man was settled and had what he needed. They both would make trips down the left wing and ask after the men. They would see if they had any nearby relatives that they would want with them and if they needed anything else. It's what a good leader did for his men. It was something he learned to do under General Pierce's guidance many years ago. After things were settled here, he would go to the bunk at their headquarters and see to the rest of the men. Usually, he gave them leave after the debriefing was over. but this time after the main "official" debriefing, there would be another covert meeting. He and the General would disclose chosen truths about their new Merc brothers and sisters. Then he would have them sign papers so they would be liable under law not to disclose anything they learned at that meeting. If they did, they would be a guest at Ft. Leavenworth for the rest of their lives, in solitary.

"Quite the crowd, hey, O'Hara?" General Pierce nodded his head toward the right wing.

"What's the count and the info you have?" O'Hara needed the Intel. He wasn't going out blind again on anyone in his unit, Merc or not. The more he knew, the more he could have done.

"I had a hell of a time getting this whole group through clearance. Only a handful had the badges and passes needed. The head of security is still having fits. Major Stewart is working him over and trying to get those passes cleared ASAP for those who don't have them yet. The children were the hardest to get past, but they wouldn't leave them outside with an adult to watch over them. So I got them through. Two sisters, each have three mates. One brother also has three mates. Several children and three of them are Cat's."

O'Hara's eyes widen at that. "Which ones?"

"See that big, light-brown haired one, the one with the Bo? That's her youngest at sixteen, Craven." He nodded to Craven who was standing next to another man with blond hair and piercing blue eyes and who was armed to the teeth with more guns and knives than O'Hara could count.

"The blond one?" O'Hara nodded to the one standing next to Craven as if guarding the entrance to the wing.

"Her brother, Grant. He is now a Corpus Christi detective. You should see his record. When not in hot water for excessive force, which he manages to wriggle out of every time, he's bringing in the worst of the worst. He's had more arrests then five men put together in the department while he was in Houston. He has already made three arrests of some real scum suckers since he's been here," General Pierce sounded impressed.

"A real go-getter, huh?" O'Hara remarked.

"It's why the police department puts up with his ways. He gets results. Won't take a partner though. Always works alone." General Pierce provided this tidbit.

He thought about that, "Will that make him hard to work with on a team going out with us?"

"Word is, he is close with Cat. They've worked together before. No problems. She could keep him in line, if it came to that," the General sounded sure of this, so he took it that way. "Good to know."

The General continued the run-down on Cat's children. "That one there, the dark brown haired boy with a sword—that's Crimson. He's eighteen. Watch how he moves."

O'Hara watched the boy moving back and forth like a caged animal. He never stopped. His footsteps light and smooth. He would bet this kid could move like lightening. He would place bets her youngest, Craven, could move through a brick wall, too, if he wanted to.

"Moves like a panther, that one," O'Hara said to General Pierce.

"Yeah, I thought you'd see it. He and his younger brother have some serious potential. I don't know their personalities yet. If you find out before I do let me know," General Pierce told him.

He nodded, "Will do. Where's the other one? You said three were hers." O'Hara was real curious now to see her eldest.

"A blond one with blue eyes, real long hair for a male, though." The General was too used to men being short haired due to the military influence. "But you can tell he's got moves, too. Two swords on his hips, but he isn't out here. He's inside with his mother. All I know is he is twenty and protective of his mother. His name is Christoph. Wouldn't give up his weapons. None of them would. I had a hell of time over that clause, too. The adults were difficult, but getting her kids, who are armed, onto the base, took some serious threats," General Pierce grunted.

"Three boys with serious potential and three mates who look like they can get serious is good to know," O'Hara reflected.

"That's why I'm filling you in. Good job by the way. Your whole team did real well. We've got the information data and I sent it up the food chain. Your team has their number one status back. I told them you needed to find the right tool to pull off a mission you knew wouldn't be able to be done otherwise. You found that tool, used it and that's why you succeeded this time. They are now singing your praises again." The General slapped him on the back.

"She was the one who got the data," he protested.

The General got his no-nonsense look back in his eyes. "You're the one who made it work with her. You didn't have to do that. You're the one that held off the remaining enemies from behind, so she could have time to get the data. You were also the one who called in the diversion so she could finish her work, but I didn't put it that way in the official report. Too bad we can't give her and hers the credit they deserve. But, also it was your team that neutralized the nuke. So take your just due. Yes, she did a phenomenal job, but that's because she had you to partner her. You both did a damn fine job!"

"True, we all did well. Damn fine team that went out with me. I liked that Sergeant Miller. Not only did he take out several guards, but he stood behind Cat when she needed it. A very loyal man, once you get his respect. Damn fine fighter. Good head on his shoulders," O'Hara told him.

"I'll make note of it in his file," the General said. "Any trouble?" He was asking if O'Hara had any lip from any of the men on that squad.

O'Hara shook his head. "No sir, a very cohesive squad. Followed orders well. They kicked some major ass out there. I won't mind working with that squad again."

A Special Forces team usually consisted of 8 to 9 men with a leader of high enough rank at the head. O'Hara never could find anyone else that fit in with his group on a permanent basis, for one reason or another, other than the three he had now. So he would have to borrow from marine squads to make up the man power he needed on most of his missions, or other Special Forces men would fill in for that mission only.

General Pierce tilted his chin down the hall where one of Cat's sisters was coming towards them. "Look, O'Hara. Seems like she is coming to us."

O'Hara turned to see a small, black-haired woman walking down the hall towards them, smoothly side-stepping around children playing in the hall. She moved like a dancer or a dagger in the night with all the weapons on her body. Her long black hair was braided, too. Something he noticed Cat did when she was getting ready for a fight. He couldn't tell if it was going to be good news or bad news from the expression on her face. Her face was unreadable; O'Hara made a note to himself never to play poker with her.

As she passed Craven, she gave his shoulder a gentle squeeze. "How's my mom?" Crimson glided over as well, but he didn't say anything, just held her eyes in a steady stare.

She looked at them and said, "We're doing everything we can. Your mom's a fighter." She didn't bullshit them. Just told them straight. They both heard what she wasn't saying. It was looking bad in there. O'Hara and General Pierce could tell from their eyes that the news was tearing them up bad, but their faces just hardened in determination. Both were ready to fight The Reaper himself if it came to that. O'Hara approved of the boys' stoicism. Their aunt gave them each another gentle squeeze on their shoulders and looked back down the hall to one of the women sitting there. A small blond woman got up and moved towards them, ready to offer motherly help if the boys needed it. Crimson went back to pacing, back and forth, ignoring the comfort offered. His steps were a bit more agitated then before. Craven leaned up against the wall and allowed the blond woman to place a hand on his shoulder and leave it there. Solidarity was obvious in this family.

The black-haired woman continued towards where O'Hara and the General were standing next to the nurse's station. At the same time, the men that Cat had helped, came into the main wing and walked to them as well. Ridgewood was placed in the left wing or O'Hara knew he would be there, too. Sergeant Miller was among these two men. The black-haired woman reached them first.

"You heard?" she nodded at them.

"Yes. Is there anything else we can do? Any medications that might work?" the General asked.

"No," shaking her head, "medication would most likely kill her right now, but we do need a few things, if you'd be so kind? I know we've made things difficult for you in getting us through and we do appreciate it, General Pierce." She talked in a quiet, but precise voice. With her Oriental cast, she was a very beautiful woman. Beautiful and deadly. O'Hara looked at her knives in her vest.

"I will do the best I can. It's Cassie, right?" The General didn't promise, because he didn't know what, exactly, she would request.

"Thank you. And, yes, it's Cassie Wong or Chameleon when out in the field," she nodded to the General. "Our two other brothers, their mates and children are coming down to Corpus Christi. They will need passes when they get here."

"I can arrange that when they arrive," the General agreed.

"We also need to convert the big room at the back of the wing in there into a play area for the smaller children. We can outfit it with TV and games for them to play, if that is all right?" she asked him.

This idea pleased the General, who could see the nurse getting irritated at the noise the young ones were making now. "That would be a good thing for the kids."

She turned and nodded her head to one of the males waiting in the hall. He did an abrupt about face and went to work on the proposal. These people got things done with no time wasted, O'Hara thought to himself. He approved.

Sergeant Miller and the two men had made it to the station, but waited politely for the conversation to be finished.

"Is there a cafeteria in this hospital?" she continued her list.

174

"Yes, there is. Down that hall and take a left. There's an elevator, take it down to sub-basement 2, turn right and it's there," O'Hara filled her in on the directions.

She nodded, "Good. Some of the children are vegetarian, so it will do for them, but does the cafeteria have any red meat that can be barely cooked here?"

O'Hara shook his head, "No, I am afraid not."

She asked, "Then can we order in food for those of us who need very rare meat? The pregnant wives, especially, have need of red meat often."

The nurse, who had been eavesdropping on the conversation, looked about to add her two cents on pregnant women and red meat. The General gave her a hard glare. She sat back down, trying to look like she was minding her own business.

The General spoke up for this question as O'Hara turned to him, "Yes, I'll leave word at the gates. If Detective Windham, who has a badge and a pass, could be sent for pick up, it will be easier for me to arrange."

She acknowledged the request, "It can be done." She looked sideways at the nurse, as if trying to figure a way to ask this next request without it being overheard by those who shouldn't know. The General, seeing her dilemma, helped her out.

"Nurse, why don't you go do rounds or something and leave us for a few minutes." At that moment, a doctor had made his way to the station and lent down over the desk, filling out forms and glanced at the monitors. He stopped what he was doing.

"Nurse, why isn't this patient on code blue?" he demanded.

"That one is in the east wing; it's off-limits now to medical personal. I have no authority in there," she informed him, sounding put out from this fact.

"General, may I ask what the hell is going on? That patient obviously needs some serious medical care. The blood pressure is way too low and the pulse rate is in the danger zone. There isn't anyone I can see in that hall who should be there...."

The General cut off his tirade, "I appreciate your concern, but anyone in that wing is to be left strictly alone. They have their own physicians who will tend to their own wounded."

"Why wasn't this cleared with me? I am in charge of this section when there are wounded stationed in here." The doctor was outraged, General or no.

"I cleared it with the Administration just yesterday morning. If you haven't been notified of it, that is not my problem. Meanwhile, Major Burns, you will stay out of that wing no matter what happens in there, is that clear?" The General was now going toe to toe with Doctor Major Burns.

Major Burns looked at the monitor again, "This isn't right. That patient is going to die if something isn't done now. It may already be too late..." He got cut off by Cassie's hiss of anger.

Man, this lady can get pissed fast, O'Hara thought.

"Watch what you say about my sister. Those two boys are her children. They don't need to hear your tone of doom. You will not be allowed near my sister. You will stay away from all of us." Her hands were slowly going towards her knives.

Doctor Major Burns looked closely for the first time at those in front of the hall, and those sitting within it. He noticed that they were all armed and not regular military.

"These people are not military. What are they doing in my hospital in the first place? Don't tell me they're mercenaries?" he sounded disgusted and fearful at the same time.

"Fine, I won't tell you they're mercenaries," the General answered, "but you will stay out of that wing from now on, period."

"I won't stand for this, not in my hospital. Not only are you stopping me from doing my job, but you brought a bunch of swords for hire in my hospital, bleeding and God knows what else. With weapons to boot!" and with that statement, Cassie snapped her fingers.

Instantly, the mouth of the hall was covered. Even Cat's sons held their weapons at the ready. Every male and a few females were taking a two barrier stand in front of the hallway waiting for the next signal. The smaller children were being hustled into the far back room they had requested by the pregnant females. It would be a blood bath. But O'Hara and the marines who came in to visit all turned their backs to them and stood ready to stand between the doctor and whatever else he brought. The rest of the family saw this and in that moment they knew they were one team. The rest of O'Hara's team came in from the front. Most likely coming to visit and see what they could do, when they stopped and took in the scene. They looked at O'Hara who nodded back in a sign to stand in the back of him and they moved. They too, stood with the family, figuring out what was going on by the tension alone.

The doctor didn't know what do. "I could get the MPs and the hospital administrator. You have no right coming in here or stopping me from my job. I'll get the MPs and bust into that room and try to help that sword for hire when I get there," not backing down, "then I will throw them all out and have you written up for putting the security of this hospital, this base, in jeopardy. Now, I want to know what's going on in there."

"You will be the first to die if you do," Cassie growled. Now she had an emotion, and it was scary.

The General barked a laughed at the doctor, "I'd like to see you try it, but for the mess I would have to clean up; plus getting good men hurt for your ego and your curiosity." He stepped close to the Major. "Now, go call the Administrator and find out what you obviously missed earlier today." As the doctor reached for the phone, he said, "No, not here. From your office. I'll be making a phone call to him myself." he barked, "O'Hara!"

"Yes, sir?" he clipped out.

"Why don't you and your men escort the good doctor out of this section?" he ordered.

"Yes, Sir. Men form up." They walked over to the doctor. Romeo took one side and Wizard the other. All four of them made him move down the hall leading out of the section of the hospital with the doctor sputtering all the way.

The General picked up the phone and hit the numbers for the hospital Administrator. "Hello, John? We've had a bit of a problem with one of your doctors here." He paused to listen. "A Major Burns." He proceeded to have the Major removed from the section, with orders to stay away from here, on out. Another doctor would be coming, that would follow orders better and keep his mouth shut. Cassie eased when she heard the orders being passed and flattened her hand in a step down motion.

Everybody in the hall relaxed. The General kept his relief to himself. Cat had warned him things could trigger these folks into a real bad mood in a second. She obviously wasn't kidding.

He ended his phone call and looked at the nurse. "Would you like to be reassigned as well?"

"No, Sir, I am leaving now," and she fled to the left wing.

Cassie turned to look at the marines who stood with them and asked, "Are these the ones Cat helped?"

"One of them, yes. This is their squad leader, Sergeant Miller," General Pierce introduced them.

"Good men. O'Hara's teams too. Cat said they were honorable." Cassie gave a small smile and offered, "We can help with the other wounded if you'd like. They will heal faster if you allow us to do this."

"That would be most welcomed, seeing as how Corporal Howard is up with no down time needed. If you could do it without taking from what Cat will need, it would be an honor." He remembered part of the ritual words of accepting a gift and thought it would be fitting here.

She smiled and bowed her head. "We would never take from Cat. We have many talented healers. And Craven needs the practice as well." She

177

nodded to one of Cat's sons. "We, however, may need blood until our other family gets here to help replenish."

"We'll find willing donors for you," the General promised.

"I'll give again. I don't mind," Corporal Howard said.

Cassie shook her head, "No," looking at his wrist and seeing the bite marks, "you have already given and need time to regenerate your blood cells. You shouldn't donate again for at least four days." She raised her gaze from his wrist to his eyes. "Thank you for the further offer. It speaks well of you." Corporal Howard actually blushed.

"Not to worry, there are plenty more to ask for donations. It won't be a problem to fill what you all need in there," the General assured her.

"Thank you, General Pierce," and she turned and walked back down the hall.

CHAPTER FIFTEEN
Bonds of Tempered Steel

Over the next two days, Cassie had become the new liaison between her family and the General and his men, often spending time with them at the nurse's station or cafeteria. She filled them in on the family antidotes of each family member there, when not helping with the healing for Cat. The family had, one by one, healed his men who were wounded, and they left the facility totally fit and ready for the next mission in record time. The new doctor was wise enough to look the other way when he would come in to check on a soldier and the soldier would be sitting in his bed requesting to be released early. The doctor just filled out the forms, showed them to the General, who would nod his head, and file it away. Doctor Major Burns wasn't heard from again, having been transferred to another base. In the Arctic.

The official and unofficial debriefing took place the day after the fiasco with Doctor Burns, in hopes of stemming any other incidents with these volatile people. Captain Holland wouldn't believe it until Cat's mates and other family members came in and proved to him beyond even his ability to be skeptical. They almost had another 'incident' when Captain Holland stormed out of the room saying under his breath, "Knew she cheated somehow. Goddamn blood sucking sell-sword," to which Andre snarled and started going after the Captain, with death in his eyes. It took both his brothers and other family to hold him down and calm him. O'Hara guessed Captain Holland missed the part of the meeting that brought up the exceptional hearing these people had. At least the meeting cleared some things up for him.

Not all of the family was vamped out. Only Cat and her mates were, but the rest of the family did need red meat, very rare, because they burned so many calories very fast, when using their powers. They metabolized faster than a regular human, apparently. The General and O'Hara could tell the family was learning to trust and relax at the base more than before, by the fact they wore fewer weapons and would take their children home to bathe and sleep, not returning until later that day.

There was still a guard for Cat and her mates, who were wearing themselves out healing her and not leaving her side except when absolutely necessary. They were all looking pale and worn out, when O'Hara would see them eating in the cafeteria. None of the three talked to others much, nor to the other family members. They would eat, pick up their stuff and return right back to the room. General Pierce and O'Hara would look at the monitor at the nurse's station and see slow progress every six to eight hours. It was like she was fighting for every inch of life, making slow but sure progress. Her family looked like they were fighting right along with her. It was nerve-racking for everyone.

Every now and again, O'Hara and his team would see an orb of light bouncing down the hallway of the right wing. It would zip out of Cat's door and zoom down the hallway. The family members would give a smile and some would shout 'all right,' and Cat's monitor would pick up a beat or more. Then the orb would zip back into the room. The Doctor and the nurses learned to ignore and go blind when these things happened. They learned to ignore the scent of sage being burned, when lighting anything flammable was against hospital regulations. They didn't want to be transferred as well.

General Pierce, O'Hara and his men were sitting in chairs next to the wall, watching down the hall for any news, when a tall dark haired man in a business suit walked towards the nurse's station with Major Stewart guiding him. Cassie had come out of Cat's room running towards the nurse's station, trying to beat the man there. Everyone who was in the hall stopped what they were doing and waited. How they could see this guy coming before he reached the station, took O'Hara off guard, until he remembered what Cat had said about the energy pulses of people.

They all must have felt this guy coming. He had black hair and had a strong Italian cast to him, but for the blue of his eyes, which were startling. He had a cold, hard look with a gaze that took in everything around him at one time. O'Hara would bet he had weapons stashed on him somewhere, as there was a slightly suspicious bulge under his Armani suit jacket. The tailoring must have been good to make O'Hara have to search for it so hard, but it was there.

Cassie had made it to the station before the man did and he stopped and nodded a greeting at her which she returned with a quiet, "Hello, brother."

"Sister. Progress?" was all he asked.

"Some, yes. She is stabilizing," Cassie answered.

"Good." He turned to look at the General and his men watching the exchange. He nodded his head to them, but didn't greet them in any other way. He just turned and walked down the hallway towards Cat's room.

Cassie, for the first time, seemed to not know what to do.

She opted to smooth things over with the General and his men." That is our youngest brother. His main concern is for Cat's health right now. I am sure he will greet you more formerly later. And you'll meet Gaston as well. He is at their new home with Gerard's wives and their three babies. They are too young for anything like this and Gaston has many, many children and even a great grandchild now. Gerard and Cat are very close, since they both share the same biological father. That is more than the rest of us do. It makes the blood ties stronger between the two, as do the family heritage protocols."

General Pierce looked confused, as did the rest of the men. "I thought you were all related?"

"We are, but we don't have the same physical mother or father as those two do," she answered.

O'Hara asked the next one. "How is that possible, for you all to be related then?"

Cassie frowned at him, saying, "You haven't read the books yet have you?" She shook her head, "Never mind. We, you, and everyone are born on the spiritual astral plane first; some are born right away onto the physical plane, while others are not. Everyone born on the spiritual plane is, sooner or later, born again on the physical plane. If you recall your John in the Christian Bible, it says, "'That which is born of the flesh is flesh; and that which is born of spirit is spirit' This was learned from the Egyptian Book of the Dead and is true. To enter into any of the higher astral planes or heavenly bodies, you must be born first of spirit on the spiritual plane, *then* of flesh here on *this* plane. Some Christians just twisted this for the reborn again dogma they got wrong," curling her lip. She further explained, "We six are all born to the same mother and father astral being, but were placed into different physical mothers and seeded by different physical fathers; except those two. Cat and Gerard have the same physical father. It wasn't supposed to happen. But then again, all things happen for a reason, we are taught," she shrugged her shoulders at a loss to explain the difference.

"So you all have the same parents on the astral plane, but different parents on this physical plane, right?" Romeo asked for clarification.

Cassie nodded yes. Then her face changed and her eyes got wide. "I have to go. Gerard is calling for a power circle. There are enough of us here now to do it." And she went back down the hall at a fast pace. The hallway cleared of children and adults. Most went into the room that Cat was in, with only a few to watch the children in the back room. Otherwise, the hallway was cleared for the first time in days.

Romeo joked, "Fifty says they blow the place apart." The tension was broken with bets being placed on whether the family would blow the place apart or heal Cat.

The General just shook his head and refused the betting with a small smile.

Wizard took O'Hara aside and said, "Do you know who that was?"

"Who, besides being Cat's youngest brother?" O'Hara dreaded the answer.

"Only the son of one of the most powerful Mafia Dons, who controls the West coast. The son of Leon Gianinni, Gerard Gianinni," Wizard added with wide eyes.

O'Hara groaned. That family was notorious for being the hardest crime family to pin a crime on. Also, for being the most lethal and ruthless family in America, next to those of the New York crime families.

"And this is Cat's father, too," O'Hara was floored.

"I never heard of a daughter until now. If she is, it is the best kept secret. I have a friend in the FBI. He makes a hobby of knowing everything there is about Mafia families. The only thing I've heard from him about this particular family is the son wouldn't go under the tutelage of the father for taking the mantel of Don when the old man was ready to step down. Fifteen years ago, he was a mere boy then, maybe 16 or 17, and they had a falling out. The old man was furious. It wasn't until about a year ago, they had made peace with each other. But the son still refuses to take over the family business."

O'Hara whistled long through his teeth. "That kid has balls. Huge ones. Why did he refuse? Isn't it a natural thing for families like that?"

Wizard shrugged his shoulders, "I don't know, maybe my friend does. Want me to dig into it?"

O'Hara said, "Oh yeah, but don't dig so deep we compromise them."

Wizard just looked at him. "Go teach your grandma to suck eggs, Rock." Wizard left to find a computer and a phone.

The General watched him walk back to the remaining group and asked, "Anything I need to know?"

O'Hara nodded and filled them all in.

The General's face paled a bit. Then he shook his head, "Well, from the frying pan into the fire. What is the difference, I have always asked." He looked back at O'Hara." We'll deal with it. But let's try to keep this inner circle only. No need for the rest of the platoon to know this."

They all agreed with that.

The scent of sage grew stronger as they went back to watching the right wing. O'Hara was glad the General was able to get control of this section of the hospital; the right wing for his Mercs and the left wing for his military soldiers. If he hadn't, he was sure they would be having kittens at the burning of candles and sage, as well as the chanting that was going on now. They all watched, as a bluish white light shone from under the door, growing stronger by the minute.

The floor started to shake a bit and Romeo said, "Hot damn, lap dances for me tonight." Then the light was gone and the shaking stopped.

"Shit," Romeo said. "They didn't do it." O'Hara walked over to the nurse's stations monitor and saw a significant difference in the readings there. Then people started filing out of the room, looking drained, but smiling. Cassie came down the hall to them with a small smile on her now tired face.

When she reached them, she said, "She'll be fine. She'll sleep for a while, but she'll be fine."

"That is good news. Thank you, Cassie." The General looked very pleased. O'Hara felt lighter himself. No one wanted to lose a soldier he had fought with.

Even Babyface cracked a smile and Romeo said, "OK, that's worth losing the lap dances."

Cassie turned a confused look at Romeo. O'Hara said. "You don't want to know," and grinned. She grinned back.

"The family would like to invite you to a party we are having at our new club house when Cat is on her feet. We want to celebrate her coming home and those who were with her. You are all welcome, as is the rest of the platoon."

O'Hara knew this for what it was, and was gratified the family was including him and his men with the celebrations. "We would be honored to come. I'll ask the others when I see them. Where is the new place?"

"Just down the road on S. Padre Island Drive - about five miles." She handed him a slip of paper with the address on it. "We came up with the idea before this mission. We thought it would be good to have a place to relax, have drinks and dancing. There will be food there as well. The Club house idea was thought out by all of us, and we knew you and your men should be with us to have fun when we are not out in the field. We thought this a perfect idea to have an exclusive club for those of us who fight together have a place to relax together. It shouldn't be all about the fighting."

"You thought to include us even before the first mission?" asked O'Hara

Cassie's eye grew wide, "Why, of course. We are all a team now. With a place to have fun together, we will learn to be family," she smiled and walked away.

The General had a suspicious gleam in his eyes and O'Hara felt touched by this.

"Wow, a place to play and relax. I wonder if they'll have dancing girls there?" Romeo said.

Babyface groaned, "Man, don't you ever think about anything else, but your dick?"

"No, why should I?" came the flippant response.

Later that same day, Cassie sent a memo to the General's office requesting that the men learn the rules of the club house, which will be strictly enforced.

1. NO touching of another's mate. Male or female.

2. No driving back to the base drunk. Someone from the club, not inebriated, will drive the soldier back to the base to be turned over to one of the platoon's squad leaders to avoid the MPs drunk tank.

3. Any differences are to be taken to the pit. NO weapons allowed in the pit. The winner buy's the beer for the two of them after the strong discussion is over.

4. All from General Pierce on down to Alpha 53rd Recon is a member. No others from the military base are allowed. (In order that our family can be themselves.)

5. What happens in the club, stays in the club.

6. If any rules are breached, the offender will be put in the time out room until a squad leader or superior officer can come get said offender. No charges will be made.

7. At the first party only, the night is free for all. Afterwards, food and drink will be charged at club prices, including for family members.

The General breathed a sigh of relief. This should keep the local police and the base MPs off his soldiers. The fewer incidences, the easier it will be to keep a lid on his new team. It looked like the family had thought of everything to help keep his men from being picked up and having marks on their records. Too many marks can ruin a soldier's career. He was happy to see the family taking care to watch over the Special Forces team and platoon soldiers, who could play rough sometimes. He okayed the memo and had Major Stewart make copies to be given out to the men before the party.

The Major asked, "Sir, are you going?"

"Yes, I will the first night, I think. You should go, too. Tell O'Hara that on any other night, if anyone steps out of line, to land on them like a ton of bricks. They're going out of their way to make a place for our men. I don't want them to have a hassle over it."

"Yes, Sir. I'll see to it."

Damn nice idea, the General said to himself.

Three days later, Cat finally woke up. O'Hara could tell, when everyone shouted in the hall, 'She's up, and she's hungry!' They were hugging and clapping each other on the back. Her sons broke into wide smiles, even the quiet Crimson. One of Cassie's mates went rushing towards the cafeteria to get Cat something to eat. O'Hara was sure an order of rare steak would soon follow at the gate. He broke into a grin himself. Family members were going in for short visits to say hi to her.

Cassie peered down the hall after most of the family were done and motioned for them to come on in. He tapped Babyface, who had been standing watch with him that morning, and they went down the hall for the first time. Cassie opened the door for them and he saw Cat's brothers, her mates and her sister were all that were left in the room.

The room itself was filled with burning candles and crystal stones placed everywhere; even on the floor, where he had to side-step a few of them. The scent of burning sage was still strong in the air. Cat was sitting up with pillows gathered under her head. She still looked pale and weak, but she was smiling, with both her hands being held by a mate. Demitri was on one side and Andre on the other. Antonio was at her feet, sitting on the bed.

"Hey, Captain, Major Harris, good to see you," Cat said, her voice sounding strong.

"Vincent; and it's good to see you up. How are you doing?" he asked

"Starving!" She even sounded hungry.

"That's a good sign, though," he replied. Everyone quietly agreed.

She gazed at O'Hara solemnly. "I wanted to thank you and everyone on the team for taking care of me and getting me home so my family could heal me. I appreciate it. Tell the others for me, please." Everyone murmured their thanks as well.

"No problem; I would have done it for anyone on the team. No one gets left behind. It's a ranger motto; Romeo used to be a Ranger before he joined Special Forces. We've adopted a lot of the different attitudes on our team since we're such a mixed bunch," he explained.

"A real mixed bunch now, huh?" she said, laughing.

"No kidding. But, it's a good mix," O'Hara smiled. Even Babyface cracked a grin, silently agreeing with him.

Shamus shimmered into the room, startling O'Hara. He didn't think he could ever get used to having someone or something just pop into a place like that.

"We, at Trinidad, heard you were up, Princess. Be expecting much company later. I will try to hold them off for a while," Shamus informed her. "But, be prepared for the horde to descend upon you. Your people were worried. They will need to see you eventually."

O'Hara couldn't follow what they were talking about, but Cat gave him a look that said she would explain later.

She then turned back to Shamus, "Thank you Shamus. Let everyone know I have missed them, too."

"I will. How are you feeling now?" She knew what he was asking.

"Like I got hit by a brick wall, then Godzilla stomped on it with me under it," she said, not in a joking tone. It sounded like she meant it.

"All seven levels on your inner selves were disrupted. The bonds and chakras were perforated. Now would you mind explaining how the seven hells it looked like someone had put a grenade into your soul and blew you up?" Shamus was sounding grouchy again. Gerard moved closer to the bed, his face a mask of cold stone. Like he wanted to know who it was he needed to kill, then he would simply go do it. O'Hara knew then he would be good for the team if he had even a shred of a conscious. He wouldn't know that though until he got a chance to speak to him.

"The dark God was a bitch, but I got through him. Kicked him in the nads," she smiled evilly. "I got through the so-called prince pretty easily. The dark adept type they had, took a few more moves, but I got him, as well. It was the vortex that kicked my ass. Until I got to the vortex, I only had a standard protective shield up. I've closed portals and vortexes before with just a standard protective shield with no problems. But this vortex was different. Stronger than anything I'd ever seen before. It was pulling on the edges of my soul just from approaching it. I couldn't call you, Shamus, because I was afraid it would just suck you right in. So, I gathered my energy for a standard closing." Everyone else in the room nodded as if they understood the operation of closing a vortex. O'Hara was lost, but just listened to see what he could learn. Babyface too, was engrossed in the telling.

She continued, after looking around at everyone, "I started to close the edges together. I invoked the power of The Goddess and Her Consort and poured the power on. It was like trying to close a tarp together in a strong hurricane wind, then sealing it with gusts of wind blowing in every direction. It was the hardest closing I'd ever done, but I finally did it. When it snapped closed though, that's when it happened."

186

'What's'? erupted around the room.

"It felt like an EMP blast on a psychic level and I was standing at ground zero. I felt like I had gotten blown apart. My shield was nothing against it. It had physically thrown me into the wall behind me," she shook her head, "and then afterwards, my telepathy was gone. Everything was gone, except the healing. But it wasn't working very well for me. It did a good job on the others, though. It was slower than usual and took more energy, but at least I had that left to me," she finished her telling, sinking back into the pillows.

O'Hara's ears pricked at the word 'telepathy'. That would explain a lot.

"Sweet Mother Goddess. You're lucky you're alive," Shamus sputtered. "No wonder you were so shredded. But, by all rights, you should be dead."

Everyone in the room seemed to have followed along and they were all amazed, struck in wonder she had lived through something like that. Andre and Antonio were holding her tighter. Demitri had bent down and hugged her, saying a prayer of thanks under his breath. Everyone in the room bent their heads and added their thanks.

Gerard, in a strong deep voice, offered a suggestion. "Maybe she survived because she has been changed." Even he had closed his eyes. O'Hara could tell he loved his sister. It was good to see them together, to evaluate their relationships with each other. It would make it easier later to form up teams for different missions.

"Never again, Cat. I can't go through this kind of thing again. At least one of us has to be with you on any further missions," Demitri spoke in a harsh voice.

"And a sibling," Cassie interjected. "What if you are both injured? Three is a good number. A power number for us."

Gerard nodded his head, "A vote?"

'Agreeds' all around the group.

"Fine, so long as it applies to any one of us. Three is our number from now on at the minimum," Cat agreed in a tired voice, like she knew she wouldn't be able to argue so didn't even try. O'Hara silently agreed with her, noticing all the hard eyes around the room. None of them wanted anything like this to happen again.

"We also have to come up with a stronger shield. The standard sucks for this level of operation," she added.

O'Hara was glad there would be more on the team from now on, if they all fought like she did. Looking at her mates and Gerard and

Grant—oh yeah, these guys could hand out a can of whoop ass, easily. None of the women looked soft in that department either.

He cleared his throat to get their attention. "I will need to know individual strengths and any weakness, so we can all watch each other's backs better. If I knew more about Cat when we went out, maybe I could have done something. Also, any individual skills you may have. It would make it easier for me to put a team together for specialized missions in the future."

They all looked at each other silently, but he watched who looked where first. Cat looked to her mates then turned her gaze to her brother Gerard. They all nodded at her. Then the rest of the group nodded. So they did have a slight hierarchy within their group, most looking to Cat and Gerard first, before each other.

"We'll make some time for a get together with you and give you what you need," Cat addressed him. "But only your team and the General may know everything about us, to a point, regarding what would be critical on a mission. I still haven't gotten clearance for the rest of it." Her grin turned rueful, "Of course, I have just had my ass handed to me psychic style, so I may have word soon."

He nodded, and noticed whoever this 'person' was that even she answered to, wasn't in the room. So, there was still someone higher in the chain of command. That eventual meeting should be interesting.

The next day, O'Hara was shocked to see her walking down the hall, though she was supported by two of her mates, one on each side.

He walked up, stopping in front of her. "Sure you should be doing this?" eyeing her mates in question as well.

"Yeah, physical therapy. Good for you," she sounded out of breath and in pain.

Her mates had a hard look to them like they didn't like it, but agreed with her as well. They just hated seeing her hurting.

"How are you doing?" he asked.

"Dizzy, feels like I am not quiet aligned all the way through, inside yet. But it will come." She shook her head, "Bed." Apparently she was done, and they helped her back to her room and into her bed.

Shamus was there and after they got her settled, he went to work with the glowing hands thing again. "Good job, Cat. I'll help ease the strain to your muscles and chakras."

O'Hara shook his head. Even Shamus seemed pleased she was pushing herself.

Shamus appeared to be done when he pulled his hands away. "A few more days and you should be fine. Maybe some weakness, but some time in the water will restore your energy. Lots of swimming when we get you home. Doc Shamus' orders," he grinned at her.

"Cool, it will be so good to feel the water on me. Take me to the beach, baby, please?" she pleaded to Andre.

"Absolutely, we'll be your floats," he said with a wicked grin.

O'Hara, shocked, had to ask, "That fast?"

Andre looked at him, "Sure, once she gets in the water for a day or two she'll be good as new."

"Water heals me," she expounded for Andre." It was a bitch in Tucson to get healed. I had to use a pool, which took ten times as long. And most of the time, I couldn't afford even a pool to swim in, so had to use the tub, which was a bitch at the time." She sighed heavily.

"We're taking her home tonight to put her in the pool in our backyard." Then he turned to her, "Tomorrow, we'll hit the beach."

"Awesome." She turned to O'Hara, "I didn't get a chance to ask yesterday, but how are the rest of the team and the squad? They all make it home ok?"

He nodded, "A few wounded on our squad, some on the other squads. Your family took care of most of them after they were done with you. There is no one in the left wing anymore. Everyone is home. No casualties."

She blew out a breath, "Thank the Goddess. That is great news." Then she frowned, "Damn, that means that I'm the only one here, and I was supposed to be the bad ass."

Everyone laughed at that. There was a knock on the door. Her sister Cendra poked her head in, saying, "There is a Ridgewood and his family asking for a visit. Is it all right?"

Cat nodded her head, "Sure, let them in."

"All right." She popped back out the door.

A few minutes later, there was another knock, and Ridgewood entered with his family. He had an infant in his arms and his wife had a bouquet of flowers in one hand and was holding a small child's hand in the other.

As they approached the bed, Ridgewood said, "Hi, Cat. This is my wife and children. She wanted to come by and give you these."

His wife handed her the yellow roses saying, "Thank you for helping my husband come home. He said he wouldn't be here if it wasn't for you. So, I wanted to say thank you."

"These are wonderful, thank you." She smelled them, and then looked to her mate, Antonio. "Can you find a vase to put these in, please?"

He took them, saying, "Sure, hon."

Then she turned to look at the baby Ridgewood was holding. "May I?"

Startled, Ridgewood said, "Sure," and handed her the baby carefully. Cat took the baby in her arms and looked at him. "He is gorgeous, you did well," speaking to the wife. O'Hara was fascinated by how she treated the baby. He couldn't ever imagine her as having such strong maternal instincts.

He watched, as she hugged the baby to her closely, smelling the baby's scent deeply. The look of longing crossing over her face was so strong, Andre had to turn away. Antonio just looked on with longing on his own face, almost as strong as hers. She then kissed the baby on his forehead and handed him back to his father.

"You're very blessed. He is a sweet child." She looked to the three year old and held out her hand. The child shyly reached out and touched her fingers with her small ones and smiled at Cat.

Then the little one moved towards the bed and Cat asked her in a gentle voice, "How old are you?" The child shyly held up three fingers.

"Wow, that many, huh? Three. You're very pretty. It's nice to meet you."

The child again held up three fingers which made Cat smile hugely." Three, I got it. You are awesome." Ridgewood and his wife were smiling at the meeting, but he also noticed Cat's tired eyes and said, "We just wanted to stop by and have you meet the family. Honey, can you take the kids and meet me at the nurse's station?"

She nodded and said goodbye to Cat, again with a thank you and took the kids out the door.

Ridgewood turned to Cat. "I didn't tell her *how* you saved me. I'll keep the secret to my death. I just told her you had to do some heroic shit to get me home. She understands about military type secrets, so she knows not to push. She's a good wife. I just wanted you to know that and tell you thank you myself."

"No, problem; it's what we're here for," she said quietly.

He nodded and said his goodbyes to everyone and walked out the door.

"Did you see the baby, honey?" she asked her mates.

They both nodded.

"It was worth it." Then tears welled up in her eyes and started to fall down her cheeks. "No one has ever said thank you, before." Andre groaned, and bent to wrap her in his arms and Antonio went to her side, enveloping her.

O'Hara walked quietly out the door to leave them alone.

Children. A child is her weakness. It was the fact that Ridgewood had an infant at home and a small child that made her decide to put herself over the line she knew would be bad to cross. She had read the files on every person in the platoon, committing the stats to memory, just as he had. She couldn't forget the fact that there were kids at home waiting for Ridgewood, and she didn't want them to be without a father. He could see it in her eyes. It was the strength of a leader, but it was also her greatest weakness. His eyes hardened. He would have to watch for that in the future.

CHAPTER SIXTEEN
Celebration of Life

Three nights later, the party was on. The General gave everyone leave to go, if they desired. It was a hot, humid July night, as O'Hara pulled up with his crew in a base SUV he'd borrowed for the evening. No one was sure how to dress. They did say a club, so they opted for casual nice. O'Hara had left home early because he wanted to get the feel of the place first. They got out and looked around, as was their habit, whether on a mission or not.

O'Hara looked the building over. It was huge, with dark wood paneling. The windows that used to be there were painted over in black so no one could peek inside. At the door, was a picture frame that said, 'Authorized Club Members only—NO exceptions. Bouncers on premises.' The door was open, surprisingly, but as promised, there was a bouncer waiting to see them through. Grant, himself, was manning the door and smiled a greeting at them. It was a shock to see a smile on this man's face, after knowing him only with the grim stare most had had during the family crisis. It changed his whole face, making him look younger and more open.

"Come on in. Cat has the honor of showing you guys around tonight," Grant said, as he waved them in. O'Hara nodded to Grant and a few of his men gave him a greeting, following him in. Cat was by the bar, which was on the east side of the building. The bar was about 20 ft long, with bar stools, bottles, glasses and a huge gilded mirror on the wall behind it. The motif seemed to hearken back to an older time in the West. It was like a refurbished saloon—if it wasn't for a small pentagram etched on each wall.

Cat started to walk over, and he was stunned by the way she was dressed. Her leather jacket (which she seemed to favor) was on, sure, but she had high black leather boots with black hose, a black mini skirt, and a black dress shirt. She looked great; both sleek and dangerous at the same time. He could see where she had blades in boot sheaths in both boots. He was willing to guess she had blades on her forearms as well, but for the jacket hiding them. Probably why she hadn't taken her jacket off, he thought to himself. She was still armed, but not as thoroughly as before, he was glad to see.

Cat came over with a smile on her face, and said, "Hey guys. I'm glad you all came." They all nodded and said their greetings to her. "Check it out," as she swept her hand over the whole place. "Isn't it cool? Come this way first." She led them to the south side of the bar where there was a wide staircase of about seven steps leading down to a lower floor. In the middle, was a boxing ring with a table on one side and a bell for ringing.

"This is the pit," she said. "Every one of us has their own version of this at our homes. It's a place we go to work out our differences between mates. For instance, my mates, they're brothers, right?" She looked at O'Hara who nodded. "They get in fights every now and again which I stay out of. All of our mates have differences every now and again, even the women. So if talking doesn't help, or it's past that point, we take it to our ring at home. Makes the marriages work real well."

She grinned. "This, too, your guys and our people, are like a marriage. We'll have differences from time to time which we can work out here if it's past the point of conversation. Afterwards, no hard feelings; winner buys the beer. I thought it would be a good bonding thing, since it works at home so well for us."

O'Hara was impressed with the idea. Sometimes shit happens - someone gets angry, and if they could hash it out here, it would help keep the bad vibes out of the teams on a mission.

O'Hara had a thought. "Hmm, some of you guys have too great of an advantage with the strength thing. All of you have powers. Kind of makes things a bit uneven in the ring."

"AHH," she said, and pointed to the wall. On each wall was a sign, or really, a rule. One said, 'NO powers'. Another said, 'No weapons'. On yet another wall it said, 'No fighting for sport'. And on the final wall it read, 'You cheat, You get hammered'.

"A referee will be here for the dispute. One from your group and one from mine, so we can tell if there is cheating or not. I would like to have one of each for bouncers, too. One of my people and one of yours. If someone needs to moonlight or just be here, it does pay, by the way. Except me; I am going to offer my time for free."

O'Hara and the guys nodded, impressed with the safety taken for both sides and the fairness.

O'Hara spoke up for them, "I will offer my time, too, for free, if you'll have me?"

"Awesome, you and I could be head bouncers. Split the responsibility and no one can claim unfairness." Exactly what he was thinking. It was good to see they were on the same wavelength. With both of them here, it should keep the need for the pit down to a bare minimum.

"There is a schedule in the staff room I'll show you. Just pick the hours you want. There is also a copy and another sheet for pay and hours for those who want to moonlight, as well as rules for being a bouncer."

She moved back up the stairs. "Come on, you haven't seen the best part yet." They walked past the bar and several tables for dining. He supposed this was the dining area. It was spacious and could easily fit the whole platoon at one time, plus hers if everybody showed up at once. Hopefully that wouldn't happen much, he thought to himself; nothing like a tired marine on a training field. She led past the dining area to the farthest end of the building, which opened up to yet another very large room.

On the far wall, were places to sit and drink and eat if you wanted, and in the middle of the huge room was a dance floor. On the other end of the room was a stage with several instruments. A karaoke machine, as well as a DJ station was next to it. The sound system must have been state of the art. There were lights and even a disco ball hanging from the ceiling. They had something for every taste and a way to pull it off.

"Cool, huh?" she asked, pleased of the work they did.

"You did a really good job here," O'Hara complimented her.

"Oh, no, not me. It was mostly Cassie and her mates, with help thrown in here and there from some of the others. I was down, unfortunately, for being a part of this." Her eyes got sad for a minute and he watched her shake it off. "Come on. Let me show you the time out room."

She led them back to the dining room, but to the west side of the wall where there was a door she opened and stepped through. They followed her into to what looked like a staff room. There was a table and chairs and a desk with a phone. To the far side of the wall, were two cages. Much like a jail cell, except for one of the cages looking like it was reinforced with sterling silver mesh and coated with a substance he couldn't identify.

When his eyebrow rose at this, she explained, "Your men can be contained if they're out of sorts in this one. It's normal. But, for our kind, we need this kind of cell." She pointed to the cell next to it. "It's mostly titanium and sterling silver, but this stuff here is what stops the magicks. You see, we work well *with* sterling silver. It empowers and channels our power, but with this substance, the sterling silver empowers *it* and we can't do magicks out of it. I thought it was pretty ingenious of my brother, Gerard, to think of it and manufacture it."

"What's it made of?" O'Hara asked

"I don't honestly know; he won't tell us," she shrugged. "We all have our own little triumphs we keep to ourselves," she paused. "Until we make another breakthrough with a new one. Then he might share," she smiled, laughing. "Rules for being a Practitioner: To Dare, To Will, To Succeed, To Keep Silent. It makes the best of the best of the practitioners of magicks."

"This place is great Cat, but what's with the pentagrams?" Wizard joined in.

"Oh, those. If you could '*see*' they are empowered, so that no dark practitioner can send or do magicks against us. It's a standard 101 security measure for us."

"Oh, you have problems like that?' O'Hara wouldn't be surprised with the things he has already seen now.

"Yes, we do. Even our homes and cars are warded against dark practitioners. It's mandatory," she said in a serious tone.

O'Hara was thinking out loud, "Hmm, maybe we ought to have one of you do the building and barracks at the base."

Cat's face went white. "Why didn't I think of that sooner? The General's office ought to be double warded, as well. It only a matter of time before some dark witch gets wind of something odd here and tries sending a watcher or something. I promise we'll get on that first thing tomorrow." She looked so concerned and he caught the unfamiliar word.

"What's a watcher?" And can he shoot it, if one shows up, he was thinking.

She thought for a minute on how to explain it. "Well, you know how you see those orbs before someone pops all the way in?"

He and the others nodded, having seen orbs during the past week.

"A watcher is a ball of energy from a practitioner that's sole purpose is to watch and see everything that an enemy may be doing. The reverse is true, too, though. A watcher can be used for good—like my mates used to use one to keep a watch over me when they couldn't do it astrally themselves, before we got together physically. The orb won't turn into a being, but it will record like a camera. The witch who made it can tune into it like a TV and see through its eye. Most mundanes can't see the orbs unless there are a lot of people around who are like us, to reflect the power like back at the hospital."

"That's not good, then." O'Hara was thinking that these guys can't be everywhere all the time at the base. "At least we'll be covered by tomorrow."

Wizard jumped in, "Wait, you mean because there were so many of your kind there, anyone with no training could see the orbs, but if there weren't any of you guys around, then a regular person can't see a watcher or an orb?"

Cat shook her head seriously. "No, not usually, and that could mean someone can send a watcher to the General's office and spy on him at any time and he wouldn't even know it.

"Shit, that's bad," O'Hara was worried.

Babyface agreed, "No kidding."

Cat said, "Not to worry; we'll be on it tomorrow. For right now, let's go eat. I'm still hungry!"

"Just when I thought the twilight zone episode couldn't get any weirder," Romeo sighed.

Wizard looked at him, "Yeah, I know."

Cat led them to a table back in the huge room where they could also see the stage. It was big enough to seat at least thirteen people, if not more. It had a half moon-shaped bench with thick leather upholstery and a roundish table with even more chairs around it.

"Best seat in the house," she said. Then she turned and let out a whoop. She had spotted her son, Craven, coming in, obviously looking for her. "Hey handsome, have you met the guys yet?"

"Hey mom; sort of." He looked at them and said, "Hello." He was slightly taller than her and was wearing a black leather trench coat with black pants and a black shirt with a dragon on it in blue. His hair was short and spiked with gel. He had the biggest blue eyes O'Hara had ever seen on a male, though his face almost seemed androgynous.

They hugged and he asked her, "Mom, do you want me and my cuz to sing tonight?"

"Hell yeah; do my favorite, ok?" She looked pleased.

"You got it, if you sing, too," and they pounded closed fist and he nodded as he walked off.

"That's my youngest, Craven. I think he's going through a semi Goth phase, but I think it's a cool look for him. Helps him look rougher," she mused.

"Isn't he only sixteen?" O'Hara asked.

"Yes. Club rules state you can be sixteen or older, but you can't have any liquor whatsoever until you're twenty-one. We consider our kids adults at sixteen if they have gone through all the training with weapons and fighting styles. Also, their schooling must be complete. We all home school our kids because...well...they're different. They can't get along with other kids very well. Regular kids seem to subconsciously pick it up and torment the hell out of our kids. They wind up in trouble, which affects their learning. So we home school. It fixed that dilemma," she explained.

O'Hara nodded, seeing the validity of it and admired their way of fixing the problem. Looking at her boys, you really couldn't call them kids.

They were an odd mix of something in between. They seemed adult-like, ready to rumble, but they still had their innocence. They also had an uncanny way of coming off just as adult as any of the older people around them did, with their speech and behavior, but you could still see purity in their eyes.

Their parents must have kept them out of the line of fire, so far. Teaching them how to fight without letting them get bloody yet. O'Hara hoped that for their sakes, their parents would be able to keep it up. Looking at Crimson on the other side of the room, checking on the sound equipment, he doubted any of them would stay clean for much longer. The way Crimson held himself and acted, it was like he knew what was coming—and he was ready for it.

Romeo nodded to the stage, "You all gonna sing and stuff?"

Cat smiled, "Yeah, we're all musically inclined. Well, the others more than me. I haven't had time to learn more than a few songs on the guitar. My voice is decent. The others though, they rock. Some of these guys are really talented. Wait 'till later. There are quite a few who'll take turns up there and supply the entertainment for you guys. Plus, if anyone wants to karaoke, they are more than welcome to get up there and go for it."

"It sounds neat. A real family bar everyone can have fun in. I like it," Wizard said appreciatively.

A few of the other family members made it over to their table and sat down. Cassie, with one of her mates, Cendra with two of hers, and two blonds O'Hara remembered as being Grant's mates. They said hi to all around. Cassie gave Cat a hug.

"Have you guys met my sisters?" Cat asked.

They all nodded their heads.

"Good, now you know I'm the ugly duckling of the trio," Cat laughed.

Cassie reached over and smacked her on the shoulder, "You are not."

"I am so. You two are gorgeous. I'm barely pretty and that's on a good day." Cassie frowned at her. "That's all right," Cat continued. "My mates tell me every day that I'm beautiful. I don't believe them, but it's nice to hear," Cat sighed happily. Cassie smiled with her.

O'Hara had seen Cendra's eyes narrow over this statement from Cat. He wondered what was up between the two sisters.

Romeo nodded to the other women, "Will they sing too?"

A few nodded, some shook their heads no.

"Any free women around?" he asked, as he watched a young blond girl with a really nice rack walking over to the sound system Craven and Crimson was working on setting up.

Cat reached over and smacked his hand. "That's Gaston's young daughter. She's only seventeen. Off limits, buddy."

"We should have thought of that, Cat. Every female here will be someone's mate, sister, or daughter. There is no one for the guys from the military to spend time with. Not safely." Cassie looked worried.

"Shit, you're right," Cat looked concerned herself.

"We wouldn't be able to talk shop though, if we bought in outsiders," Babyface spoke for the first time. "There are no females in the platoon, so that's out. Your family is protective over the females you have, which is the way it should be. They're relatives. Makes a difference. I think if we spread it around the platoon that the club is just a place to talk shop and hang out, they'll get used to no women for play here. They can go somewhere else for that, if that's what they want." It was the longest conversation Cat had ever had with Babyface. She agreed with his views on the club house, but still felt bad for the lack of companionship for the men.

Cat nodded, "That would be great. We'll try to think of something though, in the meantime.

"So, I won't be able to find out if those are real or not, damn it," Romeo snapped his fingers.

Cat laughed, "I can tell you that every female in our family is one hundred percent home grown from the tips of her hair to her toenails. We don't do well with chemicals for hair dye and having plastic surgery is anathema for us. A mutilation of the body. Remember, we can see auras and souls of a person. When a woman has had that kind of surgery, it leaves a black dusty spot on her aura. Kinda gross, really."

"No kidding, and these women think men can't feel a difference. Bullshit. They can, even if it's only on a subconscious level and then they become nothing more than live plastic Barbie dolls. The man's attention goes from thinking about making her a mother some day to just fucking her because her tits are fake."

"And men who want their women to get a boob job are obviously the wrong man. A soul mate will love his woman the way she is," Cat added.

"Here's to women everywhere that will learn to love what they were given by learning to love themselves just as the Goddess made them," Cassie toasted.

The girls raised their drinks and took a sip.

O'Hara even joined in the toast. "I'll drink to that. I like my women natural."

"Shit, I like my women any way I can get them." Romeo snorted.

Cat burst out, "That's because you're a hound dog."

Romeo tilted his head back and barked, "Hell, yeah."

Cat laughed, "Someday you'll be a wolf. I can tell. Wolves mate for life. Dogs fuck anything that moves or stays still long enough."

"She is right; someday you'll be a wolf," Cassie was looking at him, her eyes slightly unfocused.

"Oh, hell no. There are just too many beautiful women in the world and I haven't done even half of them yet," Romeo shuddered at the thought of just one woman. Forever.

Both Cat and Cassie turned to look at each other and smiled, shaking their heads. O'Hara raised his eye brow and wondered what it was they both saw.

Andre came up from behind Cat and kissed her cheek, then bent down to whisper in her ear.

She nodded at him and addressed the group that had gathered around their table, "I'll be back later guys, O'Hara," she nodded at him. "Kitchen staff needs stuff."

"Vincent or Rock is ok, Cat. Remember, we're trying to learn to be family." His eye brow was back.

"Rock, then," she decided. "You call me Cat all the time, so it would be fair to call you Rock." He laughed.

Cat walked away with Andre, and O'Hara noticed as Cendra watched them leave, her lips pressed tight in annoyance. Again, he wondered what the problem was. Cendra had her mates. Two of them were by her side, though they were talking with each other and not with her. Something to keep an eye on, he thought.

Andre led Cat to the staff room. He closed and locked the door.

"Hmm, honey, what's up?" She backed up against the wall. "I thought the kitchen needed towels and stuff."

"They do, but they can wait." He pressed himself up against her, kissing her deeply.

She melted into the kiss as he dragged her jacket off and was touching her. She didn't feel any panic coming on, just a red hot heat as she felt him harden against her.

He went to her neck and started to kiss and nibble his way down her throat and back up to her ear. "I need you now. I can't wait anymore. Please tell me I can have you," his pleading whisper reached her ear making her shiver.

"Yesss," she responded.

He groaned and slid his hands down to her thighs and back up under her skirt. He groaned again as he realized she wasn't wearing any panties and felt her wet heat immediately.

He slid a finger in and pressed it into her, moving his finger in and out of her moist heat slowly.

"Fuck, I can't wait, Catrina," and he pushed away. He unzipped his pants, pulling out his cock which was hard and ready.

He lifted her leg up, wrapped it around his waist and put his cock to her hot core. "Last chance, baby. You want this?" rubbing himself up and down between her slick folds. "You want this in you?"

"Fuck me. Fuck me now," Cat pleaded and he slid in. She cried out in pleasure in feeling him fill her. He pushed up, claiming her with his hard cock, pumping into her harder and deeper. She started moaning getting close to a climax already.

"Gods, I knew you would be hot. Fucking bite me. Fuck the ritual words. I give permission, just fucking bite me. Make me come in you with your teeth in my neck," Andre begged.

She reached for his neck and let her teeth drop. "I love you," she said and bit deeply into his neck.

He moaned, "I love you, too," and pumped harder. They both went over that shining edge together. It felt like they melted into one for a moment. He kept pushing in, bringing her again.

"Fuck, that was hot." He was sweating and panting.

Cat was breathing hard as well. "Damn, that *was* good," kissing him. "Can we do it again?"

He smiled and kissed her. Then there was a knock on the door.

"Hey, we need those towels, damn it." It was Gaston, who was in charge of the grill for the steaks.

Laughing, they quickly got themselves cleaned up and put back in place.

Opening the door, "Brother, your timing sucks," Cat poked him.

Gaston look annoyed and clueless to what they had been doing. "What? I need those towels."

Andre tossed them at him. "Here; now get the fuck out," and closed the door.

"Well, we broke the place in. At least I got to do something here," Cat grinned evilly at him. Andre laughed, and then grew serious. "Are you ok, though?"

"Fine. I think I've finally got it beat or it was the near death thing. No worries. I got it covered now," hugging him.

"That's good. You know the other two will pounce on you now," he smiled.

"Good, I just hope they wait 'till we get home. This place is filling up," Cat said.

"No shit, huh," Andre could hear the voices growing many and loud.

And they went back out to the bar, smiling and holding hands.

O'Hara noticed that when Cat and Andre came out of the staff room, Cendra was frowning. Cassie, however, was smiling and nodding her head about something. He wished he knew just what was going on; to have two extremes of attitude as to what Cat and Andre were doing. Cat and Andre had gone to the bar to get a drink and collect her other two mates before returning to the table. They all greeted him and his crew and settled in around Cat.

O'Hara sat back out of most of the conversation around the table, just watching the by-play of everyone seated there. A woman came by and asked them all for their orders.

After everyone ordered, Cat asked her if she needed help. "No, dear, we got it. You guys have had a rough week. This night is for you, for the clubhouse. Enjoy it this one time," she winked and walked away. He watched as Cat settled back in, looking a bit guilty for not being able to help. He watched as Demitri leaned in and whispered something in her ear. She smiled, gave him a peck on the cheek and settled in again, looking eased. O'Hara was getting a clue. He saw her mates all around her, gently touching her, talking with her, with others, but always each one had his hand on her. One played with her long hair. Andre had his hand on her knee. Demitri had rested his hand on her shoulder and kept it there, gently kneading her shoulder from time to time.

All innocent touches, but touches and attention, none the less.

Cendra's eyes just narrowed and her lips stayed continuously pressed now. Her mates, at least the two that were there, were seated back from her and speaking mostly with themselves about some car they were restoring. Guy stuff. Neither touched her, nor gave her a kiss, they just talked their car shop talk. Jealousy? Or was it something more?

Cat never looked at Cendra. Rarely even spoke to her. When Cat did, her smile would vanish, even though her responses were polite with an even tone of voice. But she treated Cendra, not as a sister, as she did with Cassie, but as someone she has to work with that she didn't like much, but put up with.

Gaston and another light brown haired woman came over with the food.

Cat's smile again vanished. "Rock, have you met Gaston? And this is one of his mates, Heather. You've already met the other two sitting over there." They had come over to sit with those at the table when Andre and Cat left for the staffroom.

"No, I haven't. Nice to meet you," Rock said.

"And you, Captain," Gaston greeted him politely.

"Just Rock will do," O'Hara smiled a bit at Gaston.

"Rock, it is then." Gaston looked at his two sitting mates, "Sara, Joanna, I need you in the kitchen." The ladies got right up. "I'll have them bring the rest of the food and drinks for your table." He nodded and went back to the kitchen with his mates trailing behind him. O'Hara turned to look at Cat, whose eyes were closed now and her own lips were pressed tight. It looked like she was counting.

Demitri again leaned in and whispered to her. The only thing he heard was Cat's response to Demitri."I know, I know. My bad. I am trying."

Andre had leaned from the other side and her attention shifted to hear his remarks. "I know. It just caught me off guard. I'll work on it," this she practically growled and Andre dropped it.

She pasted a fake smile on her face and started eating the food that was placed in front of her earlier. Antonio had scooted his chair farthest away from Cendra O'Hara noted, and began his meal, too. He hadn't even greeted her when he came to the table, O'Hara now realized, and the other two just nodded at her. Hmm, interesting by-play with them all in one area. He was learning a lot about the family dynamics from just this one dinner with them. They obviously had no problem fighting side by side in an instant when one of theirs was threatened, but in a relaxed atmosphere there were definite favorites.

He could tell when Gerard walked up to the table (with his mates beside him), because Cat's smile had turned genuine and she got up from the table to hug each one, with her brother getting a hug first. She smiled at each wife and asked after their young ones, who apparently had a babysitter or two for them so Gerard's mates could come and have a night out for fun. All three of Gerard's mates had a strong Eskimo/Indian cast to them and he found out they had all belonged to the same tribe in Alaska.

Gerard warmly greeted Cat and asked after her and hers as well. He was very conscious of his mates, too. He and Demitri went to get more seats for the wives and they resettled around the table. The dynamic of the table had switched again with Cat talking to Gerard's mates much more animatedly. Cat's mates and Gerard were talking about various business ventures.

Gerard's gaze constantly roved back to his wives, and he would smile a small warm smile, watching his sister talk with them then turn back to her mates. This group got along well and already had formed a tight knit group within. The only other sibling he saw her smile at with genuine warmth was Grant. So the problem spots were Cendra and Gaston. Cat seemed to have a very strong reaction to those two, but for different reasons, maybe?

Until he found out what the exact problem or problems were, he'd keep this trio separated on any missions in the near future.

Now that he had a general idea of what was what, but not the why, he would compartmentalize it for later. He joined in the eating and the flow of conversation around him, relaxing with the group.

A short time later, General Pierce walked in with the Major, who for the first time ever, O'Hara saw in street clothes. Everyone, out of habit, started to rise and General Pierce said, "No, sit down, sit down. This isn't the base, and I am not in uniform, so call me Richard. It's my first name, Cat, if no one has told you already."

Cat responded, "No, Sir, it's a first." She sounded suspiciously cheeky.

"No 'Sirring' me either. Richard. Use it," his tone firm.

She grinned an evil smile." Yes....Richard."

"You like causing trouble, don't you?" Richard returned the teasing.

"Who, moi? Perish the thought. I am an angel," she said, with an innocent tone, to which several people around the table started laughing. Even Gerard chuckled.

"Well, I am. Just ask my mates," her eyes widened with fake innocence.

"We can't lie, hon. You know that," Demitri squeezed her shoulder again.

She shrugged, "Fine, don't back me up. Brandon there will, won't you?"

He put his hands up in surrender, "Don't drag me into this," shaking his head. Everyone laughed. Richard got his food ordered and a drink, as did Brandon. They all had a good time enjoying the food and company, when they heard a tapping on a microphone echoing in the room.

Craven was up on the stage and was getting ready to do the first song of the night with his cousin, Deuce. Everyone turned to face the stage.

"This is for my mom, Cat, who kicked ass beating The Reaper. Either that, or hell just didn't want her taking over." Everyone laughed at the joke." She likes vampire songs even if they're dark, so here goes." And he started a rap song that sounded to O'Hara like it was about a vampire born in 1431. It was dark, as promised, but she loved it. He went into another rap song about 'white trash renegades' where every time that part of the song came on several people around the table, including Cat, would pump their fist in the air to the beat. He ended his rap set with what Cat said was called Tucson Monsters. That one was really dark and violent, but the younger set enjoyed it, as did Cat.

Her mates smiled through at her antics. Craven and Deuce did have good voices for rap. Everyone clapped and whistled when they were done. Sweating now, he and his cousin turned the mic over to Cat saying, "You promised, Mom."

She turned to Cassie, "Need a rhythm guitar girl, come help me." They both went up on the stage. She then proceeded with a song more to O'Hara's liking—Crystal, by Stevie Nicks, to which her voice was a close match. Not exact, but close, and she held the tune well. She played the guitar with her sister, who would add her voice as back up. All the time she sang, she looked at her mates. She went into two more love songs and her mates were smiling at her through the whole thing. It was a good set and everyone clapped again as she and her sister finished.

She said out to the crowd, "Ok, who's next for the executioners block up here?" Antonio stood up, kissing her as they crossed paths and said something in her ear which made her blush. He went up the stairs to the stage and sat at the piano. He belted out a couple of Elton John tunes and was really talented with the piano. He turned the set over to Christoph who was followed by four other young adults and they went into some heavy metal tunes with him on lead guitar.

The night went like that that for a while, with various members playing something and singing. When they rolled out their favorite's tunes, everyone clapped and joined in, singing along, if everyone knew the tune. It was a great show really, thought O'Hara. Very eclectic.

The General looked like he was enjoying some of the music and only grimaced with the heavy metal sets, but he was a good sport about it and would clap with everyone else after the young adults were done showing off their skills. They did have some real talent in the family.

The DJ, one of Cassie's mates, then went to work putting in tunes everyone could dance to. Cat requested Silverback songs often. It seemed to be one of her favorites to dance to and man could that girl dance. She would get all of her mates out there and dance with all three of them at once. Now that took talent.

Others would join on the dance floor with their mates. Some would allow their mates to dance with other platoon soldiers so long as they knew not to touch even while dancing. Everyone was on their best behavior. Gerard would watch his mates like a hawk when one would get asked to dance, once everyone knew it was ok. Just don't touch the females.

Even Cat would dance with others from time to time, with her mates looking on just as intently as Gerard did. It was impossible to get a conversation out of them once their females were dancing with someone else. Cendra was the exception, he noticed. Her mates didn't watch her too intently, though they would glance over from time to time just to check. Then they would get back to their conversation. Not so, with any of the other women. Their mates or father would watch until they came back to the tables they were sitting at. Letting their women dance with others was an obvious concession to the fact the soldiers didn't have any of their own there. Otherwise, O'Hara doubted even that would have been allowed. But they were good about it. No incidents happened on the dance floor and everyone, he thought, was breathing a sigh of relief. He knew he was.

All in all, the night was a great success since no bloodshed happened and everyone left smiling in two or threes. Those with young children left the earliest to get home. O'Hara made it a point to be the last, to make sure nothing broke out. Just in case.

"Think the men had a good time?" Cat asked O'Hara when the last of the soldiers had left.

O'Hara gave her a small smile, "They sure did. It was a very interesting evening. Surely, not the norm for anyone, but in a good way."

"This place will be opened for three nights on the weekend. We have more cousins and such coming in. They aren't related astrally per se, but they are physically blood-related and practitioners themselves. So, we'll have more help here soon. They aren't as touchy about the female thing as we are, who are astrally related and mated. Few of our second tiers of relatives are mated," she told him.

"What's the difference between mated and not mated, but together?" he was curious.

She took a breath, and said, "We who are mated, are with our truemates, soulmates. Touching someone who isn't our mate physically makes us ill. At least my mates and I get that way. I haven't asked the others if it happens to them, too, but I am sure there is a lot of discomfort at the very least. Others are married to kindred soul types. They aren't their truemates, but they love them nonetheless. They learn together, grow together and maybe in the next life they'll be with their bondmates." She shook her head, "It's a real mess when someone on the second tier has married a kindred soul, and then later finds their soulmate. Out of honor, they can't leave their marriage and be with their bondmate. Luckily, that doesn't happen often. Actually, only once. I hope it never happens again. It was sad to see."

O'Hara nodded, "But you and all your siblings are with your truemates? Not kindred, right?"

She affirmed, "Yes, every single one is with their bondmates. No other can ever take their place." She snorted, "It would take an act of a God."

He groaned, "I'm going to regret this, but a God?"

Her eyes wide, "Yes, there are many."

Just to clarify, he asked, "For you and your family?"

She nodded, "Yes. My siblings and I bow to the Triple Goddess and Her Consort, a Celtic pantheon. My mates bow to Isis and Osiris, an Egyptian pantheon. Gerard's mates bow to their Eskimo heritage and so on. Most of our mates bow to a different pantheon of Gods and Goddesses. There was a book on the different Gods I put on your list. You should read it."

His eyebrow rose, "And you all don't mind this. I mean there is no conflict because of the differences?"

She shook her head, "Oh, no. I even show honor and respect to my mate's pantheon. I serve my pantheon first, but I respect theirs, as well. And the reverse is true. We all respect each other's pantheons and learn about them, so as their mates, we can honor their times when they need to worship or have a job to do for their God or Goddess. We help when it's allowed, back off when it's not our business. Absolute tolerance is key. Respect for all paths and faiths are a must."

Surprised, O'Hara asked, "So no one is better than the other or tries to convert to another's faith?"

She practically hissed, "No, that is also anathema for us. None are so arrogant to believe that any one way is better or more valid than another. Look, you have many different ways of getting to your base right?" He nodded. "No one way is better than another. The most the difference is, is where you are and the best and fastest way to get there for you. Imagine trying to go the same way on the same path, day in and day out, no matter where you're at. It would be a bitch, wouldn't it?"

He agreed, "In some cases, yes."

"Religion and faith. The Gods and Goddesses are just the same way. When you are talking mind and spirit. When you are talking about astral blood ties though, that's a whole 'nuther ball game."

"How so?" O'Hara was fascinated with the subject.

"Remember being born of spirit? Well, each have an astral spirit blood tie that ties that person to a particular God or Goddess. When born of the flesh, they live, they grow, and they may or may not choose a religion to follow, right? But, say a particular person is born on this plane and decides to worship Buddha, for instance. He worships, he lives, he dies; but, if his or her astral blood ties are Egyptian, then they will first face that God or Goddess before they face Buddha. Blood ties on the spiritual plane overrule everything else."

His eyes were wide now. "So, no matter what you do here, you'll go before the God you're tied to before the God you worshiped on Earth, if it's not the same one?"

"Yes; my physical mother is a classic example. She now worships as a Christian, which would be absolutely fine with me if she worshiped that pantheon because of her heart. Unfortunately, she doesn't. She worships that God because of fear. Her new husband is Christian and brainwashed her into it. He's after her money. She doesn't want to lose him, so she converted to his religion so she could keep him. Bending her life to his to keep him with her, because he is so much younger then she is. He is my age, you see," Cat rolled her eyes in disgust. "Anyway, her spiritual blood ties are to The White Buffalo, an Indian pantheon, if you will. She has already transgressed on another problem much earlier and will face the Elders and The White Buffalo when she passes on, before all else. I know this, because I went to the astral plane Elders to plead her case and see if I could get her transgression lifted. They refused my request. The matter is now out of my hands and I will be sad for her when she passes. It won't be an easy time for her."

"You and your siblings don't seem to like the Christian religion much, or am I wrong?" he asked, confused because she said tolerance was a must.

"You are right and wrong. I like God and Jesus very much. Jesus loves everybody. It doesn't matter who or what they are. I can get behind that. I at least respect the God Yahweh, even if I don't agree with some of his tenants, or the way he wiped out his own pantheon, but that's a whole 'nuther story. It's the church and some of the people who use the religion for their own gains. They use it to control others, twisting the idealism to a dogma, to suit their own purposes. Mostly to control people's sex life, ergo, control their money and lives period. That's the part that we all can't stand. And most people aren't even aware of it, just wanting their religion spoon-fed to them without even looking into the history or political influences at the time the religion was made. So, they become sheeple and their souls aren't being fed properly. Actually, they are starving, hence the imbalances we see around us today. Crime, drugs, mental illness and so on."

Shaking his head, "I thought God and Yahweh is the same God?"

She barked a laugh, "No. Ask any Rabbi worth his kosher meal and he'll tell you, if he is honest, they are two separate Gods. Damn, the Bible has been rewritten at least fourteen times already. Lots of information and gospels were taken out that didn't fit the churches' need for control, or added to, when political climates changed. Just look to the King James version for that one."

An eyebrow rose again, "What do you mean?"

"The King of England at the time, paid that reigning Pope hordes of money to change the Bible, all for the ultimate goal of, not just more control over his subjects, but to be able to divorce, which wasn't allowed in the previous Bible versions, before the one he paid for. Lots of things have been taken out or added to, so the idealism of the teachings of Jesus has been twisted over the centuries. I bet He weeps in His Heaven seeing this happen. But, free will being what it is, none of the Gods or Goddesses can force a change over the evil some men do."

Wizard asked, "So, there is no Christian God?"

"Oh, no, I didn't say that. You have had millions and millions of people praying to this God for over two thousand years. If He wasn't real before, He is now. I can't tell you personally, because I wasn't born two thousand years ago physically, and didn't see for myself. Praying, however, *is* psychic energy; psychic energy over that amount of time becomes a reality. I do know, however, that the Archangel Michael is real and he and I get along well. He always comes to protect me when I am up against something a bit big for me to handle. He is cool. I like him. I owe him and his boss much. But, the people on this plane who profess to have God in his pocket if you just pay fifty dollars to their church and they'll heal you and you will go to the kingdom of heaven, and so on." She shuddered, "Those I can't stand."

Babyface joined in. "So how can a person tell the difference?"

"Read the books. There is a lot of information out there in books, on the web. There is a book I respect the researcher on; they said that when Israel became a state in 1948, the US backed them on the proviso that a certain document that had, up until that year been on display, not be shown anymore. An ancient document, which said Mary and her father, stated that Jesus was a product of rape. The story went: Joseph took Mary from his best friend, who she was originally engaged to, and got her pregnant. The Tabernacle law said she must marry Joseph then. Her uncle later had Joseph assassinated, which is why you don't see any more Joseph in any of the later gospels. Making Jesus not a son of a Deity, but a simple prophet, just like a lot of other prophets at that time. You ask most normal everyday people what the meaning of 'The Messiah' is in Hebrew, and they will, nine times out of ten, say 'Son of God'. It actually means, 'teacher of knowledge', hence a prophet. That's why some Jewish sections rejected Jesus."

Romeo snorted, "Damn, I didn't know that either."

She shrugged, "Most people don't. Most want the spoon-fed religion and when you are spoon fed, you can be lied to so easily; led around by the nose because you don't know any better. And you shouldn't even listen to me. I am not even a Messiah. I may be a High Priestess, but that is another job. You should decide for yourselves what you want to believe, if anything at all. Read the books; learn each religion and their history. Follow your own heart and soul. You will have a better chance of feeding your own soul, the way that is right for you. Don't listen to what I, or anyone else, tells you. Find out for yourself what you want."

"OK, say I do? And I want to be Christian. A lot of the books on chakras and astral projection would be considered evil—the practicing of witchcraft. How would that float?"

"One, if that is what you personally come to believe, then more power to you, but there are Christian witches. I like them, too. The whole tenant that, 'thou must not suffer a witch to live,' was changed from its original meaning many, many years ago. All of us witches know that. Like I said, read the books."

"You're shitting me?" Wizard said.

"Nope, you'd be surprised how much was changed in the Bible. There is talk of changing it yet again, to make it more PC for the times; more today. I guess that whole tenant that, 'anyone who takes a word out or changes a word will burn in hell,' went out the window," she snorted. "It went out the window hundreds and hundreds of years ago when they changed the original. I won't even go into HOW the original Bible came to be, in the first place. I'll let you find out on your own." Her face turned to them with mock seriousness, "You will be graded on it."

They all laughed.

Richard, and Brandon and Cat's mates had wandered back over from sitting and talking at the bar.

They were all sitting back at the table when Demitri reached over for a hug and asked, "What's up?"

Romeo answered, "She's been giving us history lessons in religions," wagging his eyes.

Demitri groaned, "Don't get her started on the Popes. Please for the love of the Gods, don't get her started on the Popes."

Wizard got a wicked grin and said, "What about the Popes?"

Every single one of her mates groaned aloud. Andre started beating his head on the table.

She grinned evilly. "Did you know that the first through the 14th Pope were married, and had kids, as did the rest of the church officials?"

"No way," Wizard exclaimed.

"Way," she nodded. "It wasn't until the 15th Pope, whom I think was a closet homosexual and/or just hated women, made it against the church law to be married if you were a church official. That's why you have so many priests now running after little altar boys. They have been running after little boys for a long, long time."

"So this whole thing the church has been debating over, about on letting their priests marry, being against the Bible, is bullshit?" Wizard asked.

"Yep; control, gentlemen. It's all about control," she nodded her head. "Did you know the first Pope was pagan?"

"Here she goes," Andre said. "She's on her band wagon now."

She glared at Andre. "The first Pope was a pagan Roman Emperor, Constantine, who saw his people being slaughtered by what was then considered a Christian *cult*. Their tenant was convert or die. Nice, huh?" she looked around. "So, to save his people, because they were losing and being massacred, he adopted the Christian religion as a national religion to be worshiped. He became the first Pope, but still worshipped as pagan in private. Thus, the Catholic Church was born. It wasn't until his death bed, when the next Pope-to-be, forced a shriven on him and stated that he had totally converted to Christianity before his death. The man wasn't even conscious enough to make that decision, but the church needed the rest of the populace to believe it for political and religious reasons."

Richard said, "You must have studied history very well."

"Twenty five years tracking down books from different sources, then hours of time meditating on which is true and which is victor's written history," she said.

He grinned." Yes, the victor of any conflict will write history to make theirs look good. It may not be the truth, just their view of it. It's hard to weed out the chaff from the wheat when they do that." She nodded. "But tell me, what does all that have to do with what you guys do? And the things we have been into lately with the dark Gods and vortexes?" He may have been relaxed earlier tonight, but now he was fishing again, O'Hara noticed. He wanted to know too, and listened avidly.

"It relates to what those evangelists say about 'the end of times'. The first time, was at the year 2000. Well, it passed and nothing happened. Then, they spouted that when 1948 and two scores passed, that was when the end of times was going to happen, because the Bible said so. That man is an idiot; oh, and a dark side practitioner, too. But, he spouts Christianity on TV for the money." She flipped off an imaginary enemy.

"Which TV evangelist?" Wizard wanted to know.

"The asswipe who'd said that hurricane Katrina happened because of the gays and the voodoo they practiced. That it was God's way of punishing them for being so free and accepting about it. He is really a dark adept. You should see the private jet he has, the three thousand dollar suits he wears, as well as the political pull - which he pays off with the money he scams from people watching his show. It's disgusting," she was snarling now.

"Oh, yeah, I remember hearing about that. The guy's a skank," he told them.

"Notice, he didn't have anything to say later when an F-5 tornado hit Kansas and did tremendous damage in the heart of white bread, good 'ole Christian folks. I guess God didn't send that one, huh?" She smiled while they laughed. "But then, he turns around and says crap about the earthquake in Haiti—saying it was God-sent to get those people for practicing voodoo."

"When bad things happen in controversial places, it's 'God's punishment'. When bad things happen in so-called good places, it's a 'tragedy'. I know. It sucks," O'Hara agreed.

She shook it off. "Back to what I was saying. If you add two scores and 1948, you had 2008. Well, '08 passed and nothing happened. We knew it wouldn't. Then, they adopted the Mayan prophecies—of 2012 now being the new 'end of times'. That one is the problem. At least, it's what we personally believe. Half is due to science; facts that are empirical. Half is because of what our pantheons are telling us."

Richard, looking relieved, said, "Give me the facts first. Facts, I can work with. Then, give me the rest and we'll go from there."

She took a deep breath. "OK; a shift is happening. It has been happening slowly over the last dozen years or so, but it is now speeding up. You can find out that the polarity of the earth will shift and the axis will tilt even more. Some of the earthquakes we've been having will help with that axis change. It will get worse. The closer we get to 2012, is when the shift will be complete, flipping North to South and South becomes North. The tectonic plates will shift, causing even more natural disasters the closer we get to 2012, because the shifting of the poles will speed up, causing friction within in the earth. Hence, lots of people, more than we have already lost, will perish. Those are the facts. The general populace has been misinformed into believing the scientists are wrong or exaggerating and so forth. Because there is nothing we can do to stop it. Panic won't help. A lot of our kind has power over the elements. I can slow or stop a hurricane, help ease floods and such, but I can't stop an earthquake. Those that can are very rare and we don't have one of those in our family ...yet. I am hoping and praying, but until then, we'll do what we can. The shift is a fact, though. The metaphysics that are related to it we can't prove, but there are myths and legends, which is why I keep telling you to read the books. There are grains of truth in many, many of them."

O'Hara nodded, "We will get on that ASAP. Meanwhile though, give us what you think or what you believe will happen and we'll go from there."

She took another deep breath. "Between the myths, legends and what our pantheons are telling us is this: When the shift happens, portals from other dimensions will open up that were closed the last time that this happened. Shifts naturally occur roughly every 2500 to 5000 years, but smaller ones. The North point will shift from this point to a few degrees in either direction. Small earthquakes happen and so forth. No big deal. But full shifts like this, not only will cause the damage I mentioned, but also open portals. Beings such as dragons, werewolves and vampires (and not the just nice ones) will return, as will other magickal races that haven't been seen since the last Great Shift. They were pushed in there or deported, if you will, by the ancient Gods and Goddesses. You have the nicer races, too, such as the elves and other types of Fae that haven't been seen in thousands and thousands of years. But they are talked about in our myths and legends still to this day. The problem is, gentlemen, portals and vortexes have already been opened up or cracked that shouldn't have happened quite yet. Point in case, the vortex that almost killed me. A vortex of that magnitude hasn't been recorded in our history since the last Great Shift. I came across one earlier than I expected. Then even *I* predicted. That means someone very powerful and someone very dark is making changes, or has made a change, but I can't pin point where or who yet."

Wizard spurted out, "Whoa, you're telling me we will be seeing werewolves, dragons and more weird shit?"

"Yes, but not all of them are bad or evil. Like any walk of life, you have good, bad and everything in between. So it is, with the Great Magickal Races. Our mandate, if you will, is to make peace treaties when they come, if we can. Defend the humans against those we can't. And meanwhile, save as many lives from disasters that we're able to." She shrugged, "The God and Goddesses aren't asking for much. Piece of cake," she snorted. "No, seriously though, we'll do what we can. We aren't the only Coven working towards these goals. There are many of our kind. But some are dark-pathed and will work against us, too."

O'Hara spoke, mostly to the General, "That's why we need to have them ward your office and the base with magick. As well as the barracks, is my recommendation, Sir. Until we can figure out what we're going to do about the information she's given us. Just to be on the safe side."

The General got a hard look and ordered, "Explain."

O'Hara told him about the wards around the club house. The protections they used on their houses, cars and the reasons for it. How it was mandatory for all family members.

The General took all this in and then seemed to come to a decision. "I'll back this. You said you can get this done tomorrow?"

Cat nodded, "First thing, I promise."

He gave a nod, "See to it then." Then he turned to her mates, "Do all of you believe in the portals opening?"

Demitri spoke for the trio after a quick looking around. "She knows her history, she knows her religions. She also has degrees in science and astronomy."

Andre added, "Many degrees in many subjects, actually."

Demitri nodded."True, but we also have our own pantheon and they tell us the same thing. They all are. If you get that many pantheons telling you all the same thing, it's time to listen. Plus, her predictions are rarely wrong."

"But I have been wrong," her face looked so sad then. Antonio reached around her, hugging her.

He said quietly, "But rarely." She just leaned back and closed her eyes.

O'Hara wondered what had happened the last time she was wrong. Whatever it was, it was still tearing them up inside. At least it was for her.

"The fact that we're here, and needed, is proof enough. We're the big guns. The Gods don't pull out the big guns unless there is a need. We wouldn't have been born on this plane otherwise," Andre said.

The General asked, "What makes you the 'big guns'?"

They all looked around at each other.

Cat patted Demitri's hand, but looked at the General. "Right now, we've dumped a lot on you. Things we can't just show you as being true, even with magick. I have a feeling though, things will happen that will prove us true, and when that happens, we'll have another heart to heart. I am afraid, at this point, even if She told me it was ok, you wouldn't believe it. And I wouldn't blame you either."

The General didn't look too thrilled, but let it go and asked instead, "Why would those that are like you, but dark path, try to cluster fuck the situation? Wouldn't it hurt them, too?"

She lifted her lip, "It's the old, 'take over the world ploy.'"

Andre popped in with, "The Mummy."

"No, The Mummy Returns, you owe me!" She was grinning now.

The General laughed, then said, "But you and yours don't want to rule the world yourselves?"

"Oh, hell no," she snorted, "why the fuck would I do that when I have my own world already? Mine is much better!"

"Excuse me?" the General's eyes were wide. O'Hara, too, wasn't sure he quite caught that right.

Her eyes were wide as saucers and Demitri rubbed his hand down his face groaning. "Oops," she said, "Forget I said that. You didn't hear it."

"Ah, yes we did, "O'Hara said. His eyebrow was totally high now.

She groaned and leaned back against Antonio. "We can show you later, maybe, but not right now. You'll have to wait."

Romeo let out a low, "Whoooaaa."

"And the hits just keep on coming," Wizard said.

"A Few Good Men," replied Demitri, Cat and Andre almost simultaneously.

The General started to speak and Cat held up her hand, "Not now, General. Not even for a King's ransom." Her face took on a determined look."Read the books. Then you might believe it." She looked brightly to the rest of them, "Who wants a good night beer?"

Nice change, O'Hara thought, but he wouldn't forget what she'd said and he'd worm it out of her. Sooner or later.

CHAPTER SEVENTEEN
Hunt of the Hellhounds

General Matthew Robertson glowered in the seat of the plane about to land at Navy Air Station base, where he would personally see what was going on. When he had received word that this General Pierce's Special Forces team had successfully cracked the terrorist compound in Pakistan that he and his cohorts had worked so diligently to help set up, he was furious. The amount of man power, time, and money (not to mention the magickal energy spent on making that compound functional and foolproof—to be used as a tool for his black cover.'s ultimate goals), had been blown out the window in one night.

He'd sent inquiries out to find out how it had happened, only to be stone-walled at every turn. Even using his magick didn't get him any results, which had forced him to call in favors and get him a meeting with General Pierce himself. A face-to-face with the man should yield the information he needed to find, so he can then deal with the situation.

He refused to be held up, now that he was so close to getting what he and his coven needed for their plans to become a reality. As he stepped off the plane and went down the stairs to the ground, where a waiting car would take him to the building where General Pierce had his office, he started to get an uneasy feeling. The feeling grew stronger the closer he got to the building. Even his attaché was feeling the charge in the air. He gritted his teeth and strengthened his shields. This has already gotten interesting. And annoying.

The closer they got to the building, the feeling of unease started to turn into a slight queasy feeling in his gut. His attaché was looking a bit green around the gills. He sent out a feeler and got zinged back. Like a sharp electrical charge zapping in defense. He thought it would be prudent not to try anything else until after his meeting with General Pierce. Though from what he remembered, General Pierce had never even had so much as a rumor to being a practitioner of any path that he knew of. He wondered that if it wasn't General Pierce's doing, who was the practitioner that spelled this place? When they passed through the door going into the building itself, he got a strong wave of vertigo. He clenched his fist in anger of being magickally treated like this. How dare they. When he found who was responsible, he would happily drag them back to his sacred chamber and sacrifice their screaming soul to his Dark God. The feelings grew, the closer he got to the office of General Pierce. They were escorted to his attachés office, where the door on the left side was the General's office.

The Major stood when he walked in and saluted him, "Good morning, Sir. How can I help you?"

He returned the salute, "I am here with an appointment with General Pierce."

"Yes, Sir, if you will wait here, I will see if he is ready for you." Major Stewart walked directly to the General's door and knocked. He walked in when he got permission to enter and returned a second later.

"General Pierce will see you now, Sir," and opened the door for him to step through. Going through Major Stewart's door was bad enough, but it took every ounce of his shielding abilities to get through this last door. If he hadn't gotten an invitation, he wouldn't have been able to do it at all. Even the Major's door was hard to get through without an invitation. The General couldn't be the one who had done the wards and protections. This level of power would have been known to his people if it were true. The General would have been flagged as a potential threat long ago and dealt with. He pasted a smile on his face after they saluted each other then shook hands.

General Pierce waved him to the chair in front of his desk, "Would you like a drink? I know it's a bit early at twelve hundred hours but…," he let the sentence drop off with a question hanging on it.

"I would love some scotch if you have it, General Pierce." He agreed to the drink so it would give him time to glance around the office to get a read on exactly what type of wards were around the place. His attaché sitting out in the Major's office will be doing the same thing. He didn't get any level of power from the General himself as he shook his hand, but he could be really good at hiding what he might be.

"Here you go, General Robertson. It's twelve-year old scotch, you should like it," the General said, as he handed him his drink.

"Matthew, please, and thank you for the drink," he said, politely offering his name to try to establish friendliness with the General. They were both four-star Generals, so posturing wasn't an issue for them.

"Richard, then please. What can I do for you?" he asked, as he sat back into his chair with his own drink.

He cleared his throat, "I heard you and your team finally cracked that hard nut down in Pakistan. Your man got his shiny gold star back over his head. Congratulations, by the way!"

Richard nodded his head, "Thank you, but I thought it was top secret? Only a few should have heard about it." He took a sip of his drink.

"Oh, I have connections all around, and when I heard about it, I had to come see you personally. You see, we may have another hard nut to crack, and I wanted to see if you and your boys might want to have a run at it." He gave General Pierce a fake admiring look.

Richard's eyes widened, "Oh, that sounds intriguing, but I do have to listen to those over my own head. They are the ones who say when and where we go."

Robertson nodded his head in agreement, "I understand that, but you know as well as I we both can get around that if we chose to. Or, by making a call, maybe they would give you the go ahead, after seeing the file I brought on the mission. I would consider it a personal favor to me."

Richard took a good look at him. "Why is it so important, and why my men?"

"Would you like to see the file?" At Richard's nod, he bent down for his briefcase and opened it. He took out the file and gave it to him. "It's a tricky mission, for one. A diplomat and his daughter were kidnapped in Saudi. You know how things have been between the U.S. and Saudi lately. We can't go in officially. Things are hot enough over there as it is. But a covert mission, under the wire, might be the trick. Your men have a reputation for getting the impossible done. It would be imperative though, to get there, and get the diplomat and his daughter back again without leaving any footprints."

General Pierce was reading the file. Robertson already knew everything about it, since it had been on his orders for the kidnapping to take place from the beginning. He was going to use the event for another reason, but decided to use it now as an excuse to find out more about Pierce's team. Someone had to be a strong practitioner in the team, if not the General himself. He doubted it was him, but he had someone close to him that was. That was obvious from the sickening wards that surrounded him now. Pierce has to know who it is to have had this done. Pierce had no photos on his desk. No personal items he could knick to use as a focus. Damn the man. Someone had schooled him well on not leaving anything personal out that someone could take and use against him.

"Well, this looks like it has the potential to be a bad situation if not handled well and soon. I take it we don't have much time before the father and daughter will be killed?" Richard asked.

He shook his head, "Eighteen hours on the outside. The sooner we can get someone out there the better. I heard your team also did a terrorist situation stateside just a few months ago. No casualties other than what the terrorists did already and got the plane down on the ground in one piece. That was some coup. It was what made me think of your team for this stint. How did they manage that one?"

Pierce answered cryptically, "Very carefully."

Robertson kept his poker face on, but the short answer told him more than Richard wanted known. The mission itself wasn't top secret and something like that, most would want to boast about. He was being extremely closed-mouthed about a mission that had made the news and made his team look damn good to those in the Pentagon. Hmmm, maybe he should look into that one more carefully. He had only used that mission as a reason for thinking of Pierce's team for this kidnapping case, but it seemed there was more about it than meets the eye.

Getting back to his original goal, "How did your boys get that hard nut? It was very impressive as well, he asked."

Pierce looked up from the file, "We had the right tool this time, is all."

Robertson smiled at him, 'Must be some tool. Isn't that mission the one that almost sunk your man, O'Hara, because he backed off the first time?"

"O'Hara knew he needed something more to get the job done right. Losing the second team proved him right, unfortunately. O'Hara got what he needed and went after it again. Did his job and got out," Richard fed the same party line that had been floating around. There had to be more to it than that. No mundane could have gotten through otherwise.

He smiled at Pierce, "Some tool there. Anything any of the other teams could use? I have a team or two that I use from time to time. They might benefit from learning about this tool from your men."

Pierce shook his head, "No, I am afraid not. I wouldn't want to lose any of our personnel. If you have your own team or teams, why don't you use them for this mission instead?"

Damn the man.

He pasted a fake smile on, "Your team has a much better average in getting the job done right. I want to give the diplomat and his daughter the best possible chance." Robertson was losing his patience and started to twist the ring on his finger. Maybe it was the room. He needed to get out of here soon to get away from the wards.

At that moment the phone rang on the General's desk. Pierce picked it up with an annoyed look on his face.

"I am still in ..." He stopped and listened to what his attaché was telling him on the other end. "Ok, put her through." He paused, as he waited for the patch through, "Yes, what can I do for you?"

He watched as Pierce had his conversation on the phone, which ended with a yes from Pierce before he hung up.

"Sorry about that, Matthew, but it was important. Now, about this case. I will kick it up the line with a red alert on it for a fast response. If we get the all clear, my men will go out. It's the best I can do."

"That's all I am asking for," he stood up to shake Pierce's hand. "I'll be at the Suites here on the base waiting for your answer, if that's all right?"

Richard nodded, "That would be fine. I'll call as soon as I know anything." Pierce walked him to the door and he collected his attaché as he left.

General Pierce had barely gotten off the phone when Cat came storming into his office armed to teeth and looking to kill something. She was followed by Cassie, Grant and two of her mates.

"Where is it?" she asked Pierce.

"If you mean him, he is at the Suite here on the base waiting for my yea or nay on a mission. What, exactly, is the problem?" he looked at her, trying for patience.

She wouldn't be this on edge for no reason.

She breathed the air and looked around slowly and carefully. "You had a darksider here. It tripped my astral alarm system, so we came running. Who was it that was here?"

"General Robertson. He was asking a lot of questions about the mission in Pakistan which he really shouldn't have known about, as well as the attempted hijacking in New York. I noticed two odd things about him. He took the drink I offered him, but didn't so much as sip it. Then he played with a ring on his hand. Not an exact ring like the one Williams wore, but a close proximity of it." He was looking worried now, as he put all the pieces together about the meeting. It had felt off from the start, and it looks like his gut was right about the whole situation not being right.

"He wouldn't take a sip if he is what I think he is. At least the smart ones don't. A lot of times it could be poisoned or hexed. Going into an enemy's territory, you never eat or drink anything offered to you. It's astral protection 101. What did he say he wanted?"

Pierce grabbed the file Robertson had given him and handed it to her. "This mission he wants O'Hara to go on. It's a tight one. A diplomat and his daughter have been kidnapped in Saudi. We can't do anything officially and we can't give into their demands. He was proposing a covert op. He requested O'Hara because of the missions he has done lately, he said."

"What would he personally gain from having O'Hara do this for him?" she mused.

She paused, and turned to look at her family. "Cassie, Grant, can you two go clean up the black sludge that prick left behind? I'll get the General's office."

They both nodded, Grant saying, "On it," and they went out the door.

"Andre, go to O'Hara's office and see if any clean up is needed there. If O'Hara is there, bring him back with you." He kissed her and left to go do what she asked.

She turned to Antonio, "Sweetheart, can you check the rest of the building? Track and clean only to the outer door. Don't go outside of the building and do any clean up. I don't want to tip off our presence here, yet."

He kissed her goodbye too, "You've got it, babe."

She put the file back on the desk and went to pick up the incense to start her own clean up.

When she was done, she sniffed the glass Robertson had held. "Yup, it was definitely him that's tripped my alarm. If there was anyone with him, he most likely is one, too. They don't like to roll with anyone not their kind."

She looked him up and down intently. "Nope, he didn't do anything to you. Your aura is clear. So what did the big bad want? Really?"

"Like I said, he was asking an awful lot of questions about things that weren't really his business in the first place. He isn't part of the committee I answer to. That much I do know."

O'Hara and Andre walked in. "Got him, babe. Nothing in his office. It was free and clear, except the flowers on his desk. I smelled them, but they weren't there for ill intentions."

"Flowers, O'Hara?" she asked him.

He sighed, "It's been going on for about a week now. I keep finding these flowers on my desk and things keep getting moved around. I thought at first I was just misplacing things, but I don't usually do that. What's going on here though?" He seemed to be trying to change the subject.

"A visit from a big bad. A General Robertson has been asking questions about your recent missions and wants your team to go on another one." She reached over, looking at the General, "Is it all right?"

He nodded to her, "Yes, please."

She handed him the file, "Read it."

O'Hara scanned the Intel with Andre reading over his shoulder. Everyone else was obviously done with their chores, when they sauntered back in.

"What's up?" Grant asked.

O'Hara read out loud so they could all get the gist of the situation.

Grant whistled low, "So, what do they want in return of the girl and her dad?"

"Something we couldn't give. People released and getting our bases out of their country," General Pierce sighed. "Same thing, different group, all the time there lately."

The Major knocked and received a come in from the General. "Cat's children are here at the front gate. What do you want me to do?" looking from the General to Cat, not knowing which one had the voice in this particular situation.

The General saved him, saying, "Cat?"

"I wonder what they could want. Let them in, if it's ok, General. Tell them to come here." She looked puzzled by the visit. "By the way, I am sorry I used the emergency code that interrupted your meeting and then when I just barged in with my family in tow. But when that alarm got triggered, I felt it was best to get to you fast. Just in case." She did look contrite, knowing she'd over-stepped her bounds on one level, without showing due respect to his position, but she did it for the right reasons and he could forgive her for that. It also showed she cared for his well being, as did O'Hara. He was starting to care for her as he would for his own daughter. If he had one.

He smiled gently at her, "You were just worried and did what you thought was best. Just don't make a habit of it, shall we?"

"I'll try," she said, and Andre snorted.

The General caught that, but ignored it. "If you truly feel repentant, can you see your way clear to do me a favor?"

Her eyes got a suspicious gleam in them, "What?"

"The administrator of the hospital noticed how fast our guys healed, and how well. He was wondering if the medic I used could come take a look at two of our other soldiers." She snorted at the 'medic' label. "One of them is in a coma, the other is critical. I know they aren't a part of our platoon, but I was hoping for a small miracle, or two?" He watched her face and knew she wouldn't be able to say no.

"The critical one should be no problem. I won't know for sure until I take a look at him. The one in a coma is another matter," she stated.

"How so?" The General was curious.

She went to grab a juice from his cabinet. "The one in a coma, I will have to astral out and follow his 'aka cord' to wherever his spirit, soul or astral subtle body is. That's why he's in a coma. One of those parts of him is out on a walk-about. It doesn't matter which part of him is out. When I find the part, I can only ask him to come back. I'll guide him back if he says yes, but if he says no, I cannot, nor will not, force him back," she sounded determined on that.

"What's an 'aka cord'?" Pierce had never heard that term before.

Surprisingly, it was O'Hara who answered first, "An 'aka cord' is a cord that goes from the solar-plex chakra to each of the seven levels of a person's inner being. It can also go to those who have bonds with others. Like a mother-son bond, father-daughter bond, and so on."

Cat looked pleased. "You've been reading the books. Good job!"

"Well that sounds all right, then. How long will something like that take?" the General asked Cat.

She shrugged, "Depends. Sometimes they're hanging around in the room near their body. Sometimes they are out on the physical plane back at their home or somewhere they felt safe. The main reason for a coma is because the person suffered a severe trauma, so part of them escapes from the body, wandering around wherever they feel safest. Some even go to the astral planes—and those are the hardest to talk into coming back."

O'Hara asked before he could, "Why is that?"

"Because the astral planes, lower or higher, can fool a person into believing that is their own heaven or hell. Convincing them that they are still alive, and their body is back on the physical plane waiting for them, can take some doing. It's easier when the person tracking them on one of the astral planes is a relative or someone they trust. I'm a complete stranger, so he may not believe me." She finished her drink and threw it in the garbage can next to his desk.

"So, what I'm getting is, it can take longer than fifteen or thirty minutes?" Pierce asked her.

She nodded, "Yup."

He sighed, "Ok, then can we take care of the critical one now and save the one in a coma for when you come back. I still haven't decided what to do about this," pointing to the file. "O'Hara, what are your thoughts?" They were interrupted when there was another knock on the door.

It was the Major with her boys. She waved them in and motioned them to sit back and wait 'till they were done. O'Hara looked at her, as if asking her if she really wanted them in the conversation, to which he got an affirmative.

He shrugged at it, thinking to himself they weren't his kids and answered the General. "It's a tight situation. We can fly to the base in Saudi and drive out from there to a point about twenty-four clicks away. But the Intel doesn't cover exactly what kind of resistance we may have. There is nothing about any land mines that may be strewn around, tripwires or booby traps. We also don't have any photos on the building they think they may be in. The Intel is suspiciously light. I have to wonder what he is really after and how did this wind up on his desk? The only good thing we have going for us is the location of the building being on the outskirts of the town. We won't have to worry about civilians giving us away. The chances of any civilian casualties are at a minimum, as well."

The General looked at Cat. "I know your people are only to do the weird, but he did come to the office with this and is a darksider like you said. I know this looks like a normal job of a kidnapped diplomat and his young daughter, but would you consider going along? If so, what do you think of it?"

"One, I think he's after something. Two, I think he knows you now have magickal help. That could be what he is after. Somehow, someway, you stepped on his toes and he's trying to figure out how you did it. Once he has enough Intel on the how, the who and the what, he'll most likely come after you." Everyone murmured their agreement. "This job here, I think we should go for." She turned to O'Hara, "I know the Intel is light. Too light. But with us along, we can see and sniff out more things than a regular human. We can help you sidestep any land mines and such. That's not the problem."

"What is the problem you see?" O'Hara asked her.

"This could be a way for that General to see what you have up your sleeve. He might have someone watching. If so, once we get ID'ed by his spies, they may decide to come after the General here right away, while we're stuck in Saudi. It's what I would do. He may be thinking General Pierce is left here without protection, because all of us, your team and your ace up your sleeve, is over there dealing with this," jabbing her finger at the file.

The General got a smug look on his face. "But what they don't know is that we have more than one ace up our sleeve."

They all got grins on their faces over that remark. She looked at the General, "So you wouldn't mind being in protective custody until we get back to the base?"

"What kind of leader would I be to ignore a clear threat?" he responded lightly.

225

She grinned at him. Then her eldest boy cleared his throat, saying, "Mother."

"Yes, son?" she glanced at him.

"We would like to be a part of this. We are all old enough now and we think we can handle the lower class jobs, if you like. But we want to get started now on more serious learning."

O'Hara held his breath. He was wondering why she'd allowed her kids in, on what he considered a delicate matter; not for public consumption.

She caught his look, "O'Hara, General, I let my boys in on this meeting because, as he said, they have learned all we can teach them at home and in our private dojo's. I wanted them to see how my mates, siblings and I work together. By *watching* and *listening,* they can learn much of how to be a leader and when to fall back and let someone else lead." She got up and walked to face her son. "However, I did not allow them in here to go on a mission with us so early in their training for this level. They still have much to learn."

O'Hara saw the General nod his head. He was wondering if the General was agreeing with her assessment or knowing the reasons for allowing the boys in. Maybe both?

She continued, "Is this why you followed us to the base? To be allowed on a mission?"

"Well, yes. We need to learn more, Mother." He held her eyes steadily and refused to lower them to her.

"Watching and listening on how we handle a situation isn't good enough for you for now?" she asked him, her voice getting a tad threatening. O'Hara and the General could hear it. Both of them also noticed her mates were just watching, not interfering whatsoever. Her brother and sister looked curious about the situation.

Craven stepped up and looked his mother dead in the eye with an expression of sincere honesty, saying, "Sweet Mother of all that is beautiful and gorgeous; stunning in your perfection of radiance; glowing in your…"

"STOP," she turned around, so as to not show she was biting back laughter.

Crimson said in a quiet voice, "Suck up."

"Both of you shut up. This won't help," Christoph said in a biting voice.

Her mates walked outside the office, closing the door, but it didn't stop the laughter both O'Hara and the General heard coming from Major Stewart's office. Her siblings were biting their lips, looking up at the ceiling.

The General cleared his throat, "I may have a solution to this …umm… dilemma."

Cat's eyes widened. "Oh, please enlighten me, oh fearless leader."

He gave her a mock glare, but continued, "They can help guard me while you're gone."

O'Hara and Cat looked shocked, and then she broke first with a grin. "Yes, that's perfect."

Craven spoke again, "Fine, these two can stay and guard the General. That is the most important job, a high priority job, and I'll go with you to Saudi."

"What? No way," she turned back to him.

He looked determinedly at his mother. "Yes way, Mother, because like you said, I can watch and learn. How can any us of learn anything if we don't see anything? Meetings are nice, but all we'll learn is how to have a meeting. It won't show us how to follow orders in the field. How to deploy men on a job. How to take down the bad guys. How to sneak; when to sneak. When to charge, when not to charge. When to use magick. When to use mundane means. We won't learn anything like that and that's what we really need now."

"Yeah, so we get stuck babysitting, while you get all the glory?" Christoph snorted.

"No, he is a General. A very important man and like Mom said, if that bad guy send anything or anyone after him, those left behind will have to deal with it. You two are better suited for that. All I'm doing is tagging along, watching and staying out of the way." He looked at his mother with his big blue eyes, doing their damnedest to get her to agree. "I promise, Mom."

Both O'Hara and the General could see this young one working her down and admired his strategy.

Christoph and Crimson both nodded their heads, with Christoph adding, "He'll probably send something or someone really nasty. We'll be here for that. We'll have your back, General Pierce."

"Umm, thank you, son," wondering what he had gotten himself into. Her mates had snuck back into the room to watch the last half of the scamming this young one was doing.

"Maybe that's not such a good idea then?" she asked the room at large.

"Mother, you know I can handle anything thrown at me. You trained me yourself. Crimson, too. He's wicked with a blade," Christoph spoke fast.

"What about the girl, Mom?" Craven added to his argument. "She is how old, General?"

"Nine years old," he told him, trying to figure out where he would take his argument.

"See, you'll need me. You know I'm good with young kids. She'll be freaked out, needing someone close to her age who can calm her. Hell, I can carry her if she's too tired, instead of you or another soldier carrying her, which would give you another gun free for protection. With me carrying her, we can move faster."

The General and O'Hara look at each other, knowing they had the same thought. This kid was slick.

She actually stopped to think about that. "You're right, it would free up another gun. Of course, the nasty stuff could hit us there if Robertson wants to take out O'Hara and not the General. Or he could try for a two for one and send nasty things to both. Both ways, you could all be in the line of fire and it would be best to keep you all home," she raised her own eyebrow with that.

Craven held up his hand to stop his brothers. "Then how will we ever learn? Time is running out, Mom. You said so yourself, that things are happening faster than you predicted. If you wait too long, it may be too late to teach us the really rough stuff. Then, when shit happens, where will we be, huh?"

"Shit, I fucking hate it when you do that Craven, I really do," she stomped away, breathing hard.

"Babe?" Andre asked lightly.

"No, he's right. That's why I am so mad." She stomped back over to him and grabbed his shirt and pulled him close to her face. "Hear me well son. I will take you, but you had better follow my orders to the letter. Or when we get home I'll have your ass in the pit. No more grounding, no more spankings. You want to be treated like a man? Fine, you will be. And it's the pit for you, if you step out of line, even once. I will not treat you any differently then I would O'Hara's men or anyone placed under my command. Do you understand that, son?"

"I understand," he said seriously.

"I am serious. No different than anyone else under my command who did not follow my orders. I will beat your ass black and blue. Are we clear?" she growled.

"Clear, Mom," he said quietly.

"Are we clear?" she asked louder.

"Crystal clear, Mom," he answered louder.

228

She let his shirt go and dropped him gently back to the floor. "Don't call me 'Mom' on the job. You have to call me Cat. Trust me, it's a leadership thing. Just ask O'Hara or the General for that matter."

"Yes, Cat," Craven said, promptly obeying her.

This seemed to have satisfied her and she went to her other two sons. "Both of you will be under Grant and Cassie's command. You will follow their orders precisely, or you too, will find yourself in the pit with me. Is that understood?"

"Yes, Cat," they said simultaneously.

Growling, she said, "Guard that man well. Make me proud. Don't let anything happen to him."

"Yes, Cat," they both repeated.

"Grant and Cassie, you have my sons at your disposal." Turning to the General, "These two will be in charge of setting up protection for you while we are gone, if you send the rest of us. It's your call."

He cleared his throat, 'Yes, well, I am waiting for word from upstairs about that right now. I'll also try to find out how he knew of the Pakistan mission."

He picked up the phone and got Major Stewart to get the ball rolling.

He looked at everyone, "Why don't you all meet me in the war room. I'll be there once I get this all settled. O'Hara, get your team and a squad together just in case. Pack for Saudi."

"Yes, Sir," O'Hara clipped out.

The General looked at Cat. "Cat, you should pack too, and pick your team, other than what you've already decided. Let O'Hara know your configuration. I'll have the Major get a plane on standby. Also, you or one of your people can see to the critical soldier."

"Yes, Sir," she snapped out as well.

Everyone else just nodded and walked out the door.

When General Pierce walked into the war room, he noticed that O'Hara had called in Sergeant Miller for the briefing, also. The rest of O'Hara's core team was there, as well. The soldiers came to attention and he waved them to go at ease.

He got to the point. "It's a go. The Pentagon, as well as others in power, would very much like to see this come to an end, quickly and quietly. It is imperative we are not caught doing it. That is priority one. Rescuing the diplomat and his daughter is second to it. I trust you have already hashed out a rough outline?"

O'Hara nodded, "I've spent a lot of time in Saudi and have friends on the base there. We'll be able to get set up with what we'll need once we get there."

General Pierce said, "Good." Then he turned to Cassie," I got a call from the administrators office. Thanks for the healing. The man is doing well now." She nodded back at him. "You'll take care of the coma patient later?"

Cassie shook her head, "I was going to let Cat do it when she got back. She is the best out of us at astral projection. She's done things on the astral planes none of us have touched yet. If he's there, she's the one most likely able to bring him back."

The General nodded at her, "Good, it can wait then. I called General Robertson and told him the good news," he said with slight sarcasm. "He thanked me and said he was taking off for another meeting somewhere."

Cat interrupted him, "When?"

"He has requested our tower for permission for takeoff in 30 minutes."

"Good, then fill me in with the rest of it later. I'm going to go get set up where he can't see me." As she started to walk out the door the General stopped her. "What are you planning?"

"A watcher. I'll tag it to him when he leaves," she explained.

"Won't he notice something like that?" General Pierce asked her.

She grinned evilly, "Nope, I have a way of cloaking mine. Not many know how to do it and it's undetectable. True, it won't get past any place he's got shielded, but it will hang around until he comes back from under it and follow him in open places. We'll at least get Intel of that much." She looked at her people, "You guys need to hide your power levels. Antonio, show the boys how. Try to mask our numbers, too." The General nodded a 'go' at her and she whipped out the door.

General Robertson smiled to himself, pleased with the results of the meeting so far. He had put together a nasty surprise for Pierce when O'Hara landed in Saudi. He'd noticed that the shield around the building itself was a young one, and weak, with people going in and out of it every day. Easy enough to punch a hole through it and send the hell hounds in after anyone inside the building. True, they wouldn't be able to get past the more personalized shields of the Major and the General's office, but he would bet money Pierce would be the type to come running to back his men, leaving him open enough for attack. O'Hara and whatever this so called 'tool' they had, would have their own surprise waiting for them as well, once they got close enough to the building that the hostages were being kept in. But just in case this doesn't get every one of them, he'll go to New York and gather more information. Always good to cover your bases, he thought to himself.

Four hours later, he wasn't smiling so much anymore. After his illuminating talk with Special Agent Williams, he had learned much about this 'tool' General Pierce and O'Hara had picked up. He also found out Williams belonged to another dark coven and was using the fear card to make an incumbent look bad, so another would get elected in the following elections. His coven wanted people who were coven members themselves or at least handpicked by them, who would then take over their districts. His own coven has been using the fear card with great success in getting people replaced in the Pentagon, one by one. Another good thing coming out of the meeting with Williams was an alliance of sorts. Their covens would help each other get their people in place, with his taking over the Pentagon and William's people controlling as much of the Senate and House as possible. 2012 wasn't too far off, though they should both be controlling a vast majority by then. And when more portals opened, they'll be the ones making the deals with the greater magickal races and eventually controlling even them. He smirked to himself. Like the one they had made in Saudi.

This Catrina Garcia though, losing his smile, he had thought she was dead from tangling with another dark God. True, the dark God Orochi was no more, having been thrown back into his own dimension. But the rumor was, she herself had perished in the fight. That rumor was obviously not true. Now, she has also has taken out another dark God, Kalim. The one he had helped those puppets in Pakistan to call up. That makes her more of a threat than he had thought. He made a call to Saudi and demanded a larger contingent then he'd originally ordered. One of those beasts weren't going to be enough. But three. Yes, three should do the trick. She won't be expecting them and one of those beasts can take out a whole squad in under three minutes if it didn't stop to feed right away. He had to offer up the young girl in return, who he'd planned on sacrificing at the next Sabbath. Oh, well, there were many others he could get a hold of to replace the child.

CHAPTER EIGHTEEN
Shadow of Intent

Cat was praying under her breath to her Goddess while holding Andre's hand. She prayed for protection for those at home and for a successful mission here. She prayed for the well being of everyone involved with this mission. She prayed and hoped she was heard. Andre squeezed her hand while he said his own prayers. Both of them were nervous for their young son; but Craven and his brothers were right. Time was running out, and they did need experience in the field. Better a simple kidnapping then what she had just dealt with for a first mission, she thought to herself.

Craven was wearing his own uniform, for real, for the first time, and it almost made her cry. So far, he had done exactly what she'd said, when she said it; playing the perfect soldier. So far, only Romeo and an Ensign in the squad had warmed up to the boy. They were talking during the last leg of the flight to Saudi about weapons, such as what kind of gun would be good for certain kind of areas and situations. Romeo was partial to the SOCOM and his Glock. The Ensign liked his Desert Eagle nine mil. On and on, they argued about accuracy and dirt with each type of gun or rifle.

Craven just soaked up the information. She knew when he got home, he would ask to be able to use the small arsenal they had there for practice, and see exactly for himself what these guys were talking about. She knew O'Hara wasn't happy, but only asked her if she knew what she was doing. When satisfied with the answer, he asked for his abilities with weapons and magick. He seemed impressed with all the kids fighting abilities and with various types of weapons.

Craven just preferred his Bo, but he did take his knives and swords with him for this mission. O'Hara raised his eyebrow when each of them wore not only the blades, but had their gun of choice strapped onto their waist belt, with the bottom of the holster tied to their thighs, so the holster wouldn't flop against them and make noise when running. He seemed to approve of the added weaponry, at least.

Eleven hours later, they landed for the final time in Saudi Arabia. They had all put on their head wraps and, if asked, O'Hara would only say to others outside of their squad that a few of their men were using different tactics and the new gear was necessary for that. They figured that way, if no one saw their faces, they wouldn't be able to tell that they weren't military by trying to look them up in the military data base.

They used the vehicles that were waiting for them on the base and took off right away. They needed two vans to hold everyone plus have room for the diplomat and his daughter. Cat had learned it was Ambassador Roger Hubert and his daughter, Melody, while reading the file back at the office. Why anyone would bring his young child to a hot zone on a job was beyond her. Then she mentally kicked herself, thinking about what she was doing.

She sure couldn't throw any stones on this one. Cat got ready to work by putting her game face on and shutting down any part inside that wouldn't be good for the mission at hand. They got about 4 clicks away from the building and hid the vans as best they could before hoofing it out, fast, because they were running out of time. Right before they were about to split the squad, approaching the building from three different directions, she fell to her knees, as did Andre. Craven's eyes looked panicked and wide open with shock.

O'Hara slid up by them and asked, "What's wrong?"

Cat was breathing heavily, "They're under attack at the base."

"By what?" O'Hara demanded.

"I don't know. I'm only getting glimpses of teeth and screaming. Are either of you getting a better picture?" she asked her mate and her son.

Both shook their heads.

Craven asked in a shaky voice, "What do we do, Mom?"

"Cat," she corrected him, "and we finish this job. There isn't anything we can do back there now. We'll find out as soon as the fight is over. I don't want to get in contact with your other fathers or your brothers and distract them at a critical moment. It could get them killed. You," pointing to Craven, "go with this group here around the side like we planned. I'll go with the group up the front. Andre can watch for trip wires and mines and take the back with the last group. We finish this, then we go home and see who we need to kill."

They all agreed to that and took their positions, splitting up, each going with their assigned group. Cat was in O'Hara's group, as they made their way carefully to the building. In three minutes, they were all hidden behind trees, bushes, cars and debris lying in piles in the street near the building, waiting for the go signal, to hit the building at the same time. Cat waited for O'Hara to send the signal, when they all heard the growling start off to the east side, and shortly afterwards, gunfire. The side of the building that her son was at.

The sounds were bound to alert those inside and O'Hara looked at Cat, seeing tears in her eyes. She shook her head and said, "Go. The job first. Go." And he sent the signal. They hit the warehouse building with gunfire blazing on both sides, now that the element of surprise was gone. They laid waste quickly, since there were only nine terrorists in the building. The last two had guns pointed at the ambassador's and his daughter's head, threatening to blow them away if the soldiers didn't back off now.

Cat looked at Andre, who had come up behind, and O'Hara watched as they both raised their guns, took aim and fired; hitting both their targets almost simultaneously. Cat caught the one terrorist in the forehead and Andre had blown away the back of the head of the other one.

O'Hara shouted out, "Are you fucking crazy?"

Cat turned hard eyes at him, "They couldn't pull their triggers. Andre and I made sure the guns could not work. The man and the girl were never in danger, I promise. We have to go now. I feel his pain." And they both ran out the door towards the position her son was last at, while O'Hara got the father and daughter untied and made them move. The girl was hysterical, but the father was comforting her.

Right before the go signal

Craven was excited and scared at the same time. His adrenalin was pumping. He made sure he followed his mother's instructions to the letter, because he knew she wasn't kidding about the pit threat. So he stayed in the back, with the group of three men who were to take out the side window of the building so they could fire at any enemies, causing even more of a distraction. His job was to watch their backs. The safest job his mother could think of, he was sure, but still, he was here.

He was a part of a mission. It was all he had ever dreamed of as a kid. Being in the back of the group was what made it possible for him to hear the low growling off to the side. He warned Eric in front of him and the group turned to see what the problem was. At first, they thought it was only a stray dog hungry for food and making noise or maybe a guard dog, but what came at them was no Benji. And there was more than one.

Three hulking wolves, the size of small ponies, came at them, slowly advancing. Teeth were bared, snarling with a low threat as they advanced to the group of men that had been ready to hit the building's window.

Eric turned to Bobby and said, "Wolves aren't indigenous to Saudi, right?"

Shaking his head, "Nope."

They had put Craven in the middle of their group and raised their guns and began firing. They had no choice, because these wild big assed wolves were going to attack. Craven saw wound after wound heal on these so-called wolves right before his eyes. Although they were using ammo that could knock a nine inch hole through a side door of a car, it didn't seem to do anything but piss off these animals. That's when he put his gun away and drew his sword made of silver.

He shouted to the men, "Those won't work. Move it. Move it." He saw the lead werewolf, for werewolf it was, about to attack the man in front of him, getting ready for a spring. As the werewolf leapt, he pushed aside the soldier and sliced the werewolf's neck and it went down yelping and gurgling this time. It didn't get back up. The second werewolf came at him then with a furious growl, leaping at his throat. Craven knelt with one knee in the dirt, bringing his sword tip up and driving it through its heart. He didn't have enough time to move before the third werewolf had grabbed his shoulder with his teeth and was tearing at his flesh. Craven screamed in pain and tried to roll away, dropping his sword. Two of the men saw how well the blade worked and grabbed a few off of Craven's tactical vest and started to stab at the animal. The werewolf had let go of his shoulder and tried for his throat, when the tip of a blade came sticking out of its chest.

Eric had grabbed Craven's dropped sword and stabbed it clean through from its back to the front of its chest, going right through its heart. The rest of the team made quick work of whatever even twitched, just to make sure of the kill and then ran for the building while Eric staunched the wound on Craven's shoulder.

The other two soldiers had gotten to the window just in time to see Cat and Andre both fire their weapons. Cat then flew out the door with Andre hot on her heels, heading for the spot where she felt her son in pain. When she got there and saw the carnage lying all around and blood soaking from shoulder to left arm, she fell beside Eric, who was field dressing the wound.

She pushed his hands away and tried to heal the wound but got zapped back for her trouble.

Craven was panting with pain. "Mom, werewolves. They were werewolves."

"Sweet Mother Goddess," she cried out.

Andre echoed her.

She gave up on the wound and went to his heart; trying to go through a part of him not infected yet and 'push' the virus out. It didn't work.

It just caused Craven to wince, hissing with pain, saying, "It burns. It burns." So she stopped. O'Hara soon joined them. "We've got three wounded, one seriously. We need help in healing so we can move. We're about out of time before we have more company and the local authorities make a big fuss over this."

She nodded, "Andre?" He took off for the wounded men and would soon be joining the rest of them gathered around Craven.

"I'm sorry your son got hurt, but heal him so we can go." O'Hara was confused that she hadn't already done it.

Her voice shaken, "I can't. He was bitten by a werewolf."

"Come again," he said it like he couldn't have heard it right.

She nodded to the corpses lying on the ground. "Look—they have changed back to human form. It's how you can tell they are really dead. If they don't change, keep stabbing them. That's the rule on killing a werewolf."

O'Hara looked around at the three now naked men, when all he had seen was dark fur when he had come up at first. The men had dark hair and tattooed scroll work on their faces in black ink. "Shit. What the fuck?"

Some of the men were muttering about more weird shit.

Andre had come with the rest of the men, one who was moving slowly. For the seriously wounded, even after a healing, it would take time to get their strength back.

Eric grabbed her shoulder, then removed his hand quickly when Andre growled. "He saved us, Cat. We wouldn't be here if it wasn't for him. We didn't know what we were up against and kept firing our guns. It didn't do any good. He knew what to do and he did it. Like any good soldier would do."

"Saved me too, buddy," Craven groaned as the fire raced through his veins as the virus spread.

Cat looked at Eric as he said, "I got the last one going for his throat. He was down at the time."

She nodded at him, "Then our family owes you a debt."

"We are family now, Cat," Eric said quietly and moved away. The rest of the squad murmured their agreement.

"What does this mean for Craven, Cat?" O'Hara asked.

Bowing her head, "He'll turn, most likely by tomorrow night. He'll be werewolf."

"Ah shit, Cat. I am sorry. What can we do?" he didn't know what else to say.

She looked up at him, 'We need to get him home to the silver cage. It'll be the only thing that can contain him. Otherwise, we may be forced to kill him. The blood lust will be too strong for a newly changed werewolf to overcome."

"Then let's move. Craven, can you walk?" O'Hara asked, looking down at the kid.

He pushed himself up slowly, grunting with pain, "I'll make it."

Andre went to aid him in standing, since the kid weighed about 250 pounds of solid muscle.

"Ok, let's move it. We've got to get out of here and get Craven home to safety. Fall in," O'Hara ordered. "We also need to find out what happened back at home base, so let's hustle."

Once they were in the van, Cat moved over to O'Hara, "I got word that the base was attacked by hellhounds. One dead, nine wounded. My family is helping with holy water. They'll be scarred though, after the healing."

"Werewolves here, hellhounds at the base. That shithead General sure didn't fuck around, nor did he wait for very long." O'Hara was a bit overwhelmed. "General Pierce?" he asked quickly.

"Fine. He was kept safe. Not a scratch on him. My boys made sure," she smiled.

"How did you get word?" O'Hara gave her a hard gaze.

She pointed to Andre and then herself, "We have a bond that is as strong as it is with my other two mates. No matter where we are at, we can always hear each other in here," tapping her head. "Unless we close the connection during a battle, because it can be a distraction and very dangerous."

He raised his eyebrow, "And you didn't tell me, why?"

She shrugged, "Security. We needed to make sure we could trust you first. I would have told you sooner, but the subject hadn't come up until now."

"I had a feeling there was something like that going on. I don't blame you for being cautious. If the wrong people caught wind of what you and your kind could do, you would never have another moment of peace." His expression was serious.

She snorted, "If they didn't burn us at the stake first."

He just grunted. He couldn't deny the possibility, even in this day and age.

"For Craven, can it be reversed?" he asked quietly.

She shook her head slowly, "Nothing in the books we have mention anything for a cure. Other than the myth of killing the one who bit you, but they did that. Yet, he is still changing. So, I guess we can cross that myth off the list as bullshit. Or it could be just with this particular tribe of werewolves, that it's not a true myth."

"There are different *kinds* of werewolves?" O'Hara asked, with his raised eyebrow.

"Yes, there are different kinds of werewolves, different breeds of vampires and so on. They are just as diverse as humans are with their African, Chinese, Whites and so on."

O'Hara took all that in. "Not that I am not soaking up what you are telling me, but why aren't you over there with your son?" Knowing her feelings about kids and how absolutely vicious she could be in protecting her own, he expected her to be hovering over Craven like a worried hen over a baby chick.

"I promised him I would treat him no differently than I would anyone else here. We are still on the job. His wound was tended to as best we can. We aren't home yet, so I'm salvaging his pride since I can't salvage his future." She nodded towards Andre. "Look at him. Though he is a few seats away, he is watching over him closely; letting me play leader while he is acting as Craven's protector until we get home, but not being obvious about it." Andre looked over at the word 'play' and frowned at her and then turned his head back towards Craven. She snorted back at him.

O'Hara could see now why she wasn't hovering. It would lower Craven's status in front of the other men. Men he had already put his body on the line to protect. He had to give it to her, she was a good leader and she held her promise to her son. The boy had earned his place tonight. O'Hara could agree with that.

His thoughts turned back to the base, "How did hellhounds get past your shield?"

"I think because the shield was new for one, and lots of people go through it every day; the best we can do for that kind of situation is a weak shield. That's why we hit all of your offices so hard. Nothing can get through them very easily."

He thought about that for a moment, trying to understand the logistics of different shields and their weaknesses." The wounded? Will they turn, too?" half-afraid of the answer.

"No, but they could die if not cleansed fast enough. Hellhounds and werewolves are two very different creatures. A bite of a hellhound is poisonous. Not to worry though, I am sure my people are on that, but the treatment is very painful. Unlike our healing, the results will be scars that'll never go away," she said sadly.

"At least they'll live," He said reassuringly, "That's the main thing. One lost, you said. Who?"

"Ensign Richardson, twenty-two years old. No wife, no children, but his parents are going to be devastated." She closed her eyes and leaned back.

Captain Holland would notify the parents, but O'Hara empathized with Cat. He hated losing anyone, even though there was nothing he could have done about it and it was their job. The men wouldn't have joined if they weren't ready to put themselves in harms way. Death was sometimes the result of that commitment. It still sucked knowing someone would be mourning Ensign Richardson tonight for the rest of their lives. He will be missed by those who fought at his side, too. And they would find a way to avenge his death.

Cat and her family slipped into the airplane, which was waiting to take them back home via a stopover for fuel on the African coast. They were being as unobtrusive as possible, to escape the Ambassador and his daughter's view. They didn't want to be remembered later, which could lead to awkward questions. The Ambassador was too busy thanking the soldiers and assuring them his daughter would be all right as soon as she was reunited with her mother. There was something about the man that rubbed her wrong, a smell that was a tad off; but being too worried about Craven, and wanting to get back home to check on everyone else, she put the suspicions in the back of her mind and climbed aboard the airplane. They left the Ambassador and Melody safe at the base where they would be debriefed and assigned help if they needed it. Soon O'Hara and his men were all loaded up. Mission accomplished. The General would be happy about that, at least.

CHAPTER NINETEEN
Berserker Wolf

They reached home base later the next day. As soon as they hit the tarmac and stopped the plane, a Black SUV pulled up and loaded her family into it. The General was inside waiting for them, which surprised her.

"I thought you'd be in the war room with the men, getting them all debriefed and such?" she asked him, confused.

O'Hara climbed in, moving her aside. "Yeah well, one of ours is down. We can't leave him until we know he is on the mend; or in this case, is going to be ok. Or whatever," he said gruffly. "Whatever happens, we'll be by the young man's side throughout it all."

The General nodded along with the explanation, "Debriefing can wait, until we know the status of each of our men."

Cat's bottom lip trembled a bit, which she quickly bit down on. She turned to Andre, "Move this thing, hon."

They headed out to the bar, ignoring the speed limit the whole way. She didn't even notice the whole trail of SUV's behind theirs.

They rolled up on the clubhouse a short while later and hustled Craven into the cage; first taking all of his weapons off him and giving him a gi (a uniform for martial arts) to put on instead of his mission uniform. Much easier to replace if he shifted and tore the hell out of his clothes.

They had several GI's there at the clubhouse for those who wanted the pit, but didn't want to mess up their regular clothes or uniforms. The rest of the family that wasn't already on the base were there waiting for them to show up.

Crimson and Christoph came running out to help their brother get inside the bar. They started trading their first war stories to each other. Cat had grabbed them both, hugging them tightly, telling them how proud she was and how much she had missed them.

Then Cat turned into the mother hen O'Hara had expected, asking Craven if he wanted or needed anything.

She fussed over him, to which he smiled gently, but fended off, "Mom, I'll be all right. I am hungry, though."

Her eyes shone brightly at a new thought. "Hey, maybe if we feed you really extremely bloody rare steak, it might stave off the blood lust." She turned to Gaston who was waiting anxiously in the back of the crowd. "Bro, go cook a steak extremely bloody. Barely cook the fucking thing."

"Got it, sis," and he went off on the errand.

O'Hara noticed that when Cat had shooed the older boys out of the cage, they both started pacing back and forth, one on each side of the room to give each other space to move. Craven never paced, that he noticed. He was calmer than the other two boys were.

"Mom, maybe you should get out of here?" He looked concerned, bending over every now and again, as another wave of cramps and pain shot through him.

Her look got determined. "No, I'll know when it's time to go. You're not there yet." The look on her face got contemplative as she rubbed his back through his waves of pain. O'Hare had to hand it to the kid. He didn't bitch and moan. He took the pain like a hardened soldier.

"What are you thinking, Cat?" Demitri came up in the cage which was still wide open.

She looked up at him. "Remember when I was cursed and sick? There was that one spell that I did that almost worked, but I accidentally fucked it up at the very last minute. Then, the curse adapted and it didn't work the second time I tried it. This is like a virus, but on both a physical and spiritual level. The same as the curse and the sickness was. Maybe we should try it?"

He looked at Craven, "We should try anything that may work. Show him how, hon."

She waited for the spasms to pass and then helped him stand upright. "Ok, you need to try this one spell, sweetie."

He looked at her, shrugged his shoulders, "Anything. I'm game."

"Good, now breathe in through your nose, out through your mouth. Get centered."

He did as she instructed. "Now remember where the water here is from? The beach isn't too far. Tap into it. If we had a shower it would work, but this should be easy enough for our kind. The body of water is close enough. Find it and connect to it."

O'Hara watched as Craven closed his eyes and focused.

"Good job, son. I can see the strong connection. Now repeat after me. 'Dear Lord and Lady, banish all the negative entities and illnesses out of me, out to the water, into the sea, to be purified, as I Will so mote it be.'

Imagine small black worms coming out of you on every level and going into the sea. Do it."

She repeated the chant over and over until he had it. Repeated the visualization until she was sure he understood. Then a white glow started to shine around his whole body, which seemed to trigger convulsions in him. He bent over, moaning loudly now. The first loud complaint O'Hara had ever heard out of him since he was bitten. Craven moved down to the floor, whimpering now.

Cat was repeating, "I'm sorry honey. Mommy is sorry. Shit, Demitri what do I do?"

He placed his hands out spread over Cravens body, "Let's try to take his pain, at least."

Cat moved into position and they went to work. It seemed to help as Craven's breathing eased. Antonio and Andre had joined the circle around Craven. Everyone was adding his or her power to help ease his pain. The convulsions stopped and he was sitting up again, breathing hard.

"Should he try the spell again?" Demitri asked. "It's not as black now. More gray then anything."

"No, look deep," Andre cautioned him. "It's attached to his DNA now. If he takes it any further, his internal organs could shut down. I think this is the best we can hope for."

Cat looked at Andre, "Will it make a difference now?"

He shrugged his shoulders, "Won't know until the moon rises. We'll have to wait and see. Craven, how do you feel now?"

"Hungry and sore." His eyes were closed and he was holding his stomach as if it hurt.

Cat bent down and hugged him. "Gaston is coming with food."

A few minutes later, Gaston came through the crowd with Craven's plate. "Why don't you guys have a seat? I've got my mates cooking in the back and a cousin will man the bar. You all need food after what everyone has been through lately."

They weren't usually opened on a Monday, but with Craven needing the cage, they might as well be comfortable while waiting to see what would happen. The crowd around the door had thinned out as they took their seats and ordered food. The only ones left were Cat and her mates, with O'Hara standing guard at the door with the General. Craven tore into the food as Gaston left. Cat would glance at her mates every now and again with a helpless look on her face.

O'Hara could only imagine what kind of pain Craven's parents were going through, seeing their youngest son suffer and not being able to do anything for him. It must be especially bad for people like them, who are used to pulling off the impossible, until now, when they needed it the most.

The General broke the silence, "Will that cage contain him?"

"Yes," Cat responded first, "It's made out of titanium and silver as well as a substance that blocks magick from going through the bars once the door is closed. He won't be able to do anything from inside."

No one asked what would happen if Craven broke out and became a threat to innocents. Cat seemed to have picked up the unspoken question because she shut her eyes tight and reached for Antonio's phone. She walked outside to the dining room and O'Hara knew what she would ask for; silver ammo.

She came back in with her face tight and sat back down next to Craven. Like she wanted to spend every second she could with him before the time came. Her mates looked shattered, knowing what she would have to do, and that it would be her that would do it. No one else would be allowed. It would kill her to be the one to pull the trigger, but she would do it.

"I am sorry, Cat," the General spoke gruffly.

She turned with a confused look on her face, "What for?"

"If I had ordered that silver ammo and silver blades you told me about from the beginning we might not be here right now." The General was feeling guilty for not having the proper equipment for his men out in the field, equipment that could have been used to avoid this exact situation.

"It's my fault if it's anyone's. I didn't nag you for it, not thinking we would need it so soon. I was counting on our own blades being enough for now. Shit, we have silver ammo and I didn't even think to bring it. It was just supposed to be a simple kidnapping. It turned into more than it seemed. My fault, not yours." Andre reached down to grab her hand.

"Mom, it's no one's fault. Shit happened. Who would have thought werewolves would be in Saudi Arabia? I don't think they ever had them, even in their own legends," Craven was trying to comfort his mother.

"How or why would werewolves be in Saudi in the first place?" O'Hara threw the question in the air.

Cat gave her opinion first, "A portal. I would bet a hundred it's a portal, O'Hara. A recent one too, or we would have had reports on it before now."

Demitri added, "We'll have to send another team out there General, one of ours, to find it and close it. If the werewolf tribe is using a new portal to come into our world, then they're hostile. We won't be able to make a treaty with them."

"We should also send a message through the portal. A 'If you come back here we'll kill the whole tribe' note then shut the portal," Antonio said.

Cat nodded, "Mind you, it won't stay closed. When the shift completes, all portals will be wide open again, but it will give them pause about coming through a second time. We'll at least have the location of that portal for a future opening on our map."

"You mean that dark God could come back too?" O'Hara asked.

Shaking her head, "No, portals and vortexes are two different things."

"You have a map of potential portals?" the General didn't look pleased not to have been informed on this.

Demitri seemed slightly embarrassed. "It's not a good map. There are not many points on it. We can only add to the map when we come across a portal. So at the moment, it is very insufficient. Not worth mentioning really."

This seemed to satisfy the General.

"Can't you use magick to find a portal from here?" O'Hara wiggled his fingers.

It made Cat smile. "No, we would have to...oh I don't know," waving her hand through the air, "send our power through the airwaves or something to find portals all over the earth. I am afraid it's the old fashioned way of tracking; then magick can be used at close range."

Antonio laughed, "Yeah, the only thing that had come close, was that fucking psi-tracking device that university used back in Tucson. Remember Demitri, the one they used to track you before they kidnapped you? Cat and Dar had to break you and the others out. Then they used that thing to try to track Cat for years, but I think its range was only about an eight block radius. I don't think they had anything longer ranged at the time, or they would have nabbed all of us years ago."

"What device are you all talking about and who is Dar?" General Pierce was curious.

Cat got a really sad look on her face. "Dar was my best friend. She was the one who trained me in the High Magicks and the Astral Planes. She's dead now."

"My condolences, Cat. And the tracking device?" he prompted.

"It was some kind of psi-tracking device that was able to track anyone with substantial power to their lair, or home, I should say. It picked up any psi-waves, when a person was using magick. Like a tracking device, but for those using psychic power. They had this whole mad scientist thing going on there, until Cat and Dar busted up the lab. I had never seen her so pissed. I was surprised she didn't kill them all. Although, with the way they

treated people and beings there, I wouldn't have blamed her at all."
Antonio looked at Cat with compassion in his eyes. "They would have
deserved it babe, but I'm proud you held yourself in check, with being so
new to your power at the time." He blew her a kiss with that, making her
blush from the praise.

"And this device could possibly track portals?" O'Hara was surprised.
He had never heard of it before now.

It was Antonio who answered him. "Maybe if I had the machine, I
could reconfigure it to pick up the frequency of a portal; since portals and
psi-energy are just two different frequencies, it wouldn't be a problem. Just
take it to a portal, get a reading on it and reconfigure. The problem would
be range," rubbing his chin. "Though, if I could hook into a satellite and
come up with a computer program to make the machine work with the
satellite, it might do the trick."

General Pierce got a thoughtful look on his face. "Later, tell me
everything that happened at that university. Make it a part of your
debriefing. We'll see if we can come up with something. Right now, there
are more important things to consider."

He regretted his words as he saw the pain cross over Cat's face.

There was a soft knock at the door to the staffroom and Cendra asked
Cat to step outside. When Cat returned a few minutes later, she looked even
more depressed. O'Hara would guess her gun didn't hold normal ammo
anymore. He and the General stepped out for a bite to eat in the dining
room, while Gerard and Grant had arrived to take over manning the door.
The siblings first gave Cat a hug and touched Craven's shoulder gently, as
if afraid to hurt him, more than he was already.

"You know if she has to pull that trigger we could lose both of them?"
O'Hara told the General.

General Pierce sighed, "Yes, I saw that look in her eye. She'll do it to
protect the others, but she'll use that gun on herself right afterwards. She
won't be able to live through having done the deed."

"Excuse me, Sir?" Eric had stepped over to their table, which was
situated nearest the staff room door.

"Yes, Ensign?" the General said.

"Is he going to be ok? Can they fix him like they did Ridgewood and
the others?" his eyes looked hopeful.

O'Hara and Pierce looked at each other, each knowing what the other
was thinking. How much to tell the troops, if anything at all. At the
moment things didn't look too good in there and they both knew it, if she
had loaded her nine mil. with silver ammo.

O'Hara got a nod from General Pierce.

"Right now, it doesn't look good, Ensign. If he turns out to be a danger, there won't be much we can do for him." He told the truth, because too often, they were in the field together. You had to trust who was leading you and who was following. This squad had already come through for him and his team twice. He couldn't lie to them or cover the harsh truth of the matter.

The Ensign's look turned determined. "He fought for us, sir. He saved our asses out there, even though he's just a kid." Nodding his head toward the staffroom door, "Can't they do anything for him? I mean, she's his mother."

Romeo had come over, listening to the news, as well. "He's a good kid, Rock. Not like most kids. He's tough as nails and damn smart. Be a shame to lose him now." He, too, had spent time getting to know Craven and had obviously formed a bond with the kid.

O'Hara gave them a hard look, "She'll do the best thing for him. You both know that. We won't be able to keep Craven in that cage for the rest of his life. It wouldn't be fair or right. And their race is long lived as it is. It would be twice as bad for one of them than one of us. Knowing her though, she'll move heaven and earth trying anything before having to do anything drastic. So let's hope for the best, ok?"

Eric nodded glumly and walked back to his table with the others that were waiting for news.

O'Hara knew it would make the rounds in minutes here.

General Pierce looked at Romeo. "Sit down with us."

"Thank you, Sir," he said, as he took a seat.

O'Hara looked at all the glum faces around the room. The family members, too, looked bleak. Cassie was sitting at a table farthest away, with a book opened before her. It looked like she was trying to find something in it. Most likely something to do with werewolves and finding a cure for them. Clearly, morale was low at the moment. He looked at Babyface, who was seated across from them. His eyes were as cold as ever, but even he had a hard time when a young one was involved. He just hid it better than the rest of them.

Glancing at Romeo, O'Hara said, "This clubhouse is a good place. We can come here and be ourselves. We can talk shop, but we don't have to watch out for military protocols. The name 'The Clubhouse' is just too generic, too bland. We should suggest to the family a new name. What do you think, Romeo?"

"Yeah, we should spice it up," Romeo agreed.

"We've never regularly had enough man power in our team for a name to stick and take hold," Babyface added. "Maybe we can have both, since Alpha Recon is with us now. A moniker for both the clubhouse and our whole force."

"Hoorah, I like the idea," Corporal Howard joined the new topic of discussion that O'Hara had started, to get their minds off the doom and gloom atmosphere.

"Just so long as we don't get called 'the spook squad'. That would bite," Wizard said, with a grimace on his face.

Romeo grinned at him, "Yeah, but lately it has been nothing but the weird and things that go bump in the night."

"Well, we can't use Ghostbusters. It's been done for one, and we go up against more than mere ghosts," Corporal Howard smiled.

"Nighthawks?" Someone else in the crowd added, now involved in the debate over a new name.

"Nighthawks blows. What do hawks have to do with us?" another voice rang out.

"Well, we do our stuff at night and hawks prey."

"Still blows."

The argument was stopped cold when they heard someone yell from inside the staffroom, "Get out of there now."

A loud clang resounded, and O'Hara headed for the door and opened it. He stopped dead in his tracks, seeing a full sized mahogany haired beast growling and snarling from inside the cage Craven had been in. Only this wasn't Craven anymore. The eyes were glowing blue like no wolf he'd ever seen, and so bright, he couldn't tell if the beast had pupils or not. No white showed, just a pure glowing blue that held hate and menace, despite the bright color. The contrast was even more unsettling. He was ready for weird red or black, but never in his wildest imagination could he have foreseen this glowing blue that could actually pour anger from them. The size of the creature's mouth could bite his head off in one snap of the teeth, which looked long, white and dangerously sharp.

"Craven?" his mother called to him.

The beast threw himself against the bars, snarling and snapping at the mesh that would sizzle in his mouth and make him back off for a second. Then the beast would throw itself against the bars again, despite the pain of the burning.

"Craven, calm down, son. It's me, Mommy. Come on boo bear," she tried cajoling him into being calm.

Nothing worked. The creature just kept trying to come at her. If the cage hadn't kept him contained, he would have torn into his mother without a second thought.

She tentatively reached her hand out, trying to get him to catch her scent. "Come on Craven, it's me, Mommy." This only infuriated the werewolf more and it was actually making progress in bowing the bars. It kept ramming its body into the side of the cage, over and over again.

"Craven, calm down. Don't break the bars," she said, as she reached for her gun and drew it. He kept crashing into the side, making progress inch by inch. O'Hara wondered if he ought to clear the clubhouse before the werewolf broke loose. He looked over his shoulder at the rest of the men who could see through the door and were watching as she raised her gun to aim dead center for his head. She pleaded with him to calm down and not break the cage. Others who couldn't see everything were asking what was going on and getting sporadic updates from those who could.

Her hand never wavered in her aim though O'Hara could see tears forming in her eyes, threatening to spill over.

"Please, boo," she pleaded again.

"Babe?" Andre looked at her, helpless, not knowing what to do for her or for Craven. None of them did. Her lips trembled and the tears fell, as she slowly squeezed the trigger.

At the last second, her wrist jerked towards the ceiling. She snapped around, her face furious and said to O'Hara, "Catch," tossing the gun to him, which was a dangerous move in itself, but he caught it without it firing on him.

She rushed to Andre and grabbed the key out of his hand and unlocked the cage, slamming it behind her.

Suddenly, everyone was screaming at her almost all at once.

"Catrina, no," Demitri shouted.

Her sons screamed, "MOM."

"Fuck, are you crazy?" Antonio sounded pissed.

But it was too late. The werewolf lunged at her. She grappled the hulking wolf and threw him into the side of the cage. He landed on his paws and leapt for her again, snarling and snapping his jaws in her face. She rolled over him, getting on his back and then pushed the werewolf into the ground with one hand on his head, the other hand around his throat, squeezing his air passage. She used her body to hold his almost lying flat to the ground. Her legs hooked around his hindquarters so he couldn't get his back leg up under him.

"Craven, I taught you better than this. Fight it. Fight the fucking thing. Find your center. Get control," she demanded.

She slammed his head to the floor a few times. He snarled, and then whimpered.

"Don't let it control you. Ride it, Craven," she yelled in his ear.

He kept trying to get his paws up underneath his body so he could buck her off. He went from growling and snarling to whimpering every time she slammed his head into the cement floor.

O'Hara had the gun aimed at its head, but he let Cat try to get through its hate and blood lust first. This, he could do for her. He could be the one who pulled the trigger. Her mates couldn't do it. Not and ever be with her again. But he could. He owed her this. He liked Craven, too, but that wasn't Craven in there right now. He went to his quiet place inside, where he could pull the trigger and not let his conscious get in the way. Babyface, too, had his gun out and O'Hara was betting he had his loaded with silver ammo as well, since Cendra had brought three boxes of the stuff; each a different caliber for the various guns in the bar.

She slammed his head a few more times. "You are stronger. Fight it. Look, smell me. It's Mommy," and she blew her breath at his nose. He actually paused a bit and then went back to trying to scramble to get his paws underneath himself for leverage against her.

She let go of his throat and put her hand in front of his nose, blowing the scent from her wrist to his nostrils. "Smell me, damn it. Remember me. Remember who you are, what you are. You're my son. A Prince of the Blood line. Smell me and remember." She fisted his fur on the top of his head, holding him tighter, then focused and breathed. The hand she held in front of his nose started to glow white and she kept blowing the scent of her wrist to his nostrils. The werewolf stopped and closed his jaws. He moved his nose closer to her wrist. O'Hara held his breath, hoping it wouldn't take her hand off. He didn't bite at her wrist, just sniffed at it and then gave a tentative lick to her hand. She let him sniff and opened her hand all the way out and held her palm to his muzzle, all the while blowing her scent with the power that O'Hara could still see with his eyes.

"Good, that's good, son. Now relax. Stop trying to fight me," she said with a gentle voice.

The werewolf obeyed, slowly relaxing his muscles one by one. Everyone breathed a sigh of relief.

"That's right, submit. You may be werewolf, I may be vampire, but I am still Alpha bitch. I told you I would take you to the pit if you fucked up," she nuzzled into his furry neck.

He growled back at her lightly.

"Ok, I'm going to let you up. We are going to take it slow and easy. Ready?" she asked him.

He just lie there, waiting for her to move. She let go a bit at a time and moved slowly off him. He got up, shook himself off and sat down looking at her.

"Good job. How much of my Craven is in there now?" She cocked her head at him, as if trying to see inside his head.

He growled at her, which she took mock offense at. "Don't you growl at me. I'll bite back," and flashed her fangs at him. "Alpha bitch, remember?" pointing to herself.

He growled again, but ended with a yip, though it sounded loud as hell.

Everyone started clapping and whooping, knowing Craven wouldn't have to be put down now.

The sound startled him though. He turned and growled at the noise behind him.

She yelled out, "His hearing in this form will be extremely sensitive. Once he gets better control, it won't be so bad, I think. But for now, let's keep startling noises down to a minimum." She looked at the werewolf. "Craven, chill. It's family out there. They're just happy that I don't have to slam your head into the ground anymore."

He backed up, his growling slowly subsiding, when Cassie slid her way into the room. "Cat, why don't you try to get him to change back? It isn't the full moon. It's only a quarter moon, so he should be able to shift back if he is strong enough."

She nodded her head to her sister. "Good idea. It will also let me know how much of him in there is in control." She turned to her son, "Craven, focus on your inner self. You know what you should look like. Picture your image in your head and push. WILL it to be so. Try," she urged him.

The werewolf looked at her, lips pulled back showing his teeth.

Sadness filled her eyes, watching her son trying not to growl at her.

Then he whined and sat down. For a minute nothing happened. Then, there was a popping sound and suddenly he was there on his legs in human form.

She burst out, "Fuck yeah, way to go. Hey, check it out, your gi came back with you. That's cool." She went to him and threw her arms around him, hugging him close. "You did it, son. You did it. You won over the beast inside! That's my Prince."

Everyone clapped and cheered loudly now, still making him wince, but at least he didn't growl at anyone. Andre opened the cage and his family rushed inside, crying and hugging, giving each other turns with Craven. Then Cat grabbed him again and was kissing him. "Ahh, Mom, not in front of the guys." He was blushing, trying to be tough for everyone. But he still bent towards her and hugged her back.

"I'm still hungry, Mom," he told her.

She pulled back, looking at him, tears shining in her blue eyes. "Then, let's get you fed."

CHAPTER TWENTY
Howl of the Nightwolves

Everyone backed up, giving them room to come out. They got Craven a table near the bar where everyone was having a drink to celebrate the victory.

Eric came over and pounded him on the back, "Way to go man. That was fucking close, buddy. Don't do anything like that again. Righteous?"

They pounded fists, "Righteous! Feed me though, because the smells are driving me crazy," he said seriously.

Eric backed up, hands in front of his neck in mock fear, "I don't taste good, trust me." They laughed and sat down.

"Hey—Nightwolves," Ridgewood shouted out. "That's what we can be. Nightwolves! We have nightwalkers," pointing to me and my mates, "and we have a wolf now. We work in the night. It's perfect. What do you all think?" Ridgewood looked around and Romeo broke out with a howl. Everyone joined in, toasting the new name for the force and the bar.

The General said loudly, "The next round is on me in honor of the new name! And to Craven's well-being."

Everyone had to howl at that, too. I looked archly at my son, "No alcohol for you though, son. I'll have a virgin Margarita with you though. How's that?"

He nodded, "Sounds cool, Mom." He, too, knew his control was already on edge and alcohol would only make it worse. Even I stayed away from liquor ever since the change, not willing to test my own control.

Eric spoke up, "I'll have a beer for you. That way you can't get thrown in the pit."

Laughing, they all agreed it would be a good idea.

They got him another extra rare steak which he went to work on right away. I walked over to O'Hara and took my gun back. "Thanks. I know it wasn't fair to put you in that spot, but I couldn't think of anything else to do."

He shook his head at me, "Not to worry. It all worked out right. That's all that matters."

I smiled at him, "You're all right, Rock."

"You're not bad yourself," grinning back at me.

The General came up and waved O'Hara's team to a table close to Craven's group. "I've been thinking about that psi-tracking device you were talking about before. If I can get a hold of one, or at least the schematics, do you think Antonio can put it together and get it tweaked for tracking newly opening portals?"

I thought about it. "It would go faster with Wizard's help. He'll know how to get around the military satellites a lot faster than Antonio. Antonio has a knack for twisting devices into doing things they weren't meant to do in the first place. Put those two together and yeah, I think they can whip one out in no time."

"Great," Pierce said. "We'll get on that tomorrow after the debriefing. Now what about sending a team back to Saudi for closing the portal there once its exact location is found?"

"Gerard, Gaston and Cendra have already been chosen for going back there and deal with it. Why?" I looked at him curiously.

"I think it would be safer if another squad was with your team when you go, which should be soon since we just left a fracas back there. It'll be harder to get it done if we give them time to put up road blocks and such in our way," Pierce advised her.

"I agree with you. They can be ready in an hour. How are you on time for getting another squad together?" I asked him.

"Give me four hours to get the necessary things in order and we'll be good to go." Pierce turned to Rock, "O'Hara, we should go so you can pick the next squad to go out with her family."

"Yes, Sir." He stood up and waited for the General, who turned to me, "I am really glad your son was able to get control of this. If there is anything he needs, let us know."

"You might want to think about having a cage built at the base like this one here. You never know if we might bring in a hostile and will have to use one. We'll be building one at the house ourselves just in case he has a bad night and such," I told him.

"Good thinking. It seems we keep having situations where we need something extra to deal with what's going on now." General Piece frowned, "I'll get on those silver blades and ammo as well, though how I'm going to explain this to acquisitions, I don't know."

I laughed, "Try telling them psi-ops said that it would strike fear into the hearts of terrorists. Put the blame on them."

254

"I don't think that will work," he chuckled, "but it is tempting. Have your brother's team at the base in three hours. I'll see you and your team in the morning; we have quite the chore list for tomorrow. Get some rest."

"I will." I walked off to thank those who came to support me and my son until I reached Antonio. He stood in the background just watching me as I made my rounds. When I finally made it to where he was standing, I looked up at him with a contented smile until I saw his face. He wasn't smiling. There was no expression on his face at all, in fact.

My smile faded away as I looked at him. "What's wrong, love?"

In a neutral voice he asked, "Are you done?"

"Well, yes I am, actually. I told Gerard the new orders and he's on his way with the others. So I'm done with my job until tomorrow." I watched his face, trying to figure out what his problem was.

He didn't say anything, just grabbed my hand and damn near dragged me outside to where his car was.

"Sweetheart?" I tried again, but he didn't answer. He just opened the passenger door and gently, but firmly, put me inside. He closed my door with a slight slam and moved around the car to drive.

He headed for our house. Several times, I tried to get an answer from him, but he just ignored me. He had never done that before. When he pulled into the driveway, he got out and opened my door for me. He pulled me out of the car, again gently, but firmly, and guided me through the house to his room upstairs.

He slammed the bedroom door closed and turned to me with an order, "Strip out of your clothes now."

"Antonio, what's wrong? What did I do?" I tried to get him to talk to me, but he was past that.

He just started to take off his own clothes, waiting for me to begin. When I didn't move fast enough for him, he walked up to me and with a low, cold voice, "You are only making it worse for yourself. Get-Out-Of-Your-Clothes-NOW!"

I started to strip. I narrowed my eyes in anger though, because he wouldn't tell me what I'd done wrong. If it had been anyone else other than a mate, I would have told him to fuck off and walked out.

When I was naked, he told me, "Get on the bed face down and reach for the headboard. Do it now."

I didn't try reasoning with him anymore and did what he told me. He reached up and snapped the hand cuffs he had hanging there to my wrists. Then he lifted my hips and placed pillows under me until he was satisfied with my position. My ass was up in the air, as I waited for him to finish whatever he was doing.

"Umm, honey what exactly do you think you are doing?" I tried once again to get through to him, but still he ignored me. I heard him moving around then, getting up on the bed next to me. Then I felt oil being rubbed on my ass and even between my legs. He got every nook and part of me, including my anus.

"Never scare me like that again." Then with one hand, he slapped down hard on my right ass cheek and with the other slid a finger into my ass. I yelped in surprise. He moved his finger in and out of me, making me moan with pleasure enhanced by the sharp pain. Keeping his finger in my ass, he took his other hand and slid it around to my hot core, rubbing me between my legs, building my desire even higher. He would rub, circling my clit, then slide a finger inside my womanhood, in and out, in time with his other finger in my ass. I was moving on the bed shuddering with longing for an orgasm. My channel was getting wetter and hotter, tightening around his finger.

His hand moved from my front and slapped down on my ass again. "Never put yourself in that kind of danger again."

I yelped, then moaned with pleasure.

Panting, "But, honey what else..." He cut me off with another hard slap to my ass, "Don't you dare talk to me right now."

Again, he slid his hand under me and rubbed me between my legs, mixing the pain he was giving me, with love.

Then, he whacked my butt again. "You hurt Demitri as well. I don't like seeing him that upset." He went around my front again, rubbing fast enough to get my labia to swell with excitement, despite the spanking he was giving me.

Another hard smack. "Andre is hurting, too. We all shielded from you, even after the danger had passed with Craven, but you didn't even notice. Demitri and Andre were both damn near crying, thinking we were going to lose you both right in front of our eyes."

Three hard smacks came down on my ass. I cried out with this, going more to pain than anything else. He made up for it by rubbing me long and gently, in and out of my still wet, hot channel.

One last, hard wallop landed on my butt. "We've just gotten you in our lives. We can't go through the experience of losing you now." Then, he bent down to kiss the spots he'd spanked, using his tongue to lick and nibble. He moved up behind me and put his cock into my opening, and in one hard thrust, he started pumping himself in and out. He moved harder and faster in me, while stroking my clit, until I came in one long howling moan.

"You like being fucked, don't you?" he growled.

I was too wrapped up in the feeling to answer right away. He smacked me lightly on her other cheek. "Don't you? You like this big cock fucking you, don't you?"

"Yea, yes," I panted.

Satisfied with my answer, he grabbed my hips and pushed in hard, making the headboard slam into the wall.

"Remember, don't come in me," I warned. We had talked weeks ago about more kids. We all decided to wait until the shift was complete and things were more settled.

"Don't worry, I wasn't planning on coming in you here," as he thrust forward, harder.

When he was about to spill, he took his cock out of my pussy, put it to my ass and slid in. I moaned deeply with this, and he moved inside me, giving my ass light slaps until I came again.

As he was about to join me in pleasure, he bent over me, urging, "Tell me I can bite. Tell me now."

"Bite me," I panted.

He bit down into my neck and came in my ass with a loud groan of his own.

Lying on top of me, he whispered in my ear, "I love you. Don't ever put us through anything like that again, or so help me, you won't be able to sit for a week."

"I would like to know what else I could possibly have done?" I asked sarcastically.

"You didn't even stop to think. You just reacted. You didn't ask for any advice, any input or any guidance from anyone at all. What are we together, if you exclude us from the most important happenings in your life?" his tone was serious.

Defeated, I relaxed into the pillows. "I am sorry. I'm not used to this though. None of it. I'm doing the best I can, but I feel overloaded with too many things to take care of all at once."

He kissed my cheek. "That's why I'm here with you and not out beating the shit out of something else or drinking."

"No, you're here beating my ass. Literally," I snorted.

"Ha, this isn't beating. This is discipline with love. You know none of us could ever hurt you. We'd go out and tear up a tree or something."

He un-cuffed me and moved me into his arms.

I snuggled into him sighing, "I know that. You're the only three men in the world I fear in a fight and yet each of you would cut off your own hand first before raising it to me in anger." I bit his chest gently. "But the spanking still hurt, you ass."

He chuckled, "Your body said otherwise, as you came several times."
"Fuck you," I sighed.
"Anytime, lady love," nuzzling my neck.

CHAPTER TWENTY ONE
Mission across the Veil

The next morning, they all walked into the war room for a debriefing. The General was there at the head of the table and took in their appearance.

"You people really don't do well in the day, do you?" He was watching us slide down into our seats with a groan, looking like something the cat dragged in. No pun intended, I thought to myself. But the General smiled as I sunk my head down on the table with the aim of someone who was going to go back to sleep and damn the consequences. My mates seemed to do better than I did. At least Demitri was looking at him with his eyes open.

O'Hara and his team, as well as Sergeant Miller, walked into the room and took their seats. "Morning Cat, "O'Hara said loudly.

"Coffee, my kingdom for some damned coffee." I groaned.

General Pierce chuckled, "There is some on that trolley over there," pointing to the far wall, "as well as donuts and fruit cups."

"Donuts?" I perked up on that remark.

"I'll get it for you, babe," He bent close to my ear, "I know your butt is still sore this morning."

I hissed back at him, "Shut up or your ass is going to hurt tonight."

"Promises, promises," he laughed.

Romeo was watching us whisper to each other. "Hey, no fair. Share with the class."

I looked up and glared at him. "If we shared with the class, everyone else here would be blushing red." I laid my head back on the table muttering, "Damned humans, always so touchy about sex. It's one of the most annoying things about your kind."

General Pierce cleared his throat, "Yes, well please refrain from sharing that particular aspect and instead let's get to the debriefing part. First, go through everything on the last op. Then I would like to hear all the details of that dust up you all had with that university some time back."

"Fine, so long as you understand that if they become aware of us and come after us again, we will most likely have to take them out. I don't have time to waste anymore, in playing nice with a bunch of wannabe mad scientists, who obviously have no understanding of what they're dealing with," I growled.

"Nor any respect," Demitri added.

I gave him a sharp nod in agreement.

"They acted like they had the right to do anything they wanted. I wonder how many other labs are operating like that?" Antonio asked.

"If we find anymore, I'll try to get a go ahead from upstairs and see if we can't take them out with extreme prejudice. After a few examples like that, they'll hopefully stop with things they have no right or business messing with," Catrina promised.

"She is grouchy without her coffee," Romeo quipped.

Andre grunted, "You have no idea. You should see her when she is PMSing and has no coffee. Time to run for the hills then, my friend," Andre handed me said coffee, to tame the beast that was shining in my vengeful eyes. I sneered at him, but took the coffee.

Romeo laughed.

I looked around, "Where's my donut?"

"Sorry, babe," Andre got back up and got me one.

The General took over. "Ok, let's get down to business, if everyone is at least half human now with their coffee?" I turned to sneer at him as well.

We debriefed on the whole mission and then related the story of our victory over the evil lab many years ago. O'Hara then debriefed as well, and on down the line it went.

"Good job on the last mission, everyone. It really bought us some brownie points with the upper brass. Cat, if you, or anyone, hear of another lab running like that one did, I might be able to call in some favors in getting their funding yanked out from under them. That would be a lot less messy then your preferred method, I think," General Pierce arched his eyebrows at me.

I grumbled, "Fine, so long as we get to rescue our people or any beings they have trapped and get them released. The damage those asswipes are doing is monstrous and cannot be allowed to continue."

Pierce nodded his head, "Agreed. Just try to not use bloodshed doing it. Now, are you in any condition to help the soldier who is in a coma today?"

I downed my coffee. "Yes, after a few more of these and another donut or two, I'll be good to go so long as I don't have to be in anymore sunlight."

"Excellent. I'll clear the way for you and make sure you're not disturbed." He stood up to leave to get the ball rolling for my healing time.

"Demitri and Andre can guard me while I'm out and about. If my body gets moved while my astral self is out, it could do a lot of damage," I informed him.

"That will leave Antonio to talk shop with Wizard and see about that computer program. Good, that works out for all around. Good day to all and good luck Cat." He headed for the door.

"Thank you, Sir," I said, as I grabbed another cup of coffee.

O'Hara walked over to join her. "How is Craven this morning?"

I was carefully sipping the fresh hot cup. "Sleeping. Last night wore him out."

Babyface asked, "What if he changes while you're all here?"

"Strong emotions seem to trigger it. If he stays mellow, he should be fine. If not, I gave the other two boys syringes filled with triple doses of Thorazine. Between that and their magicks, they should be able to hold him until I get there if he should wolf out." I grabbed another donut and started eating it.

Wizard looked concerned. "It would take you at least twenty to twenty five minutes to get home. A rampaging werewolf could do a lot of damage in that amount of time."

I looked at my mates, silently asking them a question mind to mind. They shrugged and I turned back to O'Hara's men. "I can translocate from one point to another in an instant."

O'Hara's eye went up at that. "You mean you can physically go from here to home just like that?" snapping his fingers.

"Yes, but it has problems. One—I had to have been there before and seen the place. Two—if I fuck up, I could wind up as part of a wall or something like that, which can kill me. Third—it takes a tremendous amount of energy. And last, but not least—I really hate doing it." I scanned the dazed looks on the men's faces and almost laughed at them.

"You are just full of surprises," O'Hara said.

"You ain't seen nothing yet," showing an evil grin.

O'Hara just shook his head. "I can wait. Really, I can wait."

Major Stewart walked back in the room. "If you're ready, I can take you to the soldier you need to heal."

I put down my now empty cup. "Sure, let's rock and roll on this. Sweeties, ready?" I asked the two of my mates who are going with me. Demitri and Andre nodded at me.

"See you guys later," I said to the men and we followed Major Stewart.

"This is Lieutenant Juan Rico, Air Force. I can't tell you the exact details of how he came to be here, but he had several broken ribs, a collapsed lung and a broken leg. He also had slight head trauma, but no cranial bleeding. He has been on some heavy pain killers. Will that stop you?" Major Stewart handed over the hospital chart to Cat.

"Yes, actually. You'll need to stop the drip now." I read the chart myself, seeing what was done to him to get him this far.

"I'll do a healing on him first, before I go after his spirit. I can see from looking at his aura that's the part that's missing." Closing the chart, I waved my mates over to help me heal him fully.

When we were finished with that part of it, I looked up at Major Stewart. "Ok, just make sure none of the nurses or any doctors come in here and I'll get to work on the hard part."

"Easy enough. Good luck." He walked out the door and left us alone. My mates took up guard in front of the door and I pulled a chair over to Rico's bed. Taking his hand in mine, I relaxed and started my breathing ritual. I chose a spot on the wall opposite of where I was sitting and closed my eyes. Mentally, I put up a protective shield around my body and then one for my astral self. I opened and connected my chakras. Then I visualized on that spot on the wall and WILLED myself there in spirit. Soon, I was floating about an inch away from the wall I wanted to be at. Turning my astral spirit around, I looked at Rico lying on the bed. I didn't look at my own body because that would cause me to snap back into it. I focused on Rico and his solar-plex chakra, looking for the aka cord. Finding it, I followed the thread out of the room, up into the air and felt the shift from the physical plane to the astral planes.

Here I WILLED myself into a white flowing dress, so I wouldn't seem a threat once I reached the place where Juan Rico's spirit was. Catching the scent of his cord, I followed through to a place that appeared before me that seemed peaceful enough. There were tall trees, birds were chirping and the grass was tall. It was green and seemed to go on forever. Well at least he didn't go to a lower astral plane, I thought to myself, and enjoyed the walk through the forest. Soon, I heard the rushing of a river and saw two young men standing beside the river with fishing poles in their hands. They were laughing and joking with each other as they cast their lines out to the middle of the river.

One of the men was Juan Rico, or at least it was his spirit, but the other young man's spirit didn't feel the same as Rico's. It had a smoky thin feel to it, whereas Juan's felt much thicker and more solid. That told me a lot. The man who felt less dense than Juan was just spirit. He was not alive on the physical plane anymore, but had died some time ago. Juan, since he was still technically alive, had more substance to his spirit. Therefore, his spirit felt denser. I walked up slowly to the two men.

"Hello," I said gently.

They turned around, startled that I was there.

"Hi," the younger man greeted me. "What are you doing here?"

"I came to see him," I motioned to Juan.

Juan Rico asked, "What do you want, and who are you?" his face showed confusion, but not fear. That was good, I thought.

"My name is Cat. I was wondering if you would like to come home now?" still keeping my tone gentle.

"I am home, with my brother," Rico replied.

Shaking my head, "This isn't your home. It's not really his either. He is still in transition."

He frowned at me. "Transition? What do you mean?"

I sidestepped his question for the time being and asked instead, "What do you remember right before you saw your brother again?" Information was flowing into my mind now that I was here on one of the astral planes, where some go to when they die.

Some, like this young man, had to work through the fact that he was actually dead, and there were other things that he would need to work out first, before he went to a higher plane. Each plane higher would aid in cleansing his soul, so he would eventually end up in the heavenly plane he belonged to.

Until then, no one but his own personal guide should be here.

Ahh, I thought to myself. Juan was his guide, though he didn't consciously know it. He'd probably been having dreams of his dead brother, not knowing part of his soul has been guiding his brother though his transition.

Information on these two came into my consciousness. Since they didn't know how to block my power, I could tapped into anything personal on their previous or current lives on this spiritual plane. Details of them both flowed in and I scanned for things that would help me talk Juan into coming back to his body. Juan loved his brother deeply and felt guilt over his death. That's what brought Juan here now, that he, himself, has been through trauma in his own body with the injuries he sustained. Roberto, that's his brother's name. Roberto had died in a car crash when Juan was seventeen years old.

Someone else had been driving the car while drunk. It killed Roberto, but Juan lived, with minor injuries. When Juan was nineteen, he joined the service and he still misses his brother every day. Since they were together that night and were close before death, Roberto chose Juan to be his guide, an aid through his transition. A live person doesn't have to be consciously aware; they just have to agree on a subconscious level to help the loved one through their transition time.

"I don't know. I can't remember much," Juan answered.

"Try really hard; it's important," I urged him.

He stopped fishing and drew in his line while he thought about it.

"School. I remember school and the prom is next weekend, huh, bro?" He turned to Roberto who grinned at him. "Yeah, lots of chicas, huh, bro?" They chuckled at each other, eyes wagging.

Juan went too far back. Prom night was the night of the accident.

"Juan, can I talk to you privately please?" I politely asked.

He shrugged and handed his fishing pole to his deceased brother. He walked over to me and I guided him even further away to make sure Roberto couldn't overhear.

Behind my back, I mentally WILLED a mirror into my hand and brought it out to show him.

"Look back at your brother," I told him.

He did and then looked at me, still confused.

"Now look at yourself," I said, and brought up the mirror so he could see the changes in his own face. He looked and saw a face of a slightly older man of 25, not the seventeen year old who had cruised around with his younger brother.

Shock filled his eyes and he kept looking at his brother then at the mirror. "What does this mean? I don't get it. This can't be right." He handed the mirror back to me. I took it and right before his eyes, I made it disappear.

"How did you do that?" he asked with wonder.

"You need to remember what actually happened. You need to try really hard to go beyond prom night," I implored him, ignoring his question.

"But that's next week,' he said

"No, it was a long time ago. You know this somewhere inside. You know this." I felt sad for him, but I had to get him to realize this wasn't his place.

"That would mean..." he broke off with tears filling his eyes. I shielded his feelings of grief that were starting to pour out of him, so the spirit of his brother wouldn't see or feel it and become upset. This would not do Roberto any good and might slow up his transition.

Juan sank to his knees. "But we were fishing like we always did."

"I know. I am so sorry, but this isn't your place right now. You are needed elsewhere. Something important. Remember?" I was trying to jog his memory of the service and his duty there.

Juan was crying now. "I don't want to leave my brother. It shouldn't have happened. We were supposed to have a good time. Momma made me promise to watch out for him and bring him home on time. I can't bring him home if I leave this place." He was starting to remember everything.

"It wasn't your fault. Bad things happen to good people sometimes. But he can't ever go home again. It's not his place there anymore. This isn't your place to stay, either. You can visit, but you can't stay. He is where he needs to be right now."

Sobbing, he said, "I miss him."

I wrapped my arms around him. "I know. I, too, have a dear friend in a place a lot like this. She passed a while ago. She chose me to guide her through her transition and I get to visit from time to time when she needs me. You are your brother's guide here, so you will be able to come and visit when he needs you. I can promise that much to you."

He cried while I held him, until he got his grief out. "You promise I can come back?"

"I can promise when your brother needs you, your soul will know it and will come to help him. That's how it works. You'll see him in your dreams." I helped him stand up. He looked at his brother, fishing without him. "Will he be okay?"

I smiled at him. "Nothing can hurt him here. He'll be fine."

"Do I have to go back?" he asked, sounding tired now.

"The choice is yours, but if you stay, you'll only hurt yourself. That won't help your brother," I answered honestly.

He nodded. His brother, Roberto, turned to look at him, as if he knew Juan was leaving. Roberto smiled and waved. Juan waved back with a sad smile and Roberto went back to his fishing. "I don't know how to get home from here," he said sadly.

I took his hand. "Do you give me permission to show you?"

He gazed at his brother. "I'll miss him."

"I know. But he is a part of your heart and your soul. He'll always be there because of that love," I squeezed his hand.

Nodding glumly, he asked, "Take me back, please."

"Hold tight," I said, and WILLED us to the room where his body was lying. We both floated near the bed with me still holding his hand. "I remember the pain now. I don't want to feel that again," he told me.

"We healed your body. There won't be any more pain." I waited for him to make the decision.

He sighed with relief. "How do I get back in?"

"Feel with your heart and let yourself be drawn back in. You will just slide in, like putting on a glove. It's really easy and pain free. Promise," I assured him.

He looked ready, but then stopped and turned to me. "Thank you. I hope you get your wings now for this."

I was confused. "My wings?"

"Yeah. You have no wings yet. Isn't that because you have to do good deeds before you earn your wings?" he looked so serious.

"Oh, the white dress. No, I'll never have wings," shaking my head at him. "But I have a whole world that my family and I will forever be safe on. It's what I get for doing good things," I explained to him.

His face lit up. "Hey, that's pretty cool."

I laughed. "I think so, too. Now go on. We have a world to save here, so we need to get to work."

"This world is in danger?" he sounded concerned.

I sighed, "Well, you won't remember much, if anything of this, so yes, this world is in danger and it needs people like you and me to save it."

"My momma and sisters. My nephews and nieces. They are still here," he sounded alarmed now.

"True, and we need to protect them now. So like I said, get in there and let's get to work on our jobs," I told him.

"You'll help?" his brown eyes looked so intense.

I said truthfully, "Of course, it's my job."

"Good. Ok, I am ready." He turned and moved towards his body. Then, his spirit was gone, resettled into its' physical body.

I smiled and then looked at my own body and slid inside.

Waking up, I was a tad disoriented for a minute. I blinked several times, taking deep breaths to ground myself. I closed my chakras and breathed deeply. Then, my mates knew it was safe to touch me.

Demitri and Andre helped me to stand up. "We need to leave before they realize he is out of his coma now," Demitri told me, as he guided me to the door. We had just rounded the corner of the hospital wing, when a nurse was hustling in because his monitor had changed drastically.

Major Stewart caught up to us apologizing, "I am sorry. I couldn't keep her at the nurse's station once the beeping started. I take it though, he is back?"

"Yes, ready to save the world, too," I laughed at my own joke.

Major Stewart gave me a confused look. "You had to be there," I told him.

CHAPTER TWENTY TWO
Psychic Tripwire

General Pierce got a hold of the machine that was used to try to track us so many years ago. Antonio and Wizard spent weeks getting it reconfigured to detect portals that were opening too soon before the Great Shift. We quickly found a correlation between the earthquakes that were happening with greater frequency and intensity and an opening of a portal (with the exception of the one in Saudi Arabia).

The Magickal races that were seeping into our world went mostly unnoticed by regular humans, mostly due to the fact they were too busy cleaning up the mess an earthquake did to their city or country. The damage of the magickal races were hidden by the death and destruction left behind. Missions were put together with greater regularity due to this. We soon fell into a routine with General Pierce, O'Hara's team and the platoon.

My mates and I would trade off missions with my sibling's and their mates as well as my sons and some of the older children in the family who were battle ready. We became an unstoppable force, while of course, all the credit had to go to the military base and we were still virtually unknown in our participation of their success. But we didn't mind. We were doing what we were made for and making inroads in fulfilling our destiny, with one exception.

None of the magickal races we ran up against wanted to have a treaty with the people of this world. So far, six earthquakes had hit various countries. Of those, five magickal races had been thus far unwilling to try to live in peace with the humans who have lived here for millennia. Instead, they wanted what they thought was their rightful place—being ruler of all here. Each team would try to negotiate, but when that failed, we would fight back their scouts, sending them back, sometimes in pieces, through the portal they came from. We never lost a battle.

Japan also had an earthquake, and a blip appeared on our scope that a portal had opened up, but we didn't send a team out there right away for several reasons. There was minimal damage done by the earthquake, even though it registered a 6.6 on the rector scale—a record even for Japan.

There were no reports by U.S. operatives in Japan of any odd occurrences or unexplained deaths. Things were relatively peaceful there, so a mission plan for Japan was put on the back burner until we had time to scout it out personally just to make sure.

After every successful mission, we would all meet up at the Nightwolves Lair, as the bar came to be called, and we would celebrate. Each mission brought us all closer. The most unusual band of brothers and sisters any military force had ever seen, but we were a fighting family nonetheless. We outfitted the bar with a warning system row of lights, like a signal light at an intersection; this would tell us if any big brass was coming through the door.

As a private club, we had the right to keep anyone out who weren't members, but a military official with a wild hair could muscle his way through with the law on his side. To help General Pierce hide the fact that he'd hired Mercs, we made fast exits and built in hidden rooms all throughout the bar. When the light started flickering red, all Mercs had to run and hide. If the light turned green, it was the military personnel who had to bug out. If the light turned yellow, caution was being issued that we had someone coming in who wasn't one of ours, but needed to be there for whatever reason. Deliveries, repair people and so forth. A yellow light meant keep the conversation normal. Don't show claws or teeth, for those who had them, and otherwise behave yourself.

Ensign Eric Hawkins and my youngest son had come in one night with matching tattoos of a wolf howling at the moon with sabers crossing and Nightwolves stenciled above it. It soon caught on, and more of the men started showing up with that tattoo on them. Even my mates and I sported our 'wolf howling at the moon' tattoos. Of course, the rest of the family just had to get theirs, as well. We thought it was a cool idea since Special Forces teams often sported their own tattoo insignias. Even though the membership was small, it made it easy to identify those who belonged there from those who didn't. The bars' personnel grew, as extended family members moved to Corpus Christi.

We didn't let them in on missions, but they worked the bar for those who did, on a regular basis. They also babysat the younger children when their parents were out in the field and so on. Some were training hard, in the hopes that someday we would take them out on a mission, or to just get ready to defend those at home if things ever broke out in our front yards. Some not only did the military training when we could sneak it in, but quite a few had magickal abilities they practiced daily.

They became our second string and quite deadly in their own right. I was the only one who didn't have any extended family to offer for our home defense. My physical mother was all that was left from that side of my family and Gerard dealt with our physical father and that side of the family (so I could stay out of the way and not restart the feud we had settled a few years ago). My other brothers, sisters and my own mates had more than enough extended family to go around.

In between missions, I would work hard on learning how to be a partner at home with my mates. I also would spend time training, not only myself, but my sons, bringing their skills to a frightening level of proficiency. Craven took the longest, learning how to control his new strength, but eventually he learned to cope.

Crimson worried me the most, lately, taking off for hours at a time. I didn't pry, since he called promptly every time he was paged for a mission, but I couldn't shake the feeling that something was not quite right with him. He had always been the most distant of my children, often preferring to be left alone. Whereas, his other two brothers always wanted attention. Now that Crimson was eighteen, I didn't poke my nose into his private business, hoping he would come to me when he felt like sharing what he had been up to when not at home. So long as he didn't neglect his duties, I wasn't going to interfere.

The hardest part to hide, was our healing missions. None of my family could stay away from the military base or city hospitals when someone was in there and in serious condition. One of us would have to sneak in and do the healing as fast as possible, while another stood look out or ran interference for the patient we were trying to heal. So we ran two man teams for those days when feeling the pain echoing through the halls, reaching even to our war room, became too much to ignore on the base.

For the city hospital, it was easier to hide, by volunteering time as candy stripers or nurse's aides, and using our abilities when no one was looking.

The military base's hospital administrator set the tone for the rest of the staff by ignoring the 'miraculous' healings, being happy to conserve the budget that was set for the hospital, since the downsizing of personnel and funds sent to the base from the government. Once the staff saw how he reacted with feigned unawareness, they emulated the attitude, and no one else was transferred in the dead of the night.

However, we had to keep a weathered eye on the city's hospital administrator, who was not as pleased. This was due to the fact the longer a patient who had medical insurance coverage paid the hospital more money, the longer they had to stay. If they were cured too fast, the hospital didn't make as much money off of their patients. Very few doctors were genuinely happy to see such fast recoveries, since most didn't adhere to their Hippocratic oaths and worshiped their bank accounts more. This fact disgusted my family. I, personally, wasn't surprised, having seen this attitude in hospitals for years in many different states and it was growing worse everywhere.

All in all, we were fitting into our new homes and our new jobs, finding a rhythm of living that let us breathe, a way of life where we didn't have to look over our shoulders as much as before. We knew we had the General and the soldiers of Truax Field that would step in and have our backs. It was a nice change and it let us focus on what we were meant to do. I would sit back and wish I could let the stress flow away from me as easily as other members of my family did. Too often in my own life, on the streets, when things got too good, when things got to be relaxed and seemed easier—that was the time the shit would hit the fan.

BIBLIOGRAPHY

(These include the books O'Hara was directed to read to get him and his team properly started in their training in the arts.)

Scott Cunningham, "Earth Power"
Scott Cunningham, "Encyclopedia of Magical Herbs"
Scott Cunningham, "Living Wicca"
Denning and Phillips, "The Practical Guide to Astral Projection."
David Krieg, "Modern Magick"
Ted Andrews, "How to See the Aura"
Ted Andrews, "How to Heal with Color"
Ted Andrews, "How to Speak with Animals"
Silver RavenWolf, "To Stir a Magick Cauldron"
Silver RavenWolf, "To Ride a Silver Broomstick"
Gaston and Yvette Frost, "Astral Travel"
Raven Grimassi, "Ways of The Strega"
Raven Grimassi, "Wicca Magick"
D.J. Conway, "Celtic Magic"
D.J. Conway, "Astral Love"
Charles Fielding, "The Practical Qabalah"
Sayed Idries Shah, "Oriental Magic"
Dael Walker, "The Crystal Healing Book"
Phyllis Krystal, "Cutting"

Memoirs of the Nightwolves Series:
Nightwolves Coalition   2nd Edition
Nightwolves on the Prowl   2nd Edition
Nightwolves Siren's Song (Dec. 2010/Jan. 2011)
Nightwolves Dawn to Dusk—Semi Prequel (TBA)
Nightwolves Battle for Kla' din (TBA)
Nightwolves Union on Trinidad (TBA)
Nightwolves Twilight—The Last Battle (TBA)
Nightwolves Companion (What was Real,
Mundane and/or Magick) (TBA)

Paranormal Erotica by Clarrissa Lee Moon
Celeste's Nites Novelette First Trilogy (short stories—Claiming Celeste, Hunting Celeste and Sharing Celeste)
Celeste's Nites Novelette Second Trilogy (short stories-Protecting Celeste, Contemplating Celeste and Loving Celeste) TBA

AUTHOR BIO

Clarrissa Moon would like to live like a tumbleweed, going from different states often, but her home base is in Tucson, Arizona. She's an avid reader and owner of more books and DVD's then any used book shop; she also enjoys Martial arts, swimming and raising pure bred Japanese Chins. She has written as a journalist for two E-magazines. She is also, the author of 'Celeste's Nites' Novelettes. She considers herself unique, unusual and unconquerable.

Celtic Circle + Pyramid 3-7-14-24

Connect with me at the Nightwolves Lair Blog -

http://clarrissamoon.blogspot.com/

In Honor of our Planet's wild animals:

Please help these Organizations that save our Endangered Species such as the Wolves and Silverback gorillas.

http://www.defenders.org/
http://www.bigoakwolfsanctuary.org/

http://gorillafund.org/